No Time for Triage

"The roof is falling in! You have to move!"

Stoner ran up the stairs to the second floor and glanced in at the nursery. It was empty of babies. Out by the foyer, Gena was just pushing an Isolette into the elevator. "This is the last," she calld back to him.

"This is the last from Three," Murphy shouted, hurrying past him in the stairway, a boy in one arm, a toddler crying and kicking in the other.

Stoner turned to go up the stairs, when he heard a tearing sound. He looked at a center wall and saw it crumble and lean; chunks of plaster and tile and wood supports rained down. Walls began to crumble inward. The fourth floor of A Building crashed down through all the other floors into the basement, smothering everything under layers of plaster and steel.

Stoner spotted Sally, lying on her back under a mound of fallen tiles, pinned by a steel ceiling beam. She looked up at him anxiously. "I can't feel my legs," she said. Her eyes glazed, went out of focus, focused again. "Will I be all right?"

He stretched forward to try to estimate her total damage, to see how bad it was going to be to move the beam—and then he saw. Sally's legs had been cut off by the beam. They were separated from her body by at least six inches.

Stoner reached for her hand and squeezed it. "Of course you're going to be okay, Sally."

JOSEPH PILLITTERI

PINNACLE BOOKS
WINDSOR PUBLISHING CORP.

To Al Hart, Jr. for believing

This is a work of fiction. All the characters and events portrayed in this book are fictional, and any resemblance to real people or incidents is purely coincidental.

PINNACLE BOOKS

are published by

Windsor Publishing Corp.
475 Park Avenue South
New York, NY 10016

First printing: November 1989

Printed in the United States of America

Chapter One

The White Horse Medical Center was a blend of giant brick and steel buildings on the south side of the Niagara River. A few days after Christmas as this was, patient units gleamed with expensive stainless steel equipment. Rows of posted Christmas and New Year cards proclaimed that everyone there was one big family, celebrating a holiday, even though half of them were too sick to celebrate and some of them weren't even going to live to see the new year in.

The S.A.W.M.P.—officially the Sylvester A. Warren Medical Pavilion but known all over town as "The Swamp"—was an extension facility, located across the river on Bird Island. It presented a marked contrast to the spiffy new medical center on the other side of the river. A raised copper plaque in the front lobby of the A Building proclaimed that it had originally been a part of the county penitentiary, before being converted into hospital space through the "enduring compassionate understanding" of Sylvester A. Warren. As a reminder that it was originally a prison, patient room walls and floors were still covered with the bile-colored tile of the original jail cell decor. The few scant Christmas decorations that were hung on the crumbling walls only accentuated the deterioration of the buildings.

Gena Portobello aimed her white Ford Escort into a whiteout of blinding snow at the Bird Island Bridge. A first-year resident at the medical center, she'd thought when she drove to work that she'd be off by twelve that night. She'd be able to spend some time soaking in a hot tub, or polishing her nails, or trying out a new brand of English eyeliner she had bought two weeks before and hadn't gotten near her eyes yet. Instead, her red hair caught into a clip at the back of her neck, dressed in a white skirt and blouse under her ski jacket, her nails and eyebrows undone, she was driving over the bridge to the extension facility to put in another shift.

The whiteout of snow in front of her momentarily cleared and revealed the gray steel beams of the bridge. Snow had drifted two feet high, across the center span and up over the guard rails at the sides. Gena started to pull off a glove to wipe away the condensation on the inside of her windshield, but her engagement ring snagged the lining of the glove and threatened to tear it. Damn! She didn't need that level of aggravation. Impatient, she worked to free the ring, peering ahead as she did, trying to spot some clear pavement under the drift across the bridge.

She was driving over to the S.A.W.M.P. because Zack Appleton, the chief resident of the center, had called her at ten and asked her to cover the Pediatrics floor at the extension facility until morning—in addition to the twelve hours she'd already done that day. He'd also told her to help out the resident who was on Obstetrics there, because he'd broken an arm. He'd be in to cover the S.A.W.M.P. obstetrics service, but he would need some help.

"Which resident?" she had asked him cautiously.

The staff called Appleton "Ape" because he looked like

one—closely shaved black hair, a big forward thrusting head, huge hairy arms, an almost waddling gait.

"You gals are so fussy about where you're working or what you're doing," he'd said. "What the hell's it matter who you're helping out?"

That was really why people called Appleton "Ape"; he had the sensitivity of a primate. No recognition that she was exhausted from the long string of days she'd just finished, or that she could resent being referred to as a "gal" or "fussy" for being asked to cover an extra shift at the S.A.W.M.P. Not even that she might have had something more important to do on this night of the year; it was the evening before New Year's Eve.

She couldn't tell him why she cared who she would be working with tonight. She couldn't tell him that Lou Jefferson, a resident she had had to work with on her last rotation, had constantly had his hands all over her. She didn't want to work extra duty tonight if she had to work with Lou.

"Just help me out, Portobello," the Ape had finished his telephone conversation sourly. "Without a lot of fuckin' grief."

Through the window of the medical center, Gena had watched snow pelting against a corner of the building, sweeping into drifts in the parking lot. "Why can't a student go down and help him out?" she'd asked.

"Students are off for the holidays. Besides, I need someone on peds as well."

Gena could remember being a student—walking out of a hospital just before Christmas and not looking back, barely noticing that the resident watching her leave looked exhausted. She was now seeing the view from the resident's side, and she was as tired as a resident without sleep for a week could feel. "Why can't I stay at the main center and whoever's coming in here go down there?" she'd tried next. She didn't want to go outside if she didn't have to. It was a long slippery drive from the main center to Bird Island.

"Chrissake, Portobello," the man had scolded her. "I've got people out sick with flu and now with a broken arm, and emergency rooms starting to fill up because of this fuckin' storm, and you're whining about where you're going to be working. Why can't you just be a good sport and help me out?"

"I'm not whining," Gena had corrected him. "Just trying to get the deal straight."

"The deal is that you're needed at the S.A.W.M.P. tonight. Now are you going to help me out or not?"

"You know I am," she had agreed. That was the nature of being a first-year resident. "But as long as I am, I have a right to know who I'm working with."

Silence from Ape.

"All right," Gena had compromised. It was so obvious that Lou Jefferson was the person with the broken arm. "I'll work with Jefferson. I'll work with anyone but Scott Stoner."

Ape had started to clack his receiver back into place, then changed his mind at the last minute and rescued it with the connection still intact. "Lou says to remind you that you've got a full pediatrics board at the S.A.W.M.P. Watch out for the Downing girl with leukemia. And a new three-year-old with diabetes, two with croup." He clacked his receiver again, then changed his mind one more time. "And drive careful on the bridge. It's sure to be slippery as hell."

Gena had dropped her receiver, surer than before that she was going to be working with Lou Jefferson. Not because Ape had gotten so angry with her, but because he had told her to be careful on the bridge. Because he knew that she knew the bridge would be slippery that time of night. She had been raised in White Horse. She was part of the legend of that city.

Twenty-five years before, on the eve of her parents' wedding, her mother and six bridesmaids had all sat on the living room floor of her grandparents' house, tying pink ribbons onto a thousand white roses to be distributed to wedding guests the next day, when Maria Portobello would marry Gene Warren, son of the same Sylvester A. Warren that the hospital complex had been named after. Not a perfect wedding from the Warrens' standpoint; the daughter of a first-generation Italian, Anthony Portobello, was beneath their status. Aware that Gene Warren was going to marry whom he chose—no matter what—they were carrying out their social obligation, allowing the marriage the next day. Gena's mother, Maria, had nearly finished with the roses when the best man stopped to say that the bachelor party had spilled over onto the ski slope, but that as soon as they had finished Devil's Run, they would be back to help.

Maria and her bridesmaids finished the roses and tucked them away in the refrigerator. The flower girl fell asleep on the couch. And still Gene Warren didn't return. Maria took everyone upstairs while she tried on her wedding gown a final time. A dress handsewn of yards of satin and Chantilly lace, with leg-of-mutton sleeves and a twelve-foot train, everything imported from Italy; grander than any bride in White Horse, New York, had ever worn before. She had opened her hope chest and sorted out one more time the hand-embroidered dish towels, Wedgwood china, silver-rimmed Waterford—all sacrifices the Portobellos had made to equip their only daughter to marry the richest boy in town. And still the groom didn't show.

At ten o'clock, Maria Portobello was still sitting on the floor, still wearing her wedding gown, the hope chest collection still spread out around her, when the police came and told her that Gene Warren was dead. A moment's poor balance—perhaps one too many bachelor beers, one inch too much ice, one moment's faulty judgment—and he had plunged one hundred feet off the second curve of the Devil's Run. Three days later, the Warrens buried him in a casket covered by a thousand white roses tied in pink ribbons.

That was not the end of the story. Two months later, Maria Portobello presented herself to Sylvester Warren and told him she was four months pregnant.

Gena could imagine the scene: Sylvester Warren leaning across his desk, the plans for the conversion of the Bird Island penitentiary to a hospital before him; Esther, his prim and righteous wife, standing by the french doors of the library, looking on in amazement; Bruce, the younger son, and Ann, a younger sister, spinning the giant globe in the corner of the room. And Maria Portobello, wearing her last-year's coat, sitting in one of the carved walnut chairs in front of the desk. No longer interested in the Portobellos, Sylvester Warren had told Maria that her child couldn't be Gene Warren's, because the Warrens' moral principles were too high for that to have happened. She must have gotten pregnant since the funeral and now was saying that she was carrying Gene's baby in order to get their money. If she was smart, Sylvester Warren advised, she would have an abortion and be done with her charade.

Instead of following that advice, Maria Portobello had her baby, named her Gena after her father, and raised her by working at a checkout counter at K-Mart, never asking the Warrens for a dime. One less beer, one moment's surer judgment, one inch less ice, and Gena would have been the daughter of one of the richest men in White Horse. Instead she was White Horse's disgrace; raised in a rented flat along the Creek, dressed in do-gooders' hand-me-downs, mothers' example of what could happen to nice girls if they weren't careful.

The front wheels of her Escort hit a patch of ice on the bridge surface and leapt forward toward the side rail. Panicking, Gena whirled the steering wheel away from the railing to force the car out of the skid. It didn't respond, just careened closer to the edge. She was reacting backwards! Lesson one for winter driving in White Horse: Foot off brake. Turn into skid. Pray. Gena lifted her foot free of the brake and steered toward the gray railing and the hundred foot drop. Still nothing happened. The front wheels jumped the curb and continued toward the railing, not responding. A foot short of the drop down into icy water, the front wheels locked against the drift of snow along the rail and jerked to a halt. The rear tires spinning, Gena swung back out onto the roadway.

Thank you, Streets Department, she thought, maneuvering cautiously across the metal surface of the bridge and down the ramp onto the island. Thank you for doing such a damn poor job of plowing tonight that you let snow drift that way along the sides. She remembered the second lesson for winter driving that was written in the House Staff Manual: Wise up. Spend the winter in Florida.

A hundred gulls winged into flight off the snow bank in front of the hospital, as she pulled in under the overhang by the front lobby and eased into a place next to an aging orange Beetle. It was a No Parking zone, but she'd be gone by seven in the morning, so it would be all right. As happy as she was to find a spot close to the overhang, she was unhappy at seeing the Beetle parked there. It belonged to Scott Stoner, and it explained why the Ape had been in such a hurry to drop his telephone receiver. Scott Stoner was the resident with the broken arm.

Scott was from White Horse, too, although he had lived on the Hill while she had lived on the Creek when they were growing up. He had driven a cute orange Beetle to get to high school; she had walked. And now, ten years later, she recognized the car; it was the same one he had owned in high school. That had to reflect how many bills he had from med school. Although, in debt or not, deserving her compassion or not, she didn't like working with him.

Her first week at the medical center—looking for Scott one night to initial a report so she could start work—she had cut across the connecting bridge between the S.A.W.M.P.'s C and D buildings and glanced into the recovery room. In the first bed, she had seen one of the nurses from the obstetrics service, Lynn Curtain, lying stripped to the buff, with her legs spread. The man on top of her, bare-assed, pumping into her, was Scott Stoner. Gena had screamed out of sheer frustration, thinking of all the energy she had expended looking for him. Once she had loved him so much, she had felt her whole body melt into jelly every time he glanced her way. She had thought that she would die—as if air were being sucked out of her lungs—the morning he had married Sue Ellen Morrison, the daughter of a White Horse lawyer. To make up for all the years of anger she'd felt because he had rejected her, the least he could have done was to be loyal to Sue Ellen. Thinking about that, she had screamed loud enough to bring down plaster from the old ceiling. Her scream brought Security on the run and caused grief for a resident who had been shacking up rather than covering his service.

She sighed, remembering his anger, her humiliation.

Nothing to do now but go inside, find him, ask what he needed her to do, and get through this night somehow. Get home in the morning and hope she wouldn't be assigned that way again. Some things in life never changed. Despite the fact that she had earned scholarships to Princeton, and then Harvard for medical school, and he had stayed in White Horse and gone to the State University at Buffalo, she still felt like shit around him. Second best. Once he had loved her as much as she loved him. And although she had never stopped feeling the way she had about him, he had certainly changed how he felt about her. Resigned, she pulled her glove back over her ring hand again and, head down, stepped outside the car into a bitter sharp wind.

She glanced back at the bridge just before she stepped on the rubber mat in front of the sliding glass doors that opened to the hospital lobby. The distance to the bridge was distorting the view, she decided. It had only been moments since she had left the bridge, but already the drift that had stopped her from plunging over the side looked deeper and taller than it had before.

Braxton Hershey, M.D., stood gowned and gloved at a surgery table on the third floor of the C Building of the S.A.W.M.P. He was amazed at his good luck. On any normal night, he deliberately avoided the emergency room of the S.A.W.M.P. He hated the sound of crying babies, or threatening drunks coated by the smell of fresh vomit, sounds and smells that always permeated the place. This night, though, coming in from parking his BMW in the lot, the wind had been so cold that he had sacrificed the possibility of odor contamination and used the emergency room door. Halfway across the room, walking rapidly, trying to escape smelling like someone's bad dinner, he had bumped into Dan Gallagher, a former police chief of White Horse. Literally bumped into him.

Gallagher was short and fat and his ears stuck out of the sides of his head like the handles on a loving cup. Hershey had been impressed with how close the man's appendix had been to rupturing, and yet he had just been standing quietly, leaning on the emergency room counter, waiting for someone to notice him. Incredible.

Equally incredible was the fact that now, not even twenty minutes later, thanks to the efficiency of the S.A.W.M.P.'s emergency service, Gallagher was lying anesthetized and unconscious on the table in front of him.

Hershey was thirty-two, with brown hair, brown eyes, and a nose that was straight, but a little too big for his face. Only seven years out of medical school, his hair had already begun to thin on both sides of his forehead, making his face look elongated, and his already too big nose look even more out of proportion. Over the last seven years, he had spent so much time leaning over OR tables that his shoulders had started to round; the hair in his nose, affected by the constant low level of anesthesia gases in the rooms, had burnt away worse than a coke addict's. He wore thick glasses to correct severe nearsightedness, but even with those in place, he tended to squint—an odd motion, as if he were trying to peer around the nose that every day he felt looked more and more like Pinocchio's.

He had been voted most likely to make a million by his medical school class because of his natural dexterity at an OR table. Unfortunately, instead of having accomplished that prophecy, he was skirting a figure closer to only a hundred thousand a year, buried in a department of equally good surgeons at the White House Medical Center. He was growing old more rapidly than average, he felt; by the time he fulfilled his medical school prophecy for riches, he would be a freakish, stoop-shouldered, distorted old man, too deteriorated to enjoy it. He accepted a nod from the anesthesiologist at the head of the table, squinted at the clock on the operating room wall to confirm his opening OR time, and poised his skin blade.

This last year had been a turnaround one for him. Socially, he had met a female resident at the medical center who was both delightful and beautiful. Professionally, he had noticed that there was a high association between patients who had peptic ulcers and those who had atherosclerosis (a disease where fatty plaque formed along the arteries until the blood vessels became so narrowed they plugged and caused strokes or heart attacks). In a moment of sheer genius, sitting at a patio table at The Stonehouse, the only decent restaurant in White Horse, he had devised the theory that falling blood pressure from bleeding episodes such as occurred with stomach ulcers was the trigger for the atherosclerosis process. It was well accepted that peripheral vessels constricted whenever blood pressure fell. If blood pressure was extremely affected, as it could be during a GI bleed, vessels would constrict so tightly that the walls of some of them would crack. His theory proposed that the body repaired those broken vessels by lining the broken portions with fatty plaques: atherosclerosis. He needed one more patient, and his research sample of patients with major GI bleeds would be complete, confirming his theory. That was the wonder of this man in front of him. He had a stomach full of ulcerations. His hospital insurance would not only pay Hershey a little end-of-the-year appendectomy bonus here, but his condition would allow Hershey to complete his research sample.

By June, Hershey planned, he would be married to the most beautiful woman in western New York, and he would be world famous for the Hershey Theory of Plaque Repair.

In contrast to that good luck, Hershey felt the operating room he had been assigned was bad luck. Everything at the S.A.W.M.P. was old-fashioned; the table light glared off white tile walls; the X-ray view-box mimicked a prop from the *Bride of Frankenstein;* and the operating crew he had drawn was equally bad. Next to Hershey, as the scrub nurse, stood Lynn Curtain. She was about twenty-four, he guessed, a competent, pretty woman, even with her blond hair caught up under a green cap and her face half-covered by a green mask. Seven-months pregnant, she looked big enough to be nine-months pregnant. Her ankles were swollen; her abdomen was protruding so far in front of her she had difficulty reaching across the table. He had had to stretch uncomfortably just to reach the skin knife from her. And as a basic premise, he hated to start surgery with a pregnant scrub nurse. They always had to leave to use a bathroom before it was finished.

The resident across from Hershey—Scott Stoner—was working one-handed, his broken right arm covered by a plaster cast up over his elbow. Even if he'd had two hands, Stoner wouldn't have been that helpful at an OR table; he was an obstetrics, not a surgical resident. He had been pulled in there to help out only because it was Sunday night and the surgical resident was busy in the emergency room with an auto accident victim. Even before he'd scrubbed, Stoner had expressed concern that he had a woman in labor who might need his attention shortly. Hershey saw him as no use for anything but retracting. But again, that was the only thing Hershey should need him for during such a simple procedure.

Stoner was a tall man with deep blue eyes, a square clefted chin, and blond curly hair that had frizzed from the damp operating room atmosphere into miniature ringlets under his cap. It always made Hershey feel inadequate—short, ugly, and wimpish—working across from Stoner. To counteract that feeling, Hershey always tried to point out flaws in the man or his work. For the Christmas party the week before, Stoner and one of the nurses from the Obstetrics service had dressed in clown costumes and entertained children on Pediatrics at the Main Center. Hershey groused that the man should choose between being a song and dance man or a physician. Stoner was from White Horse; his father owned The Stonehouse.

Hershey wished he had decided to be a restaurant manager rather than a doctor.

Stoner had a noticeable curved scar at the front of his neck that showed over his scrub gown. Stoner claimed that he had gotten the scar from running into a barbed wire fence as a kid, but even Hershey—who deliberately spent very little time in emergency rooms—could recognize what that scar was really from: a sharp knife had been held there at some time, and sliced into his skin down to his windpipe.

The anesthesiologist at the head of the table was Jack Kissell. He was a decent anesthesiologist, but Hershey disliked him intensely. Kissell was no better-looking than Hershey, lank brown hair and a face that had been ravaged by acne. It wasn't jealousy. Kissell was always complaining, about the type of equipment he'd been furnished with, or about the general ridiculousness of building a hospital on the wrong side of a bridge.

Hershey had heard that the first time Kissell had stood at an operating table as a medical student, he had vomited on the table. The combined sight of steadily oozing blood, bright red liver, greasy abdominal fat, and coiled churning intestine had made recently eaten scrambled eggs and coffee come up all over the Mayo stand and the side drapes. Hershey loved to tell the story and did so at every procedure Kissell helped him with. To Hershey, the sight of an open abdomen was invigorating. On days he wasn't scheduled to be operating, he wished he was, so he could feel that high.

Another thing wrong with Kissell was that the man was always more interested in what horses were running at Hialeah than with the body in front of him.

Hershey glanced at Stoner, to be certain he was as ready as he was going to be, accepted a final nod from Curtain, and made his skin cut. Gallagher's skin pulled tight under the pressure of the blade. Either the man had stomach muscles of cast iron or Kissell hadn't taken the level of anesthesia down quite deep enough. Hershey glared at Kissell, sure that the level was wrong. The anesthesiologist, though, was making a routine check of the dials on his gas machine, as if nothing were out of line. That meant the problem was tight muscle. Hershey pressed harder and made the cut.

The ritual of a surgery procedure began. Lynn Curtain slapped hemostats—metal clamps to seal off blood vessels—one after the other into Hershey's palm. Stoner sponged away blood. Hershey ringed the incision with the offered clamps to halt the bleeding. Stoner sponged to be certain it had stopped. Hershey cut again. Stoner sponged. Hershey checked to see that no oozing blood remained. He wanted blood loss kept to a minimum during the operation so that Gallagher would have a quick recovery. That way, he could be included immediately in the research group.

"Remember that this is an emergency setup," Lynn Curtain said breathlessly, over the sound of metal instruments slapping one by one against Hershey's glove as he began a second round of ligation, slashing down into subcutaneous tissue.

Hershey waved at air. An emergency setup meant that he had fewer hemostats, but that was no problem. He had made such a small incision that he wouldn't use half of those on even an emergency setup.

"Do you know this fellow's hemoglobin came back at only 9.2?" Kissell asked, shuffling papers on the patient chart, pushing black-framed glasses up onto his nose, and stretching forward from his place at the head of the table.

It was important, and something Hershey hadn't known. Hemoglobin represented the number of red blood cells the man had in his circulatory system. A normal count was at least eleven. Hershey felt himself squint as he began to dissect anterior fascia, and he deliberately stopped squinting, hating the way it made lines form around his eyes.

"I'm keeping the incision small," he told Kissell. "That should compensate."

He glanced behind him at an ice bucket with a plastic bag of blood resting in it. It was a rule at the center that no surgery began without a pack of emergency blood—O negative, universal donor—within the anesthesiologist's easy reach. "I may choose to transfuse him to give him optimal recuperation potential," Hershey continued, cutting muscle quickly, leaving a second trail of hemostats.

"No transfusions." Kissell held up the man's chart to show a red-lettered note on the front of it: *No consent for blood transfusions.*

"Why is that?" Hershey raged. "Why am I being handicapped this way?"

"He's afraid of contracting AIDS," Stoner answered.

Hershey attacked the last inch of muscle he needed to carve out of his way to reach the appendix.

"Then, obviously, following my first plan of just keeping the bleeding down to a minimum is best." Hershey glanced at Stoner, assembling one-handed another pile of sponges for the next cut. "You do recognize that this is a smaller than usual appendectomy incision, don't you?" he asked the man.

Stoner nodded that he knew.

The hell he knew, Hershey thought. Letting women hang all over his six-foot-high broad shoulders was a more important interest for him than any theory about surgical incisions. The summer before he had been caught in a recovery room, on Medical Center time, making out with Lynn Curtain. That was seven months ago; the baby inside her was quite possibly a blond-haired, blue-eyed product of that evening.

Hershey cut through the peritoneal lining and exposed intestine. Curtain handed him a flat metal blade—a retractor—the instrument used to hold the edges of the incision open and allow him an easy view of intestines. He slid the curved part of it into place. As soon as Stoner had put a hand on the retractor and pulled the incision open, Hershey recognized his error. To do that surgery cleanly and without complication, he had to reach into the open incision at McBurney's point (a hand-span distance from the iliac crest), immediately put his hand on the appendix theoretically located at that point, and pull it up out of the man's body. That way, if it ruptured from handling, it ruptured on the skin surface. If it were to rupture inside the man, it would spill shit into the entire abdominal cavity. If that happened, the man would never be eligible for his study. He would still be hospitalized in two weeks, fighting off a massive infection.

Hershey felt himself begin to squint again, and blinked to make himself stop. He had made his incision so small he was going to have difficulty locating the inflamed appendix, unless it was *exactly* at McBurney's point.

If he took his time and explored the intestine with his gloved hand, he would eventually locate the appendix no matter where it was. But he couldn't afford to spend the time feeling through miles of intestine to locate the cecum where the appendix was attached, because the very presence of his hand on intestine could rupture the appendix. "Give me better retraction!" he snapped at Stoner.

As if to irritate him, Lynn Curtain shifted uncomfortably from one foot to another, the motion of a pregnant nurse who had to use the bathroom.

"Perhaps a little wider incision . . ." Stoner suggested.

No first-year resident told Braxton Hershey what size incision to use! He had been marked for success (most likely to make a million) before anyone else at that table had even opened an anatomy book.

Hoping he would get lucky and identify the appendix immediately despite the poor exposure, he slid a gloved hand into the open abdomen at McBurney's point. Instead of appendix, though, all he could feel was coil after coil of small bowel. Not a lucky stab. But then, his hand was in the abdomen of a stupid man. God knew the risk of dying from getting AIDS from a blood transfusion was nothing compared to the danger of dying from hemorrhaging during surgery.

Hershey pulled his hand free of the incision and glared at Stoner one more time. "Either give me wider exposure," he shouted, "or give the goddamn retractor to Kissell to hold!"

Kissell rocked back to his position at the head of the table and concentrated on checking oxygen dials, horrified at the thought of having to come that close to an incision.

"I believe that is the upper limit of tension that muscle's going to bear," Stoner said.

Angry, Hershey grabbed the retractor from the man's hand and jerked it against the side of the incision himself. The skin at the side of the cut was so taut it didn't give. Hershey raised up on his toes and jerked even harder, willing the muscle to obey him. *He* was the surgeon there. *He* was the expert. Still the incision didn't open anymore for him than it had for Stoner. As if to irritate him further, Lynn Curtain kept shifting from one foot to the other. Hershey threw his whole weight against the retractor and forced the incision open.

The lower edge of it tore. Blood—dark red—arterial blood—spurted upward in a four-inch arc. Holy shit! He hadn't ripped only muscle, he had ripped the iliac artery open! Hershey's throat froze with fear. The iliac artery was a major blood vessel. Torn, it made the blood, that should have gone into the man's legs, spill into his abdomen! A stream of splashing blood soaked into the skin towels and overflowed still farther onto the abdominal drapes.

"Rochester!" Hershey commanded, holding up his glove. His voice broke, mucus clogging the back of his throat. In all his years as a surgeon he had never done that before, had never even seen it done before. He tried to calm himself. He could repair a torn vessel. He grasped the Rochester clamp Lynn had handed him and poked it at the spurting stream of blood to clamp and close the ripped vessel. Spurting blood obscured his view. He couldn't tell exactly where to stab. Good Lord, the man in front of him could die from a torn abdominal artery, because he couldn't see to place a clamp!

Stoner tried to help him, dabbing quickly with a sponge along the incision line. The attempt was ineffective. Blood bubbled up again the second the sponge came free, and clouded the field. Hershey's heart started racing. It skipped a beat and threatened to stop. He couldn't get his hand to work smoothly! It jerked so badly as he reached for the artery again, his stab slipped off center. This was simple surgery, and now a man was dying in the middle of it! He stabbed again at the spot he thought would be right. It wasn't right. The bubbling didn't stop! The man was going to stop breathing. In another moment, his blood would congeal in his veins, and his heart would not be able to force it forward any more, and he would die there.

"Pressure's dropping," Kissell said quietly. His face over his mask was white, his eyes wide and staring as he ogled the spurting blood.

"Of course his pressure is dropping!" Hershey couldn't believe an anesthesiologist would even have reported that to him. "What in hell is the matter with you? *The man is spurting blood from a major artery!*"

Kissell took the criticism badly, stepping back against the

wall and folding his arms over his chest rather than offering any other suggestions.

Hershey drew back the Rochester clamp to try to use it again. In his panic, he couldn't get his blood-smeared fingers into the handle of it correctly to open it again. He tossed it over his shoulder at the wall instead. "Another Rochester!" he shouted over the sound of the metal striking the wall and sliding down to clank onto the floor, a streak of bright red blood trailing behind it on the white tile wall.

"There's only one Rochester in an emergency setup," Lynn Curtain replied, handing him a miniature Kelly in its place. "You remember it's an emergency setup."

Sweat broke out on Hershey's forehead. Obviously he hadn't remembered, or he wouldn't have thrown away the big clamp. Using a Kelly would be like trying to put a Band-Aid on a main water line. It wouldn't do any good! As surely as if a Mack truck had run over him and crushed his abdomen, the man in front of him was dying! And it was his fault! Helplessly, Hershey gripped the small clamp Lynn had handed him and stabbed it at the spurting bloodstream again. No effect. The abdominal cavity had completely filled with blood and new blood was splashing up out of the incision in a solid stream. Stoner tried to press gauze against the spurting vessel, but Hershey knocked his hand away. Pressure that way would burst the appendix, and cause a major infection—peritonitis—on top of the blood loss. Although why was he worried? What difference would it make how the man died? What kind of death was better than any other?

"One hundred over sixty," Kissell repeated the man's blood pressure again from his place back against the wall. "Pulse 120."

Hershey wiped sweat from his forehead onto his gown shoulder. Totally out of control, he stabbed at the bleeding artery with a third clamp. No improvement in the bleeding. A fourth clamp. Still nothing. A fifth clamp hit a section of the artery. The bleeding slowed. Hershey aimed a sixth clamp with vengeance and hit the center of the artery. The squirting stopped. *Thank God. Thank God. Thank God. Thank God.* The worst of everything was over. Now if he could just get the man's pressure back up . . .

Hershey glanced enviously at the bag of blood resting behind him, wishing he could use it. No. He turned back to the table firmly, discarding that option. He could patch a torn vessel and direct everything back together again. He could be sued for directly counteracting a patient request. "Turn up his fluid!" he shouted, angry because Kissell was still standing against the wall. "Get his pressure back up!"

"Damn cheap setup!" Kissell fumbled with the valve on the blood administration setup he was using to infuse a glucose solution. "Who gave me this system?"

"*All* surgery IVs are set up with blood infusion filters, whether you're giving blood or not," Lynn Curtain answered stiffly. Obviously, she was the person who had furnished it for him.

"Bad enough to run a hospital away from civilization," Kissell fumed, "I get bad equipment as well."

Hershey was too busy thinking to deal with their arguing. He could feel blood, warm and sticky, soaking through to his abdomen from his blood-stained gown. To provide an adequate blood supply to the man's legs, he would now have to make a plastic repair of the artery, hoping all the while that the man's collateral circulation held up. He didn't want to lose the man's leg. And then he still had to remove the appendix before it ruptured. Simple surgery had turned into a very complicated repair.

"You know, if you'd given me adequate retraction, this wouldn't have happened," he criticized Stoner.

Stoner didn't look intimidated.

"And, of course, even that wouldn't have happened, if I had had adequate skin relaxation," Hershey attacked Kissell.

Kissell backed squarely against the wall.

"And, of course, all that happened because emergency setups only have one Rochester," Lynn Curtain said.

She was laughing at him! All three of them were laughing at him! Well, he'd show them. He would pull this off, despite their opinion of him. He'd save the man's life and still have him well enough to include in a study group the next week.

"Get new equipment to change this table setup!" Hershey snapped at Lynn, unable to stand the sight of all the blood on the table for another second. "And before you come back, go to the bathroom!" he finished by shouting at her. "You're going to be here a long time."

Lynn Curtain lifted her hands away from the table to break scrub.

"Call labor and delivery!" he shouted at Stoner. "Tell that woman in labor to wait! You're going to have to be here a damn long time, too!"

Stoner tossed a final sponge, dripping with blood, into a kick bucket, and stepped back from the table, mimicking Lynn Curtain's hand-raised position.

"While you're waiting for a new setup, call to see if your horse won!" Hershey shouted at Kissell. "Maybe one of us can hear some good news today!"

Hershey stayed at the table and kept his own gloves in place. "I am going to detail in my note," he said to the three of them when they had reassembled around him again, "how I noticed the obvious weak point in the iliac artery, as I entered the abdominal cavity and repaired it. If any of you want to ever stand around an OR table with me again, I suggest you agree that that is what happened here."

The rest of the operation passed in absolute silence, except for Hershey criticizing the size of the sutures Lynn was handing him. It didn't occur to Hershey, even after all that time, that none of his three assistants would *want* to stand at the same table with him again.

It was midnight.

Snowflakes the size of quarters hung silhouetted against the black sky, then sliced in frantic attack against the plate glass windows of the airport weather station.

Despite the fury of the storm only inches away from him, James Evers, the chief meteorologist at the station, wasn't paying any attention to it. He was sitting at an old scuffed desk, green earmuffs hugging the sides of his bald head, a khaki army blanket tugged across his narrow shoulders, reading a purple-covered book, *The Easy and Profit-producing Way to Grow Orchids.* He was thirty-nine years old, so he had seen a night sky before. He had predicted weather outside Buffalo for eleven years, so he had seen snow before, too. What he hadn't seen before was a scheme to get rich as easy as *The Easy and Profit-producing Way to Grow Orchids* promised. The book told him that he could force orchids to bloom in his own kitchen greenhouse.

The radar screen in front of him blipped. Irritated at being interrupted, Evers glanced up, turned back to the book, then glanced up again at the screen. He had never seen a pattern as black as the one that glared at him from the screen. To make that solid and intense a pattern, the storm that was starting to strike the city had to be fierce. But then he already knew that. He had been tracing that black pattern on the screen for the last four days, since it had first begun to move south down out of Alberta.

Despite three days of warning, no one seemed to care; people were more interested in the erratic Dow Jones or the coming Super Bowl. But then, people were always sure that predicting weather meant telling jokes, or congratulating women on turning a hundred, while pointing to gray clouds or flashing lightning bolts on a United States map. The day before, the morning paper had condensed his ominous prediction of the storm into an innocent-sounding "More winter white on the way." The major evening news had summarized it as merely "More of the same." Frustrated by both news treatment and the radar screen, Evers tossed the book back onto the desk.

The biggest problem with the coming storm was going to be the wind. Once, when he was in college, he had lain on a Key West beach—rocks pressing into his gut, sand blowing into his mouth—and watched a hurricane sweep in from off shore. One second it had been only a black cloud heading toward him; the next, it had been slashing at him with wind so strong—seventy miles an hour and laced with pounding rain—it had torn the black tarp over his head into shreds, and tossed his Kodak into the hotel wall behind him. He had been lucky to escape without being thrown into the wall as well, or drowned in the seven-foot wave that had followed the storm's rim and completely inundated the beach. Twenty years later, he could still remember the biting force of that wind, the raw power that it had unleashed against him. Yet as strong as that wind had been, it had been warm. He'd endured it in bathing trunks and a cotton shirt. This storm was freezing; seventy-mile-an-hour winds accompanied by a zero temperature, ready to lay down eighteen inches of snow in as little as only four hours, on its way into Buffalo. Hardly "more winter white."

He was still at the weather station, that late on a Sunday evening, because his last duty every day was to tape a final weather report and leave it to play on an answering machine for any disc jockey who wanted to phone in during the night for a report.

He rubbed his shoulders and blew his hands to keep warm. He was tired of being ignored. Why should he bother to repeat a warning of the worst winter storm he had ever predicted? He picked up the microphone of the answering machine, tugged the brown blanket closer around his shoulders, and said in his best *Poltergeist* impression, "It's h-e-r-r-e." After a minute, he decided to modify that slightly. "Morning will be hell," he added.

He was all the way home, pulling his car into his driveway, tired from driving through whiteouts swirling across his windshield, before he realized that leaving an incomplete report hadn't been a smart move. His driveway was a sea of ice. At the rear of the house, water from a broken pipe had bubbled up, flowed forward, and then frozen the cement surface into an ice rink. His furnace must have gone out and the cold had cracked his pipes. Great. He was supposed to be predicting weather, and he'd listened so little to his own report that he'd let his own pipes freeze.

In his kitchen, he realized what had happened. The orchid greenhouse attached to the window—he'd built it according to the book's direction—had been blown in by the wind. The giant plates of glass were reduced to razor-sharp shards. Snow was blowing in through the open space as far as his living room. Barely able to stand upright in the force of the wind, he knelt in the snow blowing across the kitchen, and picked up a frozen purple orchid.

Despite what the book had predicted, he wasn't going to get rich this year. He tried to stand up and think of some way to cover the window, but the wind left him breathless and gasping. He also realized he had underestimated things when he'd said that the weather would be hell by morning. The storm had moved faster than even he had anticipated.

It was hell already.

Zack Appleton was leaning against the desk in the lobby of the S.A.W.M.P., obviously waiting for her, as Gena Portobello cut across the space on her way into the building. He rubbed a chunky hand into his right eye, something he did whenever the fatigue behind his eyes had grown so painful he couldn't stand it any longer. A bad sign. If the Ape was that tired at the beginning of a shift, it was an ominous sign.

"Come outside to the foyer," Ape said sharply to her.

Gena recognized trouble. Appleton had a habit of reaming out his residents no matter where they were or who they were with, so it was big treatment—but also very ominous treatment—to be invited outside a main lobby. She rubbed her fingers to brush the cold out of them and followed Appleton out to the narrow emergency entrance.

"Do you know I've got a memo on you that says you left forty-five fuckin' charts without final summaries on them from your last rotation?" Ape demanded as soon as they reached the foyer, pinning her against the glass door with a gorillalike arm, hunching his massive primate shoulders and chin forward until his face almost touched hers.

Gena raised a hand to show she knew she hadn't finished all her charts. She would have guessed the number was closer to twenty, rather than forty, though.

"You told Norm Redhoe last week that he should stay with his fuckin' mothers in labor—" Ape continued a list of faults.

"I didn't tell him *fuckin'* mothers," Gena protested. Norm Redhoe was an important obstetrician there; she had some tact.

"*I* said fuckin' mothers," Ape corrected what he had said. *You* said he should stay with them."

Gena had said that, but she could defend it. Although Norm Redhoe brought a lot of patients there, he treated his patients as if they were slabs of meat. The more important or wealthy they were, the worse he treated them. And patients loved him. They were convinced he must be a very good doctor, or otherwise, how would he dare to treat important people so badly? "The man *should* stay with his mothers in labor," she suggested.

"But that's why this hospital pays fuckin' *residents,* Portobellow." The Ape sounded as if he were struggling to keep his voice under control, but it rose despite that. "That's why *you're* here."

"Does it pay its *non-fuckin'* residents more?"

When Ape was really angry, a vein popped out on the side of his forehead. The man rubbed at the spot as if that were about to happen if he didn't reach the end of his list soon. "And that's the biggest problem, isn't it?" he demanded. "How *could* you have gotten all the way through medical school and still be shocked that residents shack up on slow nights?"

Gena didn't feel she needed shouting at for six-month-old news.

"You know David Frank is a very moral guy!" Ape shouted. "How could you have made an issue out of something like that?"

He should have been angry at Scott Stoner for *doing* that rather than at her for letting the medical administrator *know* he had been doing it. Gena watched Ape press his big hand even harder against his forehead, massaging the popping vein. "What I called you out here to tell you is that David Frank wants to see you in his office first thing Tuesday morning."

Gena felt a vein begin to pulse at the corner of her own temple. "Why is that?" she asked. Everyone knew that the S.A.W.M.P. was going to be closed in the spring except for some research space in D Building. When that happened, it seemed unlikely that the medical center would need as many residents as it currently employed. At least four, maybe five residents wouldn't have their contracts renewed.

Appleton scuffed at the floor with a shoe, a spotless white wingtip; he stooped and brushed a speck of dirt off it. He was fussy about the appearance of his shoes. David Frank always looked at and judged men by their shoes. "Frank talks to all residents, to see who isn't going to be here next year at this time," he said.

The pulse at Gena's temple started to throb. She had turned down a John Hopkins residency to come here. The center owed her loyalty for that. "I do a good job here, Zack." She looked down at her boots and realized she was leaving a puddle on the floor from melting snow. "I know my carbons don't always come through, so that's a problem for the business office—"

"Nobody gives a shit about the quality of your carbons, Portobello."

"I know I don't always polish my shoes."

"Nobody gives a shit about that either."

"Then what is the problem?"

"You made a major medication error."

That was six-month-old news, too. Back in August, she had neglected to ask a boy with asthma if he was allergic to any drugs before she had prescribed aspirin for him. Fortunately, when it had been offered to him, he had known enough not to take it, so nothing had come of the incident, but the Ape had used it as an example of why residents checked for allergies in patients. And the boy's father—Peter Warren—had heard about it, and asked that she not be assigned to his son any more.

"Nothing came of that," she defended her action.

The vein on Ape's head was starting to quiet. "But that's not the principle of it, is it?" he said.

"There are residents here worse than me." Gena tried another approach to defend her position. She couldn't believe she was defending a job that never let her sleep, that left her exhausted. "Jefferson is an idiot. Waldon is lazier than hell. Retagglio—"

"Ryan, Jefferson, Waldon, and either you or Stoner. That's the list of who's going."

Gena's heart stopped, not just because her own name was on the list but because Scott Stoner's was. His name was there because he'd been in the recovery room that day in July. Was that why *her* name was potentially on the list, too?

"Seriously, what's the main reason for me, Zack?" She rubbed her arms, stimulating her heart to keep beating. "It can't be the recovery room thing."

The Ape pressed harder against his forehead. "The Warrens don't like you, Portobello. And the center relies heavily on Warren money. How's that?"

"If that's true, then you never should have taken me here, Zack. Everyone in this town could have told you the Warrens have never liked me."

"Frank was delirious about having a Harvard graduate."

"Come on, Zack!" Gena struggled to find the solution. "There must be something else. Another reason."

Ape made another face. "*I* don't like you, Portobello. How's that?"

She waited for the rest of the explanation.

"You're too unsure of yourself. You let everyone push you around."

"I'm better than Stoner," she said surely. "Just tell me what I can do to prove that."

"Don't screw up anything between now and Tuesday morning, before you have to see Frank. How's that?"

"Come on, Zack! I ate shit in med school for three years to get here! I've eaten it here since July! Give me better advice than Don't screw up!"

"Easy, Portobello. David Frank doesn't describe a residency here as eating shit. He thinks it a rare opportunity for learning to develop personal responsibility. To say nothing of enduring compassionate understanding."

"Tell me what to do, Zack!"

Ape started to stride across the lobby toward the elevator. "How about, don't screw up anything between now and *morning?*" he asked, letting the elevator door slip back into place, cutting him off.

"Shit!" Gena said out loud to the foyer. A first-year resident asked to leave a hospital because a hospital was overstaffed would have trouble getting another position *anywhere.* Everyone would guess she was the one asked to go because she was the worst of the hospital's staff. Only she knew that was not based on her ability; the Warrens simply wanted her far away from them.

What was the matter with Ape that he expected her to work with Scott Stoner tonight, when he knew they were in competition for a position here? And how could he have asked her, after she had already spent twelve hours on duty that day, to spend an extra shift at the Swamp, at the same time that he planned on telling her she was going to be asked to leave? Surely even his primate brain should have been able to function better than that.

Scott Stoner had been sitting on the edge of Mary Nightowl's bed on the fourth floor of the Psychiatric Lockup in the A Building at the S.A.W.M.P. for ten minutes. He was trying to decide if he could begin some intravenous fluid in the woman's hand by himself, or if he needed help. How could he wrap a tourniquet around an arm, swab alcohol on a hand, insert a needle, and open a fluid valve over her head, all one-handed, and left-handed at that?

The last time the woman had been in, in July he remembered, she had said it was because she was afraid that she might prick her finger on a needle and fall asleep for a hundred years. This time she was afraid she had swallowed the Good Witch of the West and if she ate anything, she would drown her. Mary obviously had a hard time keeping the real world straight from that of the Brothers Grimm.

A small woman, she was sitting propped up by two pillows, her deep glowing black eyes prominent over stark cheekbones, an aged lace bedjacket stretched over her shoulders; only a wisp of the woman she had been before she had stopped eating last month to save the good witch's life. In July, Stoner also remembered, she had listed her nationality on the admission form as Seneca Indian. Her age as ninety-nine. This admission she had listed her nationality as Indian again, but her age as twenty-one. He could believe she was Seneca all right, but because of the way her face was crossed with a million age lines and capped with pure white hair, he couldn't believe she was younger than he was. It seemed more likely to him that she was closer to a hundred than just reaching drinking age.

He knew from her history that she had been admitted to the center off and on since 1974, when her husband had fallen into Lake Erie through a hole while ice fishing. She had walked across the ice to the place where he had disappeared and dived and dived under the ice cover to search for him, long past the time anyone else believed he could be rescued. Frozen brain cells, Ape said about her. That was her trouble. Stoner believed it was simply a lack of having anyone to fight or dive for any longer.

Stoner was dressed in a navy turtleneck sweater and blue cords rather than his required whites, brown Hush Puppies instead of white shoes on his feet. He had changed after surgery when he had discovered that he didn't have any clean whites at the S.A.W.M.P. His clothing was not going to win him big points with Ape. Dejected, Stoner smoothed his uncasted hand over the back of Mary Nightowl's, searching for the vein least sclerosed and caked with calcium, so that he could poke a needle into it without her screaming with pain. Or make her worry that she might sleep into the next generation.

He had felt depressed all day and wasn't sure what was causing it. Fatigue? A post-Christmas letdown? He doubted that. It was more likely a result of seeing an endless string of people who weren't going to get any better.

He had envisioned medicine as keeping a finger on life's pulse. In reality, working as a resident was no different from his father's restaurant business. A customer came to the restaurant and said he was hungry. His father suggested the Veal Oscar. The customer said he couldn't afford that and went next door to the Chinese take-out. An hour later the man was back feeling hungry again. People like

Mary Nightowl came in here; a psychiatrist suggested psychotherapy; her insurance didn't cover that; the house staff hydrated her and sent her out again. In another month she was back, hungry again.

"That's good," was Ape's philosophy about that. "Because curing people earns you little money. The trick is to keep selling them egg rolls, so they get hungry again and keep coming back. Whatever you do, Stoner, try *never* to cure anybody!"

"Dr. Portobello just arrived." Margo Torning, the evening psych service nurse, came into the room and stopped beside Stoner, bending over him, inspecting Mary's hand with him, letting generous breasts brush against his sleeve. Tremendous Torning. Fantastic tits. Stoner smelled a strange combination of French perfume, sweat, and hospital hand lotion on her. He grunted a response. His casted arm had been aching for the last hour, adding to his depression and exhaustion. He would have enjoyed falling into his own bed that night instead of sacking out in back of labor and delivery. Getting his arm raised and stopping the constant nagging pain in it was gaining importance in his mind every minute, making him wish Portobello was there to relieve him, not assist him.

"And did I tell you the nurse on 4 telephoned?" Margo added. "The patient you just did in surgery has a temperature she wants you to check out."

The S.A.W.M.P. was composed of four towers, A, B, C, and D, connected only by two overhead walkways and two basement tunnels. If any resident in the A Building was out sick, it was easier for a resident only one floor below to cover for him than for a resident from another building to come over. On paper it was easier. In practice, it was hard on the resident who was also covering a completely different service. Yet that was what was happening now. Lou Jefferson, the medical resident on 4A, had phoned in sick, so even though Stoner had a broken arm, he was covering the Obstetrics service, his usual cover, as well as Medicine A, which should have been Jefferson's.

"Are you off in the morning?" Margo asked him, moving still closer to his shoulder and trying to make certain that he caught the scent of Jean Naté from the space between her breasts. "Can I meet you somewhere?"

Stoner glanced outside at the snow blowing so fiercely against the window that he couldn't even see his car. Fatigue swept over him like a giant blanket. "Coffee shop?" he asked absently, thinking more about Gallagher than her question. It was too soon for the man to be developing a complication from surgery, even as stupid as his surgery had been. The man should barely be awake by now.

"No!" Margo traced a finger along the inseam of his right leg. "Come to my apartment!"

Stoner had lived by himself since Gena Portobello had screamed outside a recovery room in July. His wife had taken their children and moved in with her mother. He sighed, thinking about the fact a new year was almost here and his old year was still such a mess. He had over fifteen thousand in bills from college and med school that had come due the June before, and still had nothing paid on them. His house needed a new roof. His car needed tires. He had a car insurance premium due. Sue Ellen had bought their seven-year-old daughter a three-hundred-dollar doll house for Christmas, along with over a thousand other things, and billed them to charge accounts still in his name.

He was an only child. Two girls, born before him, had been born premature and had died. His mother would have been a good mother to those girls, he was sure; she had hated a boy's constant roughhousing and scraped knees and worry about his batting average. His father, on the other hand, wouldn't have been a good parent to anyone. No child would have been concerned enough about the secret for hollandaise sauce to make him happy. Because he had found so many faults with his parents, Stoner always meant to be a better parent to his children than his parents had been to him. Now for the last six months, he hadn't been doing that at all.

He glanced up at Margo's breasts, evaluating what she'd said. She'd felt free to suggest her apartment because everyone at the S.A.W.M.P. knew he wasn't getting anything at home. He'd be red-eyed and wiped out by morning, though, he reasoned, especially if Gallagher was developing a surgery complication. Although the only reason a person would have a temperature that soon after surgery was because he was dehydrated. He could bet the nurse on 4 had botched the post-op fluid order.

"What's the word on my apartment?" Margo urged.

Stretched out on her apartment couch and drinking cupfuls of cheap white wine was the ideal way to end a twenty-four-hour shift, Stoner admitted. Deep thought wasn't necessary for conversation with Margo. No big action necessary but a good fuck. Although he shouldn't even think about that. He had agreed with Sue Ellen to give their marriage a new try beginning with the new year. "By the time I shovel out my car and get to your apartment in the morning," he said, deliberately looking at the blowing snow outside and not at Margo, "I'll be too tired to do anything but sleep."

"I'll come to *your* house then," Margo said. "In fact, I'll go there now and wait for you."

He shouldn't! He was too tired! His arm ached to much!

And if Sue Ellen learned he had done that, she'd come back at him with more bills—the way she knew she could hurt him the most.

Wearily, Stoner glanced up at Mary Nightowl to see if she was processing that arrangement. Sitting up, looking straight ahead at the urine-colored wall in front of her, she looked as if she were seeing people and images there he couldn't see; listening to voices he couldn't hear. Stoner caught a whiff of Margo's perfume again. Shit. He was already only one step away from bankruptcy. How much more damage could Sue Ellen do to him?

He located his key ring in his pants pocket and dropped it into Margo's open palm before he could think any more. "See you in the morning," he said, watching Margo pocket his keyring; a woman used to handling men's keys. "In the meantime, find me a butterfly needle for this fluid, will you? Nothing else is going to work here."

"You can't use butterfly needles for anyone over two years old," Margo protested. To counteract turning him down, she flashed him her brightest smile, one an orthodontist must have charged at least two thousand dollars to mold years before. "It's new hospital policy."

Stoner refused to be impressed with her orthodontal smile. "Get me a butterfly needle,' he repeated.

"You can't—" Margo tried protesting again but after looking at the frown he was giving her, she closed her mouth and walked out to her desk. Stoner caught a glimpse of Gena Portobello there. *Shit!* Of all the people who could have been sent to help him out, why her? Why not anyone else? He turned his back on the desk area, to try and keep from thinking about her.

He had known her forever. All the way back to first grade, when for Mother's Day everyone in their class had brought in paper milk cartons, cut them off two inches from the bottom, filled them with dirt from the school flower bed, selected a white bean from a plastic bag on Miss Armstrong's desk, pressed it down into the carefully watered soil and then waited expectantly for the dirt and the warmth and the water to evoke the miracle of life.

The Friday before Mother's Day, everyone's plant had grown to over a foot tall with at least two lush green leaves pushing out on the sides. All but Gena's. Hers had still been only a cut-off cardboard carton from Mesmer's Dairy, filled with unsplit brown dirt, a barren and unfulfilled promise of life.

Stoner had stopped her in the alcove outside the school door—where no one could see him and razz him about it later—and given her his bean plant. First grade. First love.

He tried not to think about her being there. It was crazy to have been in love with someone for that long a time and never have done anything about it. It was crazy that just seeing her this way—unexpectedly appearing at the edge of his vision—still made his heart jump. Don't be a fool, Scott Stoner, he told his body, sitting back down on Mary Nightowl's bed. What ever—if anything—Gena Portobello ever felt for you, died a long time ago. Concentrate on pulling your present life back together, beginning with taking Sue Ellen to a New Year's Eve dance tomorrow. Moving home the first of the year. Getting through a residency here without curing anyone. . . .

"What if you had it to do all over again, Mary?" he asked the woman in front of him. If she could separate the sane world from her witch-swallowing one, she could simply drink some fluid and then wouldn't *need* an intravenous line inserted. "Would you do anything differently?"

Crazy Mary didn't answer him, but then she always took

a long time to weigh facts before she answered, so that didn't mean she was out of touch with the world. Only cautious. While he waited for her to process his question, he glanced down the hallway at Margo again. He watched her pull on her coat to get ready to leave. He probably should have been more careful than to have given a nurse his house key, he thought. After all, he didn't need David Frank on his back again.

In July, the night Gena had screamed outside the recovery room, David Frank had called both of them into his first floor office of the A Building. The office was big; filled with its own safe, an oversized marble-topped desk, a shaggy Scandinavian rug on the floor, black-and-white prints in steel frames, beside bookshelves filled with bound journal volumes that just went on and on. A tall, gray-haired man, Frank was the director there because he'd done some very creditable research with growth hormone and its association with blood glucose levels. He was the kind of man everyone wanted to be able to say they had interned under. He was one of the reasons a White Horse staff appointment was a valued appointment.

It had been midnight when he got to the S.A.W.M.P., dressed in a tuxedo, a ruffled shirt, and very shiny black shoes. And he hadn't been given a clear explanation of why he had been called away from the dinner party.

Clenching his teeth, cringing with embarrassment at being called on the carpet that way, Stoner had stood there in his wrinkled resident whites, his scuffed and knicked shoes next to Frank's shiny ones, and explained inanely that no patient had been involved in the incident; a nurse had.

"What are you talking about?" Frank interrupted him after only a few sentences. He must have come from The Stonehouse, Stoner decided, and this interview was making him miss a flaming dessert of some kind. Or maybe an ice sculpture in the center of his table was melting into a formless blob without him.

"I was in the recovery room sleeping with a nurse, sir," Stoner had managed to explain, wishing he had polished his shoes before he had come on duty, aware that Frank was looking at his shoes.

Frank had honed in on the word sleeping. "I understand that residents get tired on long stretches, Stoner," he'd said charitably. "I know that happens to everyone at least once."

"I was sleeping with a *nurse,* sir," Stoner repeated the explanation.

Frank had looked bewildered, as if he couldn't understand why a tired resident would share a bed with a nurse. Not an efficient way to get some sleep, certainly. Half of the lectures he gave to house staff were either on being certain to press hard enough to make three carbon copies of everything, or on efficiency. *You're not with the system if you're not carboning. You're not thinking holistic care if you're not thinking efficiency.* What Stoner meant seemed to dawn on him slowly. "You don't mean *sleeping,* do you?" he asked primly.

"No, sir," Stoner answered. Would Frank simply tell him to pack his things and leave? He could have done that, he had the ultimate power in that hospital. He was capable of throwing a resident caught with his pants down out on his ear, contract or no contract.

Frank had looked as if he were trying to be fair, to understand the nonunderstandable. "Do I have you confused with someone else, Stoner?" he had asked. "Aren't you married?"

"No, sir. Yes, sir," Stoner had contradicted himself, feeling his face turning bright red and hating Gena Portobello for doing that to him. "No, sir, you're not confused. Yes, sir, I'm married."

His first morning there, when he had walked into the auditorium for orientation—almost numb from fear he'd been unable to tell the secretary handing out name tags who he was—he had caught a glimpse of Gena Portobello. She was pouring herself a cup of tea from a silver urn at the side of the room. His knees had gotten so weak from just seeing her that he literally hadn't been able to walk over to talk to her. The realization hit him that she had been following the same path he had been following all those years. All the nights he had sat memorizing rhymes to remember the names of cranial nerves—"On old Olympic's towering top, a fucking German viewed a hop"—she had been memorizing the same list. But now, only a week after that reunion, after being so deliriously happy at seeing her there, she had lined him up for trouble with David Frank.

"Would I be correct to assume the nurse with you was not your wife?" Frank had asked solemnly.

"Yes, sir. That would be right."

"Do you know who *my* wife is?"

"It wasn't your wife either, sir."

"I asked you, if you know who my wife is, Doctor Stoner," Frank had said slowly, each word dropping like a weighted stone, "because she is the former Ann Warren, the daughter of the man who built this hospital. To point out to you how far back the ties to this hospital go in this community."

"Yes, sir. I realize that." Stoner tried to correct what he had said. "I never meant—"

"And because I want you to know the level of commitment that is expected from house staff here," Frank had cut him off. "When I was as far into my first residency as you are, I had already completed my first research project: the analysis of fat absorption from the gastrointestinal tracts of rhesus monkeys. To do that accurately, you have to gather all the subject monkey's excreta. I was such a dedicated researcher, I went down to the lab evenings and did that myself. Scraped excreta off cage bars if I needed to, to obtain it all. I expect nothing less of anyone who works for me."

Stoner just stood silent in front of the man, feeling guilty that he had never read the famous "scrape the shit off the monkey bars experiment of 1935," although he knew it had been included in the bibliography list given out with house staff orientation.

"Are both of you still on duty now?" Frank had asked finally as the silence in the room grew acute.

"This whole thing is my fault," Gena had interrupted, moving closer to the Italian marble desk. "I shouldn't have made an issue out of it."

"As long as you're both still on duty," Frank glared at Gena to silence her—the man who decided what needed to be made into issues there and what didn't, "we'll finish talking about this some other time." He had turned to look out the window of his office, as if he had never noticed the Bird Island bridge out there before, or as if he were estimating how much time it would take to get back to The Stonehouse and dessert. "And next time you're on duty," he had looked at both of them equally, "would you be sure your shoes are polished? I like to see residents with polished shoes."

Stoner had felt relief at Frank's solution. Especially since in the six months since then, the man had never brought up the subject of the recovery room or the shoes again. But the incident hadn't ended there. Over the next few weeks, the story had spread through both the main center and the extension facility. The more the story was told, the worse the versions grew. In one version, Gena Portobello had screamed because she had found Scott Stoner in bed with a patient.

"If I had my life to do all over again," Mary Nightowl interrupted his thoughts, staring at Stoner through narrowed, deeply lined eyes, speaking through badly decayed teeth, "I'd do a lot of things differently."

Stoner managed a grin for her. He turned to listen to her and continued the conversation that he had forgotten he had even started fifteen minutes before.

Chapter Two

Ryan McFarland had been aware of the pain in his left shoulder for over an hour. He smoothed his huge right hand over it, trying to make the pain go away. No reason to think it was anything serious, he was sure; just a sign of getting old. He could remember a time when he could work for twelve hours at a stretch and never feel a thing. Now he was able to get no farther than the door of the White Horse City Garage before his whole chest and arm ached so much he could hardly walk.

He was a big man with a full head of tousled gray hair. He wore a black peacoat, jeans, and linesman's boots to protect himself from the cold. He still spoke with a deep brogue from spending the first six years of his life in Ireland, although he had lived in western New York for fifty-five years. He had been the supervisor of City Services of White Horse for the last three years. On a storm night like this he was responsible for sixty square miles of highway, including four thruway ramps and seven bridges, and with only twenty-eight men, fourteen plows, and ten salt trucks. Still rubbing his shoulder, he walked past the lineup of trucks pulling one by one into the city garage for a change of shift.

"Think we'll get a lot more of this stuff?" Ted Melcamp, the shift foreman, hurried along beside him, clapping his leather gloves against a plaid mackinaw as he walked, trying to keep warm. Melcamp paused beside the Number 3 truck as he passed it and aimed a hard kick at accumulating ice on the back splash.

Ryan aimed a kick at the ice as well. Ice in back of the front wheels of the big plows was one of his biggest problems. Too much accumulation and it completely blocked the front wheels from turning.

Melcamp's kick had loosened a chunk of ice and it fell away onto the garage floor. Ryan's kick had been ineffective. But then, his shoulder hurt too much for him to raise his leg high enough to have any force. "Can't be too much more snow up there," he answered Melcamp's question, counting how many plows were in as Jerry Horowitz backed in the last one, equally ice-covered. "It's all down here."

Ordinarily, McFarland rotated plows—seven out and seven in—so that they had ice-melting time. This day, with snow coming down hard since early morning, he had ordered all fourteen of them out. Now he realized that all he had accomplished was to create fourteen plows with difficulty in steering.

The barn was cold. Up in the rafters two doves cooed and huddled together against a gray cinder-block perch to keep warm. As cold as it was up there, it was still a hell of a lot warmer than outside. Horowitz pulled on his brake with a grating squeak and jumped down from his cab to stand in front of McFarland. Like everyone else there, he stood blowing on his hands and stomping his feet, obviously trying to look alert and ready to go, although he had to stifle a yawn to do it. Ready to start a new overtime shift while he was still exhausted from the last.

"What would you think if everyone took the rest of the night off?" Melcamp asked.

Ryan could think of nothing more appealing. If *he* had the night off, he would go home and fall into bed. Rest his arm and chest.

"Even four hours off would be great," Horowitz agreed. "Give the plows time for the ice to melt."

"We could start again at five o'clock. Get streets and bridges cleared enough for the morning rush hour," Melcamp urged.

"I just finished hustling snow off the Bird Island bridge," Horowitz added, his words coming out surrounded by a cloud of condensation. "It's clear as a baby's butt."

McFarland didn't believe the Bird Island bridge was that clear, but if the wind was blowing snow away from it, not toward it, it might stay clear until morning. "Do it," he said quickly, rubbing his arm again, trying to will the pain in his shoulder to go away. "But remember . . . back by 5:00 A.M. We'll have a hell of a lot of snow to push aside by then."

Drivers whooped and slapped each other's backs and scattered for the doors.

"Don't tell anybody, but I did your driveway on my way over here!" Horowitz called back to McFarland at the doorway. "You should have no trouble pullin' in."

Drivers were not supposed to do that, dip a blade by anyone's driveway. McFarland acknowledged that this evening, though, he couldn't scold. Knowing his driveway was accessible was the best news he could imagine hearing.

Outside, he gunned his four-wheeler and bounced it over a drift at the curb into the street. He was halfway home—

driving through a less well-plowed Center Street than he liked to see—before he heard a radio disc jockey predict that the storm was not going to die out, but was actually expected to increase in intensity for the rest of the night. He was pulling in his driveway—neatly shoveled by Horowitz as he'd said—when he realized that if Horowitz had been there dipping a blade to clear his driveway, the man could not also have just returned from the Bird Island bridge. That meant he might not have been near the bridge for hours.

Which could mean the bridge was full of snow. And now it was too late to do anything about that, because he'd already given everyone the night off. Damn it! Ryan rescued his keys from his ignition and started into his house. After another minute, the pain in his shoulder was so ragged, so cutting, he didn't care if the Bird Island Bridge was clear or not. All he wanted to do was crawl into bed and coax the pain to go away so he could use his arm again.

Jack Kissel, the anesthesiologist for Gallagher's surgery, signed a final OR note on the man's chart and tossed it onto the schedule desk.

"Done for the day?" the receptionist asked, talking around a mound of bubble gum in her cheek.

"Punch me out," Kissell answered her.

The girl was polishing her nails. She raised a half-finished hand—three nails a bright purple, two undone—to the name rack on the wall and slid his name file over from an In to an Out column. "Is the induction room clean?" she asked, leaning back in her chair and comparing the color of her finished nails to the color of the purple blouse she wore under her lab coat.

Kissell didn't know one way or the other if the room was clean or dirty. He said yes.

"All the garbage bags out?"

Kissell didn't want anyone going into the induction room that night. He said yes again.

"If you'll check it's locked before you go, I'll mark it okay for housekeeping. So they won't even have to go near there." She opened her top desk drawer and scooped the ring of keys on the desk into the drawer.

"Oh, what about the standby blood?" she asked one final question, turning back to him. "Is that back in the cooler?"

Kissell didn't know if the standby blood for Gallagher's surgery had been returned to the OR cooler or not. Lynn Curtain had cleaned up the OR room. As she was always conscientious, he could conclude she had taken good care of it. He nodded that was under control as well.

"Be sure and drive careful going home," the receptionist finished. "Radio says the snow outside is bad."

Kissell didn't care about the storm. He cared about the ring of keys she had just swept into her drawer. Dan Gallagher had checked into the hospital with two thousand dollars in his wallet. And just before the man had started counting backward to unconsciousness in the operating room, he had opened up his football-sized fist and entrusted the money to Kissell's care. In front of Lynn Curtain.

If no one else had been there, Kissell knew he would have been tempted just to quietly fold the money and stuff it into his wallet. Place it on Joe Dilly in the fifth at Hialeah and have it escalated into at least twenty thousand by the time Gallagher was ready to be discharged and asked for it back. But Lynn Curtain had been there, and had reminded him, as soon as surgery was over, what hospital policy required him to do with patient-entrusted money; make out a receipt for it, put that on Gallagher's chart, and then, since it was Sunday night, put the money in the safe in David Frank's office until it could be transferred to the main safe Monday morning.

With Curtain watching him, Kissell had had no choice but to make out the receipt, staple it to the chart, put the money into a manila envelope, label it, and follow Curtain through an elaborate process of taking the OR schedule desk keys, walk down to the first floor of A Building, open the Personnel office, take down a ring of keys from the wall, and walk back down the hallway to Frank's office. Curtain had opened that door with the Personnel ring of keys, crouched in front of the safe behind the desk, and spun its dial. Her back had blocked his view so Kissell hadn't been able to see the combination she had used, but inside the safe he had seen a huge stack of money. Surely fifty to a hundred thousand dollars, all locked inside an old under-the-counter safe with a simple ten-number dial.

Walking back with Curtain to the surgery suite so she could finish stripping Gallagher's OR room and get it ready for cleaning, Kissell had worked to estimate the number of possible combinations there were on a ten-number safe. While he had stopped to check Gallagher in the recovery room, he'd scribbled in the margin of the man's vital signs sheet to recalculate and arrived at ten thousand as the possible total number of combinations. That meant if a man spun a different combination on a dial every five seconds it would take only fifty thousand seconds to crack such a safe. Fifty thousand seconds was fourteen hours. That meant if a person took the key to the Personnel office from the OR schedule desk to start the process at ten o'clock some night, by sunup he could be halfway through that total number of combinations. A second night and he could finish the other half and be into the safe.

Kissell knew he was not a good-looking man. He was too tall and willowy and acne crypts still pocked his face. On top of that, he was naturally shy; conversation with strangers was always an effort for him. He couldn't be a surgeon because cutting tissue nauseated him. Based on those realizations, he had recognized early in medical school that he would not be a success as a doctor. Anesthesiology, on the other hand, was conducted largely with unconscious people who weren't capable of conversation and didn't care what the person administering it to them looked like. Unfortunately, unless he opened his own practice, being an anesthesiologist made him an employee of the medical center. That put him in the same financial category as a resident. Tired of living at that level, he had sunk into debt to his bookie for twenty thousand dollars and to a loan shark for twelve thousand more. He had taken out both a first and second mortgage on his house and now the bank was writing him letters, threatening to take his car. Which was why discovering the money in Frank's safe was so interesting. In only two nights of spinning safe combinations, he could cover all his bills and be on the plus side of life again.

What would be the chance of getting caught? Not much, he guessed. Who would ever suspect him? He wasn't entrusted with the safe combination. And if the safe's emptying happened at a time when he could verify he was on the other side of the bridge, no one would even question him about it. The whole thing came down to deciding how much of a chance he was ready to take to pull himself out of debt.

He could start as soon as the receptionist with the purple nail polish went home and Dan Gallagher was transferred to a patient room in the A Building so that the OR suite was quiet. There was one more thing he'd have to wait for: why he didn't want cleaning personnel in the induction room. The ring of keys he'd need to use were the same ones that opened the refrigerator where the blood for surgery was kept. To be supercautious, to be certain nothing was out of line, he would have to wait in the induction room for the lab technician to collect the unused blood from Gallagher's surgery before he could take the keys. That way he would be sure they wouldn't be missed.

All those things would happen before one o'clock he was sure. That would give him five hours before 6:00 A.M., the earliest David Frank would possibly come in, to spin combinations. He blew on his hands impatiently, a gambler blowing on dice, weighing his chances. If he were lucky he would hit the combination early in the game. He might even be into the safe and back in bed within an hour. By morning he could be out of debt for the first time in seven years.

Gena Portobello walked into Mary Nightowl's room cautiously, trying to evaluate how welcome she was going to be. Not by Mary. She and Mary had a lot in common as White Horse's outcasts. By Scott Stoner. Once, back in high school, he would have turned around at the faintest suggestion of her footstep. Now, he neither turned nor looked up as she approached. "You'll need to get a smaller needle than this to start," he said to the space in front of him rather than to her. "Did Margo give you a butterfly?"

"You can't use butterflies on anyone over two," she educated him on the new policy.

"Is there a policy that allows anything to get done around here?" he asked. Obviously angry, he pushed himself to his feet and strode out to the nurse's desk. In another minute, he strode back with a miniature, orange, flanged needle in his fist and slammed it down into her hand. "Or don't you know what these are?"

Gena didn't appreciate having equipment forced on her. "I know you think it isn't fair that I am the one helping you out tonight," she said calmly. "In all fairness, you should know it wasn't my choice either."

"Fair is an adolescent notion you should try and get rid of," he said, talking to Mary Nightowl's hand, not to her. "It doesn't apply to much."

"I wish—" Gena started again.

"The policy of wishing has been suspended," he interrupted again. And that was strange. Only people originally from White Horse understood that old joke. A saying like that should have been accompanied by a grin of recognition, because it reflected how long they had known each other. Stoner had a nice grin when he chose to use it, but he hadn't smiled at her for six months.

"Would you rather I just went home?" she asked.

Stoner focused unfriendly deep blue eyes on her. "I don't recommend that anyone drive tonight," he said.

That didn't mean he was going to be nice to her, or he wanted to work with her for the next eight hours. Just that she shouldn't get herself killed.

Resigned to a night of stubborn silence, Gena took the needle Torning had originally connected to the fluid line, rather than the miniature orange one Scott had given her, and began her own inspection of Mary's hand. She didn't sit on the bed as Scott had been doing. David Frank lectured frequently on how many germs were on patient beds and how he didn't like his residents sitting on them. *You're not thinking holistic care if you're not thinking safety and efficiency.*

And while I'm talking to you, could I remind you to keep down the obscenities on charts? And could I see polished shoes? I like residents in polished shoes.

Stoner looked away from her, stood up to walk over to the window, and inspected the snow outside.

"I hear you were very good in the Christmas show," she said to his back, hoping that would make better conversation. In a high school musical, he and she had done a soft-shoe number dressed as chimney sweeps, and she wondered if he had used their old routine. She could bet she still remembered it, could polish it up.

There was no indication that he had heard her.

"How did you break your arm?" she tried another approach.

He didn't answer that either, just stared out the window as if he had never seen snow before, which was crazy because he used to shovel it off The Stonehouse walk every morning before school from the time he was in grade school.

"Shouldn't you have it in a sling?" she asked, trying to find some kind of mutual topic. "Keeping fractured arms elevated is the only way to keep pain out of them."

He didn't answer again. And didn't elevate his arm.

Gena swabbed Mary's hand with alcohol and punctured what she felt sure was going to be a solid vein. The vein was so brittle, though, from age, that it rolled away from the needle point. Lost. A dry tap. "Have anyone in labor?" she asked next. She had a right to ask about his work assignment for that night. After all, she was helping him out with it.

"You don't need to worry abut having to do things for me all night." He turned away from the window to talk to her, but looked at his casted fingers as if they hurt, instead of at her. Of course, they hurt, she thought; he didn't have it in a sling. "I'm going to have a light night."

Gena tried not to show she was happy about that.

"You don't even have to worry about having to help me cover again," he said. "Or didn't you get the word yet, that you won't be here long enough for this to happen again?"

That wasn't fair. Ape hadn't said that. "The word I got is that it is going to be *either* you or me," Gena said. "Which doesn't worry me. I know I can do anything you can do."

He pushed out his chin defensively. "Name one thing you can do *better.*"

Gena had to admit there were a lot of things in doctoring he could do better than she could. He was naturally comfortable with people; she sometimes stumbled on correct things to say or was too shy or nonassertive to say them. He could convert medicine dosages instantly in his head; she had to reach for a piece of paper. He had a fantastic recall of information—

"Having trouble finding one?" he pressed, moving to stand next to her when she didn't answer immediately. Close to him, she caught a familiar odor of after-shave. Who would have believed that? All those years and he still used English Leather! All those wasted mornings when she could have woken up beside him and enjoyed that smell, except he had asked Sue Ellen Morrison whose father lived on the hill and whose ancestors went back to the Mayflower! "Come on. Name something," he persisted.

"I polish my shoes," she started. "I don't sit on beds—"

"Awesome."

"I'm more responsible."

"Screaming outside a recovery room is *responsible?*"

Gena felt her hand start to tremble. Had to put down the needle. "Look, Stoner." She lost any kindness she had felt toward him. She wasn't there as a social worker; she was his competitor. "If I'm being asked to leave here, it's because my father killed himself, and the Warrens have always resented that. If you're being asked to leave here, *you* have nothing to blame it on but the fact that you have the morals of an alley cat."

"As if you're some kind of goddamn virgin, Portobello. As if you've never done it with anyone."

Gena had no answer for that because the first time she had ever "done it with anyone" had been with *him.* Angry that he had chosen that moment to bring it up, she reswabbed a new place on Mary's hand, sure she was going to hit a vein this time. She didn't. The vein rolled again; older people's veins were like slippery rocks.

"You know, if you'd use the decent needle sitting beside you, instead of that knitting needle, you could do that right," he said.

"That isn't the right way!" Gena contradicted him. "It's the *convenient* one. And the expensive one! Butterfly needles cost four times regular ones."

"If you'd sit on the bed and use a small needle—" he started again.

"I'll what?" she demanded. "Be as good as Scott Stoner? Be able to compete with you?"

"Cause less pain."

That was a good point. Gena nodded that she had the message and started to unwrap the miniature needle by her elbow. Stoner watched her for just a second more, then turned back to the window. In another second, he whirled around to look at her hands again as if what he had seen there had only just clicked in. "Are you going to tell me about *that?*'' he demanded, reaching across her and turning the engagement ring on her left hand so he could see the stone better. ''That thing must be a full carat.''

The ring was so new Gena had barely told anyone about it. And he certainly wouldn't have been the person she would have chosen to tell first about it in any event. She remembered a morning when Sue Ellen Morrison had stretched out a hand and showed her a ring, and she'd felt such pain she'd thought she would rip in two. ''It's an engagement ring,'' she answered simply.

''Christ, Gena.'' He kept his hand on hers for a long moment, then dropped it abruptly, his pupils wide, searching her face. ''*Ape* could tell it's an engagement ring. The question is, who in hell is it from?''

She didn't answer him. She could feel her hand shaking again, a reaction from him touching her for just that one crazy moment.

''I broke my arm when I tried to push my car out of a drift,'' he answered the question she had asked before and he hadn't answered. Some kind of a trade-off.

''The ring's from Braxton Hershey,'' she answered his question.

He stepped up beside her, frowning, looking as if he couldn't connect the name Braxton Hershey to a face.

''Hershey the surgeon,'' she explained. ''The man you scrubbed with only this evening.''

''Hell, Gena!'' For just a second his face went crooked. Then he blinked and righted it. ''Braxton Hershey is a pompous ass! How could you think of spending the rest of your life with someone like him?''

How dare he ask her that? As if he cared what she did. As if he had some investment in her future. He had had none since an evening in high school. Her hand unsteady,

Gena turned her back on him and concentrated on Mary Nightowl's hand. Just as he'd predicted, the new needle punctured skin and slid in easily. "If you're done criticizing my judgment now," Gena managed, unwilling to let him know how much he could still hurt her, "would you open that line for me?"

Stoner whirled the plastic clip on the fluid line above her head. Not to the speed of flow she wanted, of course, but open at least, so it wouldn't clot shut until she could regulate it.

"Do you know what I'd do different, if I could do things over again?" Mary Nightowl asked, suddenly sitting up straighter, as if the question had just been asked. "I'd not get married again. I'd have children though. Like you did, Dr. Portobello."

Gena stared at the woman, unable to understand why she had said that. What question she was answering.

"Easy, Mary," Stoner put a hand on the woman's shoulder protectively. "You have your two worlds confused. Or maybe Dr. Portobello with her mother. Dr. Portobello doesn't have children."

"Another thing. I'd be rich and famous," Mary continued, as if she hadn't heard Stoner's denial, or else believed that both of them would be sincerely interested in the surveyed opinion of someone who swallowed witches. "So rich, every week I could afford to ride a merry-go-round that didn't stop."

Gena continued to stare at the woman. The summer that Scott and she had been juniors in high school, Gena had gone to work at the Cow River Amusement Park, just as she had every other summer. In the middle of her first evening there, she had loaded up the merry-go-round, put it on Run, and walked away, leaving red, white, and blue horses going round and round and round on an endless ride, people pulling rings from the overhead trough endlessly until a golden one appeared. The person who grabbed the golden ring off the merry-go-round that way won a free "wish" or prize on the midway. In all the confusion that night of the merry-go-round that wouldn't stop, whoever had won the ring had walked off with it. Ralph Atkinson, the owner, had posted a sign the next day, "The policy of wishing has been suspended" because he had no gold ring for anyone to grab.

"The last thing I would do . . . is not fall in love again," Mary concluded. "It hurts too much when love is over."

Gena remembered the sight of the woman's husband—blue and bloated and reeking with rotting flesh—being raised from the Niagara River the spring after he had drowned.

Hell, wasn't that true, she thought. Walking back toward the nurse's station and unlocking the two wooden doors that led to the unit, wondering as she fumbled for keys, how a woman who seemed more sane than she herself was, at least better able to peg what she wanted to do with the rest of her life than Gena could, was confined on the inside of those doors, while Gena was allowed to walk out of them.

From the second doorway she looked back to see Scott Stoner still standing by Mary's bed. "Now you've got it straight," she heard him say to the older woman. He reached and squeezed her shoulder again. Comforting. Orienting. "Now you're talking about the real world."

Chapter Three

Zack Appleton stood by the nurse's desk on the fourth floor of A Building, staring out at the swirling snow. He hated being up all night. The only advantage to working nights was a certain feeling of power. Keeping watch while a city slept, never being surprised by waking up in the morning and finding himself snowed in. Able to see it coming all night.

He recognized that there were worse jobs to do at night. His guidance counselor in high school had told him once that working at a job, maybe a clerk in McLean's Hardware on South Peach Street in Atlanta, was probably the best Zack could ever expect to accomplish in life. His mind was too slow to make him a winner. In the end, he had never even gotten that job. McLean had given it to a pretty little cheerleader. Without a part-time job, he hadn't had money for premed. He had compensated by accepting a football scholarship to Mississippi State. There he sat for hours on locker room benches, listening to a man berate him for not enough school spirit or "goddamn fuckin' gumption," another way to say his mind was too cautious. But then, coaches hadn't been able to understand he only put on a helmet because of the tuition money, not because he thought it was important to put on a helmet. They had thought football was the only thing there was.

Never a sensational linebacker in college, just solid and steady, he had never been good enough to be picked for an All-Star game. In his senior year in college, he *had* been picked in the pro draft by the New England Patriots. Not because he was flashy, the pro scout stressed, but because he was consistent, able to hold fast, plug a line, no matter how many times halfbacks tried to come through it.

He told everyone now that he had never tried out for the Patriots; that he had chosen medical school instead. The truth was that he had tried out; even one year in a pro helmet would have paid his full medical school tuition. The hard-to-face part of the truth was that he hadn't made it; he had been beaten out by a monster from Ball State who weighed forty pounds more than Zack and had gotten off his tail seven seconds faster. Stymied, trying to find a way to go on from there, Zack had mailed admission forms to a hundred and twenty-three medical schools in the United States. After reading a hundred and twenty-three rejections, he had had to settle for admission to one in Mexico. A crazy education: His first year there he spent as much time getting his *Como Esta* straight, as he did learning pathology and the legitimate uses for steroids. He had transferred back to S.U.N.Y. at Buffalo for his U. S. license. A "fifth pathway," back door, older-than-usual doctor.

Done with school, he'd wanted to intern at Mt. Sinai in Miami Beach and spend his free time stretched out on the sand collecting seashells. Never a sensational medical student, however a solid and consistent one, a White Horse residency outside Buffalo, up to his armpits in snow, had been his only option.

Now he had decided what he wanted to do. After this year

as chief resident at White Horse, he'd go back to Atlanta and set up practice there. Get rich on the little old Southern ladies who didn't have as much heart trouble as loneliness. Inside, however, he already knew that would be a disaster. He had been beaten out of every position he'd tried for in his life. He would be beaten out of a lucrative practice in Atlanta, by someone more personable or better-looking than he was. His best move, therefore, would be to set up an internal medicine practice right here in White Horse. Doctors knew him here; they slept through the night now because he was there keeping green residents in line; they would refer to him. Slow, but consistent and thorough, had paid off for him in both line-backing and being a chief resident. As a White Horse internist—if he could keep gritting his teeth about how much he hated snow—it would continue to pay off for him the rest of his life.

Impatiently, he flipped open Dan Gallagher's chart to the temperature page as he walked into the man's room. It showed the patient had had a temperature over 103 since he had arrived from the recovery room. Zack looked from the chart to Gallagher. The man should have been having an easy recovery period. After all, an appendectomy was easy surgery. Instead, he was obviously not doing well. His eyes glowed with fever; he was so hot that sweat was clinging to his forehead in huge beaded drops; his lips were dry and cracked; he looked barely responsive. As Zack looked back at the chart, Gallagher coughed and moaned from pain and pressed a hand against his abdominal incision, as if he felt it were ripping open. A plastic tube in his nose, leading down to his stomach, should have been barely draining anything—just there to relieve any air on his stomach and keep him comfortable—instead, it was draining dark brown, evil-looking fluid.

"What in hell is going on here?" Zack pulled his stethoscope from around his neck and pressed the tip of it against the man's abdomen. He punched his pocket beeper at the same time and told the operator to page Scott Stoner, flipping through the chart again to look for Braxton Hershey's post-op orders. If an appendix ruptured, a patient had to have antibiotic coverage afterward to prevent infection. If it was a routine appendectomy, that was optional. There was no mention of antibiotics in Hershey's orders, which meant that Hershey had thought there had been no problem. Zack impatiently pushed the call light by the bed to raise a nurse, while he flipped through more pages, trying to make sense out of what he was reading. There were only two things that could make a temperature run that high: intracranial pressure affecting the heat control center in the hypothalamus and infection. Obviously this was infection. Zack punched the call bell a third time, but no one had appeared by the time he had finished Braxton Hershey's written description of very routine but lengthy surgery.

"Yes, Doctor." A little blonde nurse—looking terribly young to be on alone at night, and apparently cold, an examining gown pulled over her uniform—finally appeared in the doorway of the room. She was holding blood-smeared crumpled linens in her arms. Her shoes—white, he guessed, when she had come on duty—were also splattered with blood.

"Find Lynn Curtain for me," Zack barked at her, turning his back, not wanting to hear the story about whose blood she had on her. "And repage Scott Stoner."

"He just got off the elevator," the nurse said in a soft, little-girl voice and left again with her pile of dirty linen.

"What in hell did you do to this fellow in surgery?" Appleton demanded of Stoner as the man walked into the room.

"He was an appendectomy," Stoner answered, coming to a quick halt beside him.

"No chance Kissell barfed in the incision during it, is there?" Zack asked.

Stoner gave him a look that said that wasn't likely.

"How about telling me why in hell it took two hours for you two to do a fuckin' appendectomy?" Ape asked next. "Hershey can do one alone in twenty minutes. As quick as ten if he's double-parked. Five, if he has to piss."

"All I did was retract during the thing," Stoner answered, holding up his hands to show he had no hidden cards. "I didn't watch the time."

"And how many times did either you or Hershey break sterile technique while you were doin' all that?"

"Sterility was never a problem."

"That's impossible, Stoner!" Ape protested. "The man has a temperature of 103!"

"He's dry. He lost a lot of blood."

"The worst dehydration does is cause a temperature of 101. He's 103. That means, if you didn't rupture his fuckin' appendix, you cut some fuckin' gut! You should have been up here an hour ago, getting him cultured and an antibiotic started."

"I *was* up here and ordered a new hemoglobin on him," Stoner said. "Because I think that's going to come back low."

Ape had started to puzzle over what a margin full of scribbled numbers on the vital signs page meant, when Lynn Curtain appeared in the room doorway. "What do you need, Doctors?" she asked. "That Debbie couldn't get for you, that is?"

Zack assumed Debbie was the linen-carrying nurse who had first appeared. "Debbie looks fifteen," he criticized, still looking at the chart and not at her. "Why is she on alone?"

"She is twenty-one, Doctor. And licensed. And being paid to do whatever it is you want. What is it you want?"

The morning Bob Haiden had oriented Zack, he had told him that the S.A.W.M.P. used to be really loose at night. Then the center had hired Lynn, a baccalaureate nurse from Boston University, as night supervisor, and she had put a tight rein on things so that decent care could get done at night. Zack had been really worried about working at night at the S.A.W.M.P., so far away from the main center. Haiden had grinned and said there was a secret to success at the swamp, and he would share it with him, if Zack agreed to take some of his weekend calls. Zack had thought the man was going to share some overall principle on how to get tricky patients through the night until morning, some eternal secret of medicine that had escaped him, or simply hadn't translated well into Spanish. Instead, Haiden had whispered to him that the secret was: page Lynn Curtain.

Zack liked her. She had enough education so that he could talk to her about patients, not just issue orders to her, and there was an attractive sensuousness about her. But not this night. She was wearing a green cotton scrub dress instead of her regular uniform. It pulled tight across her bulging abdomen, advertising her pregnancy. A wisp of hair was straggling out of the barrette that held the hair off her collar. Her ankles looked swollen. "Is there anyone in for X-ray?" he asked her, trying to sound agreeable in light of how tired she looked.

"Debbie knew the answer to that."

Laughing at her nerve—not many people dared not to openly grovel before him—knowing she'd tell him in another minute if X-ray was staffed or not, he lifted away Gallagher's abdominal dressing to see if Hershey had put in a drain. If he had, and if his bowel sutures were leaking, Zack would see brown, fecal fluid. There was no drain.

Zack opened Gallagher's chart again and puzzled at the scribbled numbers on the temperature page. "What's your concern with bleeding?" he asked Stoner. "Did he lose a lot of blood?"

"I think Hershey rated it in the chart as the topside of normal," Stoner answered.

"Why was that?" Zack demanded.

"Hershey describes what happened in his note," Stoner answered. "While making his incision, he noticed the iliac artery had a weak place in it. He repaired that as long as he was in the abdomen. Unfortunately, that resulted in a large blood loss."

Zack had already read that, but guessed that Hershey had repaired the artery so fast his hands had smoked. That shouldn't have resulted in much blood loss. "Is there something you're not telling me?" he asked.

"I think Hershey's note says it all."

Zack questioned that, but let it go. "Get me a setup for a blood culture and white blood count." Zack issued orders to Lynn, since Stoner wasn't moving to give any new ones. "And a flat plate abdomen for fluid level." He paused to see if Lynn hesitated at any of that. She didn't. Which meant X-ray was in. "Then call Hershey and let him know what is going on here!" he shouted after her into the hallway.

Zack had friends from medical school who had already taken care of celebrities: Ella Fitzgerald, Boy George, and even the President. Western New York had few celebrities. Dan Gallagher, because he was so influential in that city, was the closest to a celebrity he had come. The story of his life, he thought. There he stood, hoping nothing would go wrong so he could set up a practice in this town, and now, his first important patient had apparently developed an overwhelming infection. Zack crossed his hairy arms in front of his chest and leaned against the wall, pondering on what to do next while he watched Lynn go for the blood tubes. He had wanted to ask her to come home with him the first time he had ever met her. But slow and consistent, trying to be cautious, deciding he should buy some better sheets before he asked her, he had taken his time. Scott Stoner hadn't been cautious. Scott Stoner hadn't worried about sheets. He'd used the hospital's. And because he'd acted that way, she was now seven months pregnant. Maybe more. Zack knew almost nothing about pregnant women, but she looked more than seven months pregnant to him.

"So what was the hemoglobin level you got on him?" he barked at Stoner, stepping back to the sink to wash his hands.

Stoner reached for the man's chart quickly to try and locate it. "I was just coming up to find that out," he said.

"Who have you been shacking up with that you didn't get up here sooner?"

"That isn't funny, Ape." Stoner stopped looking for the report to talk to him. "You know I need good things said about me these days. Don't start rumors."

"You and Curtain are only a rumor? She is so pregnant she can hardly walk, and you are only a rumor?"

"I could use some help here, Ape, not criticism. I didn't know the man was this bad."

"I'll give you help." Ape couldn't control his temper, angry over how sick Gallagher had become. "Exactly the same as I gave Portobello. If you want to stay here past next Tuesday, keep your mind on what you're doing. Don't screw up anything between now and then."

Stoner's jawline hardened. He had already screwed up.

"I'll even give you some extra advice, Stoner," Ape added, starting toward the hallway, "Don't screw *anybody.*"

Stoner glared at him, then bit his lower lip as if he was deliberately stopping himself from answering. He was well aware how much say Ape had about who stayed and who didn't.

Zack stopped by the nursing station abruptly, bringing his mind back from Stoner to the care problem. Aside from new blood work, he didn't know what to do next for Gallagher. If the man's bowel sutures were leaking, he needed to be taken back to surgery, but if his blood count was low—and the nurse at the desk didn't seem able to find a report—he was no longer a good surgical risk. Zack sighed, watching the nurse search through a pile of unfiled laboratory slips. He hated the feeling of not knowing what to do, the feeling that he had run all the plays he knew. Slow and steady hadn't worked with Lynn Curtain. Slow and steady didn't seem to be working with Dan Gallagher either.

Gena Portobello walked down to the first-floor locker room in C Building and hung up her coat. As she did, she heard a radio from a basement lab announcing that the wind outside was up to sixty miles an hour. The thruway was drifting so much snow, it had been closed to the Pennsylvania line.

"Do you expect there to be a problem keeping White Horse roads clear tonight?" a radio announcer asked the director of City Services.

"There's no immediate problem," a man with a rich Irish brogue answered over the periodic beep of a tape-recorded message. "My best plows and my best men are out tonight."

When wind velocity reached seventy, a storm was officially a blizzard, the radio announcer educated her. Gena remembered hesitating on the guard rail of the bridge, almost plunging over it. She wondered if knowing the storm wasn't a blizzard yet should have made her feel better. She was wondering also why Mary Nightowl had said she'd like to ride a merry-go-round that didn't stop. Did the woman know about the night Gena had turned one on and let it run?

A crazy thing for her to have done, yet no crazier than some of the other things she and Scott Stoner and Dale Ronald had done as kids. An odd combination of trouble, the three of them: tall and blond Scott, with not much free time because he was expected to help out in the restaurant after school; The Stonehouse still a small street-front place on Center Street back then. Dale, short and black-haired with almost no chin, was the son of the city's funeral director. Gena with red hair, the city's disgrace. Three kids without much in common, except that their names had fallen so close in the alphabet that they had always been assigned adjacent seats in school.

A lot of the crazy things the three of them did as kids had to do with the fact that girls in town were directed not to play with Gena because she was a bastard. Stoner was expected to bus tables so he couldn't socialize much. When he did get out, and they were all together, they were ready to do something wild.

In the White Horse City Hall, the name plates on office doors were metal strips that slid into metal grooves, easily removable and exchangeable. As early as grade school, the three of them had regularly changed the sign on the Mayor's office with that on the ladies room door, then sat in the lobby and watched dignitaries—and once the Mayor himself—walk into the ladies' room by mistake. One time, Stoner and Dale stole some paint from Currie's garage and painted stripes on the school principal's lawn. A week later all three of them had taken the same paint and broken into the police garage and painted Dan Gallagher's patrol car bright pink.

One Sunday, Dale had stuffed a frog under Father Henzel's domed communion tray, and the three friends sat in the back row of the church and watched the man try to conduct a mass while the tray in front of him was rattling and bouncing, as if it was actually springing into body and blood. Their reputation as real troublemakers came when it was discovered that they earned money by stealing clothing from stiffs that Dale's father had buried.

For funerals at the Methodist church, the pallbearers carried the casket into a private room off the front foyer, while the hearse was brought around to the big steps in front and Dale's dad was sealing the coffin. When Dale turned fifteen, his dad started leaving that job to him. In the few minutes Dale was left alone, he and Stoner and Gena would strip the clothes off the corpse. When the hearse was out front and the pallbearers returned to carry the casket down the big church steps, no one guessed that anything had disappeared or changed from when they saw the casket last. It cost the three of them a dollar to get the suit or dress cleaned. They sometimes got as much as twenty dollars at a used clothing store in Eagleton for a good suit or dress. They also got a very revealing—if rapid—look at a lot of naked—if dead—men or women, not a totally repulsive act at fifteen.

The day they were discovered, of course, was not during some little funeral when there were almost no mourners, but at the funeral of Harkness Nathan, a former mayor of White Horse. Being ushered into cars at the front curb of the church had been almost the entire population of White Horse. Down the front steps into that crowd had walked six pallbearers carrying an elaborate silver casket, Harkness Nathan lying naked inside it. Only two steps into the processional, on the next to top step of the church, the shoe of one of the front men had slipped on an icy patch. The man had dropped his end of the casket to keep upright. A second later, everyone else's shoes hit the same ice and they all let go the same way. The casket, silver and embossed with angel faces, bumped the length of the twelve front steps, gaining speed as it went, until by the time it reached the sidewalk it was little less than an airborne silver streak. When it smashed against the fire hydrant at the curb, the lid popped open. Out jumped the body of the city's most outstanding citizen, as naked as the day he had come into White Horse.

All three of them had spent a long time that evening explaining the incident to parents, listening to expectations of accountability. Gerald Stoner ran a quality restaurant. Never in his wildest dreams had he thought of doing anything more out of line than serving milk instead of cream in the coffee. He never even compromised as much as to serve frozen vegetables. The main reason Dale and Stoner and Gena had been able to get away with gags and jokes all those years—Gena was sure—was because after each one, Gerald Stoner invited Dan Gallagher or any other injured party up to The Stonehouse for dinner on the house; a treat for people who otherwise couldn't afford his prices. Unable to invite a dead man who had had his clothes stolen, Gerald had reacted to the silver streak incident by telling his son he didn't want him to ever speak to Dale Ronald or Gena Portobello again.

Although The Stonehouse had opened in its present quarters overlooking the Niagara River gorge by that time, and Stoner had moved up to The Hill, staying away from him had not been easy for Gena. From the day Scott had given her his bean plant, they had been more than just friends. At twelve, lying on the grass in Niawanda Park, she'd savored her first kiss from him. At fifteen, after they were no longer supposed to be speaking to each other, she would stand leaning against her locker every morning at school and watch him spin his combination, take off his coat, and comb his hair, as if he never saw her there. Except just before he turned to go, he'd flash her his grin, as if he definitely did know she was there.

The one most upset by the no-more-gags arrangement was Dale Ronald, because he had no real friends except for the two of them. Dan Gallagher, the Police Chief, was miffed, too, because he was missing out on all those free Stonehouse dinners. A short man, so fat that the buttons on his jacket always gaped open, he was a man asking to be made fun of. The best gag ever was the Great Watermelon Caper the spring of Stoner's and Gena's junior year in high school.

Scott had offered to drive Gena home from school that day because it was raining and he had his brand new orange Beetle. He was anxious to show it off, although the windshield wipers didn't work well, so it wasn't a great car for rain. As they passed Rinaldo's market on Main Street, a store clerk was just beginning to set up a pile of watermelons on the sidewalk. Just beyond the corner, pulled in next to the curb, they could see Dan Gallagher's big car, with CHIEF on the door.

It was too rich an opportunity to pass up. Stoner parked, went into the market, and paid for a melon, but he didn't pick it up. Back in the car, he drove around the block, screeched to a stop in front of the market, scrambled out, making a show of what he was doing, and darting through the raindrops, grabbed a melon, ducked back inside his car, and pulled away with a squeal of wheels against the wet pavement. To the man sitting in the police car, it certainly looked like a boy stealing a watermelon. Gena and Stoner were only half a block away when, siren screaming, the police car pulled along beside them.

"I saw you take a melon!" Gallagher's face began turning purple as he waved at Stoner to pull over. His breath was pushing out in sharp, short gasps as he ran up to Stoner's front window. Rain was running in rivulets down his face, as he shouted, "Goddamn, the two of you are going to jail for this!" His uniform had turned a soggy blue by the time he started to pull open Stoner's door, and, eyes bulging, spotted the market receipt Stoner held out to him. Gallagher kicked the tires of the car and then the door. At the last moment, he noticed the faulty window wipers. "You get out of here!" he shouted at Stoner, tugging his suit jacket back into place over his protruding belly. "If I see you again today, I'll jail you for those windshield wipers!"

Except for the rain, it had been a warm spring afternoon. They had had no place special to go, so the two of them sat in the car in the cemetery driveway, hidden by a high stone wall, and broke open the watermelon. They ate most of it, laughing at how many people they knew lying in their coffins naked.

At the end of the afternoon, after two hours of being alone that way, hidden by the rain and the wall, Gena glanced at Stoner's blue eyes searching her face, bumping a knee against hers and then pulling it back, stretching an arm along the back of the seat and touching her arm, then pulling it back. Then he had kissed her. She hadn't meant to be that serious. To deepen a relationship always led to trouble. But there would be no problem, she reasoned. At the right moment, she would stop everything and brush him off, keep everything under control. Remain only friends with him. Except when he brushed his lips along her cheeks a second time, she knew she wasn't going to stop him then or any other time.

In another minute, he had been pushing into her—a high she hadn't known before—first a moment of unyielding hymen, in pain just for that moment from the trapped pressure of tissue never before stretched that far.

By the time he had rezipped and she had pulled her jeans back into place, she had agreed to go with him to the Junior Prom the following week.

Gerald Stoner reacted to that announcement by telling his son that he was taking his car away from him for two weeks. For tormenting Dan Gallagher that afternoon, he said. But it was obviously to make the prom difficult for Stoner, and hopefully make him change his mind about taking Gena—to end an alliance with a girl so far beneath his social status.

White Horse was so small though that to get anywhere except Bird Island, no one really needed a car. Stoner walked to Gena's house to pick her up the evening of the prom, and they walked together along the edge of the railroad track and then up Hill Road to The Stonehouse (where else did people in White Horse go for their very best occasions?). She remembered she had worn a white organdy dress with miniature pink embroidered roses on the top, high enough in front to be proper for White Horse; low enough to let a sixteen-year-old date appreciate and remember what he had felt there the week before. Stoner had worn a white tuxedo with a pink cummerbund. They sat at a table near the fountain with Dale and a girl named Faye and ate excellent melt-in-the-mouth prime rib. The school dance band had been dressed in yellow blazers and porkpie hats and played Elvis Presley's "Return to Sender" over and over. And at the very end of the evening, for a reason Gena was not sure of, Dale stood up on the main table with one foot in a crystal punch bowl, and drank a toast to any guy in the class who knew which side the mole on Sue Ellen Morrison's ass was on.

At midnight, two of the band's porkpie hats stuck on their heads, Stoner and Gena had walked back along the Hill road and the railroad track to town. The end of a perfect evening. Until about twenty yards from the old train station, when Gena had realized that there was someone following them. That wasn't totally unusual; a lot of people used that route to get from the north end of town to the Creek. The two of them were all the way up to the old station house, a red brick building abandoned years before with boarded-up windows, when she realized the people following them had moved up just behind them. When she turned to see who they were, a black man grabbed her arm and pulled her against him. "Don't move, don't say nothin'," he whispered as he pressed a switchblade up under her chin.

Stoner hadn't understood yet what was happening; he tried to elbow the man aside. A second black man caught his arms behind him and pressed a blade up under his chin the same way. "Walk inside," he commanded the two of them, motioning to the door of the empty train station that a third man, a Hispanic with a tiny bobbing mustache, was holding open for them.

"Show us what's inside your pockets," the leather-jacketed man behind Stoner had demanded inside the station.

Stoner must have still believed that was a joke. When he tried to pull away from the man who was holding him, the knife at his throat sliced hard enough across his neck that bright red blood trickled down onto his white jacket.

"You gotta' follow instructions better, guy." The man snapped as Stoner pulled back away from the knife to keep it from slicing further into his neck. Two gold teeth flashed at the side of his mouth. "The blade is very sharp."

That was the moment Gena realized that this was no innocent "scare the hell out of the local cop" high school gag. They could be killed.

"Reach into your pockets now, nice and easy, just like I told you to do, and show me what you've got," the gold-toothed man instructed Stoner again.

Stoner handed the man junk from his pockets: a comb, a pencil stub, a roll of Lifesavers, a house key, some loose change, finally his wallet with six dollars in it. The man took the objects from him patiently, one at a time, then slammed everything down onto the floor. "Goddamn kids!" he shouted at Stoner, kicking at the comb and the Lifesavers and sending them flying across the room into a cloud of dust. "You've got even less than me!"

"Come on, Chez," the man behind Gena tightened his hand on her arm. "We're goin' to get *somethin'* out of this, aren't we?"

The man with the gold teeth glanced at Gena, then looked away again. Suddenly embarrassed. "Hurry it up," he said after a minute, talking to the far wall, coughing and covering his face behind his hand from the dust. "Before someone comes."

Gena hadn't followed what he was approving. She was thinking how strange it was that even in very uncommon circumstances like that, a man had remembered a common courtesy like covering his mouth to cough. It was her last thought about courtesy. The Hispanic behind her snatched at the strap of her gown and tore it off. The sound of white organdy tearing was sharp and dramatic in the empty dusty building.

"Hey!" Stoner started to pull away from the man in back of him again.

The gold-toothed black man slammed Stoner back against the baggage room wall and pressed the knife hard enough against his throat that it cut skin again. "Just keep it quiet until everything is over." His voice was the same soft, almost whispering tone he had used before, but all the while he spoke, he pressed the knife hard into Stoner's neck. New blood kept trickling down onto Stoner's jacket. "You don't, I'm going to have to kill you both."

Stoner froze against the far wall.

The Hispanic clamped a hand over Gena's mouth and pulled and ripped the rest of her gown into shreds. The second man, a black with an distinctive scar on his left cheek, held out a pocket knife and slashed off her underpants and stockings with its tip.

They were going to rape her! Gena struggled; she couldn't tear herself free. She looked frantically at Stoner to do something.

He came away from the wall in a blur of motion, clawing and pushing at the gold-toothed man. Up by her side, he plunged a hand down on the shoulder of the black man with the pocket knife, trying to turn him away from Gena. The black thrust the knife into Stoner's lower abdomen. It didn't seem to matter. Stoner kept coming. The black pulled back the knife and stabbed at least two more times.

Outside the station, a faraway train whistle shrilled, and the red lights of the Hill Road crossing started flashing on and off, turning the room first white, then red. The gold-toothed man grabbed Stoner by the collar and tossed him back against the wall again. "Don't slow things up here, fella'," he pressed his switchblade against Stoner's throat again. "Or the next time this goes all the way through to the back." The wall behind Stoner rang with the sound of his head hitting it. Gradually, Stoner sank back against the wall, fresh blood soaking his white tuxedo from both his neck and the stab marks in his groin.

Outside on the track, a switch clicked from the train's wheels striking it; the gates of the crossing thudded into place. Inside, the two men wrestled Gena onto a trunk top, scurrying to unzip and push her legs apart. The Hispanic ripped perineal skin and vagina as he pushed inside her.

Outside the station, a freight train thundered past on the side track, box cars of chemicals heading for Niagara Falls rattling and clanking. Inside, pain tore through Gena's pelvis in jolts as skin and mucus membrane ripped. As if he didn't notice, the man tore more tissue each time he pushed inside her. In and out, in and out, in and out.

Outside, the train clanked and swayed next to the building. The whistle screamed. Pain flowed through Gena in a steady stream. When the man finally did pull free of her, his penis was so smeared with blood that drops of it fell onto the floor and over the trunk.

The black man with the scar on his face didn't seem to notice that in order to take his turn he had to push in through torn tissue; that each of his thrusts tore still further until by the time he was finished Gena no longer had the strength to scream. Finally, he pulled free of her and she crumpled onto the floor in a pool of blood.

The caboose of the train passed at the same minute, leaving the room instantly quiet. "We're goin' now, guy," the gold-toothed man said softly to Stoner, slowly taking the switch-blade away from his throat. "The both of you wait half an hour here before you go. You leave any quicker, I'll kill you both."

There was the muffled sound of zippers closing and a quick scurrying of footsteps behind Gena, and then the door opening and closing.

Silence. Nothing in the train station but years of dust and aged trunks and yellowed notices of connections to Pittsburgh and Scranton. Gena curled tighter into a ball by an ancient wooden waiting room bench, aware blood was continuing to trickle down her legs, hoping the red flow would increase and continue until it killed her so she would never have to describe what had happened here to anyone.

"Gena?" Stoner's voice floated down to her finally, but as if it were coming from some place far away. She was aware of Stoner crouching beside her and trying to pull the shreds of organdy around her. "Come on. We have to get out of here."

Gena closed her eyes.

"Here." Stoner stripped his tuxedo jacket and wrapped it around her, urging her again to follow him. He was having trouble moving, obviously in pain from the stab wounds. Finally he picked her up and carried her along the tracks to Boyer Street and Richard Culbertson's office. Gena remembered ether, stitches, her mother shouting across an examining table at Stoner for not being able to stop that from happening. Outside the examining room, Gena had heard her mother arguing with Dan Gallagher. After what had seemed like a long delay, Gerald Stoner had joined them and added to the shouting: if Stoner hadn't dated that kind of girl, that kind of thing wouldn't happen.

Culbertson had quietly put in stitches to stop her bleeding, then admitted Stoner to the medical center to have his stab wounds closed. He told a crazy story that he had fallen on a broken bottle. Everyone there agreed at the end of the evening to tell no one what had really happened.

It would be better that way, Dan Gallagher had insisted. Gena could avoid having to testify in court about what had happened to her; Stoner wouldn't have to testify about how he hadn't been able to stop it from happening. The experience should have pulled the two of them together forever after, but it had been too big, too painful, for either of them to handle. Rape was too unspeakable an event in a small town to mention. And so, instead of pulling them together, it had become a hurting, uncomfortable wedge that had pulled them apart.

In another month, Gena had set a merry-go-round on Run. In the fall, to get away from White Horse, she had gone to Baltimore to visit an aunt. She didn't come back to White Horse until May of her senior year, in the hope that being away from Stoner for that length of time would kill everything she felt for him. She remembered very clearly walking up to him in the hallway of school the first day she was back, thinking it would feel strange, talking to him, watching him smile. Instantly, she was overwhelmed by pain, an actual physical stabbing bolt that started in her gut and spread up into her chest. Just seeing him again brought it all back. She watched him focus his terribly blue eyes on her, as if searching to see how she felt about him. And she noticed the way Sue Ellen Morrison's hands rested so comfortably on his shoulders while he did that.

If she had ever messed up anything in her life, she thought, it had been not telling Gerald Stoner that the episode at the train station hadn't happened because she was a creek girl—it had simply happened. Standing there staring at Scott Stoner in the school hallway that first day back, feeling that bitter biting pain in her chest—and doing nothing—meant she'd messed up again. She watched him walk away with Sue Ellen, her hand sinking down to pat his butt as they left. She hadn't done anything about those two things back then. And it was impossible to do anything about them now.

Lori Dukane was seventeen, slim with a distinctive angular jawline and rich brown skin.

She had first felt the pain cross her abdomen at noon. Not actual pain, but a sensation more like a giant belt stretching across her stomach and pulling tight. By the time Carl Dukane had called home at six to leave the message with Mrs. Manson downstairs that he had a chance to work overtime and wouldn't be home until midnight, the pressure of the band had been suffocating. Each time at its peak, it had been overlaid by the feel of someone pushing a knife into her insides, twisting it over and over until they slowly withdrew it again.

At 2:00 A.M., when she heard the welcome sound of the pick-up truck in the driveway, she lay curled into a ball on the kitchen floor, the knife slicing through her over and over again. She hadn't felt the baby inside her move for hours. Bowel had twisted around it, she was sure, and cut off its blood supply and killed it, and now the pain was killing her. Thinking about the dead baby, her tears pooled in her eyes and overflowed down her cheeks onto the floor.

"Lori?" Carl called to her from the apartment doorway. "Why are you on the floor?"

She was too exhausted to answer. If she tried to say anything, by the time he reached the kitchen she might already be dead.

"Lori?" her husband crouched down beside her and wiped away a tear from her face. "What's happening?"

Drops of moisture from melting snow on his cap fell onto her abdomen. "I'm tearing apart," she whispered through lips dry and feverish. She was so tired, her voice sounded hollow.

He urged her to sit up.

She couldn't. The pain was too sharp and too long and too hard for her to do anything but just lie there.

"Come on. You have to do something." Carl pulled her to her feet. Supporting her against his shoulder, he helped her to the apartment door. "The pickup can get us through this to Bird Island. To a doctor."

She didn't want to go to a hospital! She didn't want to see a doctor lean over her and tell her that the baby was dead. As bad as the knifelike pain was, lying there and not knowing for *sure* that the baby was dead, was better than hearing someone say it.

At the doorway of the apartment, he stretched her coat over her shoulders and helped her out into the hallway.

"I wanted to have a baby!" she cried as he urged her to start down the stairs. She couldn't stop new tears. "I wanted to have one so bad!"

He was only seventeen himself and not much more aware of how things worked than she was. Picking her up, he carried her down the last stairs. ''I think you're havin' one,'' he said. ''What do *you* think all the pain is about?''

Lori sat in the front seat of the pickup, open-mouthed. All day long, as many times as she had felt the rhythmic pressure and pain surround her belly and lock her in its grip, the thought that *normal* labor would feel like this had never crossed her mind.

Chapter Four

Scott Stoner was still standing by the nursing station on 4A, waiting for the hemoglobin report on Dan Gallagher.

He hated having to cover for Lou Jefferson this night. Jefferson always seemed to be complaining of flu symptoms he had to stay home for. Stoner suspected that Jefferson had ulcerative colitis rather than an infectious flu that kept him out so much. Either that or it was sheer laziness.

Then again maybe it was minimal depression. Four-A was the type of service that could cause that; a lot of chronically ill people were hospitalized up there. A sixty-nine-year-old woman named Peggy Ferris, who had owned a dress shop in White Horse for years, occupied a room at the end of the hall. She had dictated what was fashion and what was not to White Horse women while Stoner had been growing up. He guessed she must have been aware that she had a lump in her breast for months before she mentioned it to her daughter. Maybe she had been deliberately ignoring the lump; a woman choosing her own route and time for dying, just as she had chosen how women would dress all those years. Unfortunately, unchecked by surgery, cancer cells had crept into every bone in her body, causing such searing pain at any movement that she was left confined to the S.A.W.M.P. now, unable to walk, the very weight of her body enough to break her back and leg bones. A woman who had spent her life dictating fashion was to spend her final days wearing a blue hospital gown, gritting her teeth against pain.

Her roommate, Evelyn Corning, was the widow of Lionel Corning, the man who had been the manager of the western New York federal bank for twenty-two years before he had died of a heart attack the spring before. All those years as a bank president's wife, Evelyn had courted favors from White Horse people; people willing to fawn over her to get a loan from her husband. Now she was lying bedridden with multiple sclerosis, unable to speak, to feed herself, or reach for anything. Just move her eyes right or left. Some day she would die and no one would even be aware of it for hours, Stoner thought, except the nurse whose job it was to keep track. No one would really care, either. The banker's wife had never been important in White Horse; only her husband's signature had mattered.

Stoner liked to stop by to see the two women whenever he was at the S.A.W.M.P., just to talk. Peggy Ferris was always openly appreciative of attention, and Evelyn's eyes followed him hungrily to the door each time he had to go, telling him even more clearly how appreciated was the sound of someone talking to her, treating her like the seemingly important woman she once had been.

Next door to them was Howard Grishaven, a man who had lived next to the White Horse grade school since Stoner could remember. Coming home from school every afternoon, Stoner had cut across his front lawn; in the summer, he'd grab an apple off the tree there as he went. Every day,

Grishaven had chased him the full length of the lawn. Day after day, year after year, unrelentingly. This day, Grishaven's veins and arteries were so filled with atherosclerosis plaque that the blood supply to his brain had narrowed to a trickle. He was comatose, unable to speak or respond. Everything about him was grinding to a halt except the on-off switch in his brain. He had a tube flowing into his subclavian vein feeding him fluid, a tube pushed into his stomach through his nose siphoning off fluid from there; another into his bladder running off urine. His kidneys had stopped functioning, so he had a tube pushed into his abdomen to let highly concentrated fluid flow in and out to rinse urea out of his body. A less stubborn, less persistent man would have died a long time before. Grishaven was reacting to death the same way he had reacted to a school kid cutting across his lawn every day; not knowing when to quit, he just kept on and on. Every week, a new medical student was assigned to him to order hyperalimentation fluid to keep him in electrolyte balance and rinsed out, to prolong his vegetative state. No one considered investigating why the man's on-off switch hadn't triggered—or how to trigger it—because he was such good practice for med students. Stoner glanced in at the man as he waited for the nurse to telephone the lab, saw he was no different than usual, and came back out to the desk. In the morning a new med student would arrive with a clipboard under his arm and puzzle all day over the perfect electrolyte formula for the man. Up something a little, decrease something a little, earn an A or a D. Stoner's job was just to keep the man safe through the night so the student wouldn't be cheated out of that electrolyte balancing in the morning.

No one answered in the lab. The nurse hung up and said she'd call back in a minute. Stoner used the time to walk back over to the 4A lockup and check Mary Nightowl's IV. She said she was still certain the Witch of the West was alive and well in her stomach. Hell, Stoner thought. The S.A.W.M.P. was warmer and the food was better than what she could afford on the outside. So as long as she didn't mind the other company on the ward: a young girl with straggling yellow hair who had tried to kill herself because her parents told her they were getting a divorce; a forty-year-old man with a wide bald circle on his head, depressed because finally he realized he was never going to do half the things he had planned to do at twenty; a woman named Henrietta who paced wildly up and down the corridor, swinging her arms and scolding imaginary people to mind their own business. If Mary didn't mind the company, he couldn't fault her for being there.

He sat at the nurse's desk and telephoned Henrietta's psychiatrist to check her antianxiety order. The psychiatrist answered sleepily that it was the middle of the night and suggested Stoner increase his own antianxiety level rather than wake him up again. Stoner settled his receiver back gently despite his opinion of that advice—he'd forgotten it was the middle of the night—and increased the woman's thorazine dose himself. Sitting at the desk, he could see snow blowing so strongly out in the parking lot that it had completely walled in the first three rows of cars. His Beetle, parked under the overhang, was a little more protected. If he didn't move it from under there before morning though, he could bet maintenance would plow him in so deep it would be March before he got it out of there.

After another long minute of pondering whether the girl with the terrible hair had actually meant to kill herself, or just meant to scare her parents—Suicide a complexity that escaped him—he crossed back to the medical side to evaluate the blood report he was sure the nurse there would have by then.

Over the years, Stoner had become more and more disgusted with Gallagher, because he had never looked for the men who had dragged Gena and him into that train station. The two of them were marked for a lifetime, and the police chief hadn't done a thing about it.

Back in high school, Stoner admitted, that had seemed to make sense. White Horse *was* a small town, and he would have been mortified by explaining how he hadn't been able to stop Gena from being raped. Only a year later, he realized that that plan hadn't made sense. He and Gena had already been marked by the incident; a trial could not have marked them more.

The little 4A nurse reached across the counter and handed him the pink hematology report he was looking for.

He peered at the miniature numbers on it for the hemoglobin report. Presurgery, Gallagher's level had been 9.2. Postsurgery, it was down to 7.2. Of course it was down! Despite Hershey's underplayed chart note, he had seen the man spurt blood like a stuck pig. The normal was eleven to twelve; a level half of normal meant that the man needed blood transfused if he was going to make it. Especially because now he was developing an infection.

"Transfuse two units of packed cells." Stoner picked up the man's chart to write that out.

"I don't think there's that much of his type blood here," the nurse said. "I think the emergency room used it for the man in the auto accident."

Stoner peered to read her nametag: Debbie Chemielewski. As Lynn Curtain had said, she had to be at least twenty. He agreed with Ape that she looked sixteen. "Use emergency blood," he said.

Debbie smoothed a straggling wisp of hair back behind her ear. "I don't think you can use that."

Stoner hated working with nurses without enough education to know what they were doing. "Emergency blood is O negative. O negative blood has no antibodies in it," he educated her. "So it has no potential to react with anything. It can be given to anyone."

She nodded obediently, but not as if she really understood his point.

"It's red and it's liquid and it'll be compatible," he simplified the theory even more.

"The blood bank only keeps three packs of emergency blood on hand here at night," she explained the real problem. "And Lynn Curtain likes to reserve two of those for the emergency room on a storm night. So I don't think she'll give you permission to use two."

"Cross *one* unit emergency blood," Stoner amended his order. "Until I talk to Curtain."

"Of course, maybe Miss Curtain will let *you* use anything you want," Debbie amended her opinion.

Stoner didn't acknowledge he had heard that, tired of people linking him with Curtain. He knew the blood was rationed. He also remembered there had been an O negative blood pack in OR earlier that evening that hadn't been used. He would get that and take it to the lab to be crossmatched for Gallagher, without having to go through Curtain for more than one pack.

Although, wait! The reason that pack hadn't been used in surgery was because Gallagher didn't want any blood. *Shit!* Stoner walked into the man's room and stood looking down at him until he opened an eye groggily to see who was there.

"I know you're not crazy about this," Stoner said to

him, moving up close to the head of the bed, "But you need a blood transfusion."

The man groaned with pain and shook his head so hard his ears wiggled. "Absolutely not. I don't want anything but clear fluid flowing into me."

"How about some thick red fluid?"

"You wouldn't give me blood without me saying it was all right, would you, Stoner?"

"I want you to tell me it *is* all right."

Gallagher gripped his belly as if it were tearing in two. "What makes you think I can trust you?"

"You have a hemoglobin half what you should have. In another hour, you can trust me that your brain cells won't be able to think unless you get some new blood inside you."

"Let me hear Appleton tell me that, and I'll believe it."

Stoner shook his head. "I can't call a chief and tell him I can't convince a patient to let me do what so obviously needs to be done."

"You think I'm going to trust you to do anything for me, Stoner, think again."

Stoner clenched his jaw. As mortifying as that would be—asking Ape to come up there and confirm what he was saying—he didn't really have any choice. Without new blood, Gallagher was dying.

He caught a glimpse of Debbie just outside the doorway and motioned to her to come inside. "We're going to run some blood," he said confidently. "In the meantime, get up a clean tubing for this IV," he pointed to the blood setup tubing that Kissell had complained about in surgery, still hanging over Gallagher's head, and at a stream of old blood accumulated along the side of the plastic. "So you're sure it's free-flowing."

Debbie nodded agreeably and left to get new equipment.

"You aren't running anything, until I hear Doctor Appleton say it's all right," Gallagher contradicted.

"I'll get him for you," Stoner said quietly as he followed Debbie back out to the desk. At the desk, he decided to humble himself still further and try to get Braxton Hershey's opinion. Hershey didn't answer. His telephone rang and rang endlessly, apparently in an empty house.

Okay. That meant he had no choice but to call Appleton and listen to his opinion of a resident whose patient trusted him so little he needed a back-up opinion. Thanks a lot, Dan Gallagher, he said to himself as he punched buttons, aware that he probably deserved that, for all the jokes he had played on the man in his lifetime.

Richard Culbertson lay stretched out on a cot in one of the resident's sleeping rooms in back of Labor and Delivery. He was the S.A.W.M.P.'s Chief of Obstetrics, a long way up from being a resident.

He was seventy-four, an age where he would have retired years before if he had gone into a sensible business instead of doctoring. He had opened his first medical office in White Horse in 1959, the year he finished his residency. Eisenhower had been president; women had thought that being a housewife was a credible role; Chubby Checker had introduced the Twist.

He'd bought his practice from Joel Dirkhiem, a retiring GP. Dirkhiem had owned pretty outmoded examining equipment, but he'd insisted that half the people in White Horse came to him. The truth had been that he'd never modernized his office, because *no one* in White Horse came to him. He'd been a Demerol addict for the last ten years. His office had been on the second floor, over The Stonehouse. Culbertson should have realized that sick people didn't walk upstairs to go to a doctor.

Culbertson had been forced to live on restaurant handouts for almost a full year, until one morning a customer in the restaurant choked on an olive and stopped breathing from a plugged airway. Culbertson ran downstairs and trached him and saved his life. After that, one by one, people had heard the story of the new man in town who literally brought people back from the dead. Patients started to come to him. He bought a house on Boyer Street and used the downstairs as office space.

Once he had sick people coming to him, he needed a closer hospital where he could care for patients without having to drive all the way into Buffalo. He bought an empty office building on Center Street and furnished it with hospital beds and started the medical center. Today, people credited the growth of the center to the Warrens. Granted, Warren money had made it grow, had served as the incentive for federal grants and community contributions, but in the beginning it had been Culbertson's creation. He still put any extra money he had into the center. Ten years before, when the surgery suite had almost been forced to close for inadequate facilities, he had personally donated a hundred thousand dollars to upgrade it.

And now, David Frank had asked him to retire! Was *insisting* that he retire the first of the year. Had already named his replacement. And what did he, Culbertson, have to show for it? Almost nothing. He had little recognition at the center. Sometimes early in the morning, arriving at the main center, watching the gleam of early morning sun strike the WHMC logo on the front of the building, it bothered him that his name was nowhere on the building. Daily, he waited for someone to suggest that as a fitting reward at his retirement, at least one building there be renamed for him. He dreamed of that happening.

Except that he had made three mistakes in his life. The first had been believing Joel Dirkhiem that an upstairs office, over a restaurant, was a good location. Second was encouraging the center to expand to Bird Island. Looking back, he realized he should have encouraged expansion, but at the main center instead.

Only he knew about his third mistake. And David Frank. When Culbertson retired, like a runner passing on the eternal flame, he was expected to pass his practice on to some worthy resident, most likely Zack Appleton. The real reason Culbertson didn't want to retire at the first of the year, was that he was trying to hold on long enough to pass his practice on to Gena Portobello. He knew that she had never been the same since the evening Scott Stoner had carried her, bleeding, to Culbertson's office on Boyer Street. That involved his third mistake. He had not been the same since that day either.

Bob Haiden, the chief obstetrics resident at the medical center, woke to the sound of the wind banging open a shutter on his apartment window. He stirred and sat up, then lay back absolutely quiet again, willing the noise to stop; or else his wife to get up and do something about it. After all, he had worked sixteen hours that day, seven to eleven. He was only off now because Gena Portobello had agreed to work an extra shift at the S.A.W.M.P. to relieve him.

The wind whistled along the side of the house, scratching snow against the shingles. *Bang,* the shutter swacked open against the outside clapboard again. If one of the two of them didn't get up quickly and stop the banging, the shutter would blow off and fall on someone's head and they would be sued for half of everything they owned, Haiden thought. Or the shutter would rip shingles off the side of the house as it tore free and their landlord would sue them for everything they owned. Whistle. *Bang,* the sound repeated.

Jennifer didn't seem to notice that they were about to be blown away. In the small bedroom off to the side, their two-year-old son whimpered, coming awake from the noise. At the foot of the bed, their golden retriever, Brave, emitted a deep warning growl. Hell. Haiden buried his head under his pillow. In another minute Tony would be fully awake, thinking it was morning, and Brave would change to ear-splitting barking. And that would be the end of sleep for the night—and the end of his ability to think the next day. A person like Ape didn't seem to be much affected by lack of sleep; it only made his eyes bloodshot and the vein on his temple threaten to pop out of his head. Haiden didn't do well unless he had a full eight hours. Less than that and his brain function muddled to the level of a jellyfish.

He had the distinction of being the only black on White Horse's house staff. Originally, he had been taken on because the hospital had needed a black to fulfill its minority hiring quota: a token. The last laugh had been his, though, because he was the sharpest obstetrics resident there. If he could get adequate sleep. The year before, David Frank had been so impressed with Haiden's ability to run an OB service and conduct research on streptococcal B infections in newborns at the same time, that he had offered him the position of research director for the center the following year when the S.A.W.M.P. would be closed and the D Building converted into research space.

Whistle. Bang. Whack. Wearily, Haiden pushed himself out of bed and groped along the wall to the window. He jerked open the window and leaned out to refasten the metal hook that held the shutter against the outside wall. A blast of wind hit him so hard he felt himself being tugged outside, bitter cold snow stinging his face and neck.

"What are you doing, Bob?" his wife asked sleepily.

Haiden forced the metal hook into its matching ring and pulled himself back into the bedroom. He slammed shut the window emphatically to keep out the cold.

"It's freezing in here!" Jennifer sat upright. She was wearing a green silk nightgown with thin spaghetti straps that showed off her light brown skin. Angrily, she pulled bedclothes tighter around herself. "Why did you have the window open?"

Haiden's arms and face felt numb. He beat his arms against his pajamas and slid back under the bed covers, his teeth chattering, his shoulders shaking from cold. "Keeping us from being sued," he answered.

"You've got to be crazy." Jennifer lay back down and turned her back on him, hogging the covers. "Opening a window when it's freezing outside."

Haiden didn't answer her. Because he knew he wasn't crazy. He also knew that this was the last year in his life that he would have to put up with banging shutters on an apartment. By this time next year, he would have a maintenance-free ranch house on a large corner lot on the Hill in White Horse. And an electric blanket with dual controls.

Back in Harlem, growing up, he had spent hours sitting on the dirty stoop in front of his mother's project apartment watching women like Jennifer, Jamaican, light-skinned—a certain flare to the way they walked and motioned with their hands—coming and going from Big Sam's topless bar down the block. In college at Ohio State, he had dated an Italian cheerleader for two years, enjoying the feeling of power it gave him to realize he was appealing to a totally white girl. He had almost married her. Until in medical school an anatomy professor made it clear that black doctors with white wives were not well accepted in most communities. That would certainly have been true in White Horse. David Frank was far too stiff-backed a WASP for that. So in his last year of med school, Haiden had asked Jennifer, the lightest-skinned black he knew, to marry him. She looked good, but she wasn't a very intelligent woman, and she was no good at talking about or sharing any problem he had.

And he would have liked to have had someone to discuss things with—things such as the fact that he hadn't been completely honest with David Frank. He had written the article on streptococcal B infection, all right, the year before, but he hadn't actually obtained the data. Lynn Curtain had done that for him. He was working on a second study now. Sally Yates, the night nurse on Obstetrics, was obtaining most of his data for that. Not that that made it bad data. But it wasn't the kind of research that would stand up to David Frank's scrutiny. Not if Haiden could believe Frank's scrape-the-shit-off-the-monkey-bars story.

Fine for Frank. Haiden shuddered again and tried to ease some blanket away from Jennifer, still not totally warm. Frank hadn't been running a whole obstetrics service, supporting a wife, a child, a dog, and paying rent on an apartment that was falling apart, while he was doing research.

God, if he only had more time each day to do the things he wanted to do! To get everything together. Haiden stretched and touched Jennifer's shoulder to see if she was still awake. She didn't stir.

Hell. She wouldn't wake up, and he couldn't get back to sleep. He pushed himself out of bed, and walked the length of the apartment hallway to the kitchen, and dialed the S.A.W.M.P. to ask for Lynn Curtain.

For the last year, he had kept a count each month of how many boys were born at the medical center in contrast to how many girls. He was sure when he finished analyzing his data at the end of the year, that he would be able to see a pattern where more girls were born in the spring, more boys in the fall; more boys before 2:00 A.M., more girls after.

Lynn Curtain supplied him with that night's statistics: Culbertson had delivered a girl at ten o'clock; 7 pounds, 6 ounces.

Haiden reached under the kitchen counter for his black bag to record that in his notebook. Reached into empty space. Damn it! He must have left his medical bag back at the S.A.W.M.P. in the locker room. "Lynn?" he hurried to catch her attention before she hung up on him. "Would you ask one of the docs who are in to see if I left my black bag on a locker room bench in Labor and Delivery? And to put it up on top of my locker for me, if I did? I've got some expensive things in there."

"No problem," she answered.

He thought it was a problem that someone as pregnant as she was had to stay on her feet all night. "What about yourself tonight?" he asked her. "Are you going to get some time to get your feet up? Try for some rest?"

"It isn't too bad tonight."

"Good. Take some advice and try to do that, Lynn. I don't like to see you get so tired."

"Thanks. I appreciate that."

Haiden dropped his telephone and walked back to bed. Trying to get back to sleep, he buried his head under his pillow again. On top of his other worries, for some reason, he had a bad feeling lately that David Frank was stalling on opening the Bird Island D Building. A director of research job might not even be available until the following year, which meant that after July first, he might not even have a job. He'd have to find a way to pay for a new house and new furniture, as well as pay Sally Yates for the new statistics she was obtaining for him—although maybe he could convince her to do that free—worrying all the while that he might not have a secure job after July first. The whole thing was unfair. He was trying to be a good husband, a good father, a good doctor. All he was asking for was to get enough sleep at night to let him do that.

He eased more blanket away from Jennifer.

"Will you stop that?" Jennifer asked, sitting up to face him. "Why do you think because you're awake, everyone else should be?"

Haiden reached out and touched her breast.

"Well, who is this?" she asked, suddenly dipping her shoulder to let her nightgown slide away from her other breast as well, her voice less harsh, even teasing, "The same man who said at bedtime that getting sleep was the most important thing he wanted?"

Haiden admitted his priority had momentarily changed. He pulled Jennifer down against him, smoothing a hand up over her generous breast, rationalizing that he couldn't go back to sleep anyway. He was too wide-awake from the banging shutter. His eight hours were already blown; his mind was already jellyfished.

"Dr. Portobello. 463. STAT."

The page was followed by crackling and static from an overhead ceiling box. Gena stood, trying to associate the page extension—463—with a patient floor. STAT was a time-honored hospital code: Latin for *immediately.* Not used lightly, it was reserved for true emergencies. But what was 463? The extension dawned on her as the elevator numbers indicated a car was descending toward her: Labor and Delivery.

But it didn't make sense that they would be paging her. The only reason she would be paged STAT from there was if there was a mother in labor ready to deliver, and there couldn't be. She had asked Scott Stoner if he had anyone on his board, and he had said no.

The elevator doors opened. Sally Yates, the night nurse from the first floor delivery suite, stepped off. She was wearing a shapeless green scrub dress with an even more shapeless doctor's gown over it. "Boy, am I glad to see you." She put her hands on Gena's shoulders and pulled her into the elevator, pushing the button for the first floor. "There's a delivery in."

Gerald Stoner often sent his son doggie bags from The Stonehouse. Gena had opened laboratory freezers at both the main center and there, looking for a place to put a blood specimen, and found no place to put it because of a red doggie bag marked Stonehouse on each shelf. Gena sometimes took advantage of them—Gerald Stoner served excellent food—and opened one for a snack with Sally. She assumed that was what Sally meant.

"A *mother,*" Sally said, taking her arm firmly as the elevator opened on One and started walking with her down the hallway to Delivery. Having a baby. "And she's almost ready to deliver it."

Damn Scott Stoner, Gena thought. He'd known he was going to have a delivery all the time. He hadn't told her, hoping that would make her fall on her face.

"She just came in," Sally clarified that. "Her husband ran their pickup into a drift just this side of the bridge, so they walked from there. It's good they did, instead of waiting for someone to come and rescue them." The woman banged open the door to labor and delivery by stepping on an electric eye on the floor. "I paged Dr. Stoner first but he didn't answer, so the operator said to page you. Are size six gloves all right? We're short of everything but those."

Gena nodded. She wished she felt as confident of her role as she did of her glove size.

"Membranes are ruptured. Dilation is eight centimeters." Sally stopped by a scrub sink and started hurriedly opening glove packs, tossing brown autoclave tape right and left as she pulled. Giving details on the mother as she worked. "Gravida one; para zero."

Gena took a moment to evaluate that message. A woman pregnant for the first time, almost at the point of delivery; at least past a point of no return in labor. First-year residents didn't get a lot of delivery room experience at the S.A.W.M.P. Gena felt a thrill of anticipation run through her, a greedy ache in her belly for the experience. Eight centimeters was almost fully dilated; there would be no long labor to wait out; no problems—although she didn't know that yet. Her hunger for good experience might have gotten ahead of her judgment. Cautiously, she walked into the first labor room to see if everything was as simple as it had seemed from Sally's description.

One step inside the room door and she knew things were complicated. The woman in the first labor bed was not a woman at all, but a young kid. Pretty. Rich black skin and glistening black hair wound into row after row of cornrow braids. But surely not over fourteen. At the foot of the bed stood an Afro-haired boy looking not much older than she was, telling an exhausting story of how much they had planned on having that baby, but his pickup truck had gotten stuck on the bridge getting there, and the only thing he had to shovel with had been his snow scraper. He had had to carry his wife the whole last block. Anxiously, he rubbed his hands together and blew on them to get them warm. He looked as if he knew he was in way over his head. As if he were maybe going to cry if someone didn't say everything was going to be all right now that he was at the hospital.

The girl screamed and clutched at his hand as a contraction gripped her abdomen. Gena timed her scream to time the contraction: sixty seconds long. Working length. That was good. But not good enough to reassure the boy that everything was fine.

Labor, as a process, took three stages to complete; a long first phase, then a short second and third phase. During the first phase, the cervix or the bottom of the uterus gradually widened from a tightly closed circle to an opening with a diameter about ten centimeters. Contractions during that time became gradually longer and harder. When the cervix was about eight centimeters diameter dilated, contractions suddenly became noticeably harder and longer, a separation period called transition. A point of no return, because at that step, no matter how much anyone tried to interrupt it, labor could not be stopped; it would run its course. The second stage began with the end of transition: the woman developed a sensation that she had to push with each contraction. That natural pushing action delivered the child: stage three.

Adolescent girls were the death of obstetricians because they developed more complications during pregnancy than other women. Gena had a ninety-dollar book in a closet at her apartment that listed all their problems. Although this girl couldn't be as young as she looked, because the young boy had called her his wife. If the baby was in a good position, and the girl had received good prenatal care . . . Gena touched the girl's abdomen to feel for the baby's position, expecting to feel a firm round globe just over her pubic bone, the outline of the fetal head. Instead, her hand sank into nothing but spongy molding. Shit! The baby was breeching, being born hind-end first! Page one of her ninety-dollar book under major complications for an adolescent.

"Who is your obstetrician?" Gena asked the boy at the foot of the bed. First-year residents were never allowed to deliver breech babies. There would be no way she could defend a decision to do that alone.

"We just moved here," the kid at the foot of the bed answered slowly. "In Cleveland—"

Gena waved him quiet. It was the middle of the night. She couldn't get help from Cleveland. She couldn't even get much from Scott Stoner apparently. She had been there a good five minutes and he hadn't surfaced yet.

"Richard Culbertson is sleeping over." Sally Yates opened a cupboard by Gena's elbow and took down a green scrub dress for her to change into. "Because the storm outside was too bad for him to drive. Should I call him?"

"Great idea," Gena agreed. She wanted this baby for this girl. It was a terrible responsibility to be a kid yourself, and be about to *have* a kid. The last thing the girl needed was an injured baby.

"She hasn't been to see a doctor for a couple months," the young man at the foot of the bed seemed to wrestle with the new information, finally forcing it out. "Cause money has been such a problem."

The one stipulation Gena had made, that the girl had had good prenatal care, had just slipped away. "How old are you?'' she demanded, thinking he looked so young he should have been out playing baseball, cheating on English tests, goosing girls in high school hallways, not worrying about having a baby.

''Eighteen,'' he mumbled. ''My wife's seventeen.''

The girl bit her lower lip and licked away a drop of blood from it.

''And you haven't seen a doctor in how long?'' Gena asked her.

''Four months,'' The young boy answered for her. He looked sideways; then plunged ahead anxiously. ''But her father is a doctor. She thought he'd be able to tell if anything was going wrong.''

A sixth sense told Gena not to take that statement at face value. ''He actually checked her during the last four months?'' she asked. ''Or saw her across the table at Sunday dinner?''

The boy kicked at the bed leg and blew on his hands again. His foot had to sting from the kick but he didn't seem to notice. ''She didn't tell him that she wasn't goin' to a doctor,'' he answered, ''if that's what you mean.''

The whole scene was loused up good, Gena thought. Wishing Stoner would surface, she turned and started toward the locker room to change to a scrub dress. She hoped there was a crash cart with some decent resuscitation equipment on it in the delivery room, in case things went as bad, as she imagined they could.

''Did I tell you she's got funny blood?'' the boy asked her at the door.

Gena stopped walking. ''What kind of funny blood?'' she asked. They were black; could she have sickle cell anemia?

''She don't have a blood type,'' the boy tried to clarify his information.

A nonsense message. Everyone had a blood type. His wife hadn't had it typed, that was what he had to mean. Because she had never gone for enough prenatal care to let anyone do that.

"Are you sure you're not talking sickle cell?" she double-checked.

"No," the kid said that with certainty. "But her dad said the baby could get sick because of it."

Her father had meant his daughter could get sick, she thought. Because there was no hemorrhage worse than the hemorrhage that could happen after childbirth. And because the girl was so young, the overstretching that was going on inside her could cause that to happen.

"Not only is Culbertson coming, but Dr. Stoner is here," Sally Yates announced, coming back in from the hallway, looking bright and cheery, as if she were a tourist, just looking over the facility. "Stoner didn't hear the page because he was in the kitchen. He eats back there all the time."

Gena wasn't particularly concerned with where he ate.

"Lynn Curtain told him he's causing mice in the kitchen," Sally continued chatting, while she moved a chair away from the doorway, getting ready to move the girl's bed to the delivery room. "Last night when he left a bowl of soup on the kitchen counter to get the phone, I dropped a rubber mouse into it. You should have seen him jump when he came back. He really thought what she'd said had happened."

The girl in the labor bed screamed, then made an involuntary grunting sound that meant her uterus was now fully dilated, and all that was left for her to do was push and get her baby born. It was no time to be just standing there talking about rubber mice, no matter how amusing that must have been. Gena picked up the scrub gown Sally had given her earlier and opened the door to the locker room to change.

All doctors' rooms there were co-ed. Scott Stoner had chosen the same place to pull on a scrub suit. He had already changed his cords to green cotton scrub slacks, although he didn't have the waist string tied and was fumbling to pull his sweater over his head one-handed. "What have we got?" he asked her, looking at the sweater and not at her.

It occurred to Gena that he could check that out himself. He had more experience in obstetrics than she did. Although he apparently was having enough trouble just getting a sweater off. "A seventeen-year-old with a breech."

"All breeches are sectioned these days," he said firmly, although his words didn't sound firm because they were muffled by wool going over his head.

"This baby will be born before you could set up for a section. And besides, Culbertson is coming."

Stoner groaned and started fumbling with the buttons on the front of his shirt. There was a dispute between Culbertson and the house staff, Gena knew, over how to deliver breeches. When Culbertson had begun practice, all breech babies had been delivered vaginally. He didn't see any problem with continuing that practice, although new obstetricians had statistics that showed most breech babies were better off being sectioned.

"Do you know where Hershey is tonight?" Stoner asked next. "How anyone can get in touch with him?"

Gena didn't know, and she didn't want him back on the subject of Braxton Hershey if she could avoid it. "Hershey doesn't do cesareans," she said. "He's strictly GI."

"I need him because Gallagher is going so bad," Stoner said.

"Did you try The Stonehouse?" she asked.

Stoner stopped fumbling with the buttons on his shirt and looked directly at her. "Why would he be there?" he asked. "My dad hires a really *good* butcher."

Gena crossed her arms in front of herself, anxious to change, but unwilling to take off even her lab coat with him there. "He eats there a lot," she answered.

Stoner glanced at his watch, then turned back to unbuttoning his shirt. He seemed unable to get the last two buttons undone. He tore off the last two at the shirt bottom and ripped it free, looking to see if she was suitably impressed with the chest muscles that showed. He dropped the shirt onto a locker room bench, snatched up a green scrub shirt, and walked out into the hallway, leaving the swinging door clanging and banging behind him as he went.

Gena changed in half the time Scott had taken and was out by the sink, already half-finished scrubbing, when Richard Culbertson surfaced. He was a short man with a big nose and gold-framed glasses that kept sliding down. Despite the fact that he might be getting old-fashioned, Gena enjoyed working with him; he had a good bedside manner with patients. Where some attendings made everything a lesson, quoting articles in journals a resident should read, some tape they should listen to, he just quietly demonstrated what needed to be done.

He was dressed in a scrub suit that he must have been sleeping in, because he looked like one big green wrinkle. He brushed his left hand through his hair to come awake. Aside from his old-fashioned philosophy, another problem he had was that the year before he had had a bad stroke. Just after the stroke, it seemed as if he had survived the attack with no impairment. Only this last month, a definite weakness on his right side had become very apparent. His handwriting, always too small to be read easily, had become so tiny it was almost indistinguishable.

In a prenatal office, he was still great, Gena was sure. In a postpartum room, after a baby had been born, he was still excellent. In a delivery room, though, at that midway point in having a baby, when he needed to reach and support a baby's head for even the most routine of deliveries, he was hopelessly inadequate. His right arm just didn't have the strength to do that any more. Interesting situation here, Gena thought, watching him shuffle toward her. A chief and an obstetrics resident without right arms; a pediatric resident with good arms, but no experience in what she was doing.

Culbertson stopped by a sink and stabbed his feet into paper boots, as if he were going to scrub with her. He pulled down a mask next and started to tie it over his face, but he couldn't get the strings together into a knot because of his poor hand. Gena glanced at Stoner to see what he was doing. He was standing by the door to the waiting room, talking to the young father-to-be, making no apparent effort to scrub.

Lynn Curtain, a green scrub gown pulling tightly across her big abdomen, came out of the nurse's locker room and saved Culbertson the trouble of having to fumble anymore with ties; just fastened them for him. Really great, Gena thought, doubly angry that she not only had to spend this night at the S.A.W.M.P. working with Stoner, but she was going to have to spend it working with the woman he had shacked up with as well.

"Bob Haiden phoned to say he left his medical bag on a locker room bench," Lynn said, coming over to the sink. "Would one of you put it up for him next time you're in there?"

Gena nodded. Because it was never trouble to do anything for Bob Haiden. She would have traded him for Stoner anytime.

Inside the labor room, the girl screamed again. Gena felt herself start nervously at the sound. If Richard Culbertson didn't have coordination enough to get his mask tied, how much help would he be delivering a breech baby? Maybe Stoner had been right to be concerned. But if he believed he was right, why wasn't he scrubbing instead of talking to the young father?

Culbertson looked at the nearby scrub sink, wrinkled his nose to keep his wire-framed glasses in place, but then walked into the delivery room without any attempt to scrub.

That meant he was going to let her do it by herself, Gena thought. He would just watch. Breech births could be damn tricky. The head was the largest part of a baby, and when it was born first, the uterus stretched to accommodate it; the rest of the baby's body then just slid out. When the butt presented first, the uterus only dilated large enough for the butt; when the head finally arrived at the opening to the uterus, it could be trapped inside and the baby would suffocate before it could be born. Or the mother could be torn to shreds. It took a practiced feel, a practiced skill, to deliver that late-coming head; that's why there was a rule that first-year residents didn't do them.

Gena dipped her hands a final time under the faucets to rinse. As she did, Culbertson shuffled back out of the delivery room and stood leaning against the scrub sink beside her, watching her rinse off soap and scoop up the sterile towel from the gown pack Lynn had laid out for her. Stoner had moved closer to the door of the delivery room and was joking with Sally Yates. Culbertson had a bad habit of telling stories about how he had delivered babies on farm kitchen tables before there was a medical center, the same as David Frank talked about his scrape-the-monkey-shit experiment. Gena waited for the man to start reminiscing.

"You have a sonogram?" he asked Stoner over Gena's head instead.

"There hasn't been time," Stoner answered. "She just came in."

"Sure you know what you've got?" Culbertson asked him.

"A breech," Stoner answered, coming away from Sally to respond to a Chief the way a Chief expected to be responded to. "But without other complications, so I guess we're doing this your way. Farm table obstetrics here."

Culbertson looked at his hands and rubbed his right thumb as if it didn't have much feeling in it. "Don't get overconfident with breeches," he admonished. "They are never easy."

Stoner nodded, pulling a green cap over his curls.

"And don't make fun of old procedures," Culbertson added. "They're not so bad." He looked as if he were going to add something to that, then didn't. Pushing his glasses up onto his big nose, so they wouldn't fog up over his mask, he opened the delivery room door with a shoulder and settled onto a three-legged stool at the foot of the table.

Stoner stood looking at the door as if he were going to give his opinion of the man's philosophy, but then didn't. "Lynn?" he turned his back on the woman to let her help him with a mask, taking down a glove pack from the top shelf over the sink as he did. "Would you drop this extra pair of gloves on the instrument table for me?"

"I'm sure Sally has the right size gloves on the table," Lynn said, turning her attention from Stoner to Gena. "She's very good about that kind of thing."

"Just put the gloves on the table like I asked you to do, will you?" Stoner asked.

Lynn scooped up the glove pack meekly, as if she were going to do that, but then she just stood holding it, running it through her fingers, as if it might have been filled with something other than gloves. "I get it," she said. "Sally's rubber mouse is packed inside here. Right? When you flip open the inner wrap, it will jump out. You know I can't put anything not sterile on the table." Lynn spoke in a supervisor's voice—the supervisor who had made the S.A.W.M.P. a decent place to work at night.

"I'm not going to open it until everything is over," Stoner said gently. "Relax."

Lynn nodded, some kind of concession, pulled a mask up over her own face, and soundlessly walked into the delivery room with the loaded gloves.

Gena finished gloving, pressed against the delivery room door with one shoulder, and came up to the foot of the table. She could appreciate what it was like to be seventeen and overwhelmed by what was happening to her, need support rather than a resident horsing around with trick gloves.

The pregnant woman was lying on the center table with a green sheet draped over her belly—a really big belly—although she was so small, maybe that made it just look big. Sally had perched a green cap on the girl's head and pulled it to a fashionable angle over her corn-braided hair. Her legs were encased in green cotton boots and raised by metal stirrups to a delivery position. She was wide-awake and nervous as hell.

"Here's who we're waiting for!" Culbertson exclaimed, looking up at Gena.

Up on the table, the girl's abdomen tensed and rose with her next contraction. She panted—short catchy breaths—

and the circle of black buttocks at her vulva grew greater and greater in diameter. Her face grew elated from the sheer joy of creating life. Across the room, Scott Stoner pushed open the door and approached the delivery table. He was still not scrubbed.

"I like an inch-and-a-half episiotomy for a breech," Culbertson said as Gena came up to the table. "Episiotomies," he finished philosophically, looking from the girl to Gena. "The way to deliver heads and end prolonged love affairs. A quick cut is better than a ragged tear."

Gena lifted the scissors off the instrument table and made the episiotomy cut. Blood oozed from the incised tissue and the baby's buttocks moved perceptively downward.

"With the next contraction now, Lori," Culbertson gave instructions to the girl in the same calm voice he had used to greet Gena. "Pant a little—don't push—and we'll get this baby born."

It impressed Gena that, although Culbertson had only been with the young girl for a few minutes, he knew her name. Gena hadn't even asked it. She could learn a lot from Richard Culbertson.

"Is this when I get the bad pain?" the girl asked.

"All you'll feel is a little heat," Culbertson answered steadily.

"On television they always get horrible pain." The girl giggled with nervousness and excitement, then screamed with another contraction.

"I think that's when people get food poisoning," Culbertson answered her calmly. "Not babies." The statement must have reminded him of The Stonehouse because he said, just as calmly, to Stoner, "My wife wanted me to ask you the next time I saw you, Scott. What is *zabaglione?* She saw it on The Stonehouse menu last week."

Stoner grunted, disappointed that Culbertson saw him as an expert on food, not delivering babies. "It's custard made with wine," he answered flatly.

"Would my wife have liked it?"

"Most people do," Stoner answered. "It's made with marsala."

Culbertson nodded. "With the next contraction now, Lori," he said, leaning back on his stool comfortably. "You'll feel as if we're pouring hot water on your bottom."

In front of Gena, the girl's abdomen tensed and rose with a new contraction and the circle of black at her vulva grew bigger and bigger in diameter. The girl gave a startled cry, not from pain really, but from the surprisingly hot sensation of perineal tissue stretching taut.

In another second, the baby's buttocks delivered readily into Gena's hands. Babies born butt-first that way often had a lot of buttock compression that expelled fetal intestinal contents—meconium—into the bag of water. This baby's back was smeared with blackish green sticky meconium.

"It's a boy!" Gena said to the mother. Culbertson moved a foot and kicked her shoe, a can-the-chatter, pay-attention-to-what-you're-doing motion. And correct on his part, Gena conceded. A baby with meconium on his skin was no problem. A baby with meconium in the lungs, on the other hand, was in serious trouble. And that could happen there. She really didn't know yet.

The mother squealed with pleasure, as if it were Christmas morning and the present she had opened was exactly what she wanted, feeling lucky to have a first-born boy. Although if she were really lucky, Gena thought, she wouldn't be delivering at a place like the S.A.W.M.P., and she would have had the money to go for prenatal care. Gena looked again at the amount of tarry black substance on the baby's butt and felt less sure every second that everything was going well there. Something in the back of her mind about the size of the baby also started to bother her. It seemed smaller than she had thought it would be. Less developed. She could swear she had felt more bulk in the woman's abdomen than that.

"Get the arms," Culbertson said curtly.

Carefully, Gena swept a hand up under the baby's chest and brought down the right arm, then working even more gently, the left. She was nervous about the next step: To deliver a head from that position, she had to put her fingers into the baby's mouth and exert traction against the lower jaw. Traction too hard on the jaw and the nerve fibers as they crossed the shoulder and neck would tear and leave the baby's arms paralyzed ever after; too little traction and the head wouldn't deliver, and she would be back at Square One. Put yourself on the line, Portobello, she said to herself. Do it.

For better or worse, she slid two of her fingers into the baby's mouth and pulled toward herself. Simply, easily, effortlessly, the baby slid out into her hands.

Hell! What a lot of crap the whole business about delivering breeches was, she thought. Culbertson was right, sectioning was unnecessary. There she was, holding a fully delivered baby in her hands without a bit of trouble!

Gena tried to wipe some black from the baby's face so he'd look more presentable before she laid him on the mother's abdomen. "What's his name going to be?" Culbertson asked the mother, filling in the silence in the space when all of them should have said, "My, what a strong cry." Because, although everything about the baby was small but perfect, he didn't cry.

"Ubi Sta," the girl answered, her voice filled with awe;

her eyes sparkling with life. "That means Most Desired in Swahili."

"Ubi Sta Dukane," Culbertson repeated the name slowly, as if he were swishing it around in his mouth like a fine Chablis.

Gena always began counting to herself from the time a baby was fully born until it breathed. She had already reached ten by the time she had laid the baby on the mother's abdomen. She was at twenty by the time she had the cord clamp in place, at thirty and getting nervous by the time she had drained a cord blood sample and cut between the clamps. She liked to see babies breathe within twenty seconds after birth, although they could go longer than that without breathing and still be safe. She had reached forty seconds. The skin around the baby's mouth, his hands and feet, and his chest had begun to take on a bluish color by the time Sally had lifted him away and laid him on his side in a bassinet.

She had to move quickly to resuscitate him. Gena turned quickly to give the baby some oxygen; stopped as Culbertson kicked her foot again: a reminder to keep her eyes on the mother. Gena glanced at the girl's bottom. The afterbirth was starting to deliver with a spurt of blood. Okay. Gena had planned on looking after the baby first, but she could field things either way. She turned back to the mother and touched the cut cord to deliver the afterbirth.

"Say when for methergine," Sally said, hesitating at Gena's elbow, holding out a syringe of medicine ready to inject it into the woman's thigh to make the uterus contract as soon as Gena had the afterbirth delivered. Gena let the blood-smeared, pancake-sized afterbirth settle into her hands and started to strip her gloves, ready to go to the baby, aware that the baby had not yet breathed. Beside her, Stoner nodded to Sally to give the methergine.

"Freeze!" Culbertson barked.

Gena froze stark still with a glove half off. Beside her, Sally froze with the syringe of medicine in midair. Stoner froze with his head half raised. *Richard Culbertson never raised his voice.* Yet he had just shouted! What did he think was happening? The only thing that hadn't happened yet, was that the baby hadn't breathed, but he still had time to do that. The afterbirth was intact. What was wrong?

"I've got it," Stoner nodded that he understood. Unfolding his arms and waving that he would solve the problem, he moved over beside the mother and placed his hand on her abdomen. *Of course.* Gena remembered an old rule of delivery, from a time before fetal monitors had been invented, that said a mother had to have a check for twins before she was given any methergine. Because once she received the drug, it made her uterus clamp down, and if there *was* a second child inside her, that would trap it there. Gena finished stripping her gloves while Stoner pressed a hand into the woman's abdomen to check for a second baby. The girl was so small, Gena expected to see him push in and touch her backbone. Instead, his hand stopped abruptly against a hard firm mass, halfway down. Talk about complications there! The girl had some kind of tumor or mass in her abdomen or—Jesus! The baby Gena had just delivered was only the first of twins! Ordinarily, with a fetal monitor in place, or an X-ray or sonogram to offer that information, the twin check was little more than wasted motion. There'd been no fetal monitor in place here though. No X-ray. Farm table obstetrics.

"See what the first baby needs," Stoner said sharply to

Sally, motioning her to drop the methergine and go back to the baby.

'Is something wrong with my baby?'' the young girl asked. Blood was dripping from the corner of her mouth where she had bitten her lip again.

Gena needed four hands and she had only two. She had a baby not breathing and a second one yet to deliver. And if Culbertson hadn't said *freeze,* Sally would have given the methergine and locked a uterus down on a second twin and killed it. By the time she figured out how to deliver the second twin, it might be too late for the first one! She might lose two babies there!

''Why isn't my baby crying?'' the young mother asked again.

Stoner grabbed a stethoscope off the baby bassinet by Gena's elbow and pressed it against the girl's abdomen, ignoring her question, trying to get a reading on the second baby. ''Heartbeat's ninety,'' he said to Gena. A slow count. Which meant the second baby was short of oxygen. He needed to be delivered fast, or he was going to die inside a uterus too young to have produced him.

''What's the presentation?'' Culbertson asked calmly of Stoner.

Gena brushed Stoner's hand away from the girl's abdomen and plunged her own into the space, trying to think: *presentation.* Right. The way the second baby was lined up. Head down? Head up?

''Transverse,'' Stoner answered for her.

Shit. Gena raised her hand helplessly. That meant the baby was lying sideways to the birth canal. The worst possible position. But then that was why the first baby had presented breech. It had been trapped into a breech position by the sideways twin.

"What are you going to do?" Culbertson asked Gena.

OK! She did know. If only the first baby would breathe so she could think! *Clean gloves.* That was step one, so the mother didn't die of an infection afterward.

Gena reached for the clean glove wrapper on the instrument table. Froze. Because there were two wrappers there: A sterile extra pair for her in case she needed it and the unsterile extra pair that Stoner had asked Lynn to add to the setup—with a rubber mouse inside it. And she couldn't tell them apart. How had she gotten into this situation? She couldn't open a pair of gloves and let a rubber mouse pop out with a chief of service there!

"Transverse is like standing in the middle of a railroad track," Culbertson said. "When a train is coming, you have to jump one way or the other."

Gena translated: A baby cannot deliver sideways. Move your tail to push it one way or the other before it dies. But she couldn't tell which pair of gloves to choose.

"I usually breech the second twin," Culbertson continued. Stoner came up to the back table to see why Gena was having such trouble with equipment. *Hell.* Unwilling to use his help, Gena stabbed for the pack of gloves nearest her and flipped them open. As the inner flap released, a gray rubber mouse jumped up in the air at Stoner.

"Holy shit!" Stoner jumped back and bumped against the instrument table, sending hemostats and forceps and the placenta basin flying against the back wall before he caught his balance.

"If you're free now, Dr. Portobello," Richard Culbertson said slowly, his voice still calm despite the fact that some of the instruments she might need were now on the floor and worthless, "I'd try to breech the second baby."

Gena stabbed for the second pair of gloves on the table

and jerked them on, thinking she was going to kill Scott Stoner when all this was over. "Under control here," she said absurdly to Culbertson, avoiding the man's eyes because she *wasn't* under control at all.

Recovered from sending instruments flying, Stoner strode back to the young girl and pressed on her abdomen to bring the second baby into a breech position. Instantly, the woman's uterus recognized a good delivery position and picked up a contraction. The girl pushed the second twin free into Gena's hands.

"Got yourself twin boys," Culbertson said proudly.

"They're both dead, aren't they?" the mother asked. She started to sob against the gown sleeve of her eighteen-year-old husband. "They're both born dead."

The hell they were dead, Gena thought. It had actually been under five minutes since the first twin had been born. That gave her time to try a hundred things with him before he wrote himself out of the picture. Hurrying, she strode back to look at the first baby. Sally had been giving him face oxygen to try and revive him, but it just wasn't enough. His skin had turned blue and mottled, his chest muscles stiff from nonuse. Lynn slapped a metal laryngoscope into Gena's hand to pass down into the baby's windpipe to try and offer him air.

Gena hesitated. That was a damn tricky maneuver on small babies. Stoner could do it better than she could. Only—damn!—He couldn't! He only had one hand. That's why she was there. She'd have to do it. Hurrying, she slid the metal blade of the laryngoscope beside the baby's tongue and past his vocal cords, down into his windpipe, then slid an intubation tube into the baby's windpipe beside the metal guide to go deeper. There was a thick glob of meconium just at the junction of the bronchi, blocking the airway.

Christ! No wonder he wasn't breathing. No one could breathe through shit that way. Gena reached for the catheter attached to the suction machine to suction the glob free and get the baby air.

The suction catheter on the machine was a number ten; the intubation tube was a number eight. Number tens didn't fit into number eights; the catheter couldn't fit inside the tube. That baby was going to die even after she'd located his problem because the crash cart had the wrong size catheter on it. Hell. Even though meconium was fetal shit, it was sterile. Gena put her lips on the tube and inhaled. She pulled salty meconium into her mouth and spit it out onto the table as Stoner reached across her and pressed a blast of one hundred percent oxygen into the baby. The baby stirred as the oxygen reached his lungs and immediately gasped and pinked up. And cried.

Lynn brought over the second baby, as limp and unbreathing as the first one, while Gena pawed through the crash cart for a second intubation tube. She found one large enough for a two-hundred-pound man, one the right size for a good-sized woman. She had no choice but again to use the one too small to suction through. Stoner moved the first baby over to the side of the warmer and continued to give him oxygen while Gena struggled to find the right opening in the second baby's larynx. Push too far with a blade that way and she would put it through lung tissue and rip his breathing ability to shreds. Not far enough and she would be nowhere. A lot of medicine was exactly like standing in the middle of a railroad track. Either way, you got hit; either way there, the baby didn't make it. Jesus, why couldn't she see the vocal chords? What was wrong with this second baby's throat?

Her stomach knotted into a ball so tight she gasped from

pain. Why couldn't she find the windpipe, which was ordinarily a big tract and could not be located anywhere else but exactly where she was looking?

Lynn Curtain reached over and swung the baby's head into a straighter line. Immediately, the slitlike opening of the glottis appeared. Right. Right. Right. Rule one in resuscitation: don't overextend the head. Gena remembered that printed in the margin of Bob Haiden's house manual: overextension is the most common error of intubation. She also remembered a handwritten notice on the locker room wall in labor and delivery: "Need to know a procedure? Page Lynn Curtain."

The laryngoscope blade and tube both slid in once she had the throat in line. Gena sucked back another black mouthful of shit, spit it into a kick bucket, and pressed oxygen into the baby. He cried. Gena felt her own breathing slow. Everything was going to be all right. The mother was all right. And both babies were breathing.

"Stitches, Gena?" Culbertson asked.

Gena pulled a stool over to the table obediently and placed perineal stitches to close the young girl's episiotomy incision. She asked herself if she had ever done anything more stupid in her life than she had done in that room. Thinking that delivering a breech baby would be an adventure. Not asking *why* that baby was breeching. Coming within a breath of killing a second baby. Juggling a rubber mouse.

Struggling not to let her anger interfere with what she was doing, she finished the stitches, tossed the needle holder onto the instrument table, then stripped her gloves and started to walk out to the scrub sink. The young father reached out and touched her arm as she passed him and spontaneously gave her a hug. How great to be eighteen and in love with someone and have everything work out the way you hope it will, Gena thought. She gave him her best smile but kept walking to the scrub sink outside in the hallway. Alone in the hallway, she could not control her stomach. Everything inside it welled up and she vomited into the first scrub sink.

Finally, nothing left inside her, she raised her head to see Culbertson leaning against the wall by her side, Stoner standing back by the delivery room door, both watching her.

"Either of you learn anything from all this?" Culbertson asked a space somewhere between Stoner and Gena as Lynn Curtain held out a chart for him to sign.

"I know now that the reason you asked me if I had a sonogram was because you knew there was a twin in there," Stoner answered. He crossed his arms in front of his chest and spread his legs, a defiant rather than a meek stance to use with a chief.

Gena ran water at the sink and wet a paper towel to wash her face, not saying anything.

Culbertson looked down at his right hand for a moment and rubbed his one thumb instead of signing the page. "This business isn't easy," he said. "You get overconfident, you get stung."

Is that what he called that, Gena asked. *Stung?* She felt as if a truck had run over her. As if she had stayed in the middle of the railroad track he had talked about, and been hit by a freight train.

"I can explain about the mouse," Stoner offered, taking a step forward, his tone a little more unsure.

Culbertson signed the chart with his distinct miniature signature and waved Curtain away. "There isn't any explanation for the mouse," he said curtly.

"And the presentation," Stoner persisted. "I know I didn't feel a clean presentation."

"Then that's what you say," Culbertson berated. "I've got a breech and I can't explain it. Not, I've got a breech and it looks damn-ass easy."

Those hadn't exactly been Stoner's words, but Gena conceded that was what he had meant. *She* had thought it had been an ass-easy situation!

"Having babies isn't easy," Culbertson repeated. "Supervising a breech calls for extra responsibility."

"I didn't mean I thought the thing would be easy," Gena said, trying to defend her attitude. "I meant I wanted the experience."

"I wanted to work here another two years as a Chief and retire with a little status," Culbertson said. "Instead I learned today I'm going to be replaced next week. To be known ever after as the old man who couldn't cut it. But I can tell you this." His lips became firm. "I have *paid* to get where I am. I'm not giving it up lightly."

"The trouble with the mouse—" Stoner tried again.

"I don't want to hear about the mouse!" Culbertson shouted. "Because the trouble isn't with the mouse! The trouble is that you two never grew up! You're still kids back in high school. Locked into a time in your life that was so good for you, you can't let it go."

Gena had hated high school. She wiped the cold towel against her forehead, hating to even think about it. "The mouse was Stoner's joke," she said. Unwilling to take responsibility for his fault.

"But you could have stopped him! You could have taken some responsibility!"

Gena closed her mouth, aware that that was the same criticism Ape had leveled at her earlier.

"If either of you ever want to work with me again," Culbertson finished emphatically, "Grow up. Until then, don't either of you walk into a delivery room with me." He walked on into the locker room without looking back and slammed the door.

Stoner replaced his feet in a wide apart, don't-give-me-any-guff stance. "Do *me* a favor and stay out of my way for the rest of the night," he said to Gena.

Gena tore the mask away from her neck and dropped it into a can by her feet. "You have no right to be angry with me, Scott Stoner," she accused him. "I breathed those babies. I saved their lives."

"Are you crazy?" Stoner pounded the wall so hard it had to hurt all the way up into his shoulder. "You screamed outside a recovery room last July because you didn't like the way I used my spare time! When you spend yours opening up rubber mice!"

"It wasn't *your* spare time last July. It was duty time! And it wasn't *my* rubber mouse. It was yours!"

"Jesus, Gena, I never intended to use it with a chief of service in the room. Believe it or not, I don't even bury people without their clothes on anymore!"

"You can't knock what I did," Gena repeated. "If I hadn't been there, those babies would have died."

"If Culbertson hadn't been there, they would have been sectioned and not needed to be breathed."

"For Chrissake, Scott," Gena resented his know-it-all approach. "You don't need to make out obstetrics is so damn complicated only *you* can do it. If that girl hadn't gotten here through the storm outside, she would have had those babies alone in a car."

"She wouldn't have had the second one."

That was true. Gena conceded that point. The second

one would have died inside her. If its afterbirth had loosened while still inside her, the girl would have hemorrhaged to death in the car.

"Maybe you should have thought about this being a serious business, *before* you put the mouse on the table!"

He waved disgustedly at air and walked away to the nurse's desk. "When you're done throwing up, get the cord bloods to the lab for bilirubins for me. Bilirubins go on a pink lab slip with three carbons."

Instead, Gena walked into the locker room and sat down on a wooden bench in the center of the room, angry that he had thought he needed to tell her that she needed three carbons. Everything at the S.A.W.M.P. needed three carbons! Mainly, she was angry because of what had happened. She needed a recommendation from Richard Culbertson, and now, instead of saying anything good about her, he was going to say she was as careless as Scott Stoner!

There was a black medical bag sitting on the bench opposite her. She lifted it up and set it on top of Bob Haiden's locker.

What was the possibility that Stoner had known there were two babies in there, and hadn't told her on purpose to make her look bad, so that he could have her job, she wondered. Grimly, she stripped her scrub dress and stepped into a hot shower. Was he capable of that? She was thinking so hard about that, she forgot all doctors used one shower room. She stepped out of the shower directly in front of Stoner, standing naked, trying to pull a plastic bag up over his cast. She couldn't help but stare at the giant muscles on his chest, the old surgery scar across his lower abdomen just over a curly triangle of pubic hair, how big he was—God—no wonder Lynn Curtain made a point she had slept with him.

“The operator just beeped me that there’s an ambulance for the emergency room at the bridge.” He stood looking at her the same way, then abruptly turned his back on her as if he wasn’t as interested in looking at her as she was in looking at him. “Thought you ought to know that.”

Gena reached for a towel.

“Glad to see you don’t *always* scream at seeing naked men,” he added, keeping his back to her.

Gena didn’t answer.

“It’s also nice to see your body hasn’t changed,” he finished, obviously enjoying her discomfort. “You’ve still got great breasts.”

Gena stood staring at his trim tight butt. Finally, she picked up her clothes off the locker room bench to go and change. “You’re not bad yourself,” she said, leaving him still standing and fumbling to cover his cast. “You’re a perfect ass.”

Chapter Five

Eddie Deer sprawled at a laboratory desk in C Building at the S.A.W.M.P., tapping out a rhythm with a pencil against the wooden countertop with his right hand. He held his hand palm up, letting the pencil vibrate by only gentle pressure with his thumb on the eraser end. Because he had only a fifth finger and a thumb on that hand.

He had worked at the center for seven years. Few people knew what he looked like because they reached him by telephoning him, rather than talking to him in person. Specimens were left for him in a wire basket attached below the sliding window in the hallway, rather than given to him. He was like a giant troll who lived in the bowels of the building and came out only periodically to feed himself or use the hall bathroom.

Few people wanted to work in the lab area at night, because the basement was always faintly damp and chilly. That meant that even if Eddie wasn't the best lab technician in the world, he had job security. A rabbit, left there from the old days when rabbits had been used for pregnancy testing, was still alive to keep him company, so he wasn't totally lonely. He occupied his time listening to a ghetto-blaster—a hundred-dollar radio that furnished the music he tapped to.

The telephone at his elbow rang and he answered it by picking up the receiver in his good hand and cradling it between his shoulder and chin, so this way he could continue his drumming without being interrupted.

"Eddie?" Lynn Curtain raised her voice, aware she would be speaking over the competing sound of music. "How much emergency blood do you have on hand?"

Eddie glanced at a notebook by his elbow where all the blood that was used was recorded. He didn't move to open it. "Three packs," he answered, because the S.A.W.M.P. always had three packs at night. It was some kind of quality control rule.

"Stoner's going to requisition a unit. Cross what he wants as long as you have three."

"Got it, Chief." Eddie settled the receiver back into place and turned back to his work.

The radio song ended and the disc jockey began describing the bad storm outside. Eddie stopped drumming long enough to survey the counter in front of him. Arranged there were three blood tubes he had just brought in from the hallway drop basket. One for Dan Gallagher, to cross-match the emergency blood. Two tubes for a baby Dukane, to run for a cord bilirubin. He would run the cross match on Gallagher right away, and send an emergency pack of blood up to the fourth floor. A cord blood was not an emergency. He could take his time doing that. Writing left-handed, he logged the specimens into his intake book. Perplexed as to why Doctor Portobello had sent him two samples of cord blood on one baby, he tossed one of the specimens into the cement sink. The glass tube shattered, splashing blood across the sink bottom.

Scott Stoner telephoned him, and Eddie stopped listening to the weather report long enough to hear him increase his order on Dan Gallagher to two packs of blood. Cross two from there, he added, and he'd bring a second one down from surgery. Eddie nodded. He had an okay from Curtain to cross blood and it wasn't that much more trouble to cross two units rather than one.

The Beach Boys and "California Girls" blared out of his radio as the deejay stopped describing the snow. Deer picked up his pencil again and resumed drumming. He was so engrossed in singing along with "California Girls," he didn't notice that the reason there had been two cord specimens on the baby was because they were for a Baby A and Baby B, and Baby A's blood specimen was now running down the sink drain beside him, lost.

Ryan McFarland lay spread-eagled on his bed, watching David Letterman on the portable television set on his bedside stand. Lying absolutely still that way, he could no longer feel the shoulder pain.

Off to his right, in the bathroom, his wife was soaking in the pink bathtub they had given each other for their twenty-fifth anniversary. As Ryan looked at the television set, a blast of wind hit the side of the house so hard that the bed underneath him actually vibrated from the impact.

A wind like that not only moved snow; it packed it into rock-hard drifts. If he were smart, he would call Melcamp and tell him to roust everyone out sooner than 5:00 A.M., he thought. If he moved, though, even enough to reach for the telephone, the pain would start again. That made it better, he decided, to just lie there and watch his wife soak and listen to that evening's monologue, wondering how staying up that late all those years was affecting Letterman's health. He wondered if Letterman felt chest pain when he fell into bed toward early morning.

Jack Kissell sat in the dark in the anesthesiologist's induction room in the surgery suite of C Building, staring at a slit of light let in by the barely opened door. Impatiently, he stretched and pushed a lock of brown hair off his forehead, smoothing a hand over his pitted face. Kissell was waiting for the lab technician to come up, use the desk keys, and take the blood pack from the cooler back to the basement lab refrigerator. He had added up all his bills and his next year's expected income while he waited and reaffirmed his decision: he was going to open David Frank's safe.

Just outside the induction room, Kenny Rogers blared out a plea for a lady to love him. Kissell jumped at the sound, almost giving away the fact that he was there. It took him a long moment to be able to breathe regularly again and tell his racing heart to relax. The sound came from a radio on a cleaning cart.

Almost immediately he realized that he couldn't just ignore the cleaning woman. What if she was planning to clean the induction room where he was waiting? She'd see him. Don't panic, he told himself. That shouldn't happen. The purple-fingered receptionist had said she'd tell cleaning personnel not to do the room. He could see two green garbage bags resting against a corner, a tray of needles and dirty syringes sitting out on a counter. Obviously he'd been wrong. The room hadn't been cleaned.

Would the cleaning woman sense that? Stop to double-check the room? Outside the doorway, Kenny Rogers ended his song to jangling banjo music and a deejay's deep, sensuous voice. "Stay in tonight if you can, children. Snow up to your ears out there."

Kissell willed the cleaning lady to hurry up and leave the suite, willed her not to be a superefficient person who would check the garbage.

"Coming up, Lee Greenwood and a country classic!" the deejay bubbled with enthusiasm over his next tape. "Find yourself a warm blanket and appropriate warm companionship, children, and *listen.*" Kissell tried to shrink even more deeply into the darkness as new guitar music started. He hoped the lab technician would come soon for the unused blood, so he could go downstairs and lose himself inside David Frank's office. What a fabulous opportunity to get rich! But he was mortified that he had to sit there huddled next to bags of garbage, hiding from a cleaning woman, to do it.

The emergency room of A Building had been the kitchen pantry when the building was a penitentiary. It gleamed with row after row of stainless steel cupboards that had once held New York State stamped-metal mugs and plates. Not a great emergency room in appearance, it was filled with adequate equipment for quick care. Gena Portobello stood waiting by the admissions counter. Red lights flashed outside as the ambulance pulled in under the overhang.

In another minute, the door to the lobby banged open and two Monroe Ambulance attendants, wearing bulky blue down jackets over their whites, jerked a red-blanketed stretcher across the white-tiled floor toward her. The blast of cold wind that blew in after them was so strong, it would have toppled a metal Christmas tree on the counter next to Gena if she hadn't reached to straighten it.

The ambulance attendants stomped their feet, sending snow flying across the floor, and blew on their hands to try to get them warm. Their faces were bright red from walking just the short distance from the ambulance to the door, their shoulders were white with snow. There was even snow on the face of the big burly man with tousled gray hair on the stretcher between them. At the edges of the oxygen mask pressed against his nose and mouth, his face had a short-oxygen blue tinge. His chest heaved with the effort to pull in air past the pain he must have been feeling in both lungs.

A tiny woman, hair as gray as his, hurried along beside the stretcher. She was wearing a black wool coat and clutching a big black purse under her arm, seemingly under control. Seemingly. She must have been so frightened by the acuteness of her husband's illness, or the ambulance light flashing outside her house, Gena realized, that she hadn't remembered there were thirty inches of snow outside. Because on her feet, she had soft pink furry bedroom slippers that were now matted and stained with snow.

"That's a hell of a storm!" The ambulance attendant straightened his back and stomped his feet again as he pushed the outside door closed. "It's blown the damn bridge almost closed!"

"Where do you want an M.I.?" The ambulance driver interrupted him and nodded.

The wife with the matted bedroom slippers brushed tears away from her eyes and looked around the empty foyer at the tired-looking silver Christmas tree. Then at Gena. She immediately looked away again as if searching for help.

"Room one," Gena announced, trying to sound as if, of course, that's where people like herself who were experienced in myocardial infarctions put them. Because that was the reason the wife had looked away from her: She was looking for an experienced doctor, not a young-looking girl straightening a metal Christmas tree.

After an accident, the body starts to compensate for the injury. Most of the things it does to right itself are helpful, but sometimes they actually hurt. When hemorrhaging, for example, the body needs blood replacement, yet it invariably closes down veins to try and trap blood in the vital organs, shutting off a site to use to get fluid or blood inside the person. The art of handling any emergency is to be able to anticipate what the body is going to do—constrict arteries or dilate them, pool blood in the central core or disperse it to the periphery, increase respirations or slow them—and then run just ahead of what the body was trying to do. Give it a push if what it's doing is constructive; block it from doing hurting things.

Basically, a hurt heart tries to increase its rate to compensate for inefficiency; after an hour of that, it invariably realizes that what it needs most is to stop and rest. The important thing to do at first is to help it increase its rate. Most important, though, is to stop it from resting, because once it stops to rest, it has no mechanism to start itself again. That meant blood gases. Cardiac enzymes. An ECG. Something for pain. Gena started to count off steps on her fingers. Probably some epinephrine to stop an irregular beat. Next, a sharp nurse! A sharp nurse could stop the most inadequate of residents from goofing up. *Stoner!* She might not like to work with him, but he had to know more about heart attacks than she did. And then Ape from the Intensive Care Unit. Although she couldn't call him until all the other hundred things had been done first.

"We were held up a long time at the bridge," the ambulance attendant repeated as he let Gena help him push the stretcher into the first treatment room. "I bet you couldn't get a regular car through here."

Gena had confidence that City Maintenance had plowing under control. They wouldn't let the bridge close in.

"My husband is Ryan McFarland," the tiny wife put a hand on Gena's arm as Gena started to place ECG leads on the man's chest to get a heart tracing. "He's director of City Services here. He shoveled our driveway tonight to get his car out to go to work, but then he was so tired he simply came back home. He was in bed when the terrible pain started."

The tile in the emergency room between the steel-faced cabinets was a deep jaundiced yellow. The fluorescent light overhead glared off both surfaces to turn the man's skin a pale yellow. Gena tried to evaluate his true skin color and how short of oxygen he was as she worked.

"He was just lying there?" she asked the wife. "This was non-activity-induced?" She was sure that this was the man with the Irish brogue she had heard on the radio earlier, talking about his best men and best plows being out this evening. She wondered if she should call someone about the bridge. Contrary to what he'd said on the radio, this man hadn't been out worrying about anything.

The wife didn't answer Gena's question. A lot of people did that in emergency rooms, because they didn't think a doctor could listen to an answer *and* work. Hell. Gena could do six things at once and still get an admission history. "I'm listening," she said quickly to the woman.

The wife drew her lips together tightly and worked the strap on her purse back and forth in her hand, back and forth again. "We were—" she started an explanation again, but then seemed unable to find a word that would be right for what she wanted to say, and she stopped. She looked down at the wet bedroom slippers on her feet, red-faced, and finished by saying nothing.

Back in the foyer, Scott Stoner stepped off the elevator as casually as if he were answering a page for lunch rather than the emergency room. He had changed back into his blue cords and navy sweater since Gena had seen him in the locker room upstairs. He stood by the elevator, rubbing the fingers on his casted arm as if they hurt, and pushing his hands into the sleeves of a white lab coat, rather than moving to help her.

Gena looked up at the wife and repeated her question, confused why the woman was having so much trouble with her answer.

The woman sucked in a deep breath and shook her head again, unable to find a word to describe what her husband had been doing.

Back by the elevator, Stoner glanced at Gena, brushed blond hair off his forehead, grinned, and raised his good hand to let the woman know *he* knew what she wanted to say. "Way to go," he said to Ryan McFarland, coming up to the examining table and reaching over Gena's shoulder to set the last ECG lead in place for her. His blue eyes sparkled as he caught the man's eyes. "The day I get mine, I want it to be the same way."

Ryan McFarland's forehead was flushed and covered with beads of perspiration from the terrible pain he was feeling. In spite of that, he gave Scott an Irish grin for recognizing what he had been doing in bed. A nice couple, Gena thought. They were through raising children at that point in life, just quietly growing old together, looking forward to some good retirement years ahead. "Sorry I missed your point," Gena said to the wife. "I do know what people do in bed, as well as Dr. Stoner does."

"You acted surprised about it in July," Stoner said to her.

Gena turned her back on him and picked up the first part of the ECG strip to examine. It showed that a section of the back wall of the man's heart had blown. A heart beat was initiated by the action of the back wall. If any more wall went, his heart would lose its ability to contract and beat, and that would be it. The overhead light flickered and made the hollows in the man's cheeks stand out in skull-like depressions. A prediction of what was to come. Because, Gena thought, since the moment he had felt that first hard pain in his chest, he and his wife could no longer plan to grow old together.

"Ever since he's been in charge of snow removal, I've known this was going to happen." The wife touched Gena's arm, tears breaking on the rims of her eyes and spilling onto her cheeks. "It's too big a job for one man to try and do." She looked at Gena expectantly, waiting for her to say something comforting, such as, "Well, don't worry. We've caught this in time."

Gena bit her lower lip instead of saying that because it wasn't true. She was never sure what was the right thing to say in moments like this.

Stoner's father had taught him to say slick things like, *"May I suggest the Peach Melba? It's extremely good this evening,"* words that were helpful when there were peaches rotting in the kitchen and it was his job to get rid of them. Not helpful with people like the McFarlands. Death perched on his shoulder like a pirate's parrot.

The only real practical thing to ask the wife would be if she knew whether or not he had life insurance, or if their car was paid for, maybe how much they still owed on the house. Because unless the man's heart compensated better than it was doing at the moment, or could be persuaded to compensate better, she was going to need to know those things by morning. They were going to be *her* car payments and *her* house payments and *her* insurance money by sunup.

Gena pulled her stethoscope from around her neck and busied herself listening to the man's chest to cover her lack of words. She hated the sound coming back to her from inside the man's lungs: gurgling and crackling, the sound of fluid pooling there from ineffective heart action.

By the time Gena looked up, Lynn Curtain had come into the room, hung a bottle of intravenous fluid over McFarland's head, and laid out blood tubes and a syringe for Gena to use collecting blood gases and enzymes. Gena picked up the needle—one twice as big as the kind she liked to use—and tried a vein on McFarland's hand. It dry-tapped, his veins shut down from shock.

"Will you stop using those damn things?" Stoner grabbed the needle meant for a giant and tossed it into the waste-paper basket by her feet. "Get her a butterfly!" he barked at Lynn. "Then one ml of Lasix and ten mgm of morphine STAT."

Lynn took a step toward the counter, but had to stop and reach to support herself against the edge of the desk as she was hit by a deep pain from the baby's head pressing on her pelvic nerves. "You can't use butterflies on anyone over two years old," she said officially.

Stupid policy at that point, Gena thought, because Stoner had already thrown her first needle away. What did she want to do, pull it out of the garbage? Give the man blood poisoning on top of a heart attack?

"Where do you keep them?" Stoner asked Lynn curtly, opening a back cupboard. What he *should* have asked her, Gena thought, was "Why are you working? You're almost ready to deliver." Those words would have acknowledged that she was pregnant though, and although the baby was obviously his, that was a subject Gena had never heard either of them discuss. Stoner pulled down boxes of equipment from the cupboard and pawed through them, looking for butterfly needles.

Lynn stood motionless by the far counter and watched him empty two full cupboards and clutter half the counter space before she said flatly, "Cupboard over the sink, Doctor. Box on the right-hand side."

Stoner slammed open the steel door over the sink and scooped up a whole handful of butterfly needles. He tore the wrapping off one with his teeth, swore as he had trouble getting the plastic cap off the needle, and pressed the tip of the miniature needle against the back of McFarland's hand one-handed. The needle slid in perfectly without any resistance.

Gena straightened to look at the monitor attached to McFarland's chest leads, ready to add the morphine Lynn had prepared for the fluid line as soon as it began to drip. She had to admit Stoner had a knack for getting things done, even if he antagonized everyone and left a mess. She added the morphine and then reached for a new syringe to draw blood for enzymes and gases.

One of the ambulance drivers turned on a radio strapped to his belt and the room suddenly filled with a twangy rendition of "Auld Lang Syne." Behind Gena, Stoner grabbed the wall telephone and dialed for Zack Appleton. "Zack," he raised his voice to make himself heard over the music. "We're in emergency with an M.I." He shoved the telephone receiver at Gena and stepped back by the messy counter.

Gena laid the ECG tracing paper out in front of her on

the counter to describe the spikes and waves. Appleton was an excellent cardiologist; if Gena were lying on a stretcher there in that emergency room, she would want him to be the man giving directions over her head. When given the chance to teach about cardiology, though, he always did that, rather than just give instructions. And what Gena needed was clear one-two-three directions. She watched Lynn walk over to McFarland and begin to take his blood pressure. She always found herself watching Lynn when she worked with her, wondering what there was about her that had appealed to Stoner so much that he had risked shacking up with her in public. Her looks? She was pretty but not exceptionally so. Her personality? She was good with patients, but not any more so than Sally Yates. Not any more than Stoner himself.

What intrigued Gena as well, was how the woman blatantly made a point of being very pregnant. Gena concentrated on what the Ape was telling her about the first lead results. As she flipped a page on the long strip of paper to describe the second lead pattern she heard a second ambulance pull in under the overhang. The door let in wind that felt even colder than before against her back. She turned away from the door and put her hand over her ear so she could hear Appleton.

Despite her impatience, he told her in slow, well-thought-through phrases that the ECG tracing did indeed indicate that the man had had a myocardial infarction. Impatiently, Gena turned around to see who was being wheeled in on the second stretcher, as the Ape started to describe why he didn't like the last part of the heart tracing. It was full of inverted T-waves.

She looked down at a sandy-haired ten-year-old on the stretcher. There was an oxygen mask covering the bottom half of his face, but she recognized him under it: Mark Warren. His father, Peter, a tall man with a nervous hurrying step, slicked-back black hair, and a mustache on his upper lip like a small black rug, followed the stretcher. An important man: he was the grandson of the Sylvester A. Warren who the building had been named after. If Gena believed that Gene Warren had been her father, then Peter Warren was her uncle.

Peter came to a stop by the edge of the stretcher so abruptly that his wife, Elizabeth, hurrying behind him, couldn't stop in time and bumped into him. She was a stately, pretty woman; bright red nail polish and a huge diamond gleamed from her left hand as she crossed her arms in front of herself to press a blue cloth coat closely to her body. The ambulance hadn't been heated, Gena guessed, and she was freezing. A scarf covered half of her hair; the hair in the front, superficial blonde, was caked with snow. Mascara on her eyes had run and made black smudges under her eyes. She stomped her feet and tried to brush snow off tiny black strap shoes that had to be wet and cold.

Gena tried to ignore them. She knew them because Mark Warren was admitted frequently with asthma. Unfortunately, he was also the boy she had ordered the aspirin for the August before, whose father had said he would rather she didn't take care of his son. Too bad, unless he wanted to go back out in the cold. She was the only pediatric resident on. The boy's chest heaved as he gasped for breath. Air whistled as he forced a breath out through constricted bronchi.

"Who's the pediatric resident on?" Peter Warren demanded of Lynn, looking at her abdomen as if he couldn't believe anyone that pregnant would still be working.

"Portobello," Lynn answered, motioning to Gena.

Warren looked for a moment as if he were going to ask the ambulance driver to take his son back outside. "The telephone operator said Portobello was at the Main Center," he contradicted.

"Keep on the oxygen. Set up some D5, half saline," Stoner barked an order from the back counter as Gena hesitated. "Pull up some aminophylline."

"Are you listening to me, Gena?" Zack Appleton asked in her ear.

Gena moved the telephone closer to her ear. "You said you didn't like the inverted T-waves," she said.

"IV's ready," Lynn interrupted her in another minute over the sound of Ape describing the oxygen lack that caused inverted T-waves. Gena felt tempted to ask Stoner to start it with his butterfly and teeth technique. Being short of breath from asthma had to be one of the worst feelings going. She liked to get kids out of that feeling in a hurry if she could. She also wanted Peter Warren's consent to treat his son.

"In an emergency, you don't need consent." Stoner came away from the back counter in a blur of activity and knelt beside the boy, flipping the restraining straps free on the stretcher so she could work. "It's a given that people opt to live," he persisted when she still didn't move.

"Zack, wait a minute." Gena dropped the telephone before the Ape could argue with her and stooped down beside the stretcher. She weighed what Stoner was saying; a second sense telling her he wasn't talking about emergency care at all. He was talking about a night in a train station when he had stood frozen against a wall rather than let a man kill him. She had never faulted him for that night. On the other hand, she had never *said* to him that she didn't think he had been at fault. Had he thought all those years that she held him responsible for not stopping that? He had gotten himself stabbed trying to help. She didn't know what else he could have done.

On the stretcher between them, the boy noticed her frown. He sucked in a breath, but then almost completely stopped breathing. His eyes were blue-green, a color that gave them transparency. He closed them as if to hide how much fear was registering beneath them.

"What brought this on?" Gena asked his father, hoping Peter Warren wasn't going to say his son was coming down with a cold. It was hard to stop asthma attacks if they were part of a cold.

When she had been growing up, kids on the block had always called Peter Warren "Peter Perfect." He and Elizabeth had adopted Mark when Gena was a senior in high school. It was always a little disappointing to Peter, she guessed, who admired perfection, to find that by the time the boy was three, he had developed asthma and so he wasn't quite perfect. But then, having a wife who couldn't have children must also have been a big disappointment to Peter.

"He came home from Boy Scouts tonight wheezing," Peter answered the question.

"Mark took some Anacin." Elizabeth Warren said. "Because his arm hurt. He didn't know Anacin had aspirin in it."

The boy visibly jumped as Gena turned his hand over to try and spot a vein. Color drained from his face and his eyes pleaded for her to move it as he struggled, chest muscles tugging to their limit, to take in at least one solid breath of oxygen. In her hurry, Gena dry-tapped the vein.

"How'd you hurt your arm?" she asked. The kid had

jumped as if she'd twisted the hell out of his right arm, when all she'd done basically was turn it over.

Behind her, Ryan McFarland groaned with pain and Stoner stood up to walk back over to him. "Isn't there something you can do for my husband?" his wife demanded of Stoner.

"Jesus Christ!" Peter Warren smashed his fists together with a resounding whack. "Why in hell isn't there ever any privacy around here? Why, every time we come here, does our business become everyone else's? And everyone else's ours?"

Gena glanced around the crowded examining room. There wasn't any privacy because there was only one of *her*. If she split the McFarlands and the Warrens into separate rooms, McFarland might arrest while she was with Mark. On the other hand, Mark might arrest while she was with McFarland. As a third possibility, *her* heart might arrest running between the two rooms. But then, what made her think that both McFarland and Mark weren't going to arrest at the same time even in the same room? Especially if she couldn't get the needle into place.

The boy kept his right arm so stiffly against his side that she couldn't position it to get a good look at the back of his hand to look for another vein. After another second, she gave up trying to struggle with that arm and reached for his other one. "What happened to your arm?" she repeated. "How'd you hurt it?"

The boy closed his eyes for a response. Great, Gena thought. Always able to plan on great cooperation from the Warrens.

"He fell at school this afternoon," his mother pulled her coat closer. "But I'm sure it's only a sprain."

"Would you order an X-ray for that?" Gena asked Lynn,

crouching lower over the stretcher to try to set the IV needle into the boy's opposite hand.

"If he'd known there was aspirin in Anacin, he never would have taken it," Elizabeth continued. She stopped to peer at her reflection in one of the stainless steel cupboard doors and tried to wipe smeared mascara off her cheeks. "He knows better than to take aspirin."

The boy kept his eyes shut so Gena couldn't read what he was thinking: she knew he knew better. The evening she had tried to give him aspirin, *he* had been the one who had stopped *her*. But stop the wheezing. Figure out what had started it *later* was the rule for asthma attacks. She had to jab him twice, but finally found an adequate vein for the fluid.

"Does anyone remember that Dr. Appleton is still on the phone?" Lynn asked the room at large as Gena anchored the fluid line and slid home a syringe of aminophylline to dilate the boy's airway. Behind her, Stoner apparently decided he could solve the telephone problem and attacked it to talk to Appleton.

"Heart rate is a hundred and twenty," she heard him say into the telephone. "Spikes are falling on the monitor."

McFarland was growing worse. Creases had faded from his forehead and his sweating had stopped, signs that the morphine was working, but the heart monitor over his head showed his heartbeat gradually becoming faster. Trying to adjust for the damage done to it. A step downhill not up, because by racing, his heart would tire out more quickly than if it would just keep a slow controlled pace.

McFarland stirred and the pattern on the cardiac monitor changed. Instead of a tall spiking pattern, there was a multitude of small erratic blips. "Now he's lost all his QRS spikes," Stoner said into the telephone.

The Ape decided that teaching time was over. That monitor pattern meant that the bottom chambers of the man's heart had begun fibrillating—quivering—from exhaustion, and were ready to shut down. He gave Stoner the one-two-three directions they needed: a dose of epinephrine and a bolus of xylocaine, followed by defibrillation.

"Some consult," Stoner said, walking away from the telephone back to McFarland's stretcher, hands in his pockets, as if he were strolling down a side street instead of an emergency room. "The ambulance driver told me more than he did, for Crissake." He stopped by McFarland's stretcher and barked an epinephrine order at Lynn.

"Please help him!" McFarland's wife clutched at Stoner's sweater front. "You have no idea how much I need him!"

Gena stood up to study the cardiac monitor over McFarland's head one more time. *Try to remember where he keeps the bills,* she thought, looking at the wife. *And the checkbook.* As if she, too, could see that on the monitor, the wife grabbed Stoner's arm and pounded on it, crying hysterically.

As she did that, the outside emergency door opened again and a man and a woman, both wearing fur coats, walked into the foyer. His was a long shaggy white one. Was there such a thing as a polar bear coat? The woman was wearing what Gena was sure was black sealskin. She had a matching sealskin hat on her head, more fur on her boots and purse.

"Get that for me," Stoner nodded to Gena, wrapping his arms around McFarland's wife and walking to the side of the room with her. Why had a heart attack happened to a man like McFarland who had a wife who cared so much about him, Gena asked, when the man putting his arms around her cheated on his wife and felt fine?

"Today," Stoner added when Gena made no motion to move toward the foyer.

Gena stared at the man disguised as a polar bear, looked beyond him at the fender of a black Porsche parked outside. The man looked worried but not in obvious pain. What had Stoner seen that she hadn't?

"Some diagnoses are hard," Stoner said sarcastically, keeping his arms around McFarland's wife, motioning for Lynn to give the epinephrine to McFarland for him. "Pregnancy is a giveaway."

Gena looked closer at the woman and understood the quick diagnosis: The woman was very pregnant. To have driven there on an evening like this, she had to be in very active labor.

Behind them, the emergency room door banged open again, pushing snow across the length of the room. A ceramic table lamp by the waiting room couch crashed into fragments onto the floor. One of the ambulance men who had left ten minutes before stumbled backward into the lobby. "The whole bridge is nothing but a wall of snow." A second one struggled in after him and threw his weight against the door to close it again. Both of them had difficulty talking, they were so short of breath just from walking outside one block. "Drifts six to eight feet high, the whole length of the bridge. There's no way we can get off this island."

Gena's first thought was that no one could get in, either, so there would be no more new admissions for the night. She could get caught up. But if patients couldn't get in, that also meant that if she needed help, no one could get in to help her. And in the morning, if no one could get in, how could they get out?

"How long would you say we'll be trapped in here?" Lynn Curtain asked.

"This storm is supposed to keep up for twenty-four hours," the man in the polar bear coat said.

"Is this place adequate to manage for twenty-four hours by itself?" the first ambulance driver asked, blowing on his hands and rubbing his ears.

"We're pretty low on blood," Lynn answered. "And maybe food."

A blast of wind hit the side of the building so hard the windows rattled. The door blew open again and the metal Christmas tree on the counter blew over, tinsel and wooden ornaments spewing along the hallway to smash into the copper plaque that said the building had been built because of compassionate understanding. A lot of the medical staff, like herself and Stoner, Gena thought, had put in sixteen hours already. Lynn Curtain looked exhausted. People who were overtired made mistakes.

As if it were the answer to something, she watched Lynn Curtain begin to pick up the tree ornaments that had blown into the hallway: a teddy bear, a silver rocking horse, and an odd-shaped, handmade, gold-painted Christmas star.

Chapter Six

David Frank had fallen asleep watching an old Clark Gable movie on TV. The last thing he remembered was Clark standing by the starboard engines, instructing the engine room crew to dive. Against orders, he was taking the submarine into the Bongo Straits.

But now—as if that order were being countermanded—the telephone over Frank's head was ringing.

"David!" his wife shouted to him.

A very confusing order because he hadn't even met his wife yet. He was a young man, enjoying a bachelor's life in the Navy under the very capable command of Clark Gable. *Running Silent; Running Deep.*

"It's Zack Appleton, calling from the extension facility."

Frank came awake abruptly, peering at his watch, trying to straighten out the real world from the unreal. It was 4:00 a.m., and he wasn't in the Navy. He was sitting on an Early American couch in his family room in White Horse where he had fallen asleep. His wife Ann—dressed in a light blue bathrobe with floppy blue wool slippers on her feet—

was stretching to hand him an old-fashioned Early American telephone from the kitchen.

"The bridge to the Swamp is drifted shut," Zack Appleton barked at him as soon as he had the receiver to his ear. "Do you know we're trapped in this fuckin' place?"

Frank liked Zack Appleton, had utmost confidence in him as a chief resident, but he hated his language. "The name of that facility is the Sylvester A. Warren Medical Pavilion," he corrected him calmly.

"The bridge to the Sylvester A. Warren Medical Pavilion is drifted shut, sir," Appleton repeated. "So we're trapped in this fuckin' place."

Frank shifted the telephone to his other ear. "The bridge—"

"Has an eight-foot drift the entire damn fuckin' length of it. The city fell asleep on its ass and I'm in big trouble here because of it. I'm short house staff. Dan Gallagher has developed the worst post-op infection I've ever seen. Enough to make me wonder if the whole damn surgery setup wasn't contaminated."

Frank hadn't known Dan Gallagher was a patient there. He did know the implications of an OR autoclave breakdown. Once, years before, the center's sterilizing equipment had almost broken down; if Richard Culbertson hadn't single-handedly donated money to correct it, it would have caused a city-wide infection.

"Will you get me an estimate of how long it will be before anyone can get in here to help me out?" Appleton finished without waiting for any further comment from Frank, and dropped his receiver back into place.

Frank dropped his telephone and stood up to walk over to the french doors to see how much snow was on his patio. Unbelievably, snow was piled up three feet against the doors and blowing so wildly that he couldn't see the nearby streetlight. If snow was packing that way in the streets, he thought, opening the Bird Island bridge might not be easy. The extension facility could be shut off for hours.

Some snow had blown in on the oak floor through the narrow strip at the bottom of the French doors and Frank tried to kick it back outside. Too bad construction at the main center had been delayed this winter, he thought. Because of that, the main center hadn't been able to take the patient beds from the extension facility so that he could close it down. Because of that, he'd had to put money into strengthening the buildings of the extension facility by adding new structural cement columns to them. Now, because of that expense, all he had was an empty D Building waiting for contributions to reach a point where he could use some to equip it. And three buildings—A, B, and C—were still occupied with patients.

What could be happening at the extension facility? The Ape had said he was short house staff. Frank wondered how well-staffed nursing was. Or laboratory. He covered his face with his hands and tried to think more clearly, wishing he were on the other side of the bridge to keep an eye on things until the path was clear again. He was nervous about which house staff were in, which security officers. He had, unexpectantly, a lot of money in his safe.

He stood frozen for another five minutes, before he dared to lift the receiver of the strange telephone again and ask those questions.

Scott Stoner pushed himself up out of a chair in Dan Gallagher's room. It was discouraging that although Gena had helped him connect a central and venous access line to the man and start a new type of antibiotic, the man was really no better than when they had begun. Although the X-ray hadn't shown anything, his gut had to be leaking, Stoner concluded. Hershey had hurried so much at the last, he must not have inspected the bowel as well as he could have. Although . . . wait . . . Stoner looked back at the stomach tube that threaded down into the man's stomach and noticed that the color of the drainage had turned from dark brown to bright red. That meant Gallagher had started a whole new problem; his old stomach ulcerations had activated under that much stress. As if his gut leaking wasn't bad enough, he was now oozing blood from his stomach.

Please let no one else have used the last pack of emergency blood, Stoner thought, walking out to the desk area to find the nurse. Because he was going to need it.

With the bridge closed, no surgeon would be able to get in that morning to operate on the man if his bowel was leaking or on his stomach if he started heavy bleeding from that. It was time to get a new hemoglobin level report on him. Balancing the amount of blood the patient was losing against how much he was giving him was becoming more important every minute. On the other hand, he didn't want to use up all the blood there, if he could prevent it. Stoner picked up a capillary tube and a blood lancet as he entered Gallagher's room, trying to remember the Latin phrase that stood for *first, no harm.*

"Hell, Stoner." Gallagher coughed and sat up straighter in bed, gripping his belly with pain as he spotted him. "When are you going to stop clowning around and do something constructive for me?"

Stoner stopped tightrope walking and looked up at the ceiling to keep from looking at Gallagher. Over the man's bed, a crack in the plaster trailed about four feet into the room. A blast of wind hit the side of the building and as he watched, the crack grew longer by another six inches. "I'm not clowning around," he said firmly.

Gallagher coughed and had to hold his stomach again, the coughing caused him so much pain.

"Did you forget that I knew what you were like, long before anyone here did?" Gallagher asked.

Stoner steadied the man's finger and swabbed it off to puncture it for a blood sample. "What do you mean by that?" he asked.

"You forget that I was there the night you had your little trouble at the train station?" Gallagher asked.

Stoner felt like pushing the lancet into deeper body parts than just the man's finger.

"I knew right away, the night you told me that story, what really went on there, Stoner. That blacks being there was just a handful of shit."

Stoner straightened to stare at the man. "Tell me that again," he said. Amazed at his control. Because no one could tell *him* anything about that night.

"Come on, Stoner." Gallagher managed a nasty grin. "I figured out you took advantage of the Portobello girl that night. Then the two of you made up that story about rape, to keep your dad off your back in case she got pregnant. And you fooled Gerald Stoner. I'll give you that. But you couldn't fool an old-timer like me with that kind of story."

Stoner's mouth fell open. No wonder the man had never tried to find those three men! He had never believed that they had been real. "How can you say that, Gallagher? I watched them rape Gena!"

"I have my reason for knowin' I'm right," Gallagher said.

"Look at my neck, Gallagher!" Stoner pulled down the front of his sweater. "Does this look made up?"

"You could have done that to yourself. After all, it's only a surface cut."

The stab wounds he had inside him weren't surface stuff, Stoner thought. He stabbed the man's finger none too gently. "Talk about a handful of shit," he said, waiting impatiently for a slender capillary tube to suction off a drop or two of blood.

"I've got proof," Gallagher said. "I know what I'm talkin' about."

Stoner capped the tube as soon as it was half full and walked to the back room to spin it down for a quick readout. He couldn't believe what Gallagher had just told him. How could anyone think he could have hurt Gena Portobello that way?

"What are you going to do for Gallagher?" Lynn Curtain asked him, looking up from a cup of coffee. Beside her, Debbie Chemielewski was sitting staring into space.

"I'm going to give him another unit of blood."

"He's already had *two* units," Lynn said. "Which is strange, because I told the lab tech to only release one to you."

"There's still one upstairs in the OR cooler." Stoner felt his temper rising at the inadequacy of the S.A.W.M.P. "So even with this one in him, there'll still be an extra pack available."

He stalked back into Gallagher's room and stared down at him. "What's your proof?" he demanded. "That makes you think I did that to Gena?"

Gallagher looked up at him, surprised, as if he had never expected to have to produce that answer. "I saw her baby from that night," he said.

The man's falling blood pressure must have cut off the blood supply to his brain cells. It was causing a meltdown in his core. Because that was crazy thinking.

"Portobello never had a baby," Stoner corrected the man. No wonder Crazy Mary had told him that same thing. She had heard it from a police chief!

Gallagher raised his eyebrows to say he knew he was right.

Rule One with people who were hallucinating was never to argue with them. Respect their concept of reality, no matter how ass-backward it seemed, because it seemed ass-straight to them. Following that rule, Stone bit back his opinion of the man's opinion and walked back to the treatment room to read the spun-down hematocrit tube.

The level was 8.0; he wasn't perfusing brain cells well. "Give him a third pack of blood," he said to Debbie. "I'll get the one from the OR and replace it for the lab."

Debbie burst into tears at the urgency in his voice. "Do you believe it?" she asked. "He told me he was dying! And he's right!"

Stoner grunted because he saw that as an improvement. Ten years before, the man had gotten everything confused. This time he was right. If Frank couldn't get the bridge cleared fast, or if something happened to the last pack of blood, that just could happen to him.

"Your new admission—the pregnant lady—is Leslie Kerr." Sally Yates was leaning against the L and D desk, rubbing her eyes, trying to stay awake as Gena stepped off the elevator, returning from helping the Ape move Ryan McFarland to B Building. "She's Norm Redhoe's patient. I called to tell him she's here."

Gena nodded, but she wasn't very interested. From the

preliminary history she'd taken the woman was barely in labor. Stoner could monitor her one-handed until morning.

"Redhoe said he's not coming in to stay with her," Sally said. "She's thirty-two and having her first baby," she continued. "With a borderline pelvis. So Redhoe wants her observed very closely. External, not internal monitor, though. No X-ray. No sonogram."

Gena wondered if there were any X-ray or sonogram technicians in even if she *had* wanted that. There wasn't a hell of a lot else to do with those procedures ruled out but to watch her. She wondered how borderline a pelvis he was talking about. If it was too borderline, she would need a cesarean section and Gena wasn't prepared to handle that. And Scott Stoner had a broken arm.

"Aren't you going to ask who she is?" Sally teased, excitement bubbling up to the edge of her voice. "She's David Frank's daughter!"

David Frank, the medical administrator of that hospital, who owned a black and white office and black and white morals to go with it, who had said he'd talk to Stoner about his recovery room morals, yet never had. Who had a list with both Stoner's and her name on it. Jesus, let the woman's labor go slowly, Gena thought, that in the ER, Stoner had had his nervous arms around McFarland's wife rather than examining Mrs. Kerr. Again, she wondered just how borderline a pelvis Redhoe was talking about.

"Did you see her coat?" Sally asked. "She asked me to hang it up rather than lay it on a bed, so cockroaches wouldn't get near it."

"Why are they here instead of at the main center?" Gena asked, ready to move on to more important things than an endangered species coat. If the woman did have a borderline pelvis and she developed a complication so that something happened to her baby on their duty time, neither Gena nor Stoner would be able to get a second residency anywhere.

Sally stifled a yawn and came a little wider awake. "They were at a concert downtown when labor started, so with the roads so bad, they decided to come here instead of the main center."

Gena picked up the woman's chart outside the first labor room and walked inside to take a history from her.

Leslie Kerr was sitting on the edge of the bed, dressed in a blue hospital gown, her legs covered modestly by a sheet, a woman radiating the gracefulness and sophistication of someone used to expensive clothing and fine bed linen. Without the thick coat on, she was slimmer than Gena had first thought, except for her pregnant abdomen. Strangely, her face was a contrast to her overall appearance. She had light blue eyes like her father's, but her front teeth were not at all like his. They were markedly bucked and covered in front by metal braces. Since Lynn had said her age was thirty-two, surely this wasn't just a recent attempt at straightening her mouth. It had to have been the result of some orthodontist giving his all for years and years, and still not being able to get them into line. Gena wondered how crooked they must have been at the beginning.

Despite the fact that she was a hometown product, Gena didn't know the woman. She had attended a series of private schools along the Hudson; Vassar for college. After that, Gena remembered, she had gone to Paris on an art scholarship. She remembered one gallery showing at the Albright-Knox in Buffalo that had received mixed reviews, and probably wouldn't have even occurred except for the Warren money behind her.

"I need some history," Gena pulled a comfortable chair

up next to the woman's bed, intent on getting a detailed history that would rot off her father's socks.

Leslie Kerr nodded agreeably to questions during the entire history, yet never elaborated on any answers, which was unusual. Most women were anxious to talk during labor, a response to the nervousness and excitement of the last few hours of being pregnant. Because of that, obstetricians often got their ears filled with more information about women and their families than they wanted to hear or needed to know. Leslie Kerr shared little. Did she have any infections during pregnancy? No. Did she take any medicine? No. Did she smoke? Never. Did she drink? Never. Any recreational drugs? Never. A very righteous family, the David Franks, Gena thought, trying to determine if the woman was so confident that her baby would be perfect or she was just naive—no one had ever suggested she might have trouble with delivery—so she didn't seem worried. She was one day away from her due date. Blood pressure checked out well. Gena stretched and felt her abdomen. There was a term-sized baby in there, all right; head down, lined up for delivery. Heart sounds were a hundred and twenty. The one contraction Gena felt cross the woman's abdomen wasn't strong, just barely palpable. It certainly couldn't be doing much. Gena reached for a glove off the side table to do an internal exam, while she ticked off the rest of the important questions about pregnancy: had she had any falls during pregnancy? No. Bleeding? No. X-rays? No.

"I'm not truly as dull and stuffy as everything comes out though," Leslie Kerr added, lying back on the bed and sounding as if she were trying hard to be pleasant. "I have had my wild moments."

Gena guessed the woman's wild moments would rate on a scale of one to ten at about minus two, but gave her the benefit of the doubt that they had seemed wild to her. She stretched two fingers inside the woman to palpate the cervix.

What she discovered wasn't good news. Gena pulled back her hand to notice that her fingertips came away faintly blood-tinged. That was good in that it meant "show," the mucus plug that acted to keep bacteria from entering the cervix during pregnancy, had loosened. But the uterus had disappointingly admitted no more than one fingertip, only a one-centimeter-diameter opening. Leslie Frank Kerr was in such early labor that she shouldn't even be in the hospital. If Stoner had examined her in the emergency room when she had first come in instead of assuring Mrs. MacFarland that her husband was going to be all right, he would have sent them home. They could wait and go to the main center in the morning. Gena heard herself sigh, thinking about that.

"How long will it be before this baby's born?" William Kerr demanded. He watched Gena strip off her glove and toss it into a wastepaper basket. As if that were wasteful, or as if he were in charge of finances of that hospital, not his father-in-law. A man with prominent jowls and a bulldog face, he had taken off his bulky fur coat and was wearing a very rich-looking navy blue suit. She looked at the admissions information to see where he worked at. Right. Kerr Cement. In the summertime, the streets of White Horse vibrated with the whir of his big green mixers, Kerr Cement Company printed on their sides.

Gena kept her eyes on his broad shoulders as she answered him, recognizing trouble, because a small baby could deliver safely no matter how big the pelvic ring of bone. A baby with football-size shoulders, like this man's, could cause real trouble for a woman with a small pelvis.

"A long time," she answered, walking out to the hall desk to call Stoner with her findings.

"Lynn Curtain phoned to say your X-ray on Mark Warren is ready." Sally Yates met her at the desk, yawning again. "And that you should look at it right away. It looks like trouble."

Well, why not? Gena thought. Everything else was going wrong. She gathered up chart forms from the desk and rode up to 3A to cross the connecting bridge to X-ray in C building. Halfway across the narrow hallway, a blast of wind hit the walkway; the bridge trembled and creaked as if it were threatening to tear loose. Stepping into C Building, Gena had the odd impression that not only had the walkway moved, but the entire A Building had twisted with the blast of wind.

She held up the X-ray marked Mark Warren waiting for her in a view box and felt a new fear move through her. There *was* a break. Lord, she had underestimated the extent of the trouble she was in. David Frank was a very influential man, despite his concentration on polished shoes and his bad habit of telling the scrape-the-shit story. If anything bad happened to the Warren boy or Frank's daughter while she was in charge, she wouldn't be able to get a new residency anywhere in the *whole free world.*

Dawn Brady, the night nurse in the second-floor newborn nursery, sat rocking and giving the first Dukane twin his first feeding of sterile water. She wasn't a pretty woman, her features were too coarse and her hair was fine and wispy, and she had been a good twenty pounds overweight since eighth grade. Nursing had appealed to her because it gave her the same safety-in-numbers feeling that being a nun would have given her. It also was a profession that exposed her to handsome young doctors—some of whom were eligible and looking for nurses who would understand their long hours and commitment.

Being a newborn nursery nurse was an enjoyable type of nursing. All the babies in her care were well newborns, so there was little responsibility involved, except to be certain they were all fed, or teach new mothers how to do that. The problem with the job was that, because her patients rarely had complications, doctors rarely came into the nursery at night. She had worked there almost a year and yet had barely met any eligible doctors.

Being snowed in might present the opportunity she needed to get really acquainted with one of them—possibly Dr. Stoner. Of all the doctors in the center, he was the one she wanted most to get to know.

Dawn glanced down at the baby in her arms impatiently, urging him to drink faster. His twin had chugged down a feeding in just a few seconds. This baby was too sleepy to suck well. She sat him upright in her arms and the overhead light caught the white of his eyes. For just a second, they reflected back yellow to her. She studied the baby intently. If they really were yellow, she could call Stoner and tell him she thought this first twin was becoming jaundiced! That would bring him up here in a hurry. A baby jaundiced that soon after birth meant it had severe liver or blood incompatibility trouble.

Dawn turned the baby again, and decided she had been wrong. There was nothing wrong with him. And scaring a doctor about his condition wouldn't score big points for her. She sat rocking, urging the baby to suck, scheming further how she could attract attention to herself. As she put the baby back into his Isolette, she thought again, just for a second—as foolish as it seemed—that the sclera of his eyes did seem slightly yellowed.

"Telephone for you, Dr. Stoner."

Scott Stoner picked up the receiver by the fourth-floor nurse's desk as he passed it, happy to hear David Frank say that he was moving rapidly to get the bridge cleared. In the meantime, Frank added, he was checking to see who was covering each of his services. "Happy to hear you're on obstetrics," he finished.

The hell you are, Stoner thought. You wish Haiden were here. You must have shit when you heard me answer this telephone.

"Who is there on pediatrics?"

"Portobello."

"Medicine 4?" Frank asked for more punishment.

"Me again."

"Why are you covering two services?"

"This is the Swamp." Stoner sank into the nurse's desk chair to explain the man's own rules to him. "When anyone on Medicine A calls in sick—"

"You know I like to hear house staff call the extension facility by its proper name," Frank interrupted him.

Stoner couldn't think of the Swamp's proper name. Mumbled, "Yes, sir," in place of correcting it.

"Other than you don't know the name of where you are," Frank returned to being supportive again quickly. "Is everything under control?"

"Yes, sir." Stoner couldn't let Frank hang up without acknowledging that he knew how overall unhappy the man was with him. "Appleton told me I have to make an appointment with you the first of the year."

"That's right, Stoner," Frank agreed smoothly. "If you'll call my secretary after the first—"

"I mean he told me *why* I was making an appointment."

Frank cleared his throat, the way he often did at meetings when he wanted to change the subject and move on to something easier to discuss. "All house staff receive an evaluation at the end of December, Stoner. It's something to be done sitting down in my office, however, rather than on the phone."

"I just wondered what was the main thing. If it was the incident in July."

Frank cleared his throat again. Twice. "Well, I'm not going to tell you I was pleased with your conduct in July, Stoner. I'm sure you consider me terribly old-fashioned, but I just don't believe that people need extramarital sex." The man cleared his throat again, as if he were surprised at himself that he had used a word as risque as sex. "And it's not just my age, I assure you. My daughter is as young as you. But you can bet *she* has never engaged in anything like that."

Stoner believed him. But then he'd met the man's daughter and knew that she was thirty-two and still had bucked teeth, so maybe no one had ever asked her to engage in anything like that. Stoner pounded his fist on the desk in frustration, sensing the man was about to hang up on him again and rushed to stop him. "Do you know your daughter is here?" he asked.

"Leslie?" Frank sounded as if he had swallowed his telephone receiver. Or it had swallowed him. "Why is Leslie there?"

"She's started labor, sir." A funny family, Stoner thought. Unable to talk about sex without choking up. But even with that, surely his daughter had told him she was pregnant. In another minute he remembered the storm outside and realized the man must have thought she was there from a car accident.

"Does that mean she's in A Building?" Frank asked.

"Yes sir." A Building was Labor and Delivery.

"You know that building is to be torn down next year." Frank sounded like Appleton, taking a chance to educate. "As soon as the extension facility is converted solely to research space. It's the oldest of the towers."

Stoner knew that the A Building had been condemned as structurally unsound and ordered demolished. Only by contracting for cement columns for the building had the center been able to save it and supposedly make it sound enough to continue its use until the addition to the main center was complete.

"I don't understand why Leslie went there," Frank said, sounding as if he were thinking out loud, rather than really talking to Stoner. "I'll ask the airport if there's a possibility I can get a helicopter up to lift her out of there. Get her to the main center. Page Zack Appleton and tell him to get right back to me."

"Yes, sir," Stoner said. But he said it to a dead line because Frank had already hung up. Jesus, the man thought he was so inadequate, he was willing to risk his daughter's life in a rickety helicopter rather than leave her there with him, he thought. And all because he had asked Lynn Curtain for a few minutes of her time the summer before.

Disgusted with himself, Stoner sat staring at a temperature conversion sheet on the wall behind the desk, at row after row of fahrenheit, then centigrade numbers, and asked himself if what Culbertson had said could be right. Was he frozen in some former, more fun, point in time? Marriage to Sue Ellen had not been fun. He knew that. But then, he'd only married her because she'd said she was pregnant with his child. Then she had had a miscarriage, so there had been no child. He'd tried to pull everything together and go on to college after that. He paid for all of it himself, while he worked full-time at the Stonehouse on the side. Same for med school. And all that while, Sue Ellen complained because she couldn't have a Henredon dining room table like her mother had. Had started drinking gin and tonic at dinner. Moved to simply gin anytime. Lord, that was part his problem, because, in the beginning, he had encouraged her to drink. She didn't harp about his spending all his money on tuition rather than a dining room table after the first glass.

He sat staring at the temperature conversion scale on the wall above the desk, wondering why he had been so stupid to not wait longer before he had married her. At least find out first if it was his baby she had been having before he married her. It hadn't been his. He knew that because the fetus's blood type had been Rh positive. And because both his and Sue Ellen's blood type was Rh negative, any baby he could have had with her would have had an Rh negative blood type, too.

Gena was still staring at the X-ray of Mark Warren. Immediately obvious to her on the film was the outline of the two lower arm bones, the ulna and the radius. She wasn't great at reading X-rays, but something as obvious as a broken bone she could pick out.

And there was a break there all right, in the boy's left ulna, the kind called a Greenstick—a crack rather than a full break. Even though that was the small bone in the lower arm, it needed to be set. Technicians always took X-rays of both arms on children, so there was a norm to compare arm contour against. This technician must have confused the labels on these, Gena realized, because the one she was looking at showed a crack in the left arm, and Mark Warren had been holding his right arm stiffly. She pushed the second X-ray up into place. Surprised. There was an even more evident crack there in the radius, plus an older, duller, healing crack in the ulna. She read the labels again and put the films back up. No matter which way she looked at them, there was no mistaking it. Mark Warren had two fractures in the ulna bone in his left arm, one in the ulna and the radius on the right. One of the two on the right was very recent; the others were older, healing fractures.

What in hell could be causing that? Was there a chance the kid was taking some kind of drug that had started draining calcium out of his bones, making him more susceptible to injury than usual? Not likely. That happened sometimes to older people, but not to otherwise healthy ten-year-olds. There was an inherited disease that caused that—osteogenesis imperfecta—but the possibility of that happening to Mark Warren wasn't likely. No other Warren had it. Although wait—her brain was going numb in the middle of the night. Mark Warren had been adopted. She didn't know anything at all about his family history. That could be the problem.

What she'd do for tonight was put a cast on his arm and take away the pain. Even in the middle of the night with a bridge snowed shut, that would be easy. What would be harder would be explaining to Peter Perfect that the boy he had adopted might have an inherited bone disease. She could guess Peter Warren would like that as little as he liked the boy having asthma.

* * *

Jack Kissell still sat crouched in the induction room behind the OR schedule desk, waiting for a lab technician to come for the key for the blood cooler. Kissell was anxious to take the desk schedule key downstairs to the Personnel Office and go from there to Frank's office. His watch said 4:45 a.m. Technically, the cooler was supposed to be emptied by one o'clock, but no one had come to get the blood out yet, and he couldn't move until they did.

As if to answer his question about someone coming, footsteps sounded in the hallway outside the OR suite. Kissell listened to the sound of soft shoes enter the suite and the rustle of paper as hands sorted through the top drawer of the schedule desk. Finally, there was a jingle of metal, as whoever it was took out the ring of keys for the blood cooler.

Kissell caught a glimpse of a blue cord pants leg and tan hush puppies as the person passed the slightly cracked door to the induction room. That made it Scott Stoner. He listened to Stoner walk over to the cooler and open it with one of the keys on the ring.

"Come on. Where are you?" Stoner asked the inside of the cooler.

Kissell remained frozen, watching the man close the door to the refrigerator again and walk back toward the elevator, flicking off light switches as he went. At the desk, Stoner stopped, picked up the telephone receiver, and dialed a number. Then stood drumming his fingers against the desktop until the call was answered. "Eddie?" he asked after another minute of intense drumming. "Stoner. In OR. There isn't any blood in the cooler here. Did you pick it up already?"

Kissell couldn't make out the laboratory technician's answer.

"Trust me. I can tell an empty refrigerator when I see it," Stoner contradicted him.

The lab tech's reply was muffled again.

"Of course it's serious," Stoner said. "It means there isn't any more emergency blood in the place."

A hurried explanation from the technician.

"Look," Stoner cut him off. "Hold the new pack I ordered you to cross for Gallagher. That way we won't use up everything."

A short muffled reply from the technician.

"Damn it! You never do *anything* fast!" Stoner shouted. "Why did you choose this night to start?"

Kissell heard the telephone slammed on Stoner's ear and Stoner drop his receiver back into place. There was the click of a switch as Stoner flipped off a final light switch by his head and started to walk back toward the suite door.

That was good. It meant he was going. Except Kissell was sure that he hadn't heard the man put the keys back on the desk! He was taking them with him! Kissell started to move, to remind Stoner he had them. Only he couldn't do that! That would give him away. He'd have to explain why he was lurking in a dark room.

At the end of the hallway, Stoner apparently remembered that he still had the key ring and tossed it the length of the hallway onto the OR desk. It clattered and jingled to a halt against a metal index card box.

Kissell sat frozen until the hum of the elevator door opening and closing let him know that Stoner had left the floor. He was free to take the keys now and move to Personnel—and the next step on his way toward Frank's safe.

* * *

A strong blast of wind hit the third floor of A building as Gena Portobello stepped onto it from the third floor walkway again. The wind hit so hard that she could actually feel the building shift with the force of it. She didn't know if that always happened or not, but she guessed the sensation couldn't mean anything too serious. She had to believe the building was secure.

An older woman—Monahan, Mulligan, Murphy—something like that—was the charge nurse there at night on the pediatric unit. Gena didn't see the woman anywhere around at the moment, though, so she sank down into a chair to dial Violet Hamilton, Mark Warren's private pediatrician. Hamilton was an overweight butch woman who always made the point that she had come through medical school when women had to be twice as good as men, implying that she was twice as good as any man. Violet liked to be kept constantly informed of anything happening to her patients, always criticizing any time lag in communication. Gena described Mark Warren's wheezing and response to aminophylline and that she had admitted him and was continuing oxygen. Hamilton interrupted her before she was finished, to ask why the boy had been admitted at one o'clock and it was now almost six o'clock and she was just calling her.

"I wanted to see the X-ray before I called you," Gena said.

Hamilton had strict rules about no superfluous X-rays being taken on her patients. She gave Gena her routine lecture on the hazards of overexposure to X-ray. As long as Mark's chest had cleared initially, she said, she had a real question as to whether a chest X-ray had been necessary.

"The X-ray was of his arms," Gena interrupted her.

There was silence on the other end of the telephone as Hamilton digested that. After a long moment Gena recognized the problem: she had said that she had admitted a boy with asthma, a chest condition, and then she had ordered and read an X-ray of his arms. She rushed to tell Hamilton about the boy's second problem: the broken arm.

"Have you called an orthopedic resident?" Hamilton asked.

"There's no orthopedic coverage at the Swamp at night."

"Well, call the main center for help, dear. Don't work in a vacuum," the woman criticized.

"The bridge to the Swamp is snowed shut, Dr. Hamilton. No one can get over here."

Hamilton took an even longer time to digest that. Finally, she asked, "Well, how can *I* get in there? How can I see patients this morning?"

Gena thought it was obvious that the woman couldn't, but she said nothing.

"I'm certain you know," Hamilton began a new explanation slowly, as if she were really certain that Gena did *not* know, "that when elbows are casted, there is a very real danger of the brachial artery being compromised. Causing permanent paralysis in the arm."

Gena knew that. She'd learned it in Elbows 101 her first year in medical school. "I'll be careful," she said. "What I'm concerned about is that the X-ray shows two old breaks as well as this new one."

Hamilton didn't add anything for a long moment. Then she asked, "What history did you get on that?"

Gena hadn't asked for an explanation of the past breaks. She hadn't talked to the Warrens since she'd admitted Mark. "He slipped at school this afternoon to account for this break. I don't know about the others."

Gena waited for Hamilton to give her hell for an incomplete history, but oddly enough, the woman didn't seem upset. "That's all right, Gena," Hamilton's voice sounded very sympathetic. Taking pity on her for being stuck there, Gena guessed. Or else sure that was the best she could do. "Don't waste any more of your time on that as long as you're busy. Leave it to me to look into when I get in. And Portobello," Hamilton obviously thought of something she wanted to add before she hung up. "You know the Warrens contribute a lot of money to the center. Please don't mess up the cast."

Everyone knew the Warrens contributed a lot of money to the center. And there was no one in White Horse whom Gena's mother had not told that *she* was a Warren, so Hamilton must have known that, too. She grunted for an answer and dropped the telephone; wondering if she would have acted as smug as the other Warrens did, if her father hadn't been killed. Reluctantly, she pushed herself to her feet.

"Could you get me equipment for a cast?" Gena asked the nurse who had just appeared at her elbow.

"First-year residents can't put a cast in place without a second opinion consult," the nameless nurse answered stiffly. She was tall and thin and wore a starched white uniform and a senseless cupcakelike cap on her gray hair. The desk light glared up on the dark rings under her eyes as she frowned even more deeply.,

She was an ageless woman, the kind who had gone to nursing school before much education was required and was now sentenced to work nights because the day jobs were taken by better-educated new graduates. Since she went to school at a time when she was taught to jump to her feet for doctors, she probably resented jumping for doctors who were younger than her own children.

"Could you get that for me?" Gena asked her. She walked into Mark Warren's room to listen to his chest, to see if he was quieting down.

The boy was still dressed in the clothing he had worn in, a blue sweatshirt with the word SWATCH across the front of it, jeans, expensive Nike sneakers, and crew socks. He was lying propped up by two pillows. The gatch on the bed raised him to an almost upright position. He held an oxygen mask pressed against his face. Despite those measures, his respirations were still fast and uncomfortable. It seemed as if the oxygen wasn't reaching the deep lung spaces, therefore it wasn't doing any good, which made him have to breathe even more rapidly. A circle going round and round and round.

His mother was standing by the foot of the bed. She still had on her coat, the front of it held tightly against her as if she could not get warm. She hadn't combed her hair since she'd arrived. She had wiped the smeared mascara from under her eyes, but that had left dark tired-looking rings.

Peter Warren, in contrast to her, looked great. He was sitting on the one comfortable chair in the room reading *Newsweek*. He had taken off his coat and was now wearing a black suit with a black vest. The only thing that broke his perfect appearance was his right shoe, a very shiny black wingtip, tapping nervously and constantly against the edge of the bed.

Gena explained about the recent break that showed on Mark's X-ray and that the arm would need to be casted. "That's why it's been hurting since this afternoon," she said.

Mark looked up at her. "I didn't hurt it until ten o'clock tonight," he said between efforts for more air.

Gena thought he'd said he hurt it in school. So much for her listening ability in an emergency room. Not that the time made any difference as far as the cast went. She looked up at the plastic intravenous setup and tubing running into his left hand and recalculated the solumedrol dose he had running there. If that was running right, he should have been breathing easier by now. Asthma attacks could be triggered by stress. They could also continue because of it. "How is school going?" she asked him.

"He's missed a lot of school lately," his mother answered for him, hovering by the side of the bed. "His marks are good though. He does very well in school."

"Is your room at home allergy-proofed?" Gena asked next.

"It's stripped completely," his mother answered for him again.

"Did you take your routine meds today?"

"He always takes them," his mother answered.

Gena would like to have heard the ten-year-old answer himself for at least one of those questions, but she let that go. Peter Perfect's son was perfect; that was the message she was getting. So why wasn't the damn perfect asthma medication she was giving him settling things down damn perfectly?

Gena looked up at the sound of the equipment cart arriving at the room door. The nurse whose name she didn't know had apparently located Stoner, because he followed her and the equipment into the room. He greeted the Warrens as if they were old friends and stood, arms crossed on his chest, discussing the stock market with Peter, and their plans for New Year's Eve the next night with Elizabeth, rather than looking at Gena. Finally, he took time away from their social calendar to look at the X-ray. His eyebrows shot up as he saw the multiple fine line breaks. "Have a lot of pain?" he turned to ask the boy.

"Don't give him any aspirin," Peter Warren answered

for him, "Portobello almost killed him last time he was in, trying to give him some."

Thank you, Peter Warren, for pointing that out, Gena thought.

"Well then, let's just go for a cast this time," Stoner said. He perched on the edge of the boy's bed and steaded his arm in position for Gena to apply a cast. Gena had the bottom layer of stockinette in place. Stoner and Peter Warren had discussed the price of gasoline and both the Patriots' and the Bills' seasons before Gena decided to ask the boy the last of the routine questions for admission: had anything upsetting happened to trigger an attack?

"He came in late," his father interrupted a comparison of John Unitas and Jim Kelly to answer for the boy that time. "If being scolded for coming in late makes him wheeze, you had better give him something stronger to prevent it, because the next time, he can expect the same thing."

Gena looked up at the boy to see his response to that. Except for a glance at what she was doing to his arm, he had returned to lying back in bed, inspecting his ceiling. He made no move to show that he had even heard his father's comment.

She was sure getting a mixed picture, Gena thought. A mother who said she had a perfect son. A father who saw his son asking for trouble. A son who was only interested in studying ceilings.

"Where did the aspirin fit into all that?" Gena asked.

"He wasn't thinking," Elizabeth Warren answered immediately.

"Give the woman credit for not being a fool, Elizabeth!" Peter Perfect shifted in his chair, talking over Gena's head to his wife. "She has obviously already guessed that Mark took it deliberately. That nothing stops everything faster than an asthma attack.''

Gena hadn't guessed that at all, and if that were true, it bothered her. A ten-year-old could kill himself before he caught their attention that way.

''I seem to remember it wasn't easy being ten,'' Stoner said.

''Don't defend him, Stoner!'' Peter Perfect tossed the *Newsweek* onto the window sill and sat up even straighter in his chair. ''You were burying naked stiffs at his age! That makes you no judge of anything!''

Stoner clamped his mouth shut.

''An ambition like yours to break every rule, impregnate every girl in White Horse, by the time you are thirty, isn't to be admired,'' Peter Perfect finished his lecture.

Gena finished wrapping plaster wondering why Peter Perfect's remark had bothered Stoner so much. Having impregnated Lynn Curtain didn't seem to bother him at all.

Jack Kissell had let himself out of the surgery suite by the north stairway and darted across the short overhead walkway from C Building to A Building, then ran the length of the rear stairway in A Building down to the first floor. A bottom stairway door there brought him out by the business office hallway. Cautiously, he took a step toward the Personnel Office, listening for any sound, any hint that another person was in that wing. He heard a door open. A ring of keys rattle. Anxiously, Kissell peered into the corridor and spotted a cleaning lady with a yellow-bagged cart just leaving the Personnel office. She had huge hips and a duff that stuck out behind her as she walked. If he had been even two steps ahead of himself, she would have seen him, he thought. Frantically, he ducked behind the stairway door and watched the woman close the Personnel Office door behind herself and push her cleaning cart down the hall, away from him. He waited, concealed by the door, until she turned the corner and was out of sight.

He had had to wait so long for the blood cooler check, that it was too late to try to get into the safe. All he would be able to do now was to make certain he could get into Frank's office. That he knew the way.

Hurrying, he strode to the Personnel office door and pressed a gold key from the OR ring into the door lock. Damn! The key didn't fit. He tried a second one on the ring. It fit the lock, but didn't turn. He was wasting time. He'd be seen! The third key? No! Still not a fit. The fourth? No. What in hell could all those keys be for? He knew Lynn Curtain had used one on that ring to open the door. If he didn't find the right one soon, someone would see him. He would be exposed as a common thief. Maybe the fifth one? Damn, no! A sixth? *Yes.* The key turned and the door opened. *Thank God.* Kissell slipped into the room and closed the door after himself. He would grab the ring of keys from the wall . . . *shit!* The ring on the wall wasn't there. The cleaning lady must have taken the ring of keys to clean David Frank's office.

Dejected, Kissell slumped behind a row of file cabinets. There was nothing else to do but go home and try again another night. He pulled the telephone off the desk and dialed his wife to tell her he was coming home.

"Where are you?" she screamed with relief at the sound of his voice. "I thought something terrible had happened to you!"

"My car is stuck in snow," Kissell tried to lie convincingly to account for his time. "I'm waiting for a tow."

"I'll come and get you." His wife sounded as if she were about to drop her telephone and back out the garage. "You *are* across the bridge, aren't you? Would you ever have guessed the whole damn thing would snow-shut that way?"

Kissell asked his wife to repeat what she'd said about the bridge; he sat, weighing what it meant, as she repeated a story about a clogged Bird Island bridge. "No one can get across the bridge?" he asked her. Wonderful! It meant that no one would be able to get into the Swamp to work this morning. That would offer him a lot of time to spin safe combinations. He hung up, sure that a cleaning lady wouldn't keep the keys to Frank's office long. After all, how much time did it take to clean an office?

As soon as she brought those keys back, he would have hours to work on the safe. He sank down in back of the row of file cabinets, making certain his body didn't cast a shadow anywhere, prepared to wait, laughing at all the times he had told people it was insane to run a hospital on an island. Amazing how susceptible that made the building in a bad storm!

How rich he would be by the time the storm was over.

Chapter Seven

Bob Haiden had finished showering, pulled on a clean pair of white slacks, a light blue shirt, and a dark blue tie, and was fumbling in the dark by his dresser for a tie clip by 5:00 A.M. A list of things he had to do that day was carved into deep recesses of his mind. He was opening the door of his apartment building, when he realized the outside storm door wouldn't budge.

He turned on the porch light and peered into the dark to see what was blocking the door. He couldn't believe what he saw. A five-foot drift of snow had wedged against it. He stretched on his toes to look above it and watched a garbage can, swept ahead of blowing snow, smash into the building next door; garbage and newspapers spilled out of the can and instantly whipped away to pelt against the stop sign on the corner. No traffic was moving in the street, a drift at the far end, as high as the one on the porch, completely blocked out cars. He wouldn't be able to get into work. And he had to talk to David Frank about his research position, submit himself to the scrape-the-monkey-shit story if he had to, to get Frank to talk about research money.

Amazed, he walked back upstairs, the metal fasteners on his galoshes making sharp clicks against each step. He sat down on the edge of his bed and turned on the clock radio. An announcer was just finishing a list of school closings: "All Town of Tonawanda public and parochial schools; all White Horse public and parochial. Repeat: all Buffalo public and parochial schools are closed. Go back to bed, kids! Have a nice day!"

Bob's wife reached a sleepy hand out from under the covers to try and turn off the sound.

"Cut it out, Jennifer!" Bob batted her hand away. "I have to hear a snow report."

"It has snowed every day since November first," Jennifer answered dully, pulling covers up over herself. "What's different about today?"

The announcer began to list plant and business closings.

"When you can't open the front door," Bob answered firmly, dropping his gloves onto the floor and looking outside again at snow so thick the street was totally impassable, "*Something* is different." He listened to a report that the Bird Island Bridge was closed. "Why didn't anyone call me?" he asked Jennifer angrily. "Tell me that happened?"

"You leave orders not to be bothered at night," Jennifer answered. "So you can sleep. The only person who ever calls you is that pregnant nurse."

That was true, Haiden admitted, but surely everyone would have known he would want to be disturbed for that news. Didn't they realize the Swamp was composed of old buildings and a storm could tear them apart? He stood up and reached for the telephone to call the center, then returned the receiver gently to its cradle. *Not everyone did know that.* He was the one who had contracted for the cement columns in A Building. He alone knew how weak the basic structure of that tower was.

It was 6:00 A.M.

Gena Portobello picked up the phone on the labor and delivery desk—because no one else seemed to be answering it—and said hello.

"Would you believe it, Portobello?" the voice of Norm Redhoe, Leslie Frank Kerr's obstetrician, thundered into her ear as soon as she had the receiver in her hand. "I've got an important patient in there and I can't get in."

Gena wasn't convinced the man *would* have come in, even if he could have. That was the game he played with patients.

"I know that Richard Culbertson stayed there last night," Redhoe continued. "Does he know that Leslie Frank is there?"

Redhoe was interested in Culbertson resigning so that he could be the chief of service, Gena knew. In light of that, she guessed that he wouldn't want Culbertson near the administrator's daughter where he could make a good impression on her in his absence. "No," she answered. "I don't think he knows."

"Well, let him know. Ask him to look in on her for me, will you? Make sure he knows that she has a borderline pelvis. Whatever you do, don't start to think you can handle things by yourself. She's David Frank's daughter."

Gena felt numb, realizing that Norm Redhoe would rather risk Culbertson making a good impression with Leslie Frank than to leave her in charge. Great evaluation of her ability. Although, after the delivery room fiasco during the night, she could understand how that opinion of her ability had come about. "You have that, Portobello?" Redhoe demanded when she didn't answer him.

"Yes, sir."

"You do realize that Leslie Frank can have real trouble with this baby, don't you? I want you to keep that out in front of you all the time. And be certain that Richard Culbertson keeps it out in front of him. With a small pelvis, things start slowly, but then all hell breaks lose."

"David Frank said he might have his daughter lifted out by helicopter," Gena tried to make things sound better.

"I've already checked that out. The wind is too strong."

"Scott Stoner—" Gena tried another approach.

"Not Stoner! It's *Culbertson* I want to know about Frank's daughter. Get Culbertson working."

Gena hung up to the sound of Sally Yates chattering with the night aide and flipping pages in her black narcotic notebook as she did her morning narcotic count, as if this were just another morning. Federal regulations specified that all narcotics had to be counted at changes of nursing shifts; the nurse leaving and the nurse arriving both counted the contents of the narcotic box and signed the narcotic book, certifying that they agreed on the total in the cabinet.

Sally was making her count, apparently, despite the fact that she wasn't going to be relieved. Gena watched her hold up a box of Demerol vials, count them, glance at the book in front of herself, and initial the page.

The aide on the unit had set up a television beside the nurse's station and was watching the screen: a weatherman pointing to a radar map of western New York and talking about wind velocity and inches of snow. Night factory workers were trapped in plants all over the area and unable to get home, he said. Bell Aerospace had sixteen hundred trapped; Harrison Radiator had three thousand. The most critical problem, however, that he could spot, was the sealing in of the Sylvester A. Warren Medical Pavilion on Bird Island. . . .''

The phone rang again at Gena's elbow: the day resident for Medicine A, Mort Warzinski, calling in to say that he was sorry he couldn't get in. Gena listened to the man run through patient problems on Medicine A. ''A patient named Herkemer needs his antibiotics reordered. And Grishaven, of course, needs fluid reordered. And Braxton Hershey called me. Said a patient he has there named Gallagher might need a couple units of blood this morning,'' Mort suggested.

Gena nodded and started to write that on a list. Stopped. ''I don't think there's any more blood here, Mort,'' she said.

''Use emergency blood.''

''I *mean* emergency blood. The standby blood from OR is missing. That means Gallagher used up everything here during the night.''

''But why did you give him that much, Gena?'' the man demanded. ''No one can get in there to replace any this morning.''

''How was I supposed to know that last night?'' Gena asked, ignoring the basic fact that she hadn't given it to him; Stoner had.

Mort sighed. In the background Gena heard a woman offer him cream for his coffee. ''Okay,'' he said crisply. Gena waited to see if he was responding to the offer of cream or talking to her. ''You couldn't have known that. But what do you do now? That's the question.''

Gena guessed she had better find Stoner and ask him to get up to the fourth floor and evaluate Gallagher, for starters. If a helicopter could get up, maybe one could drop some blood, Mort said. He'd find out. Gena wrote *Check Dan Gallagher* on the top of her list.

"No helicopters can get up, Mort." She knew that from talking to Norm Redhoe. "It's too windy."

"I'll recheck and call you back." Mort hung up his phone.

"Wait a minute!" Gena shouted at him. Too late. And too bad. He had information she needed: Where Hershey was.

The telephone on the desk in front of her started ringing again immediately: Bob Haiden phoning in for her or Stoner.

"You can't believe the mess out here, Gena," he said. "From my kitchen window I can't see anything but snow." Gena had little sympathy for anyone home in their kitchen instead of on Bird Island. She pulled a chart toward herself and read him the workup on Doctor Frank's daughter.

"Holy hell, Gena!" Haiden sounded really teed off with her as soon as he caught the name. "Why didn't you call me that she was there?"

"She's barely in labor, Bob. And you don't like to be called when women are barely in labor."

"Portobello!" The man shouted at her. "Rules like that don't apply when the woman is the administrator's daughter! What are you going to do, if she's ready to deliver, and she has trouble before anyone can get in there?"

Gena didn't need to be reminded of that.

"OK. Never mind." Haiden's voice turned sympathetic. A woman's voice behind him came closer to the telephone and kissed him good morning. "Just keep a close eye on her. Let me know of any changes. Like you said, she's so early, what can happen?"

Across the room, Sally Yates couldn't find three vials of morphine that were supposed to be in the narcotic cupboard and began slamming doors on other cupboards looking for them.

"The bridge will be clear soon," Haiden said. "And everything will be all right. What about my medical bag? Did either you or Stoner find time to put it up for me?"

"I did."

"Good. Thanks." It was good to hear Haiden being appreciative of something rather than angry with her. "I've got some expensive things in there. Crazy of me to have just left it on a bench."

Across the room, Sally Yates opened another cupboard and slammed it shut.

"Have anyone else in labor besides Frank's daughter?" Haiden asked.

"No. I helped Culbertson deliver twins during the night."

"Nice experience."

"They both had tracheal meconium. I had to breathe shit twice."

Haiden laughed, then muffled a hand over his receiver and declined toast and grits. "Didn't I warn you last July that residents take a lot of shit?" he asked.

"I didn't know you meant literally."

Haiden laughed again, but Gena wasn't sure it was that funny. One evening the summer before, when she had been really tired, she had moved a lot slower than Haiden had liked. "You have to learn how to survive better," he had said to her, motioning for her to follow him. "Live with less sleep. Bounce back faster. Otherwise you're not going to make this."

"You survive because you protect your sleep like a hibernating bear," she had told him.

"I survive because I'm tough," he had insisted, and had reminded her that Norm Redhoe was another example of a man who was tough. She should always remember that when working with a patient of Redhoe's. Good to remember now, she thought, because Leslie Frank Kerr was Redhoe's patient.

"One last thing," Haiden pulled closer to his receiver, bringing her back to the present. "I know Lynn Curtain worked last night. Would you keep an eye on her for me? I wouldn't like to see her get too tired, as close to delivery as she is."

"Sure." It was never trouble for Gena to do anything for Haiden, but since a certain night in July, Lynn Curtain wasn't her favorite person.

"She's decided she wants to deliver her baby at home, and I said I'd do that for her," Haiden continued. "Don't let her get so tired that she delivers there and I lose the experience."

Gena wasn't crazy about home births and Haiden didn't need experience. He was as good as anyone could get. "Why'd she decide to do that, Bob?"

"She's self-conscious about delivering where she knows everyone. You know."

Gena wasn't sure she did know, but let that go.

"Call me if you have any problems," Haiden finished. "I'll be home."

Gena settled the receiver back into place, wishing that if anyone could be here instead of home, it could be Haiden. Across from Gena, Sally reopened the narcotic cabinet and began taking out bottles and vials again one by one to locate her missing one. The phone rang and she walked back across the room to get it. "This is for Stoner," she said, handing the receiver to Gena. "Can you take it?"

Gena guessed she could, sure that it would be an attending with a patient review and orders.

"This is Sue Ellen, Gena," Stoner's wife said. "I've been trying to get hold of my husband."

"Did you page him?"

"My husband doesn't acknowledge my page."

Gena didn't want to be involved in a husband-wife quarrel. "I'll ask Scott to call you," she said, hurrying to shift the telephone to her other ear to block out the sound of Sally Yates slamming shut more cupboard doors looking for her missing narcotic.

"While you're talking to Scott," Sue Ellen continued, "will you remind him that he promised to take me to a New Year's Eve party tonight?"

Gena had a fleeting memory of a senior prom, an organdy gown, a kiss beside a fountain, blurred immediately by the memory of Sue Ellen's hand sliding along Stoner's shoulder in a school hallway; kissing him in front of an altar; Stoner bragging the next month that she was pregnant.

"Tell him he could sleep over here afterward." Sue Ellen clicked a glass against her receiver as if she were calling while eating breakfast. "After all, no one should drive on New Year's Eve if they don't have to."

Gena had a difficult time believing the woman had said that. She must have no idea how bad the storm was or she wouldn't be talking about going to a party.

"He also could sleep over for another reason," Sue Ellen added.

Sally slammed a cupboard door so hard Gena jumped.

A glass clicked again by Sue Ellen's receiver. "Would you believe I paid over two hundred dollars for a dress to wear to a party tonight and now everything's being canceled?" she asked.

Gena yawned, not at all concerned about a canceled party or a two-hundred-dollar dress.

"Be careful, Beverly! You're burning that toast!" Sue Ellen shouted at someone behind her. "Don't touch the glass! Damn it! That's vodka and you've spilled it!"

"I'll have Scott call you, Sue Ellen," Gena repeated, hanging up. She wondered why Sue Ellen was drinking vodka for breakfast.

"OK. I fell for it." Sally Yates closed a final cupboard door and came over to the desk. She'd changed to a white uniform from the scrub dress she'd had on during the night, and looked as fresh and trim as if she had just come on duty. Which was strange, because all night, when she'd been on duty, she'd looked sleepy. "Stoner has the morphine, doesn't he? I'm looking all over for it, and he has it. Very funny."

At one time morphine had been combined with scopolamine and given to women in labor as "twilight sleep." It wasn't used that way anymore, because it had left mothers so sleepy they didn't know what was going on, and babies too depressed to breathe at birth. Stoner should never have been near her cabinet for morphine to use that way.

"He took it as a joke, didn't he?" Sally asked.

"I'm not responsible for jokes between you two," Gena said.

"*Please* say Stoner took it for a joke." Sally looked around the nurse's station for a final desperate time. "I can't call Curtain and tell her I have lost three vials of morphine! She'll fire me!"

"Everyone must lose some sometime," Gena said. Not knowing if that were true or not.

"No one ever loses *any!*" Sally screamed, clarifying that. She opened a desk drawer, glanced at pads of paper and paper clips, and slammed it shut again. "The dumb part of this is, I didn't count narcotics when I came on last night. Cris Meyer was on, and she said she hadn't given any and was anxious to get home before the roads got any worse, so I just took her word for it and signed the count. That whole box could have been missing before I came on."

Gena turned her mind to her own problems and started a new list of things to do: check Dan Gallagher, check twenty patients on 3A, recheck Mark Warren, look at the new twins, check Leslie Frank . . . The phone at her elbow rang. Sally plunged a hand down on it before Gena could and thrust it at her.

It was Bert Lewis, the center's senior pediatric resident, asking for a report on Mark Warren. He sounded really aggravated that he couldn't get in. When the Warrens were unhappy, they made everyone else unhappy, he said, especially him, whose job it was to keep them happy. She should be sure and do everything by the book, and hope the road crew was having good luck shoveling the bridge, he advised. Gena hung up feeling very angry. He should have known she would do that without his instructions.

The telephone rang abruptly again and Gena grabbed for it.

"Gena? Guess where I am?"

Gena leaned against the desk, happy to recognize Braxton Hershey's voice. She also recognized a familiar piano in the background.

"I'm at The Stonehouse!" Hershey exclaimed. "About a hundred people are snowed in here with me."

Gena envied him. The Stonehouse was a beautiful place, with plush green carpets, white wrought iron tables and chairs, white tablecloths, flowered napkins, white china with silver rims, plants hanging overhead. In the evening, with fresh flowers and white tapers on each table, it was like a quiet, unspoiled English garden. Gena glanced around at the oldest building of the Swamp, that seemed to shake every time the wind hit it. If she had to be snowed in anywhere, she thought, she would want it to be at The Stonehouse.

"The chef is making crepes—" Braxton continued.

Gena's stomach growled.

"Tonight there's going to be an ice fish on each table. Everybody's blowing up balloons—"

But then, New Year's Eve was always a big night at The Stonehouse. Red, white, and blue balloons would fall at midnight, along with confetti and streamers. Featured among diners there that evening would be Scott Stoner and his estranged wife wearing a two-hundred dollar dress that he probably could not afford, she thought. Obviously could not afford. After all, he still drove the car he'd had in high school. She had spent a lot of New Year's Eves in her life sitting home alone. She wondered how many Sue Ellen had spent wearing two-hundred-dollar dresses she couldn't afford.

"When do you think you'll be able to get out of the Swamp?" Braxton interrupted her thoughts.

"Hours, I guess."

"How's that fella I did in OR last night? My appendectomy."

"Something terrible has happened to him, Brax!" In front of her, the elevator door opened and Scott Stoner stepped off it. "Here's Stoner. I'll let him tell you about it." She extended the receiver toward Stoner.

Stoner stood frowning at her from the space between them as she held the receiver out. For a moment, he looked as if he was going to walk on past her without acknowledging she was even there, then he grabbed the receiver from her.

Lynn Curtain stepped out of the elevator behind him, looking even more tired than she had during the night. A lot of hair had crept out of the barrette at the back of her head and was straggling over her ears. She was there apparently, because Sally Yates had reported her missing morphine, Gena guessed. Gena turned to the television screen while Stoner carried on a conversation with Braxton. An announcer on the morning show described an accident during the night where a car had stopped because of blowing snow. The cars behind that one had plowed into each other until by the time the whiteout had disappeared, fifty cars, or a total of one hundred and thirteen people, had driven into each other, like a string of dominoes going down. A lot of people had pulled off the thruway during the night because of the poor visibility. Any car pulled over that way was now under snow. There was a very real possibility that people had fallen asleep after they had parked in those cars and were now frozen to death. If alive, they would remain trapped in their cars for hours. The wind was blowing the thruway shut so thoroughly that the state police couldn't even get through the toll gate.

"I put the first Dukane baby under bilirubin lights for you." Lynn came back to the desk and started to look through the desk drawers while Sally Yates watched her anxiously.

Gena was still listening to the announcer on television, more concerned with what he was saying than with a new baby.

"Did you hear me about the lights?" Curtain asked her.

All babies developed some buildup of bilirubin, a breakdown product of red blood cells at birth that made their skin turn yellow. Putting them under fluorescent light helped them evacuate it from their system by improving liver function. That didn't even start to show until after twenty-four hours though, so the baby couldn't be that yellow. "You can't do newborn lights without an order," she said to Lynn.

"All right." Lynn sighed, turning back to the medicine chest. "I'll take him out from under lights. You write the order and I'll put him back."

No reason for her to be so touchy, Gena thought, as if she were the only one who was trapped there. "The only babies that get jaundiced this fast after birth, Lynn, are ones with serious blood incompatibilities. And they're so sick, you're not going to do much for them with just lights."

Lynn pushed a strand of hair back behind her ear; she didn't move from where she was standing.

Gena looked back from reels of blowing snow to see what she had missed. *Jesus!* That was what Lynn was telling her: the baby was sick! *I put a baby under lights, Doctor,* not *wake up, dummy, you've got a sick baby upstairs. Try the peach melba,* not *peaches are rotting in the kitchen.* It couldn't be too serious, though. The laboratory technician would have called by this time if he'd gotten an abnormal cord blood, and she'd had no call. Unless, of course, there wasn't anyone in the lab . . . Gena strode into the unit kitchen to use the phone there and dialed the lab.

All around her, the kitchen smelled like a bakery. Warm cinnamon rolls were sitting on the counter. A pan of a tomato and garlic mixture was simmering on the stove. Discarded in the wastepaper basket at her feet she noticed a crumpled doggie bag from The Stonehouse. She tipped the pan to see what was bubbling inside it, but couldn't recognize what it was.

Nervously, she tapped the telephone in her hand waiting, for someone to answer it. If no one was in the lab, the cord blood could have been high from bilirubin and she wouldn't know it. The baby could have been in trouble for hours. After eight or nine rings, the sleepy voice of the lab technician finally said hello in her ear.

"This is Doctor Portobello." Gena felt her nerves straining taut. "I sent down two cord bloods during the night. Did you run them for me yet?"

The person on the other end of the phone yawned for an answer.

"Bilirubin levels on two Dukane babies," Gena urged the technician for a better response than that. "They were important."

"I got one blood from you about two," the technician said. Yawning again, "and I ran it and it was normal. I don't know about any other blood."

"There were two specimens," Gena said persistently, sure that the time had been closer to one o'clock. "A and B twins."

The man flipped pages in a book; yawned again. "I only got one sample. That's all I ran."

"You must still have a second one. I sent *two.*"

"What are you going to do to me if I don't, Doc?" the man asked. "Cut off my fingers?"

Gena remembered he was a man with only three fingers on his right hand. "I'll get you a new blood. When I do, will you run it STAT?" She hung up as Stoner came into the kitchen to check on what was bubbling on the stove.

"Braxton said to say good-bye," he said, talking to the pan, not to her.

"What does he think is wrong with Gallagher?" she asked.

"He thinks I'm too much of an ass to think anything.

And as long as you are here with me, I guess he thinks the same thing about you."

Gena watched the man take a bowl down from the cupboard and pour the bubbling sauce into it. "What about the blood from OR?" she asked, turning to new business. "Did he know where that is?"

"He said he took it down to the lab before he left. That means Deer must have had it all this time, and not realized it."

"Lynn says the first Dukane baby is jaundiced. I'll go up and write the bililight order for him."

Stoner sat down at the table and gingerly tasted what he had just poured. "How do you know that's what I want to do?" he asked.

"I assume that if a baby looks as yellow as Lynn described, you will want to order—"

"Why don't you ask me what I want? Instead of assuming it?"

"Do you want lights for the Dukane baby?"

"Depends on what the cord blood showed."

"It wasn't run."

"Why not? I told you to run it outside the delivery room."

"I assumed when I sent the specimen, it would be run."

"I just told you to stop assuming!"

"When *you* send something to the lab, you call and double-check it hasn't been lost?"

Stoner tasted the soup in front of himself again. "If it's important."

"You don't! You're too busy eating gourmet something or other back here! Or playing with Sally's mouse!"

"I don't spend it assuming." He leaned back in his chair, waiting for the soup to cool. "The only time I safely do that is at The Stonehouse. Did you know that you can guess what people will order in a restaurant by the time they're seated? By their clothes, their general appearance—''

''Try me,'' Gena said. Looking at him across the steaming bowl of soup. ''If you're so good, tell me what I would order at The Stonehouse.''

''Prime rib,'' Stoner answered immediately, leaning back an inch farther in his chair. Confident. ''Because you know for certain what it is. Consommé for the same reason. Chef salad, because you'd be worried the Caesar had too much garlic. No wine with your meal, because you wouldn't be sure what was good and what was bad, and you'd rather be safe than allow a wine steward to raise his eyebrows over your order. Nothing flaming for dessert, because you wouldn't want everyone else in the restaurant looking at you.''

Gena didn't acknowledge the fact that he had read her very well.

''Come on, tell me I was right.'' Stoner leaned back even more precariously.

''What are you eating?'' Gena asked instead of answering him.

''Busecca.''

''What is that?''

''Going to criticize because it's not usual breakfast food? I was raised on restaurant leftovers for breakfast.''

''Did I tell you your wife called?'' Gena asked. ''She's drinking vodka for breakfast.''

Stoner brought his chair down flat with a thud. ''Come on. Tell me I was right about what you'd eat at The Stonehouse,'' he said.

''Does Sue Ellen drink a lot?'' Gena asked instead.

"That's my business. Tell me I was right about The Stonehouse."

"I have no idea. Your father makes me feel like shit, so I never go there."

Stoner picked up his dish and carried it over to the sink so he could eat rapidly. "*Busecca* is tripe," he said, falling into Ape's habit of lecturing. "Something you wouldn't like. Although you were probably right. I probably did guess wrong about what you'd eat. After all, the only time I remember eating with you, you just had watermelon."

Gena gasped, not prepared for him to bring that subject or that afternoon up so blatantly. Angry, she turned and walked out of the kitchen, unable to understand why he had done that. That afternoon had been one of the happiest of her life. Not an ordinary day for him to joke about. She walked to the elevator to ride up to the third floor, unaware that his remembering it after all those years had to mean it must not have been an ordinary one for him either.

Scott Stoner started to leave his dish on the counter for Sally to wash, then decided that would be asking for trouble. He washed the dish instead, reshelved it, and walked up to the second-floor nursery to check on the first Dukane twin.

Looking down at the baby in his plastic domed incubator, Scott couldn't believe how jaundiced he had become. A tiny thing—four pounds, twelve ounces—the baby clasped his finger with his whole palm and squeezed it as he reached into the incubator.

If a baby had an A or B type blood when its mother had type O, antibodies from the mother's bloodstream crossed into the baby's blood at birth in that small space of time when the afterbirth had loosened but the cord hadn't been clamped yet. Antibodies in the baby's blood started to attack A or B red blood cells, destroying them. In order for a baby to have that much jaundice at only six hours of age, either a lot of red blood cells had been destroyed, or a lot of antibodies had crossed over.

Bilirubin—the breakdown product of red blood cells that caused the yellowing—was basically harmless as long as it stayed in the bloodstream, but if bilirubin started to leave the bloodstream, it entered muscle and brain. In the brain, it destroyed cells, and could leave the child mentally retarded, and often with cerebral palsy if the bilirubin level rose to over twenty milligrams in serum. Stoner needed a new blood sample on the baby fast.

His wife didn't have a blood type the young kid at the foot of the mother's bed had told him, stressing he had already given that information to Portobello—and Stoner had brushed him off. He'd meant she had O type blood. Angry at himself for not listening better, Stoner poked through cupboards and found tubes and syringes, drew some blood into tubes marked STAT in letters so big the lab tech would have to run it immediately, and handed it to an aide to take to the lab for him.

"Don't look so worried," the aide told him, pushing a laboratory slip in front of him to initial. "I'm an old-timer here. I know the lights'll get his color down."

Stoner nodded, but he wasn't convinced that was true. If the baby's bilirubin level came back at over thirteen, exchanging his jaundiced blood for clean blood would be the only treatment that could keep him from brain damage. Once a level reached twenty, the damage was already done and there was no reversing it. That meant it was time for him to get himself down to the basement lab and help Eddie

Deer find the blood pack Hershey had taken back to him. But if he needed it for the baby, what would he use for Gallagher when he needed more?

"Telephone for you, Dr. Portobello," an aide on 3A stretched out a telephone receiver to Gena as soon as she arrived at 3A nurse's station.

"Dr. Portobello?" a woman's voice asked in her ear. "Why are you taking Dr. Stoner's calls?"

For a moment, Gena thought it was Sue Ellen again, then realized that it was Margo Torning, the evening nurse who had left at midnight after setting up fluid on Mary Nightowl.

"I thought you were a day resident calling in," Gena said. She wondered why Margo was calling. She probably wasn't supposed to be back on duty until evening.

Margo sneezed and sniffed to clear her nose so she could talk. "When do you think Stoner is going to get out of there? Do you know it's almost eight o'clock?"

Gena still hadn't registered why Margo Torning would be checking on Scott Stoner's presence. "The bridge to the Swamp is snowed shut, Margo," she said. "No one can get out of here this morning."

Margo sneezed again. "Well, when you see Stoner," she said over the sound of blowing her nose, "will you tell him I'm only going to wait about another hour? And then I'm going to have to go home."

"Where are you?" Gena pictured the woman waiting at a restaurant or a bus stop, maybe about to freeze to death in a car on the thruway. But how could she be anywhere without knowing there was snow outside?

"His house."

Gena settled her telephone back into place, aware that someone was standing behind her, waiting to speak.

"Would you check Mark Warren for me?" the 3A nurse asked breathlessly. "He pulled his IV line out about a half hour ago, and he's started wheezing again."

Gena whirled to confront the woman. "What's your name?" she demanded, unable to shout at anyone if she didn't know their name. And she had a right to shout when she heard the words "pulled line" on a newly admitted asthmatic.

"Murphy. Ethel Murphy."

"Well, listen up, Murphy!" Gena scolded. "You don't pull IV lines on asthmatics for at least twenty-four hours! So when this happens, you can add aminophylline without racking me out of somewhere."

The woman hesitated a second, then said coldly, "The *boy* pulled his line, Dr. Portobello. *I* know not to pull them."

But Mark Warren was ten. And he'd had asthma since he was three. *He* knew better than to do that. "*He* pulled it?" Gena clarified. "Or it just came out?"

"He *pulled* it," Murphy repeated.

Mark Warren was too smart to do that, or had been the last time he was in here.

The boy was sitting straight up in bed, pulling in breaths that he then could not breathe out again. His fingertips and the circle around his mouth had turned bright blue. Elizabeth Warren, standing beside his bed, was bending over him, trying to give him whiffs of oxygen from a face mask. As exhausted as he was from the effort of breathing, he kept pushing the mask away from his nose. Finally, his mother just stood holding the mask, wringing her hands, and saying, "*Mark,*—why are you acting this way? What is the matter with you?"

Murphy had added a clean needle to the boy's intravenous setup so it could be restarted. A giant one though.

"I hope you realize this was an accident," Elizabeth Warren said to Gena, fluttering to hold up the oxygen mask again. "Or maybe the needle wasn't in right. I don't know. Otherwise, why would it have come out?"

Gena reset the giant needle into place in the boy's right foot. Intravenous needles didn't simply fall out, especially with all the tape she had put on that one in the emergency room. Murphy was standing across the bed from her, looking uninterested, stiff cupcake cap on her head, stiff white uniform, even the laces in her shoes white and clean although she'd been up all night.

"Why'd you pull this?" Gena asked Mark.

"He wanted to see if he could do without it," his mother answered for him. "So he could go home this morning."

That was crazier than saying it had fallen out, Gena thought. No one was going home this morning.

"He knows he shouldn't have done it," Elizabeth Warren continued, rubbing an eye as if it hurt. The circles under her eyes were even more prominent than they had been during the night. With her coat off, she looked like someone who had lost a lot of weight lately. Her skirt hung loosely from her waist and her slim silver belt was too big. "He's certainly been through this enough times," she said.

Gena agreed, and that made his pulling the line so strange. His respirations were still so fast that he wasn't making full use of the oxygen he was getting, that was the basic problem. How to slow his respirations down and get him using more oxygen was the question.

Murphy handed Gena the aminophylline for the line as soon as she had it retaped and she added it at a stopcock opening. Mark sat upright, gasping for air, struggling to slow his breathing. She'd have to stay and watch things quiet down—or be there in case they didn't quiet down, Gena realized. That would give her time to ask Elizabeth Warren some more questions about the boy's asthma. The loss of weight in the woman, the black and blue marks on her arms, made her wonder how long it had been since *she'd* had a complete physical, how long a ten-year-old who thought he could pull IV lines at will had been pushing her to the limit that way.

Elizabeth Warren, however, decided she wanted a cigarette. "I'll be in the waiting room," she said and stepped out into the hallway before Gena could ask her to stay.

Confused, Gena motioned for Murphy to time the boy's respirations. It was strange, she thought, that while she had been plugging a needle into him and adding drugs to his line and talking about what he was doing, Mark had just lain there with his head tipped back, looking up at the ceiling, as if it was all happening to someone else, not to him.

"Tell me about the aspirin," she said to him.

The boy gasped for breath as his only response.

"Did you take it because your arm hurt? Or like your Dad said? For attention?"

No comment from the boy. He just stared up at the most interesting ceiling in the world. Gena sensed he was also watching her reaction to his slight through half-closed eyes.

"Your mom looks tired," she offered, wondering where that might lead to. "Has she been sick lately?"

"She's sick of me bein' sick."

Look, ladies and gentlemen, he talks, Gena thought. Amazingly, he even puts words together into complete sentences. "If you've missed a lot of school lately, how are your grades?"

"You already asked me that."

Notice how quickly the human being progresses from silence to criticism, she thought. Virtually as soon as he learns to speak. "What about sports? Are you into those?"

"Swimming."

Children with asthma were supposed to swim as part of their chest therapy. That didn't mean he enjoyed it. "Into girls?" she asked.

The boy's head snapped down from the ceiling to look at her.

"Is there a girl you like?" she modified the question.

"What if I do?"

"I just wondered what's standing you on your ear so, that's all."

"Didn't you read my chart? I have asthma."

Gena didn't believe that being jumped on by a parent for coming in late had caused that much distress. If kids stopped breathing every time that happened, the world wouldn't have anyone over twelve years old in it.

"Anyone else in your house sick?" She ran her hands over Mark's head, assessing if lymph nodes at the sides of his neck were swollen or not. Could the attack have been triggered by an upper respiratory virus? No, his lymph nodes were normal. She tipped his head to the side and used the otoscope on the room wall to examine his one ear. That was normal. She couldn't see the ear drum of his second ear because there was so much wax plugging the canal. Damn. She'd need an ear curette to remove that. Those came from Central Supply. She looked into the hallway to see if Murphy was there. Nowhere to be seen. Just as well, she thought. She'd go down to Labor and Delivery and see if Bob Haiden had a curette in the medical bag she had put up on top of his locker for him. That would be simplest and quickest.

"Is anyone else in your house sick?" she repeated her question.

No comment; the boy returned to looking at the ceiling.

"I'm sure you're aware that late hours—"she tried a new approach.

"Screw you, Doc," he responded. "If I want a lecture, I can get it at home."

Gena dropped her hands and walked away from him, still not happy with the rate of his respirations, but following a sensible rule of thumb that said anyone with enough energy to cuss her out, couldn't feel desperately short of breath. "When your mother comes back, would you tell her I want to talk to her?" she asked from the doorway.

The boy pulled in a really full breath, the best one she'd seen him manage since he'd arrived there. Some sort of agreement that talking to his mother was a good idea, she guessed. She stood by the doorway counting his respirations a final time before she left, wondering how the broken bones on his X-ray were related to all of that. What could be causing such sustained wheezing? And why, when he knew not to take aspirin, had he taken some? What had been going on at the Warrens that he would risk doing that?

Stoner knocked on the glass door to Eddie Deer's basement lab.

The man looked up sourly from tapping out a rhythm on the counter to "Kocomo," a Count Down to Midnight selection.

"Braxton Hershey says he dropped a pack of O negative blood off down here," Stoner said, opening the dutch door at the side of the room and letting himself in.

"Nobody brought any blood down. Everything there came in yesterday."

Stoner opened a cooler at the back of the room labeled with a giant red cross and surveyed its contents. Hanging from metal hooks inside, slowly revolving around a center core, hung three units of blood, one marked A positive and two marked B negative. Definitely no O negative pack there.

"If it isn't in here, where would it be?" Stoner asked.

"Try the cooler next to that one," Deer answered, not moving to help him look.

Stoner opened a second door and inventoried those contents. Not hard to do: only two packs of A positive blood.

"Why two coolers?" Stoner asked. It seemed a waste of space.

"The first one is for fresh blood. It gets moved to the second one after forty-eight hours."

"Then what happens?" Stoner closed the second door and came back to the desk.

"It gets sent back to the main center."

"Did you send any back tonight?"

"You mean, did I throw some over the bridge?"

Right. The bridge was closed. "So where in hell is that blood, Eddie?"

"I don't know about any other blood."

Stoner cursed again. He wished he'd known about the shortage before giving another pack to Gallagher, because now he needed it for the baby more. "If you think of where it could be, would you call me?" he asked.

"You got it, Doc." Eddie Deer nodded and returned to drumming on the table as the next Count Down song started to spin.

* * *

A normal bilirubin blood level at eight hours of age should have been under one milligram. Gena sat by the labor floor phone at nine o'clock and listened to Eddie Deer crinkle paper by his telephone—as if he were eating a candy bar while he read her a potentially lethal lab report: indirect bilirubin: 11.5 mg. If it had risen that fast in eight hours, it would be easily up to twenty milligrams by another eight hours.

That put her in deep trouble, because the only way to reduce that baby's blood would be by an exchange transfusion. She didn't have any blood to do it with, and she didn't know how to do it, anyway. Snow was still falling and blowing outside, so the possibility of the storm letting up seemed remote. If anything, the wind was getting stronger. It was hitting the building harder and harder all the time.

Gena hung up, feeling a sharp pain start in the crevice behind her right eye. She sat at the desk debating what to do for just another moment, then dialed Bob Haiden at home.

"I've got a baby with an eleven bilirubin, Bob!"

"Put him under lights," Haiden answered quickly.

"I've done that." Gena recognized it was no time to sound overly competent. "Or rather, Lynn Curtain did that for me."

"That'll probably do the trick," Haiden turned away from the phone and said, "later" to someone at home.

"I don't think that'll do it, bob. The baby's only eight hours old."

"Hey, *listen!*" Haiden shouted at the person in the background. "I said *later.*" He clapped his hand over his receiver and cut off anything else. "Sorry," he told Gena. "My kid wants me to stack blocks with him."

Gena envied a man sitting at home playing with a two-year-old. "The baby's only eight hours old," she repeated.

"Then you're right. You're going to have to transfuse to get that down," Haiden said.

"I don't know how to do an exchange transfusion."

"Well, Culbertson's still there, right?"

"Where could he go, Bob? Don't you listen to the radio?"

Haiden laughed. "Funny, Gena. But relax. If he's there, you're in good hands. All the old-timers have done them. Call the lab. Get a cross on some emergency blood. Get the process going."

"There isn't any blood."

"I'll ask the Red Cross to send you some," Haiden refused to sound worried.

"The bridge is closed. That's the whole problem."

"Snowmobiles must be running," he said. "I'll ask the Red Cross to run you in some that way."

Gena settled her receiver back into place, feeling pain spreading across her forehead. She massaged the groove it followed, thinking she was starting to look like Ape, constantly trying to keep her cerebral circulation intact. And she was having trouble, she realized, because she was dealing with a baby and babies were very precious to her. *How did you know, Mary Nightowl?* she asked the desk in front of herself. *How did you know I had a child once?*

Scott Stoner was sitting at the side counter on the third floor of A Building—juggling an apple and two oranges despite his arm in a cast—talking to Lynn Curtain. "What could happen to blood in a lab?" he asked her.

Lynn was setting up ten o'clock medicines for children.

She glanced at an order, read a bottle label and reread the order before she looked back up at him. "Did Eddie look in both coolers down there?"

"I looked in them."

"Because Eddie was too busy listening to the top twenty to see anything?"

Stoner shrugged. "Hershey says he took it down to him. I don't understand what happened to it after that."

Lynn stopped watching his juggling to read another label. "I guess we should be grateful Hershey was still functioning well enough after that surgery to do that. Although I can't complain. He was very nice to me afterward. He helped me clean the room.

Stoner froze, his hands in midair. The fruit he had been juggling rained down onto the floor. The apple bounced. "Asshole Hershey helped clean up?" he asked. "Since when does Asshole Hershey help clean OR rooms?"

"A lot of people do things for pregnant women they ordinarily wouldn't do."

Stoner grunted. "What if, what happened to the OR blood pack was that Kissell put it inside Gallagher, to bring up his blood pressure, after we left to change?"

"I would know if he did that," Lynn said. "Because he would have had to change the IV setup to blood tubing."

"He already had blood tubing up. You said that yourself in OR."

"Afterward, there would have been residual blood in the tubing."

"Gallagher *did* have blood in his tubing! I asked the nurse on 4A to change the tubing, because there was blood in it."

"That was backup blood from the bottle of solution being lowered while he was moved from the OR table. Nine out of ten postop patients have tubing backup blood."

Stoner pondered that a minute more, then let the thought go. "It doesn't matter. I know that didn't happen, because Kissell left the room at the same time we did. And came back after me." An aide pushed the desk telephone at him, but he shook his head at her. He wasn't interested in hearing one more person talk about how tired they were, if they were inside the Swamp, or how much they wished they were there, if they were on the outside.

"It's Dr. Frank," the aide said.

Stoner took the telephone.

"I've talked to Robert Haiden, Stoner." Frank's voice was muffled by a bad connection, but very grave. "And I've asked him what he thought of the possibility of transferring my daughter over to the C Building. I think there's a good chance she'd prefer to have her first child in a building that is a little more modern than the A one, don't you?"

Stoner didn't know what to say to the man. Labor and delivery was in A Building.

"Are you still there, Stoner?" Frank asked over a loud moment of crackling. "Were we disconnected?"

"No, sir. I'm still here."

"Good. Because Robert has agreed that a delivery could be accomplished equally well in a surgery room in C Building as there in the regular delivery suite."

"Here at the Swamp—"Stoner began.

"That is the Sylvester A. Warren Medical Pavilion, Stoner."

"Yes, sir. The problem is, I'm covering the fourth floor in this building, as well as labor and delivery. With your daughter in C Building, I'd have to run between two buildings."

David Frank seemed to take a long moment to appreciate Stoner's point. "That's part of what I'm trying to tell you,

Stoner. With Leslie in C Building, you wouldn't be responsible for her any longer. Zack Appleton would.''

Stoner caught the message: David Frank didn't want his daughter in Stoner's care any longer. ''Zack Appleton—'' he began again.

''Will be calling you about the transfer,'' Frank finished his sentence for him and abruptly hung up.

Stoner replaced his receiver slowly, feeling anger start in his stomach and spread inch by inch up to his head. What Zack Appleton knew about women in labor he could lecture on in one minute flat.

''Appleton called for you while you were on the other line,'' the floor aide said. While she spoke, she handed Stoner a torn-off page from the calendar with scribbling on it. *Do your writeup on Ryan McFarland,* the note said. *And while in C Building, do a cutdown on patient in 233 for me.* Cutdowns were incisions into veins, necessary after a person had been poked so many times with White Horse's giant needles that the person no longer had usable sites for therapy. The procedure required a degree of skill that an ape couldn't accomplish, apes being unable to approximate their thumbs well enough to do that. Stoner crumpled the note and tossed it toward Murphy's wastepaper basket. The crumpled ball missed the basket and rolled into the center of the hallway.

When he looked up, Murphy was standing beside him, looking down at the irresponsible way he had littered her floor. ''Tell Appleton to fuck his cutdown if he calls back,'' he told her. Murphy continued to look at the litter.

''Do you believe that?'' he asked Curtain. ''Frank is transferring his daughter to Ape rather than letting me deliver her.''

Lynn glanced up at him, as if that didn't surprise her at all.

"Because I'm known for you asking me inside a delivery room last July, Lynn, doesn't reflect on my ability to deliver babies," he said bitterly.

"For the record. I didn't ask *you.* You asked me."

"But the only reason I asked you, was because someone bet me twenty dollars you wouldn't say yes. That's not the same thing as just asking."

She looked really startled by that. "You're making that up," she said.

"It isn't as if it was an ordeal, Lynn."

"That was all a bet?"

"So it wasn't solely for the bet. So I wanted to."

"Aside from being despicable—" she pressed on her abdomen as if it hurt and turned back to the medicine cupboard.

"OK. So I made that up," Stoner admitted. "The point is, it doesn't reflect on my ability to deliver babies."

"Telephone, Doctor!" the floor aide shouted to him from the desk area.

Stoner stood absolutely still.

"Telephone, Dr. Stoner!" the aide shouted again.

"I suppose that could be important," Lynn said, nodding toward the telephone.

Stoner grabbed it and stabbed it up to his ear. "Stoner?" Braxton Hershey's unwelcome voice sounded smoothly over the line. "As you know, I'm still at The Stonehouse." Stoner listened to the man describe how he had slept covered by a rose-colored tablecloth on the plush green carpeting of the Roman Room. For breakfast he had chosen strawberry crepes and Eggs Benedict and a Bloody Mary from an eight-foot-long buffet table. He now was sitting at the bar drinking a second Bloody Mary.

Stoner couldn't remember even putting his head down

during the night. A taste of tripe was his total breakfast. He waited impatiently for Hershey to get through describing the delights of being on the outside, and get to why he was calling in.

"I just learned that you're the HO in charge of medicine A," Hershey finally reached his point.

Stoner had trouble hearing the man clearly because there was so much laughing and general merrymaking in the background.

"As you know, I'm doing research on the effects of bleeding ulcers and atherosclerosis," Hershey, the famous researcher, elaborated. "As long as you're trapped there and have free time, I want you to help me out and add Gallagher to my study population."

Stoner grunted again, not aware that he was experiencing any free time.

"If I can include Gallagher in my sample, I'll have enough subjects to be able to scoop Dineen's results and present my findings at the March Conference," Hershey explained. "Get me a cholesterol level and complete blood gases on Gallagher every four hours for the next twenty-four."

"Blood gases?" Stoner asked. Blood gases required arterial blood; a different and harder technique than regular blood samples. Something impossible for him to do with only one hand.

"You do know what blood gases are, don't you?" Hershey asked sarcastically.

"Why do you need them?" Stoner cut him off. Of course, he knew what they were. That he didn't know how to do them one-handed was his problem, and Hershey had to remember he was working one-handed. He'd made enough remarks about it the evening before in surgery.

"The correlation between stress and atherosclerosis only appears when a person has decreased oxygen tension for a sustained period of time, such as happens with peptic ulcer bleeding," Hershey lectured. There was a jingle of ice cubes close to his phone receiver, as if someone had sat down next to him on a barstool. "Could I refill that for you, Doctor?" an enticing woman's voice asked near him.

"Well, thank you, Wendy," Hershey turned away from the phone for a moment, sounding as if Wendy filling his glass was an accomplishment next to curing leprosy. "You're willing to lay the groundwork for something this important in research, aren't you, Stoner?" he asked, coming back to his phone.

Stoner wasn't convinced Hershey's experiment was going to show anything at all, and asking Gena Portobello to get a blood gas every four hours was going to be a strain on her. On the other hand, he knew how important research was to David Frank. He'd listened to the monkey bars story as often as everyone else. If he wanted a chance to continue to work there, he really didn't have any choice, he guessed. "Getting blood run here is hard, Hershey." He thought of a practical reason why he couldn't do it. "There's only one technician in."

"I'll make certain the technician runs the blood," Hershey assured him smoothly. "Your job is just to get it for him to run."

"But how can you be so sure he'll cooperate?" Stoner asked.

"I thought I explained that if I can add Gallagher to my study, I'll be able to report findings at the spring meeting," Hershey began to lecture again. "After that kind of publicity, the funds that can become available to the center are immeasurable. I'll explain that to the lab technician."

Stoner didn't believe that Eddie Deer was going to care. He'd simply say something cute like, "What do you want to do, Doc? Cut off my fingers?" and go back to whatever he was doing.

"As I mentioned," Hershey moved in closer to his telephone. "A lot of money flows out of new studies of this kind. Not just to the initiating department, but to the hospital at large—and to people who make it clear they are interested in helping out."

"I'm not saying—" Stoner tried to restate his position.

"Money flows to people who make it clear they are interested in helping out," Hershey repeated.

What the man was saying finally sank in. "You're bribing me," Stoner interrupted.

Ice cubes tinkled close to the telephone again as Hershey thanked the waitress for a new drink. "I'll pay you a thousand dollars every eight hours between now and the time I get there." Hershey kept his voice muffled against the phone receiver but still distinguishable. "Provided that when I do get in there, Gallagher is in good shape, and the blood gases and cholesterol levels are in his chart. How's that?"

Stoner couldn't think of an answer.

"Unbelievable the knockers on the one waitress here, Stoner. Wendy Bayley." Hershey came fully back to the telephone. "Whatever you do, Stoner," he finished. "Don't let Gallagher die. Transfuse him if you have to."

"I can't transfuse him! Because I can't find the blood you took down to the lab."

"There was nothing special about that blood, Stoner. What the hell's the matter with you, you think you have to have that specific pack?"

"I need it to have *any* pack. There isn't any other blood here."

"You sound as incompetent as the technician."

Stoner clicked the button on his telephone, as if he had developed a bad connection, and started to drop the receiver back into place. Then he stopped at what he caught Hershey finishing with: "You know, you sound as if you're blaming me for what's happening to Gallagher," he said. "Remember that I'm the only one at that OR table who never broke scrub. If anyone contaminated that table and caused an infection, it was you or Curtain. And another thing, Stoner," Hershey finished, "don't get any ideas just because you'll be there all this time with Gena Portobello that you should start something with her. I know she carried something for you once. Don't try to start anything up again."

Stoner sat staring at the wall for a long moment after the man had hung up, listening to the echo of his laughter. How could the man have thought that about Gena and him? What had been between him and Gena Portobello had died in a train station when they were sixteen. He punched at the telephone, angry at Gena Portobello, because if Hershey knew about the two of them, that meant she must have discussed her relationship with him with Braxton Hershey.

Doubly angry with Gena. Because he wanted very much to start something with her again. Except she wore Braxton's damn ring on her finger.

Chapter Eight

Bob Haiden was angry with what the Red Cross had just told him. They were going to have to load blood onto a van in Buffalo and bring it to White Horse. At the White Horse police station, they would transfer it to a snowmobile and try to run it across the bridge, although they doubted if they could do that, the wind was blowing so hard. Haiden put down his telephone and picked it up again immediately to dial the weather bureau and ask for a new weather report. "It's he-r-r-r-e! Morning will be hell" was all he heard.

"How long will this storm last?" he shouted at the recording.

"Morning will be hell."

"You don't understand! I *have* to get blood into the Swamp! I have to get in there to help out!"

"Morning will be hell."

"What the shit's the matter with you?" Haiden demanded. Aware he was shouting at a recording, but continuing to shout. "The problem isn't only the blood! The problem is I don't know if the Swamp is safe in this wind or not! I need to know how strong the wind will get! If this wind doesn't let up soon, everyone in the building could be killed."

"Morning will be hell. Morning will be hell. Morning will be hell," was the only answer.

The cafeteria helpers who had been there for the night didn't have keys to the main storeroom. Macaroni and cheese, canned peaches, and coffee were all they had been able to produce to feed patients as well as personnel.

Gena Portobello left a bowl of chicken bouillon cooling on the counter of the kitchen in Labor and Delivery and walked down through the tunnel to C Building. She had to find Richard Culbertson so she could tell him that even though he had said he never wanted to work with her again, she needed his help with an exchange transfusion, assuming Haiden could get in some blood.

The minute she stepped out of the connecting basement tunnel, she could feel that C Building was a lot warmer than A. Of course, it was not as old, not as many cracks were leaking in cold. And it was busier. The lobby of C Building was filled with night cleaning and maintenance people who had no apparent duties. Giddy from lack of sleep, oblivious to the force of the storm outside, they were beginning to celebrate the day: New Year's Eve. As Gena watched, a fat woman in a yellow uniform started hanging toilet paper streamers over a door frame while a maintenance man ran across the length of the lobby, a giant streamer floating out behind him.

Richard Culbertson was nowhere to be found. She kept on walking and circled back through the basement tunnels to A Building, following a hunch he might be in one of the sack-out rooms in back of Labor and Delivery. She found him there, all right, stretched out on a metal framed cot that bowed in the center it was so old. After a moment's hesitation, Gena shook the man awake. He roused slowly, a man accustomed to sleeping soundly on any surface that would support him.

"Bob Haiden is going to send in some blood to transfuse the first Dukane baby," she told him.

"What did you say?" Culbertson sat up abruptly, looking wide-awake, clutching the blanket over him to keep it from falling away from his shoulders, obviously confused.

But, of course, he was confused, Gena thought. She had forgotten he didn't even know yet that the Dukane baby was in trouble. Shc held out the hematology slip that showed the 11.5 mg bilirubin level. "I said the Dukane baby needs an exchange transfusion," she repeated.

"They've always been done by house staff," Culbertson said lying back down again. "Haiden does all of them here."

"The real problem is getting the blood over the bridge," Gena said. "If Haiden can't get any over here, how else would I be able to get some O negative blood?"

"Ask someone to donate some," Culbertson answered.

"What are the chances there's anyone here with O negative blood? It's very rare."

"Who's on the list?"

Gena didn't know about any list.

"When anyone is hired here, they're blood-typed and their name is put on a blood-type list. Lynn Curtain can get it for you from Personnel," he said.

Gena glimpsed a light at the end of a tunnel. "When I get the blood," she started to lay out the process. "I'll phone you—"

"I've never done an exchange transfusion," Culbertson

said sharply. He pulled the blanket up over his shoulders and lay there, running his hands through his balding hair and fussing with the tip of his thumb as if it were as numb as his facial muscles.

Gena frowned. If the baby's bilirubin level continued to rise and it wasn't done, the baby would die. "Even so . . . surely you know how to do one," she said.

Culbertson closed his eyes, as if trying to shut out what she had said. "They're not easy to do," he protested. "You can puncture an artery with your catheter and then the baby bleeds to death. Or you can cause such arterial spasm his heart will stop. Or you can cut off circulation to the lower extremities and his feet will develop gangrene. Before people got good at doing them, a lot of babies died from the procedure."

"Of course there are risks—"

"Stoner will have to help you," Culbertson finished. "I can't."

Glumly, Gena walked back toward the nurse's desk, remembering vividly that the last time Culbertson told her something was not easy, how right he had been. She couldn't do it alone and she wasn't convinced that Stoner would be able to help her.

Pain flickered behind her eyes as she walked. She had to do right by the baby. She sat down on the edge of the sink in the locker room and tried to make a new list of things she had to do. Her handwriting was so shaky that her list was unclear when she finished. Was it because she was so tired? Because the pain in her forehead was pressing farther into her brain and numbing function? No. She sat up straighter and sensed it happen. Every time the wind blew, the building vibrated, the way a car did when it fought wind. A crazy comparison! The reason that happened to a car was because it had no foundation. No anchored strength. And the S.A.W.M.P. buildings were older than she was.

She picked up her list and started to look through A Building for Scott Stoner.

Jack Kissell hadn't had any breakfast and now lunch time was passing him by as well. Worse, he had no idea how to get food without someone seeing him. The diet kitchen and cafeteria were in C Building. He could go there, but surely he would be seen if he tried that. There was a small kitchen in A Building in back of Labor and Delivery where staff ate sometimes; he might be able to get there without being seen. Maybe he could find some crackers or instant coffee.

He crouched behind the file cabinets in Personnel, listening to his stomach growl. Finally, he decided he could not stand the pain of an empty stomach any longer and pushed himself to his feet. Cautiously, he inched the door open and ran the entire length of the hallway to Labor and Delivery.

From the doorway to the labor suite, he could see a blonde nurse and an aide sitting at a reception desk watching a television set. Farther back, Scott Stoner was leaning against a counter talking on the telephone. No one seemed to be in the rear hallway by the kitchen. If he was careful, Kissell was sure, he could reach that undetected. He ducked beneath the windows that looked into the office hallway and, skittering like a crab, made his way back to the kitchen hallway. As he had guessed, the kitchen itself was empty. On the table, as if waiting for someone to return for it, sat a dish of steaming soup. Kissell grabbed it and tipped it up to his mouth. It was hot and searing on his tongue, but he continued swallowing, even though it was too hot to drink. Panicking that he would be seen, he clanked the dish back into place and grabbed a box of crackers off the back counter. Ducking under the windows, he waddled, then ran the entire length of the office hallway back to Personnel, jerked open the door, and sank back down beside the file cabinet to hide himself in the gloom. His heart was thumping; his pulse racing.

Desperately, he opened the saltine box and gulped crackers one after the other, trying to salve the roughness of his tongue. What he needed was a radio, so he could know more about the weather outside and what was the chance that David Frank or someone from Personnel would arrive there before he could get to the safe. He sat asking himself how to get one while he ate more crackers, trying to keep his tongue from stinging. He wondered whose soup he had eaten. It might be missed any minute, he guessed, and someone might come looking for him. Although that was absurd. What was the chance that anyone would think an anesthesiologist, hiding in the Personnel Office, had run into the kitchen and stolen soup?

"Did you get any breakfast?" Sally Yates leaned across the Labor and Delivery desk and offered Scott Stoner a cup of black coffee as he hung up the telephone.

Stoner took the cup from her cautiously. Afraid that as long as he didn't have the toy mouse, he might see it surface again there.

"No mouse," Sally said. "Just straight coffee."

"Thanks." Stoner slumped back into a desk chair, aware that she was probably offering him coffee just to keep him there. He yawned, propped up his feet on the desk, and wondered if she would be willing to talk of other things than mice and coffee.

"If you're tired," Sally said, watching him yawn, leaning her head and elbows on the desk, "the first sleeping room in the back hallway is made up."

"I could manage ten minutes," Stoner offered.

Sally smiled and showed teeth so neat and straight they almost looked false. "You're bad, Scott Stoner. Really bad," she said.

"Come on, Sally," he tried his best grin on her. "We're going to be here a long time yet. And it's already been a long time for us."

"That's because I know who you've been making it with. It's no secret to the whole hospital."

Stoner cringed. Sipped the coffee. "You're always busy. Staying late with a patient. Having your period. Washing your hair. No one washes their hair as much as you do."

"That's not the trouble, Scott. And you know that. The trouble is you never ask me anymore. You ask *her* instead."

"And is it any wonder? I'm asking you now and you're giving me a big argument."

"I can't do anything now! What if Lynn Curtain would come down? She's already all over me for losing morphine."

"That's just another argument."

"Well, maybe the trouble is, I don't like ten-minute things. Maybe that's what's wrong. Maybe it makes me feel used."

Stoner shrugged. Put down his coffee cup. "I don't think I'm going to have time in the next twenty-four hours for a long courtship," he said, starting to move his long legs off the desk.

"I didn't say I wouldn't do anything," Sally straightened. Glanced around nervously. "I'm just being careful. Besides, I don't have anything to use."

"I do."

She sucked in a breath. "It isn't the same brand you used with Curtain, is it? If it is, it didn't work very well."

"Maybe Curtain isn't pregnant by me."

"I don't care, Scott. *I* just don't want to be."

"Come on." Stoner pushed himself to his feet and put an arm around her shoulders encouragingly. "I promise you, it'll only take ten minutes. And you won't get pregnant."

"Show me your condom supply."

"Supply? I'm only going to need one." The entire back hallway was cold from the wind hitting the building so hard it was seeping through the cracks. He stripped his sweater and cords and jockies inside the first room and stretched out naked on the cot despite the cold and watched Sally leisurely shed her clothing—her uniform, a lace slip, white panty hose, a lacy bra, bright pink panties that said WOW on the rear—revealing step by step a slim waist, small but nice breasts, slim thighs, bushy yellow pubic hair.

She snuggled down against him on the cot and let him kiss her and smooth a hand over her butt. As soon as he had located a pack of Trojans in his wallet to show her, she rolled over on top of him, traced her tongue down along his abdomen, and . . . Maybe he would never move from there again until the bridge was clear, he thought, urging her to go further, relaxing, letting distending blood start to do its thing.

"Maybe we should have used a closer room." Sally raised her head after only a minute. "What if I can't hear Leslie Kerr's fetal monitor from here?"

"You can hear it from here," Stoner assured her. Pushing her head down against him again. "Trust me."

"How do you know?"

"Because sometimes I actually get some sleep when I'm on," he answered her. "And this room is where I get it. So I know what you can hear from here, and what you can't."

Sally stopped again, listening to the monitor beat.

"Christ, Sally." It was too cold in the guard room to stay there forever. They'd both get pneumonia. "Think about what you're doing."

"You know, if you really liked me," Sally stopped again. "You would ask me to come to your house sometimes, instead of Margo."

That was a dead end. Stoner rolled over on top of her and slipped a hand down between her legs.

"Sally? Are you here?"

Sally stiffened at the sound of Gena Portobello's voice out by the labor desk. Recklessly, Stoner closed a hand over her mouth to keep her from answering. He couldn't stop now, and if they only waited, Gena would leave again. And then Sally would let him push inside her . . .

"Sally?" Gena's voice sounded annoyed as she called again. "Where are you?"

"Scott!" Sally worked his hand away from her mouth and pushed him free of her. "Get off of me! She'll come back here!"

She shoved him so hard, Stoner rolled onto the floor.

"Get your clothes on!" Sally hissed at him. "Or she'll be able to tell what's going on!"

Resigned that the moment was lost, Stoner reached for his clothes.

"Is *anyone* here?" Gena called again. Nearer to them.

Stoner had his underwear, sweater and cords pulled into place, intact except for his shoes and socks.

"Tell her I'm in the lab!" Sally hissed at his back as he opened the door to the room and eased himself out into the hallway. He closed the door after himself, stuffed his shoes up under his good arm, and started down toward the desk, hair rumpled and limping, because he still had such a hard-on.

"Have you seen Sally?" Gena asked him as he came up to the desk. She looked from his rumpled hair down to his shoeless feet, cold from walking on the bare floor. "She has to be here. She has a patient in labor."

He sat down casually at the nurse's desk and began to pull on his socks. Watch Scott Stoner try and bluff his way out, ladies and gentlemen, he thought. "I sent her to the lab with some blood," he answered. "A blood for Hershey," he added, thinking as long as he was making up a story, he should make it one that was interesting to her. "For a special study on Gallagher."

She didn't look interested in special studies.

"I don't know what you see in Hershey," he tried to improve the story to keep her mind off Sally. "He lecture a lot in bed?"

"You wouldn't understand that some people are particular whom they go to bed with."

"That may be a fault of mine," he admitted, his socks on, just shoes to go. "But I make up for it by being damn particular who I wake up with in the morning. Are you going to be able to say that?"

She laughed. "And which side of her butt *does* Sue Ellen have a mole on?" she asked.

OK. He had married the girl who had been the easiest lay in high school. At high school graduation, when Dale Ronald had stood on the center table at The Stonehouse and drank a toast to all the fellows in the class who knew the answer to that riddle, Scott realized that Dale had been toasting over half the guys in the room.

"Sue Ellen doesn't have a mole on *either* butt," he answered her. "That's the joke. Get it? That's how you know if anyone has really had her."

Gena's eyes greened the way they did when she was past angry and working on furious. "When Sally comes back from the lab—" she started.

"Christ, Gena!" Didn't she realize *she* was the one he wished he woke up with in the morning? "Who in hell do you think you are? Setting yourself up as the moral standard for this hospital? Not that it makes any difference anymore. You already ruined my chance for getting a second year here last summer. You can't do anything to me now."

"I'm sorry about last summer," she said. Very quietly. As if she really meant that. "I screamed because I thought it was a patient you were with in the recovery room."

"Thanks, Gena," he said sarcastically. "But you know the only patients I ever have in the recovery room are women who have just had babies or seven-pound newborns. Thanks a lot for that opinion of me."

"Someone told me you were there with a patient."

"And what business of yours was it, if she was? As long as she was a consenting adult patient?"

"Don't shout at me!" Gena drew back from him and started to walk toward the kitchen. "It is bad enough we are all stranded in this hellhole. You don't have to shout at me."

Stoner struggled to get a shoe in place one-handed. He didn't want to shout at her, anymore than she wanted to listen to him do that. What he wanted was to ask her to a quiet place, like a recovery room, so he could explain what a damn dumb sixteen-year-old he had felt like that night at the railway station. And how he wished he had said that to her the day she came back from Baltimore. That today he hurt when he looked at the flashy ring on her finger, and he wanted to tell her how much he hurt. But how could he say any of those things, when she had that damn dumb ring from Asshole Hershey on her finger?

"You ate my soup!" she shouted back at him from the kitchen. "Jesus Christ, Stoner, what is the matter with you?"

Stoner didn't know anything about soup. He watched her stalk back and stand beside him to slam a lab report down on the desk between them. "Actually, I wasn't looking for Sally at all. I was only looking for *her* to see if she knew where *you* were. Because the lab called back this bilirubin level on the Dukane baby. I should have known to just look in the kitchen for you! That you'd be there eating more food!"

Stoner had his shoes on but couldn't get the one tied. He had returned to a decent enough size that he could stand up without looking as if he was carrying a Magnum in his pocket. As he stood, a blast of wind hit the side of the building so hard the window behind him rattled.

As he leaned forward and read the printout—11.5 mg—another blast of wind hit the building. Accompanying the fine tremor that seemed to follow every wind blast, a loud crack reverberated at the side of the room. Shards of glass plummeted down on the steps behind them, razor sharp edges breaking into even sharper splinters as they hit the floor. Cold wind swept down from a broken stairwell window and raced across the room, sending papers and requisition forms from the counter flying against the far wall. Stoner jumped and strode to the stairway door to lean against it to force it shut again. "I never saw a storm blow out a window before," he said.

"I've never done an exchange transfusion," Gena said,

seeming to ignore the fact that that building didn't seem too stable. "Culbertson can't do one. He said you'd have to help me with it."

Stoner watched Gena pick up the telephone and ask the operator to page Lynn Curtain. He listened to Gena ask Curtain if she would check the blood list for possible O negative donors. "You *can* stay out of a sack long enough to help with a transfusion, can't you?" she asked.

Stoner didn't answer. He didn't like to see a baby die anymore than she did, but how could he do exchange transfusions, when he couldn't even tie his shoe? And he also had never done an exchange transfusion before.

Jack Kissell crouched behind the desk in the Personnel Office and listened to the sound of a key turning in the door. If he was lucky, he thought, that would be the cleaning lady returning the ring of keys for Frank's office. If he wasn't lucky, it would be Security. Security could have seen his shadow on the wall and come to see who was there. If that's who it was, he had no possible explanation for being there. He would be arrested and fired! He would not only still owe all that money to everyone he knew, but he would be disgraced.

The doorknob turned and the door opened. Kissell cemented himself behind the row of file cabinets, holding his breath. Soft flat-bottomed shoes—nurse's shoes—crossed the room. It was Lynn Curtain, he guessed, making some sort of nursing supervisor's rounds. She stopped by the desk, opened a drawer, and shuffled a few papers. If she turned on the light, she'd surely see his shadow and he'd be exposed. If she walked the other way around the desk to leave the room, or came to look in the file cabinets, she'd see him.

"Blood list. Blood list. Blood list," Curtain said out loud. She opened a drawer, said, "No," and slammed it shut again. Shuffled papers in a second drawer. Said, "OK!" Kissell listened to the last desk drawer close with a solid whack as she apparently found what she was looking for.

He was growing short of breath, holding it, waiting for her to leave. Maybe if he tried to run for the door, he thought, there was a chance he could make it out of the room before she could identify him.

He sensed her take a step toward him. Kissell almost swallowed his tongue in fright. At the last moment, she turned and walked around the desk toward the door the same way she had come in. She wasn't going to see him! He was going to be all right! If he didn't pass out from lack of oxygen.

Curtain stepped out into the hallway and pushed the door of the room closed behind her. Limply, Kissell slumped down to the floor, letting the air he had held contained in his lungs all that time escape from his throat in a deep steady hissing sigh.

"Would one of you check Mrs. Kerr for me?" Sally Yates walked out by the L and D desk and looked from Gena to Stoner. "It looks like cord compression on her monitor."

Gena followed Stoner into Leslie Kerr's room and stood beside him sizing up the fetal monitor beside the bed. Between her last two contractions, the baby's heartbeat had dipped. The pattern was that of a baby whose umbilical cord was being squeezed; his circulation was cut off.

"Turn over on your side!" Stoner barked at Leslie.

Leslie Kerr looked up at him as if he had no right to speak to her in that tone of voice.

"The baby's head is pressing on the cord." Gena reached to help the woman turn. "Lying on your side will free the cord again. Let blood circulate cleanly to the baby."

Leslie turned onto her side.

Gena stepped back by the monitor and watched what happened with the next contraction. A good pattern appeared. Great. That meant the pressure was off the cord. Now the pressure was on herself and Stoner, to figure out why that had happened. Had it been only a positional problem—an innocent correctable finding—or the result of the baby's cord having slipped down ahead of the baby's head now being crushed against the pelvic bone? A baby couldn't deliver that way, cord first. That would cut off its blood supply and kill it.

William Kerr popped up out of the chair by the side of his wife's bed and stood looking over their shoulders at the printout. "What's happening?" he demanded. "What's going wrong here?"

Both Gena and Stoner concentrated on counting the number of seconds that had been involved in the irregular pattern, rather than answering him.

"Hey, I'm talking to you!" Kerr caught Stoner's arm brusquely and swung him around. "We've been here since 2:00 A.M., and in all that time, no one has done a damn thing for my wife. The least you could do is talk to me!"

"We are doing something for your wife," Stoner shrugged off the man's arm and returned to evaluating the printout. "We're monitoring her—"

"And how much am I paying for you to be doing all of that?" Kerr asked.

"I don't know the room charges here," Stoner answered, still distracted. "I don't keep track of those things."

"God, I hate a wise guy!" Kerr turned his attention to Gena. "When is Redhoe going to be able to get in here?" he asked Gena.

"Everything is fine right now," Gena assured him, tearing off a strip of paper and explaining the jagged pen line on the monitor print that was holding continually at a hundred and twenty to a hundred and thirty beats a minute. "With this pattern holding steady, you can wait until the bridge gets clear, and Redhoe arrives, without any trouble."

"Look—" Kerr resisted taking Stoner's arm again. "I can pay for anyone in this city. All they would have to do is agree to come in here."

Didn't he recognize that Norman Redhoe and at least five staff obstetricians would have loved to be here, fussing over the administrator's daughter? Even Bob Haiden had said he wished he'd been called, and he *never* wanted to be woken up at night.

"You're being transferred to C Building," Stoner answered dully. "As soon as the chief resident makes arrangements. That should make you feel better."

Kerr nodded. "What's the difference?" he asked.

Stoner ignored his question and sat down on the edge of the bed. By the room door, Sally stifled a yawn, then came bright and alive and chatty as it dawned on her that Stoner was sitting on the bed because he wanted to talk to Leslie Kerr, not her husband.

"Why don't you step outside for a minute, Mr. Kerr?" she asked.

"Get me Redhoe on the phone!" Kerr barked at her, taking her arm and leading her out into the hallway. "There must be something else to do besides this! And you tell me how changing to a different building will help! All these buildings are trash.''

Stoner kicked the door shut with his foot, sealing the man outside, and sat looking at Leslie Frank Kerr. The average woman would have died to have had a man as handsome as he was sit on her bed, Gena thought, but Leslie didn't seem to notice. Could she know that the two of them were on her father's shit list? What a shock it must be for her to realize that she was trapped here, with these two people taking care of her.

''Having much pain?'' Stoner asked her.

Leslie smiled, but it was the smile of a hostess greeting her guests, not a woman in labor. ''Very little,'' she answered.

Gena studied her, surprised that she wasn't prettier. And how comfortable, how very calm, even bored with this whole business of having a baby, she seemed! Some women acted very serious in labor, because they were scared. Some because they were afraid that screaming or even talking would make them lose control of themselves. Some gutted it out, because that was how they thought they were expected to act. Gena guessed that was Leslie Frank Kerr's problem. She was an administrator's daughter. And she was going to act that way even while she delivered her baby.

Gena watched as Stoner rested a hand on Leslie's taut abdomen. The woman was so thin and her skin was stretched so tight across her abdomen that Gena could outline the fetus inside there clearly. She knew not only where the head and butt were, but exactly where each hand lay. She could not have missed twins on Leslie Kerr unless she was blind, she thought. Stoner traced his hand over the abdomen and down to the side where there were red stretch marks, interfaced with old white ones underneath.

"I have those because I was really overweight once and had buck teeth and no one—I mean no one—wanted to date me."

Stoner glanced up at the sealskin coat showing at the door of the closet. "Looks to me like you did all right in the end," he said. "Must be big money in cement."

Leslie breathed with a contraction and then returned a shaky smile. "Depends on how much sand you mix into it," she answered.

Gena hadn't even known there was sand in cement. "What's that do to it?" she asked.

"It stretches it farther."

"I hope that isn't the same principle as adding extra lettuce to stretch salad," Stoner said. "I know what that does to salad."

"It makes cement crumble," Leslie answered. Relaxed, the contraction over. "As soon as the guarantee is up."

Stoner kept a hand on her abdomen, while he glanced again at the monitor. "Your contractions aren't the strongest in the world . . ." he brought the focus back to why she was there. "But after a lot of those, even those start to bite. Sure you don't want something for pain?"

"They don't hurt," the woman assured him.

Stoner looked as it he doubted that, but was willing to go along with her. "It must not always be easy to be David Frank's daughter, is it?" he asked gently.

The woman's eyes clouded and she shook her head as if to discourage tears. "Please, just tell me everything is all right," she said.

"The best test of whether any woman has a pelvis big enough to deliver a baby safely or not, is that she already had one,'' Stoner answered, wiping a tear that had escaped the woman's eye away from her cheek. ''With this your first one, and your pelvis on the lower side of normal . . .''

''You mean after a woman has had one baby safely, she doesn't have to worry about pelvis size again?'' Leslie asked equally rapidly. ''I won't have to worry again?''

''That's pretty much the scoop,'' Stoner agreed.

''For this time, my husband wants a son. What are the chances this is a boy?''

''The Kerrs don't guarantee cement,'' Stoner said. ''I don't guarantee boys.''

''I need a good baby!'' Leslie grabbed his hand. ''Can you guarantee me that?''

''Your father's transferring you to C Building—'' Stoner began a list of reassuring steps.

''If I can't have a good baby, Doctor,'' Leslie interrupted him, ''William Kerr will leave me for someone who can! So I don't give a goddamn *what* service I'm on here, or what kind of building I'm in. Just get me a good baby out of this!''

Doctors getting their ears filled with more information than they wanted to hear, Gena thought. And such strange information. Leslie Kerr was an intelligent woman. Why would she have formed a relationship with a man who viewed marriage as only a way to have children? Maybe a social step for him? Up from a cement king to a an administrator's son-in-law?

''Trust me,'' Stoner said, standing up and squeezing her hand. ''I know what it feels like to love someone who doesn't love you back. But that has nothing to do with this. People don't have good or bad babies because *they're* good or bad, but because of the way the cells grow. The little cord compression you had was nothing. This baby is going to be good."

Leslie nodded and put her head back on the pillow.

"Dr. Portobello is going to get another dilatation report for me," Stoner continued, waving to Gena. "And then we'll get you transferred to a better building. Where everything will seem to be going better."

Gena reached for a glove, wishing he would just once talk to her the way he talked to patients.

Peeling off her glove following the exam, she decided she didn't like what she'd found. Not a lot of increased dilatation had happened. Scott Stoner had a bad habit of assuring people that everything was going to be all right, when that wasn't necessarily true. He had assured a woman in the emergency room that her husband was going to be fine after the back wall of his heart had blown. He had just assured the woman in front of them that she was going to have a good baby. And although slow dilatation could be happening because the woman was simply having a slow labor, it could be happening because the baby's head was too big for her small pelvis and couldn't get past the pelvic bone to press on the cervix to cause dilatation. If that were happening, the woman would definitely need a cesarean section to deliver safely. Gena tossed the glove, straightened up, and looked at the monitor readout again.

"Everything is good," Stoner repeated.

Incredible false reassurance, Gena thought. "Dilatation hasn't increased," she said to him out by the desk. "So I don't think everything is all right."

Stoner stood by the desk staring at the TV set, listening to a news announcer describe how the wind velocity was so strong—up to seventy miles an hour—the wind chill factor was forty degrees below zero. Two dead bodies had been found in cars buried by snow at the side of the thruway. Nobody wanted to estimate how many more people might be found that way.

"If you were in labor, would worrying about it improve anything?" he asked her.

"I'd expect you to be honest with me about what was happening."

"I *was* honest with her," he said. "I told her good or bad babies have nothing to do with being a cement king."

"But why in hell, if you really care, are you letting Ape move her to his service? What does he know about cord compression?"

"He shares Hershey's opinion that I do things ass-backward."

"You had the other thing backwards, you know. About you loving Sue Ellen more than she loves you. She said I should tell you that you could sleep over tonight if you wanted."

Scott Stoner continued watching the TV as it switched to a Woody Woodpecker cartoon.

"Or were you talking about Margo Torning?" Gena asked. "Did I tell you? She phoned in from your house to ask where you were."

Stoner's jawline hardened, but his concentration on the woodpecker didn't waver. Gena turned to go. She had a hundred more important things to do than stand there watching a cartoon or helping him get straight which woman he wanted in his bed that night.

"Lynn Curtain called," Sally Yates interrupted as Gena turned away, waving a hand at the side of the desk for attention. "To tell the two of you there's no staff in with O negative blood."

On the television screen in front of them, the woodpecker was blown into pieces by a time bomb.

Gena felt as if she knew exactly how he felt. "I'm O negative," she said tiredly. "If worse comes to worse, I guess I could donate some."

Stoner watched all of the woodpecker's parts fall back together again in perfect order. "Anyone who has had heart disease shouldn't donate blood and then try to work for the next eight hours," he said. "In case they have some minimal valve damage."

Gena wasn't certain if he was talking about the bird on television or her. "I never had any heart disease," she said.

Stoner turned away from the television set to look at her. "You spent a year in Baltimore during high school," he said. "Because you said you had rheumatic fever. Did I miss something? Isn't that still classified as heart disease?"

Gena had forgotten about that.

Stoner turned back to the television set, crossing his arms over his chest, spreading his legs. "You're lucky to have me around," he said pompously. "Keep you from killing yourself."

"As lucky as Sue Ellen? Reduced to drink vodka for breakfast to put up with you?"

Gena was all the way back to the elevator before he responded to that. "Just so you know, I wasn't talking about either Sue Ellen or Margo," he said. "And furthermore, I don't give a shit about your opinion on the whole damn thing."

Gena rode the elevator up to three, wondering why Zack Appleton was really taking Leslie Kerr off Stoner's service. To the best of her knowledge, obstetrics was a long way from the Ape's interest or specialty.

* * *

Jack Kissell was bored.

He had made out a list on Personnel Office stationary of all the possible combinations there would be on a ten-number safe dial, and a list of all the things he would buy with the money in Frank's safe. But now he had nothing else to do.

Unthinkingly, he reached up and tried a drawer in the file cabinet behind him. It slid forward readily. Hey! Who knew what interesting information he might find in a Personnel file?

He raised his head just far enough to peer into the drawer; but not far enough so he could be seen from the doorway or the window. The drawer contained one partition after the other of manila folders on medical center doctors.

Interesting. Kissell found his own; was relieved to find it contained nothing but his original application and yearly evaluation reports that said nothing either good or bad about him, just adequate things. True, true, true, he admitted.

He read five more files. All of them equally uninteresting. As a last try, he pulled out Braxton Hershey's. Same factual information. Except for a brief typed note. "Braxton Hershey may be an excellent surgeon, but I question his ability to carry out plausible research. Screen all projects carefully before publication. David Frank."

Well, well, well. Kissell stuffed the folder back into the drawer and returned to studying his list of possible safe combinations. Somehow he'd find a way to fit the note into conversation the next time he was at an OR table with the man. Hershey would say to him, "I hear you threw up once, Kissell." He would say, "I know something that will make you throw up."

* * *

It was almost noon. Stoner had taken a message for Gena from Bob Haiden that the Red Cross van carrying the blood from Buffalo had gotten stuck on River Road and they were afraid the blood had gotten too cold. They were loading some more onto a new van to send to her. He had expected to find kids on the pediatric ward bunked out for a rest period when he stepped off the elevator to look for her, but everyone was standing out in the middle of the hallway. Mark Warren, standing in the middle of the circle, fully dressed in the clothes he'd been admitted in, no IV line in him that Stoner could see, was shouting the length of the hallway at Lynn Curtain. His mother was fluttering halfway between him and Curtain, apologizing to Lynn for the boy's language, scolding him for so much mouth.

"Screw you! Screw you! Screw you!" His words bounced off the side walls. "I don't want an IV in any longer. You can't make me have one!"

Elizabeth Warren was wearing the same pink skirt and white blouse she'd arrived in; a silver bracelet jingled on her arm. Her eyes looked terrible, lined with dark black circles. "You're not being sensible," she said calmly to Mark, rubbing at an obvious black and blue mark on her arm.

"Fuck off!" the boy shouted at her.

Lynn Curtain walked up to Stoner. "Handle that, Doctor," she said to him, flipping a hand toward the center of the hallway, limping from sciatic pain. Her baby's head was pressing so hard on her leg nerves that she could barely walk.

Stoner didn't know what she expected him to do. If the kid wanted to shout, he guessed he could. And he didn't know what had started the trouble, so it was hard to take sides. He walked over to Mark, who narrowed his eyes as if ready to take on any newcomer. "What's going on?" Stoner asked.

"Fuck off!" Mark answered him. "Fuck off! Fuck off! Fuck off!" the boy shouted at whoever might be listening, which by then was all the children and the parents and staff on the third floor.

Stoner moved in closer, to try and shorten the shouting distance. The exertion was starting to make the boy wheeze badly. Mark obviously interpreted the move as a threat because he swung a quick right into Stoner's stomach with his casted arm. Shit! Stoner doubled over from the pain in his gut. His knees turned into rubber as Mark followed through his first motion with a rough shove, sending Stoner's head crashing back into a steel nameplate on the wall. Pain flashed from the back of his head through to the front as he went down against the wall like a rag doll collapsing, his knees no more than soft rubber underneath him.

"Mark, how could you do that?" Elizabeth Warren asked, still calm. Stoner was sure she was whacked out on Valium. Mark whirled and stomped into his room, ending his attack.

Stoner started to push himself to his feet, feeling like a slow motion film, lights blinking on and off behind his eyes. "Are you all right?" Lynn Curtain asked, reaching to help him to his feet.

Stoner brushed aside her hand. "Of course, I'm all right," he said. "How much damage can a ten-year-old do to me?"

"Go sit down in the back room," Lynn said to him. She gripped his arm, the way a nurse did with a very old man who couldn't be expected to walk very well, and led him toward the treatment room. "I'll get a towel for your head."

Stoner's head was pounding with streaks of pain going back and forth behind his eyes. The blow from Mark's cast into his abdomen had carried the weight of a Tyson punch. He sank down limply into a chair, feeling even more dizzy than he had in the hallway. In another minute, Lynn handed him a cold towel and pressed it against the back of his head.

"I can't believe he would do that to you," she said. "You have to believe I never dreamed when I asked you to handle him that he'd do *that.*"

Stoner didn't believe a ten-year-old could have done that to him either. He couldn't have if Stoner hadn't been up for over twenty-four hours. Lynn pressed the towel against his forehead. He closed his eyes to block out some of the dizziness and flashing lights. He was sitting that way, letting Lynn hold the towel against his head a minute later when Gena Portobello walked into the room.

"Sorry for the interruption," Gena said stiffly. She looked at Stoner, then at Lynn Curtain, "I need some aminophylline for Mark," she said to Lynn. "He's started wheezing badly again."

Lynn nodded and left for the medicine area.

Stoner pushed himself to his feet, took the towel to the sink to run it under water and make it cold again. "Look how you've improved since last July," he said to Gena, because it was so obvious she hadn't liked seeing Lynn Curtain fussing over him. "In July, you screamed when you found Lynn and me together. Now you just frown." He paused, then went on. "On the other hand, your patient has a strange way of acting."

Gena tried a smile of sympathy. "It's hard to believe that Peter Perfect's son would act that way, isn't it?"

Stoner grunted, not so sure of that. "The difference is Peter Perfect's father would have beaten the hell out of him for doing that," he said. He sat back down at the counter and covered his head with the towel.

"I can't believe that." Gena took a step toward him, finding it difficult to communicate with a person covered by a towel. "The Warrens don't ever get angry with each other."

Stoner knew that wasn't true. The Warrens had been on his paper route as a kid, and at least twice while he had been waiting for change, he had heard Bruce Warren slap the hell out of Peter Perfect. "No one ever really knows what goes on in other people's houses," he said, peering at her from under the towel edge.

Gena looked at him as if she doubted the Warrens could be less than perfect, no matter where they were.

"Do you know that Dan Gallagher thinks I raped you that night in the train station?" he asked, studying her face. "That's how mixed up impressions can be."

No expression crossed Gena's face, as if she didn't know what train station, what night, what rape he was talking about. She started fussing with her hair. She couldn't manage to get any more hair back into the clip on her head and pulled it free. Red hair cascaded down onto her shoulders, changing her whole appearance to the girl who had walked beside him along the track that night.

"He never got that impression from me," Stoner said, lifting the towel free of his head to see her clearly. He wished she hadn't done that to her hair. "Did he get that impression from you?"

"I never talk to Dan Gallagher," Gena answered. "He gets nothing from me."

"Gallagher also told me that you had a baby from that night at the train station. He get that from Crazy Mary?"

Gena looked away from him, trying to get her hair back up into the barrette and away from her face.

"I told him that was a handful of shit." Stoner ripped the towel the rest of the way from his head so he could really look at her. He couldn't understand her reaction—or rather, her lack of reaction—to what he was saying. He started to stand up, felt his neck ache at the movement, and sat back down quickly. "Do you know the craziest thing that's happening here?" he asked. Looking directly at Gena. "You denied that you talk to Gallagher. But you're not denying anything else I just said. You told me that you spent that next year in Baltimore because you had rheumatic fever. Shit! Yet a little while ago, you didn't remember you'd had rheumatic fever. You spent the whole next year in Baltimore, because you were pregnant, weren't you? You got pregnant from that night!"

Gena couldn't seem to get the clip fastened at the back of her head. So she simply pocketed the barrette and left her hair long. "It isn't any—" she started.

"Of my *business?*" Stoner raged. "Why do you think I wouldn't want to know if that happened? Don't you think I remember I was there in that station?"

"You never talk about that night. I don't know *what* you remember."

Stoner pressed the towel back against his head so hard it hurt. How did that possibly come down to a question of etiquette? Who should have talked to whom? Or what they should talk about?

"And I can't talk about this here." Gena flipped her hair back off her shoulders and turned to walk out of the room.

"Wait a minute!" Stoner blocked her path with an outstretched leg. "You have to tell me more than that. Tell me where the baby is now."

"He was adopted."

"By who?"

"Richard Culbertson arranged for adoption with a couple in Maryland. That's why I didn't take a residency in Maryland at Hopkins. I was afraid I'd recognize him sometime."

That was incredible! The whole thing was incredible! "Isn't the chance you would recognize him if you saw him again incredible?"

"I'd recognize the birthdate. And a birthmark. He had a perfect heart-shaped birthmark on his left foot."

Stoner tossed the towel listlessly into the sink. "Birthmarks change," he said.

"Birth dates don't."

"Why did you have him, Gena?" he asked. "Hadn't you heard of abortion? Why didn't you ask *me* what to do? I could have told you about abortion!"

Gena brushed his leg aside and walked out into the hallway, not answering that.

Hating himself, Stoner pressed his hands against his head, trying to make the last of the flickering light behind his eyes stop. He had thought that terrible night had ended the moment the big black man had taken the knife away from his throat. For her, it had not ended for nine months. But why would she have had the baby? Why hadn't she had it aborted? Mulatto children didn't always do well with adoption. Halfway between two races, they didn't know where they belonged.

Cautiously, he pushed himself to his feet, trying to figure out what must have been going on in her mind that would have made her act that way.

* * *

Jack Kissell remembered seeing a huge radio on a lab desk in C Building near a sliding glass window where blood samples were dropped off. If he could get to the C basement, he bet he could lift that out through the window undetected and bring it back to the Personnel office.

He opened the A Tower basement door and started downstairs, stopping abruptly on the first landing. It was freezing in the stairway. The steps were covered with snow from a broken window; more pelted down on his back as he ran down to the basement. At the bottom, he grabbed the doorknob and struggled against the force of the wind to pull it open. Exactly the reason he needed the radio, he thought. That wind had to be stronger than any he had felt before, to make a window blow in that way.

He turned right, out of the stairwell, and started toward the laboratory.

A woman's high-heeled shoes struck the floor tile almost beside him. She was just around the corner, walking rapidly toward him! Any minute, she would appear and see him. Running, he opened the door to the room by his elbow and stepped inside it, pulling the door closed after himself. That put him safely out of her sight, but inside a woman's locker room! As if she were following him, the woman's voice sounded just outside the door. She was going to come into the locker room! Panicking, Kissell ducked through an archway into the back, looking desperately for a place to hide.

He had run into a bathroom. White sinks lined one wall, gray toilet booths the other. Behind him, he heard the woman open the hallway door to the locker room. "How long do you think The Stonehouse will hold our reservations tonight?" the woman asked a companion.

"Not past midnight," a softer woman's voice answered.

"Some New Year's Eve," the first woman said, her voice coming nearer the bathroom.

They were going to walk into the bathroom any minute and see him! He would be discovered and disgraced, not only as a man trying to rob a safe, but worse, one lurking in a ladies' room. Desperately, Kissell grabbed the door to a stall and ducked inside it. He pulled the door closed, stepped up onto the toilet, and crouched, head down, to bring his feet up out of the way.

High heels clicked and both women walked into stalls, one on each side of Kissell. There was the rustle of clothing being pulled up and then urine falling a distance into water. Kissell couldn't believe he was crouching in a toilet stall while women peed on both sides of him! He was an anesthesiologist! He had spent four years in college, three in med school, five more learning anesthesiology! And for what? So he could hide helplessly in a john? He held his breath. If he could just get out of there without being discovered, he would go back to Personnel and stay there and not think again about stealing a radio or even any more about robbing the safe, he resolved. Just quietly wait for the bridge to be plowed and as soon as it was, drive over it to get home.

Scott Stoner walked up to 4A, past the stairway where the window had blown open, stepping over a mound of snow. Up on four, Debbie Chemielewski had pulled a television set over next to the medicine counter. He stood watching it with her as it showed the bridge to the S.A.W.M.P. lined with snow. The snow was blowing across the screen so strongly that the announcer who was trying to describe the scene was breathless and struggling to get out any words. Snow had drifted even higher behind him, he said, railing to railing the entire length of the bridge. A plow was working to move the drift, but the snow was being blown back as soon as it was pushed aside. Cutting a path through the bridge was going to be an extended undertaking.

Debbie handed Stoner the telephone to answer. He took it, hoping it was Haiden sharing good news about blood.

"Scott? What's happening to you?" Margo Torning asked in his ear over the sound of the announcer's frozen report. "Do you think you're ever going to get home?"

He had forgotten about her. "Where are you, Margo? Are you still at my house?"

"I can't get out. The street is clogged shut."

"Did you get any lunch?"

"I found some tuna fish." Margo sneezed and coughed. "But you don't have any mayonnaise to go with it."

"I make my own mayonnaise."

"Scott, I have no idea how to make mayonnaise."

Stoner sat down on the desk edge. He was grateful he'd found something he could honestly help with. "Take an egg—" he began.

"Are you crazy, Scott?" she bit him off. "It's insane to make mayonnaise when you can buy it at any store! Why do you do that?"

Margo sneezed again and apparently dropped the telephone receiver. It clacked and rang in his ear. "When do you think you are going to get here?" she asked as she picked it up again.

"I haven't the slightest," he answered. A truly honest response. "The bridge is still closed."

"Then I guess I'll make a cheese sandwich. I've never seen a kitchen as devoid of food as yours."

"I didn't invite you there for lunch."

Her voice came back more gently and no longer sounding angry. "That's nice to hear. I was afraid you had forgotten that."

"We'll get to what you came for. I promise. As soon as I get out of here."

"But when will that be? My nose is running. I'm coughing. Do you have a cat?"

"A kitten." Stoner looked up as Debbie Chemielewski waved to him frantically from a patient room door to get his attention. *"Dan Gallagher is vomiting blood,"* she mouthed to him.

"I'm allergic to cats!" Margo shouted in his ear.

"I'll have to get back to you, Margo." Stoner hung up, hoping he had misunderstood Chemielewski, but the instant he moved away from the desk, he knew he hadn't misunderstood her. The stench of vomited blood—sharp and acid—reached him from twenty feet away.

Gallagher was sitting stark upright in bed, his skin bleached absolutely white; even the top of his bald head and his protruding ears were pale. The bedding in front of him was coated with combined vomit and bright red blood. Stoner glanced at the man from the doorway and turned back to the desk to ask the operator to page the Ape. Maintaining Gallagher at that point until a surgeon could get in there meant more than just keeping intravenous fluid flowing into him.

"You remember the cut-down I asked you to start for me a while ago?" Ape asked, as soon as he recognized who was calling him. Overloaded. Exhausted from trying to keep an intensive care unit intact with his crew getting as exhausted as he was.

"You know I can't do a cutdown, Ape. Portobello will have to do it. Meanwhile, Dan Gallagher is bleeding bad."

"I've got that cutdown, plus a spinal tap, plus a catheterization that needs to be done. You still interested in me helping you out?"

"Tell me what to do with Gallagher," Stoner answered humbly. "I'll get Gena to do your scut work."

"Get Portobello over here and get her working on the cutdown. I'll go over there and check Gallagher."

"Deal."

"While you have me on the telephone, Stoner, aren't you going to ask me what I did with your mother in labor?"

Stoner guessed he was going to tell him that he had not only moved Leslie Kerr to the C Building, but had delivered her safely, and, on top of that, had called David Frank to tell him what a schmuck Stoner had been for ever worrying about her.

"What I did, Stoner," the Ape seemed to enjoy the explanation, "was tell Frank that you are the best damn obstetrics resident I have ever seen, and his daughter couldn't be better off than left over there in A Building."

Stoner had trouble believing Appleton had said that. He waited for the punch line to end the story.

"I did that, Stoner," Appleton explained his generosity, "because I'm up to my ears with patients, so I'm not moving any patient from your fuckin' load."

"I didn't ask to have her moved, Zack. That wasn't my idea."

"Well, don't get any ideas about not moving your tail, Stoner. I need that cutdown done *today!*"

Stoner walked back into Gallagher's room to tell him that

a Chief was coming over to look at him. Stoner felt relieved about that. Ape might shout a lot as he did things, but he did things well.

Gallagher glanced at him, leaning forward, gripping his belly. As much as Stoner didn't like the man, he had to feel sorry for him. He had to be hurting like hell, he thought. And be scared as hell. Because half his insides looked as if they were spilled out on the bedclothes.

"I knew you wouldn't last," Gallagher said to his news that Ape was coming. Stoner looked up at the ceiling to keep from looking at all the blood around the man.

It was strange, what had happened to the ceiling. What a few hours before had been a four-foot crack, was now a crack almost all the way across the room. Even as Stoner looked, a particularly hard gust of wind struck the building. The room shook and the crack stretched out another six inches.

"Be careful," Stoner told the man. Bringing his eyes back to meet the police chief's squarely. "Appleton'll tell me what to do, but I'll be doing it. If you want me on your side while I do that, be careful what you call me."

"I've already made it clear what I think of you, Stoner," Gallagher said.

Against the wall like he was, Stoner had to admire the guy's nerve. Half of his guts were spilled on his bed, and he still had the nerve not to be nice to the guy who could help him keep the rest of himself intact. "I guess you don't have much left to call me, do you?" Stoner asked. "You've already accused me of rape—"

Gallagher gripped his belly and bent even farther forward to try and relieve the pain. He couldn't seem to make it go away. "Because I saw the baby!" he gasped. Perspiration broke out on his forehead from the effort of speaking.

There was no use denying he knew what the man was talking about. "So seeing the baby should have been proof you wanted that it *was* rape," he said. "It must have been a black baby."

The man's voice cracked as another wave of pain crossed his abdomen. "That's what I'm talking about, Stoner! The baby was white! And had blue eyes."

Stoner wanted to punch the man. His brain kicked in at the last moment, and he pulled back his fist. One of the men in the train station that night had been Hispanic. And all babies—even black ones—had light skin and blue eyes when they were first born.

Fighting rage at the injustice of that night—the stupidity of the man to never follow up on it—to not remember one of the men had been Hispanic—Stoner turned and walked back out to the hallway to wait for Ape. He stood watching snow pelt against the window and wipe it clean over and over again as the wind pushed it free. Nature was smart. Every winter there was enough snow to wash everything clean. Let everything start over again in the spring. People, on the other hand, lived forever with their mistakes or their inadequacies. Or untruths spread about them. *Why had Gena had the baby?*

He heard the rumble of the elevator and turned away from the window to meet Ape. As he did, the crack in the ceiling that before had been confined to Gallagher's room, edged under the wall and began to split the plaster in the ceiling of the hall. As if the inner core of the building were twisting on its base and splitting in two.

Jack Kissell still sat crouched on the toilet in the ladies' room, waiting to be sure that the two women who had come into the bathroom had not only left the bathroom, but the outside locker room as well. Finally, cautiously, he stood up on the toilet and raised his head until he could safely survey the room over the toilet stall door. The room was definitely empty. If he moved rapidly, he thought, he should be able to get back to the stairway and be safe again in Personnel. Hurrying, he opened the stall door and plunged across the room. Halfway through the outer room, he spotted a box of crackers in a half open locker.

He spent the next fifteen minutes looking through the five lockers he could open for more food, disappointed at his findings: the crackers, a blond wig, two very worn pairs of white shoes, a red wool coat, a white slip with a broken strap, a half-used bottle of Air Song perfume and a box of Tampax.

All that time though, that he had opened and closed lockers, no one had come near the room. The thought gave him new courage. Enough to decide he still needed a radio so he could know when the bridge was clear. He decided to make another try at seeing if he could take the one on the basement laboratory counter.

Gena Portobello showered to come wider awake, pulled on a green scrub suit in place of her white skirt, and walked down to the basement laboratory freezer to see how many doggie bags from The Stonehouse she could find stuffed in there. Her stomach was beginning to growl with hunger. At first, she wasn't able to spot any. Some clod had really buried them under blood samples and made them hard to find. Finally, pushing aside test tubes, she recognized one of the white and red wraps behind a chunk of dry ice and pulled it out.

The bag wasn't labeled. She slid the plastic carton out of the paper bag, trying to guess what it could be. *Aigo Buillo* was written across the inner pack in magic marker. Hell, no matter what that was, she reasoned, it had to be better than macaroni and cheese and peaches warmed over—the only food the kitchen help could still find.

She carried the container up to the labor floor and popped the contents of the plastic container into a pan to defrost, then sat at the table and put her head down to rest.

"Portobello?" Zack Appleton appeared in the doorway to the room, plunked a massive hand down on her shoulder, and shook her awake. He had changed to a green scrub suit that matched hers. His shoes, usually pure white and perfect, had drops of blood on them. Edgy, he walked over to the stove and pulled the rapidly boiling pan off the heat. "Bob Haiden says he's sending you in some blood. Is that right?"

Gena nodded.

Appleton reached over her head and ripped a paper towel off the holder by the sink so hard the holder almost came down. He had to be in a terrible mood, she thought as she watched him wet the towel and begin to sponge blood off his shoes. He hated to have anything on his shoes.

"I'm going to claim it," he said firmly after a few minutes of scrubbing at the blood, "and give it to Dan Gallagher. He isn't going to make it out of here unless he gets some more blood."

"You can't do that, Zack!" Gena sprang to her feet. "I'm the one who asked Haiden to get it!"

Ape couldn't get the blood off his shoes. He pressed even harder. "You familiar with triage policy here?" he asked. Triage was a term for making decisions about who should receive care in preference to others, or who should receive care first.

She shook her head.

"Do you know who has the say on triage decisions?"

She didn't.

"The rule is triage decisions go to the senior officer."

"Gallagher is an old man, Zack," she tried to make a point for the baby. "The baby has the most future ahead. That kind of thing is supposed to be considered in triage."

"Gallagher used to be the police chief here. He's still very influential in this town."

"The baby could grow up to be president."

"A baby delivered at the SWAMP is going to be president?" Appleton came over to the stove and looked in the sauce pan with her. "Don't kid me. The best he'll do is be back here as a chronic alcoholic in B Building. That's what will happen to him."

Gena glanced up as a chip of plaster fell on her from a crack in the ceiling. Just like A Building, B Building wouldn't be there fifty years from now, she thought. She missed Ape's comment, thinking about that.

"Are you sleeping?" the Ape demanded because she didn't respond to whatever he had said.

"No. But I missed what you said."

"I said I'm going to be practicing in this town after July. And I won't be able to get a single patient to come to me, if I'm known as the doctor who let Dan Gallagher die."

That wasn't triage. That was serving self-interest! Gena stood frozen by the stove and watched him walk out into the hallway. In another minute she heard him order the lab technician on the phone to cross match the blood Haiden was sending in with Dan Gallagher's serum as soon as it arrived. Damn it! That was unfair! She punched off the stove burner and poured the bubbling soup out into a bowl to cool.

"Okay. It's done," Appleton said, coming back into the room after another minute. "I made the triage decision. The lab'll cross it off for Gallagher, as soon as it gets here."

Gena put her hands protectively around the bowl of soup at the table.

"Relax, Portobello." The Ape put his hands on his hips to talk to her, looking like the fullback he must have been in college. "I have your blood. I wouldn't take your soup, too." He slapped her on the back and left.

Gena sat down numbly, staring at the bowl of soup, tears filling her eyes from anger and helplessness. How could he just take a pack of blood away from her that way? How could he be that unfair to a baby?

"Gena?" Stoner came in from the hallway. He had just shaved, she guessed, because he looked fresh and clean again. He even smelled faintly of English Leather. "Ape just told me about the blood." He sat down opposite her and lifted the used doggie bag out of the wastepaper basket at her feet. "What of mine are you eating?"

Gena did the same thing she had done with Appleton. She put her hands around the bowl. She was becoming an animal! Protecting food like a hungry lion. "It said *Aigo buillo* on the carton," she managed.

Stoner yawned, up too long; getting too tired. "How is it?" he asked.

"I don't even know *what* it is."

"It's snails in garlic sauce."

Gena felt herself gag, just as she had reacted to the tripe.

"Any chance you're going to share some of it?" Stoner asked.

Gena closed her hands around the bowl again. You've

got to learn to survive better, Bob Haiden had said to her. Well, she was learning that very well, she thought. Upstairs, a baby's brain cells were close to rotting away from bilirubin and she was sitting there more concerned with guarding food she didn't even particularly like.

She also knew she was going to leave the kitchen and drain off a pint of her own blood for Gallagher so that the blood coming in from Haiden would be free to go to the baby. Reluctantly, she stood up and lifted four snails onto a plate for Stoner, saved the rest for herself. As Haiden had said, when all the chips were down, all the amenities dropped; survival became the only and last thing that mattered.

Chapter Nine

Jack Kissell left the women's locker room and edged along the hallway the short distance to the basement lab. From the corner, he could see the radio on the front counter as he had remembered it. Huge, but certainly portable. In the back of the lab, by a centrifuge, he could glimpse the technician. If he were quiet, he reasoned, he could reach through the open sliding portion of the window and lift out the radio. It was riskier than opening the safe would be; the technician could look up and see him at any minute. Although, if he did it right, all the man would see would be the back of his head.

If only he had something to hide behind or pull over his head. A hat? A paper bag? He remembered the blond wig he had seen in the locker room and recrossed the hall. He pulled the wig of short curls out of the open locker and stuffed it down over his own hair. It made him look ridiculous, but no one seeing the back of his head could ever guess it was him. He looked much more like Little Orphan Annie.

Centrifuges were noisy whirring machines that spun blood

tubes to allow the red cells to settle to the bottom and the serum to rise to the top. Kissell bet that when it was running, the technician couldn't hear the radio. He felt even more sure of that as he watched the technician pause with his hand on the switch of the centrifuge, waiting to turn it on, until the last of a Presley Oldie but Goodie died away.

As the centrifuge whirred into action, Kissell reached through the window and grabbed the radio. The cord jerked against the wall. Damn it! The cord would knock something over, and the technician would look up and see him! Kissell jerked again on the radio. Maybe the cord was caught under the counter and wouldn't come free. Or maybe it would tear out of the radio and ruin the radio. How could such a simple act be going so wrong? Another hard pull and the cord and a pair of dangling earphones came free.

Kissell tore the blond wig off his head and tossed it toward the locker room as he plunged back into the snow-covered stairwell. Five minutes later, shivering from running the cold stairwell, he was back in the Personnel office. He sank back beside a file cabinet. Feeling lucky. Because he not only had the radio, but over his head he could see that the ring of keys for David Frank's office was back, hanging on the wall.

Gena Portobello walked down through the basement tunnel to C Building and picked up a transfusion bag from the blood bank. Back on Labor and Delivery, she set a needle into her arm and lay back to allow 250 ml of blood to drain off into the vacuum bag.

When she stood up again in twenty minutes, the bag filled, circles of pain exploded like small hand grenades going off one by one across the back of her neck and head.

What she needed to stop that, she decided, was to do something she knew she could do well. Something simple and maybe rewarding, like examine Mark Warren's ears after she got the wax out of them. She had to concentrate on a nitty-gritty like that to avoid thinking about the impossible biggies.

She took the blood down to the lab and told the tech it was the blood Bob Haiden had sent in. The man hardly listened to her. Doctor Stoner had stolen his radio, he shouted at her. He had looked up just in time to see a head of blond curls at his window. Who else had blonde curls like his? he demanded. Gena agreed there was no one else. Too tired to be really sympathetic, she walked back to A Building and crossed the labor wing to pull Bob Haiden's black medical bag down from on top of his locker. She poked past a stethoscope, an otoscope base, a plastic medicine bottle of fingercots. Three vials of morphine. Strange. Residents didn't need narcotic licenses, because it wasn't necessary to have a narcotic number to order for hospitalized patients, as long as they were on house staff. She didn't think Bob had a number because, planning on becoming a researcher, he would never need one.

She started to drop the vials back inside his bag when she noticed a medical center stamp on the side of one of them. Of course! They were the vials that Sally Yates had lost that morning! Except that couldn't be, because Haiden had left at eleven o'clock the night before, and the morphine hadn't been found missing until that morning. Could it have been missing since eleven o'clock? Sally had said she wasn't sure of the count at eleven, because she had accepted the number blindly. But if those were the bottles, why were they in Bob Haiden's bag? All the way back in the locker room?

Gena dropped the vials back into the bag. She searched

farther and found the ear curette she had originally started looking for. She closed the bag again and put it back up on top of Haiden's locker.

Had Haiden been nervous about that bag in the middle of the locker room, because he'd known those vials were in there? He'd said he'd been nervous because he had expensive equipment in there. That much was true. Stethoscopes and otoscopes were expensive. The only thing she knew for sure, she decided, was that it certainly wasn't because Haiden used drugs. He was the most intact, competent guy there. If *he* were there, *she* wouldn't be worrying about being there.

She left the locker room wondering if she should have put the vials back in the bag or not, and if she should tell Sally that she had found them. She decided silence was the answer. There was a logical reason for them being there certainly. Bob Haiden had logical reasons for everything he did. And there would be no percentage in her getting caught in the middle of some situation she couldn't explain.

She moved to check patients on 3A. A baby with croup wasn't doing well; a preschooler with diabetes needed blood work repeated, a boy with undiagnosed abdominal pain needed to be reexamined. Mark Warren needed to be examined . . . She needed to read about exchange transfusions. She needed to worry about the Dukane baby. Walking up to Three, she stopped at the second-floor nursery to see how he was. She found his mother standing by his Isolette, looking down at him. "It's sure funny thinkin' I'm a mother," Lori Dukane said. "Like I've been split into two people."

Gena nodded, sharing a smile, because she did know what that felt like. The evening Richard Culbertson had confirmed she was pregnant, she had felt so split in two she had set that merry-go-round on run and simply walked away.

"He's so yellow," Lori Dukane said. "You're not going to let anything bad happen to him, are you?"

Gena continued her own thoughts. How had Fairy Tale Mary known that she had a child? Had Richard Culbertson—who had arranged that adoption—been less than discreet some night about doing it? Scott Stoner's name was on a list because David Frank had been shocked that he would use his recovery room for shacking up. Was her name on a list of residents to go—not because she had made an aspirin error—but because David Frank had heard she'd had a baby when she was sixteen?

"When my father hears about this, he is going to kill me," Lori Dukane said, a combination of mother and kid. A mother who hadn't gone for prenatal care, not because she hadn't cared about her children but simply because she hadn't known the importance of it.

"You didn't tell him yet?" Gena assumed that she had called everybody she knew with the news. *She* would have if she'd had twin sons.

"He's an obstetrician," the girl said. "How can I call him and tell him that I was having twins, and I didn't even know it? It'll give away the fact that I wasn't in to see anybody."

A bigger problem would be explaining to him how a medical center had allowed her to be stranded on the wrong side of a bridge with trouble getting adequate blood replacement to her baby, Gena thought. If he was any kind of an obstetrician, he was certainly going to question that procedure.

"He didn't want us to get married." Tears rimmed the edges of the young girl's eyes. "So we was tryin' so hard to make it without borrowing money . . ."

"It's over now," Gena touched the girl's shoulder like the kid she was. "But you'd better call your father. Let him know what's going on."

"I can't!"

Gena didn't have time to tell her that all fathers barked a lot, but, underneath that barking, all most of them ever wanted was what worked best for their children. She wasn't as good at talking to people as Stoner was.

"I don't have money for a call to Cleveland," the girl finished.

Hell. Gena guessed she wouldn't have had that either when she'd been her age. She searched through her lab coat pocket for change, came up with a dollar and a quarter. "Call everyone you know and tell them you had twins," she told her.

"Promise me first he's going to be all right," the young girl said.

Gena didn't know what to say to her. Who could guarantee anything in that life?

"Please," the young girl whispered. "Please make everything all right with him."

Gena had been as young as this girl was when she had sat on a bed in Baltimore and told Richard Culbertson to take her baby and give him a home she couldn't give him. Why had Stoner asked her why she hadn't had her baby aborted? Didn't he have *any* sense? Couldn't he realize she had wondered until it had been born, if it had been his? If she hadn't gotten pregnant the afternoon of the great watermelon steal the week before the rape?

Cornell Nelson couldn't remember when he hadn't wanted to be a policeman. As far back as grade school, he had pictured himself dressed in blue with silver bullets along his belt, shooting fleeing gunrunners, or dressed in brown tweed, solving cleverly executed homicides or multimillion-dollar burglaries. Instead, as a White Horse police officer, his chief duty on any day had turned out to be helping grade school children cross a White Horse street or giving tickets for speeding in the school zone. Twice he had been asked to rescue the same stray cat from the same chestnut tree. The only day in the last three years White Horse had had a murder, he had been on vacation.

That's why this afternoon was so special. This afternoon, a baby was dying on Bird Island because it needed blood, and Cornell Nelson was taking it to him. He was dressed in a black snowmobile suit and goggles, riding a snowmobile down the center of Main Street in White Horse. At least he thought it was Main Street. He was surrounded by such complete whiteouts, visibility so poor, he could have been anywhere and not have known it. He was plunging straight into a thick white blur. He could have been delivering blood to the Antarctic. This was what Christopher Columbus must have felt like, plunging toward the edge of the world.

Mounds of snow were piled along both sides of the street, hiding parked cars. In front of stores, drifts had piled up over the awnings, completely covering windows and doors. A window of a Radio Shack had blown in and he could see snow blowing through the inside of the store.

At the intersection of Taylor Street, another snowmobile suddenly popped into view from the direction of the snow-filled Radio Shack. It steered directly at him, a rider hanging on behind the driver. Thank heavens, Nelson thought. Someone else was there in case he broke down. Could help him carry out his mission. Although why anyone else would be out in that blizzard puzzled him. He waved as the second snowmobile pulled along beside him, leaning sideways to see who it was. "What are you doing out here?" he shouted.

The rider on the snowmobile cupped a glove next to his mouth and shouted something to him, but his voice was carried off by the wind and lost. As Nelson tipped sideways to try and hear better, he could see a portable TV, a new VCR, and a giant sound speaker lashed onto the back of the snowmobile. Crazy for people to be out shopping or returning things in that storm, Cornell thought. And a true shopping miracle they had found a store open. Cornell could make out the word Radio Shack on the side of the speaker. Of course! They were helping move equipment out of the store to protect it from the snow. Cornell bent over closer to show his approval. At the last instant, he realized they weren't shoppers! They were looters! They were stealing those things from the broken store window.

Nelson waved for the two of them to stop. He was, after all, a police officer. He had a gun under his suit that made it his duty to enforce law and order, even on a day as bad as that.

The second snowmobile pulled directly alongside him and the rider reached out and straight-armed him. Nelson lost his balance and fell to the side into a four-foot drift of snow. Driverless, his snowmobile careened over top of a drift and slammed into a car mound at the side of the street. Nelson blew snow away from his mouth and struggled to push himself to his feet out of the snow. The rider mounted his snowmobile. Nelson struggled to get to his feet. Couldn't. He was sunk into snow up to his waist. He struggled to pull off his glove to reach his holster. Before he reached it, the rider gunned his snowmobile and took off on it.

Nelson couldn't believe that had happened. Helpless, he

plunged through snow to the side of the street to locate a mound that had to be a telephone booth. Snow was packed so hard against it he couldn't get the door open. He broke it finally by kicking a boot against it.

"Sarge?" his lips were so cold, they could barely move to form words. "I lost the blood. Some looters took it from me."

"Damn it, Nelson," the desk sergeant didn't sound at all sympathetic. "How could you start out on a snowmobile and end up losing blood that way?"

Cornell's fingers and toes felt close to being frozen. He pressed his lips close to the receiver and tried to form words without moving them. "I lost the whole goddamn snowmobile," he said.

Dawn Brady, the second-floor nursery nurse, extended the telephone to Gena as she walked out to the desk.

"Portobello?" Haiden's voice sounded strained and curt. "The streets to the bridge are full of looters. One of them took the blood."

"Haiden—" Gena almost dropped her telephone, sharp pain creeping along her hairline and spreading over the top of her head to explode in jarring stabs at the back of her neck. "What am I supposed to do about that baby without any blood? His bilirubin is up to 14.5. His brain cells are going to be wiped out!"

"It's okay, Gena. I'll have them get you some new blood. That's all."

"How do you know the Red Cross has any more?"

"Of course the Red Cross has more blood; it's their business. I suppose if you wanted to double cover yourself, you could ask if there's someone inside there who would donate some—''

''I already donated blood! I already gave Ape *my* blood for Dan Gallagher! So I could use what you sent me for the baby.''

Haiden cleared his throat. Sounding puzzled. ''I don't think you should have done that, Gena. Because now the blood's been stolen.''

''How did I know that would happen?''

''Okay.'' Haiden relaxed again. ''You didn't. And it's all right. The Red Cross will send more blood. In the meantime, what you should do is line up Richard Culbertson—''

''Culbertson doesn't know anymore about exchange transfusions than I do.''

''Sure he does. He's old enough to be your father. Maybe your grandfather.''

''Bob—'' Gena sat down at the nursery desk and leaned forward to talk to him. ''I worked sixteen hours yesterday. I was ready to go off duty when this snow set in. It is now two o'clock in the afternoon the next day. That means I have been on my feet here for thirty-two hours at this point. I am doing the work of three services, because Stoner has a broken arm. Do you think I am in a mood to joke about whether Richard Culbertson knows how to do an exchange transfusion or not?''

''No, I guess you wouldn't be,'' Haiden agreed seriously. ''But it'll still be all right. Stoner can help you.''

''Let me repeat that, Bob. I am here because Stoner has a broken arm.''

''OK.'' Haiden refused to be upset. ''You don't even need him. You know how to thread an umbilical catheter. And after that, the exchange itself is just *removing* an amount of blood, then *replacing* that amount, over and over. Except it's a hell of a strain on the baby's heart so you have to watch it carefully. Lynn Curtain could help you. She's helped me with at least one."

Gena started to hang up again when a final question from him stopped her. "How is Lynn?" he asked.

Gena was tired of him being so concerned about Lynn Curtain. She started to hang up again.

"Don't let her get too tired, will you?" he asked. "I wouldn't like to see her go into labor. I'd like the opportunity to deliver her at home."

"That's an old wives' tale, Bob," Gena shared her opinion of his worry. "That getting tired starts labor." She stopped from saying more. Haiden wouldn't appreciate a first-year resident pointing out that he was quoting old wives' tales. As long as she had him on the phone though, she guessed she might as well tell him something else that might bother him. "Promise you won't get sore at me, Bob. But I got an ear curette out of your bag awhile ago."

That didn't upset him. "No problem."

"Why I'm telling you is because Sally was missing some morphine from her narcotic count this morning. And I found the vials in your bag."

Haiden was quiet for a long minute, then erupted. "For shit's sake, Gena! You don't think *I* put them there, do you? I wasn't there this morning."

Gena guessed she never should have mentioned the subject.

"What a stereotyper you are, Portobello!" Haiden wasn't ready to drop the subject. "Quick to think the black guy is the one into the drugs, huh?"

Gena started to tell him that she had forgotten he was black. She hesitated because she realized he probably wouldn't have taken that as a compliment. "I only brought it up , Bob, because I hope you aren't planning on using morphine with Lynn Curtain when she's in labor. Babies born when their mother has had morphine during labor don't breathe well enough at birth to be born at home."

"Who do you think you're talking to, Portobello? *I am the one who taught you that!*"

Gena backed down. Didn't add anything.

"Shit, Gena, I don't know how that stuff got into my bag," Haiden came back, sounding calmer. "Someone must have stuffed it there to keep it from being found on them. Maybe even Sally. You never know on a staff the size of the center's who's on the stuff. The nurse on Two is always complaining and asking for something for a headache. Maybe it was her."

That was so plausible an explanation that Gena felt like a fool for having even mentioned anything to him.

"But now that you've found it, Gena," Haiden continued with advice, "be smart about it. Throw it into a trash basket. Whatever you do, don't tell anyone where you found it. Or *that* you found it. Otherwise, someone will start to think that *you* took it."

Gena wasn't sure how that followed, but it did somehow, because Sally's first thought that morning had been that either she or Stoner had taken it. "I'm going to call the Red Cross now for new blood," Haiden said seriously. "Call me back when it gets in there, and I'll go over exchange procedure with you."

"What if something happens to the new blood?" Gena demanded. "The baby's bilirubin can't safely go much higher."

"For Chrissake, Gena!" Haiden dropped his receiver and cut off the rest of her comment.

Gena hung up her receiver more gently. He was right. She shouldn't have given her blood away until that from the Red Cross arrived. Or simply given hers to the Dukane baby without mentioning it to Ape that she had.

She was in the elevator, riding up to four, when a new blast of wind hit the building. The sides of the elevator suddenly grated along the shaft and threatened to stop, as if the wind had blown the elevator out of line with the shaft. That was crazy, wind couldn't reach the elevator. It was in the center of the building. Maybe the wind had twisted the shaft, brought it out of line with the elevator. But the shaft was in the center of the building! That had to mean the entire building had twisted with the wind.

After only a minute more of grating steel, the elevator swung free and continued to rise. Scared, Gena stepped off it the second it opened. Was a building safe, she asked herself, grateful to be on firm flooring again, if it could twist in a wind that way? She wondered who knew how much cement had been added to that building? If it had been enough to strengthen it or not.

Jack Kissell opened the door to David Frank's office on the first floor of A Building and let himself in. Unlike the Personnel office, with its half glass insert door, Frank's office door had solid panels. That made him absolutely safe from being detected behind it. He could be sealed into a solid cocoon from that point onward.

He sat the radio on the corner of the marble top of Frank's desk and crouched to find a plug for it on the near wall. Beginning to feel comfortable with his plan, he settled the earphones in place and scanned the dial for an AM station, admiring the quality of sound that instantly flooded into his ears. He had stolen a good radio.

Anxious to get to work on the safe, he crouched and traced the words *Armstrong Safe Company* written in raised gold letters across the door of it. Turning back to the desk, he opened Frank's top drawer and took out a page of letterhead stationery. Nice. He congratulated the medical administrator on his good taste in stationery. He lifted a black pen out of the desk set and sat down on the floor next to the safe to begin to spin and check off the first of the possible combinations of numbers. An old Simon and Garfunkel song echoed in his ears so loudly that he was unaware that a crack in the plaster above was rapidly spreading across the ceiling, as if the room or the floors over his head were being split in two.

Gena stopped to use the hall john. One step inside the room and her pocket beeper buzzed to announce that Pediatrics needed her STAT. Hey! She should be allowed a minute to use a john in peace, she thought, pushing the received button on the side of her beeper to let the operator know she'd located her. "STAT," the operator repeated, almost conversationally. But she could afford to sound leisurely. She was sitting in a padded foam chair in C Building. Hell. Gena decided to be charitable. The woman was probably falling asleep from sitting in a comfortable chair after all that time.

Up on three, Ethel Murphy met her at the nurse's desk, her uniform looking wrinkled in front and covered on the side by a bright red cough syrup stain. "I'm sorry," she said. "But the line on the Warren boy infiltrated again and he's wheezing more than he did before."

Gena didn't understand why so many lines were coming out of the boy, anymore than she could understand why his asthma wouldn't clear better. It was time to call Hamilton and ask her what she usually did for the boy's asthma attacks, because what Gena was doing obviously wasn't accomplishing a damn thing. The funny outlines on the X-ray might be the beginning of some metabolic or endocrine disease. Gena pondered over which one it might be, while she punched buttons on the telephone. She could draw blood and check for sodium and potassium levels . . . Probably calcium . . . See if any of those were thrown off and causing things to be so wrong. That would be better than just continuing to pump an indefinite amount of aminophylline into the boy to redilate his bronchioles and open him up again. As aminophylline reached high levels in the blood stream, it started to act on heart muscle as well as bronchial muscle. A very high level could stop a heart.

Hamilton picked up her telephone on the first ring, as if she had been waiting for that call.

"Always a problem regulating the Warren boy," she said in her know-it-all, I-am-good voice. "In fact, since December, maybe as far back as November, he's been extremely difficult to regulate. A couple times he's been sent home from school in the middle of the day because his breathing was suddenly so bad. Although once, before a science exam, a teacher saw him pick up a gerbil out of a cage at the back of the classroom, sniff it—you know animal hair is one of his allergies—and immediately become so distressed that the school had to call his mother to come and take him home."

Gena hadn't known all that. His mother had told her that he was almost perfect.

"So from that, we know he knows how to turn on attacks,'' Hamilton concluded. ''The aspirin he took last night is just another example of that.''

Who in hell did he think he was, Gena thought, manipulating people that way? It seemed to her that it was time to tell him that a reputation as a smartass at ten stayed with a person for a long time. ''Maybe what I'll do is just ask him to turn this attack off,'' she said simply.

''Be careful with the Warrens,'' Hamilton caught her breath, as if she, too, were developing asthma symptoms. ''They contribute a substantial amount of money to that facility every year. Whatever you do, don't do *anything* to antagonize them.''

Telling their son to get his goddamn act together didn't seem antagonistic to Gena. It seemed like a basic common sense procedure.

''Why don't you get an aminophylline level so you know for certain where you are, and then just continue to watch him cautiously?'' Hamilton suggested.

Great advice, Gena concluded. That wasn't any different than what she *had* been doing, and it wasn't working. She put the phone down gently, although that wasn't the way she felt like replacing it. How could Hamilton think she had time to just sit there on the third floor and cautiously watch a kid try and catch his breath while she was also supposed to be keeping a fetus from dying on the first floor, a man from bleeding to death on the fourth floor, and another baby from being jaundiced to death on the second? Plus twenty kids on the third floor in between.

''Are you going to restart the Warren boy's IV?'' Murphy asked from behind her as Gena hung up the phone. The woman was standing at the sink trying to scrub the red stain off the side of her uniform.

Gena didn't feel as if she had much choice; if she didn't

start it, Mark would continue wheezing until he arrested. Although another hour of constantly restarting lines in him, and he would turn into such a pincushion he would have no place left to start lines.

When she reached the room, she realized she should have hurried more. The boy was sitting almost upright in bed, struggling with every muscle to pull and push air past almost totally obstructed bronchioles. He was so short of oxygen that his lips and fingers were bright blue. Starting fluid on him was never an easy thing to do; his veins were hard ones to hit. The more he struggled, the harder it was.

Peter Warren was sitting in the chair beside the boy's bed, turned so that he could see the television screen. On the screen, an announcer was describing how store windows had blown in and looters on snowmobiles were clearing out everything they could get their hands on in downtown White Horse. The police, confined to cars that couldn't go anywhere on unplowed and blowing streets, were helpless against them.

"The world belongs to anyone with a snowmobile and a CB radio who wants to fight the cold," Peter Warren said stiffly, brushing his hair to try and cover a bald spot on the top of his head. "Absurd."

Irritated, Gena swabbed off the top of Mark's foot, thinking she was going to have to make her first stab good, or she wouldn't have a live child to make a second stab into.

Unfortunately, Murphy had given her one of the biggest needles she had ever seen attached to the end of an intravenous setup. Trying not to look as if she were enjoying stabbing the boy, she anchored a rolling vein and angled the needle into his ankle. She was angry at having to restart that line. It should have been obvious to a five-year-old that medicine by that route was important. Why did he keep pulling it out?

She added new aminophylline and watched the blue disappear from around the boy's mouth after five more breaths. Gradually, he lay back against his pillows and started to study the ceiling again. Gena looked up to see what was so interesting there and noticed a crack in the ceiling, a black line running in a zigzag pattern four feet out into the room. Gena was sure it hadn't been there before. The fourth level in the building had been cracking; not the third.

Interesting. But not her main problem there. This boy's rapid respiratory rate was her chief problem. What was she missing that she couldn't change that rapid rate? What else should she be doing?

"Elizabeth said you wanted to talk to her earlier," Peter Warren said, swinging around in his chair to face Gena and snapping off the television set with the automatic control. "But then you left suddenly."

Gena wondered why Peter Perfect could always phrase things as if they were her fault. She hadn't left. His wife had. "I was concerned with how tired she looked," she answered.

Peter turned back to look at the blank television screen. "Of course she's tired," he said stiffly. "She's been up all night."

But then so had he, Gena thought, and he wasn't black and blue from it. In fact, he was very neat and in-control-looking. Mark looked exhausted. His clothing was wrinkled; the hair on his forehead was straight and sweat-stained. She hadn't looked in a mirror, but as she hadn't put on any makeup that morning, and since it was now afternoon, and she was still wearing the same clothing she had had on the night before, she could imagine that she looked like something off a shipwreck.

Peter Perfect looked perfect. His slacks still had a definite straight crease in the legs. He was wearing a white shirt and even the back of it looked almost wrinkle-free. His cuffs were buttoned. A blue tie was fitted neatly to his collar. Everything perfect except for a single hair on the left side of his forehead that was out of place.

"Elizabeth's had flu lately," Peter said. "I imagine that's what you mean."

Gena anchored the IV line with so much tape it couldn't possibly pull out again. Bob Haiden had called, Murphy said, coming back into the room as she finished, and he wanted to be called back as soon as the blood arrived. He was getting nervous that it wasn't there yet.

"Does that mean new staff will be able to get in soon?" Peter Perfect asked, swinging back to face Gena.

"If blood can get over, I guess people can," Gena answered him.

"As soon as someone new does get in here, I'd like to go back to our old arrangement," Peter said.

Gena had trouble thinking what that had been.

"A more experienced resident caring for my son," Peter supplied the answer.

Stupid, arrogant man! Gena reached across Mark to turn off the oxygen at the wall, so that she could listen to his chest without the hissing of the gas interfering with any quiet sounds he had in there.

Mark spun in a spurt of temper and turned it back on.

"Hey!" Gena reached across the boy again for the outlet. "When I want the oxygen off, I want it *off!*"

The boy ducked, as if he thought she was reaching to punch him out. Had he been raised to believe that she was some kind of strange person who claimed to be a Warren but wasn't; who insisted on taking care of him when she was dangerous; who was probably into punching out ten-year-olds gasping for breath? Gena flipped his oxygen back on.

"Tell your son," she said to Peter Perfect, trying to sound as if this were a final ultimatum on her part, "that I am sick of wasting time in this room. I don't want this IV pulled out again, and I don't want the oxygen taken off again."

Peter Warren pushed himself to his feet, walked over to the bed, and whacked the boy's face. One. Two. Three times. All without saying a word.

Gena was unable to believe she'd seen him do that.

"Hold it, Peter!" She grabbed the man's hand to stop him. "What are you thinking of?"

"Goddamn spoiled kid," Peter said. He glared at Gena as if somehow that was her fault, then turned on his heel and walked out of the room with quick sure steps. Outside in the hallway, she heard him shout to Murphy, "Get my wife! I want to know what's been going on here!"

Gena stood staring at his son. Fighting tears, the boy pressed his hands against his face. Trying to rub aside the pain, not react to that. Maintain his usual "Joe Cool" appearance. But humiliated at having been treated that way. Gena stood helplessly by the side of the bed, unable to believe she had just admired a man because he had looked so fresh and unwrinkled in all that confusion, and then he had walked over and almost broken his kid's jaw.

"Mark?" she reached to touch the boy's shoulder.

The boy pulled in a deep breath, coughed, then couldn't breathe out again. Blue began in a circle around his mouth and spread around his eyes and down his neck. He gasped again, absolutely unable to breathe out again, or to pull in new oxygen. Wearily, he sank back against the pillows like a balloon with all the air let out of it, the color draining from his face. As the last of his color left his cheeks, his heart stopped.

"Crash cart!" Gena shouted, pushing the emergency call bell on the wall. "Code Five!"

Airway. Breathing. Circulation . . . Gena knew the steps, although she'd never done it by herself before. Could she think fast enough to be effective by herself? She jerked the boy's body over to the side of the bed, leaned over him, and started mouth to mouth resuscitation, waiting for someone else to arrive, counting the seconds since his color had drained. No one came to help her. She stopped and checked the boy's pulse. None palpable. No blood was moving in him, none reaching his brain or heart. *Think, Portobello,* she shouted at herself. Get his heart started. Breathe. Compress. Compress. Compress. Compress. Compress. Breathe!

She should have been able to feel a carotid pulse after only a few chest compressions. There wasn't any. That meant she had to be doing something wrong! What if she had forgotten a step? *Airway, breathing, circulation, drugs* . . . Hell, she couldn't think of what the right dosages for resuscitation drugs would be. A boy was going to die in front of her, because she didn't know the dose of epinephrine she should be asking a nurse to draw up for her right that minute. And no one else was there! She was all by herself trying to do that!

"Breathe!" she shouted at the lifeless boy. She flipped up the IV dial to flood him with fluid to keep his blood pressure up. It was no use. Nothing was working. If he didn't respond in another minute, it would mean she had lost him.

His father didn't like her taking care of him and he had been right. She was going to lose him. She followed the new

IV line to his ankle, wondering if the new aminophylline wasn't flowing. The boy's ankle was swelling around the needle. Shit! Her new line *was* out! In another minute she'd need to give drugs IV, and she didn't have a working line in place!

"Good going, Portobello," Zack Appleton strode into the room and nudged her shoulder out of the way to press a resuscitation mask down over the boy's face. He gave it a couple of good compressions for oxygen while she paused in chest compressions.

Stoner arrived in another second and pushed his way alongside the bed. He took the resuscitation mask from Ape and let Ape take over the cardiac massage. "Get that line in clean!" Ape shouted. Gena prepared to restart it in the other ankle, trying to remember resuscitation drug dosages. She couldn't.

Murphy arrived running with the full resuscitation cart. Ape barked an order to her for an ET tube and epinephrine as if he knew drug dosages for any age patient, including ten year olds.

As Gena swabbed the boy's left ankle, she couldn't get the line set, because the space where she wanted to stab the line was covered by a brown smudge. She swabbed the space to clean away the dirt. Murphy held up an ET tube and handed it off to Stoner. Stoner passed it one-handed down into the boy's lungs.

Gena hurried faster, swabbing the boy's ankle again. Damn! The dirt wouldn't come away. She couldn't get a new fluid line in if she couldn't see skin!

Finally, she located a vein past the dirty smudge mark and sank the needle. Bernie Kuhn, a medical resident, arrived and took over from Ape. Ape waited only a second until backflow blood had filled Gena's line and added a syringe of atropine to it.

"Heartbeat!" Bernie reported immediately, as the heart thumped under the heel of his hand the instant the heart stimulant hit the boy's circulation. The boy's heart gave a couple of healthy beats on its own, steadied, and grew stronger. Gena watched the boy gasp and then breathe. His color pinked up. Full respirations came back. He was on his own again.

Gena was sure that her last dose of aminophylline, not the slap to the face, had done that. Trying to work blind without waiting for the lab to get a report back, she'd almost killed him. If she hadn't been standing right there when his heart had stopped, his brain could be as scrambled as the Dukane baby's was going to be if Haiden's second attempt at blood didn't get there soon. Although she wasn't even certain yet how to use the blood when it did arrive . . .

Feeling her knees turn to rubber, Gena picked up a roll of tape to secure the fluid line. She tried to wipe the dirt spot away again, still couldn't make it dissolve. A wave of nausea hit her stomach. Recklessly, she grabbed the boy's chart off the overbed stand and walked into the nearest bathroom with it. Feeling the wave of nausea sweep over her again, she threw up everything she had eaten that day into the toilet.

From the bathroom, she could hear Appleton ask for a syringe to draw blood gases, and Murphy respond that he'd have to use a big needle. Appleton said he didn't give a damn, then obviously got blood with it, because he gave it to an aide to run to the lab. Gena stayed in the john, sitting on the floor beside the toilet, her head in her hand, trying not to think about what would have happened if she hadn't been standing right by the boy's bed at that moment. After another minute, Appleton came to the door and kicked her foot with his shoe to get her attention.

"Do you remember arrest forms need three carbons?" he asked.

Gena recognized what he was talking about. The first person at an arrest was supposed to coordinate the resuscitation attempt. The coordinator was supposed to fill in the forms. He was making the point that she was upchucking instead of coordinating. All right. That was well deserved. She got to her feet, embarrassed, fumbling to find some words to explain why she was so sick to her stomach she couldn't move.

"You did a nice job," Appleton added. He had changed to a pair of whites since she had seen him last and didn't look as wrinkled as before. His shoes hadn't come clean; they still had pink stains on them. "You saved the kid's life."

Gena didn't feel very responsible for saving his life. She knew that if she had been there all by herself, Mark Warren would have died.

"All the first man's responsibility to do at an arrest is keep the person alive until help comes," Appleton said, plunking a big hand down on her shoulder. She couldn't understand why he was being so nice to her. It wasn't his style to be nice to first-year residents.

"You know something I don't know?" he asked her after another minute of her still being unable to respond to him. "Something that shouldn't make you feel good about what you did?"

Gena pushed herself to her feet and flushed the john. "I couldn't think of emergency drug dosages for a ten-year-old," she admitted.

"That's why I'm here," he said. "I wouldn't expect you to know that."

Gena didn't feel much better.

"You want to know what I *thought* you might say?" Appleton asked, looking at his pink-stained shoes, his giant frame filling the doorway. "I thought maybe you'd say you know the reason the kid arrested was because you weren't on your toes with him as much as you might have been. You were being too wishy-washy with him."

That wasn't true. It *was* true that she hadn't gotten his respirations back to normal. But why they wouldn't slow down had nothing to do with what she was doing.

An inch square of plaster fell from the ceiling onto Appleton as he turned to go. He wiped it off his apelike shoulders with a quick distasteful motion, squinting at the ceiling. "Look at this mess, Portobello," he said. "Your whole building here is a disaster."

The crack on the ceiling over Mark's bed had lengthened to reach all the way across the room, spreading not only longer but wider apart. Why plaster was falling. But, hell, this wasn't her building, Gena thought. If it was, she would have torn it down last year, not tried to add cement to it.

"I think the wind is tearing this building apart," she said seriously.

"Easy, Portobello. I want your mind on people here, not construction problems." The Ape worked to wipe plaster dust off his fingertips. "I don't know if you've noticed it or not, but you're not swift enough to handle both."

"Thanks, Zack. I need encouragement."

"You need reminding that I have a bargain with Stoner and you for helping out with Gallagher?"

"I'm going to get to your damn cutdown."

"Damn right you are, because that was the deal. And the

catheterization and the tap. Because those were part of the deal.'' Appleton couldn't brush all the plaster off. He shouldered past her to the sink to wash his hands.

''That was my blood you gave to Gallagher,'' she said ''I feel I've done enough for him.''

''I am the triage officer. I had a right to do that!''

''Literally, Zack. That was *my* blood. I leached it for you.''

He stopped scrubbing his hands and looked over his shoulder at her. ''What happened to the blood that Haiden sent in?''

''He couldn't get any here.''

Appleton nodded, then shook his head. ''That wasn't smart, Gena,'' he said. ''Because you don't know how much longer you're going to be here.''

''I needed some blood for the baby.''

Ape nodded, as if that solution never would have occurred to him. ''What's the scoop on this kid?'' he asked, back to his old self. ''Why the hell did he arrest?''

Gena guessed that was all the sympathy she was going to get. ''I can't get his respirations to slow to a point that he can use oxygen.''

Appleton grabbed six paper towels to get his big hairy hands dry. ''Why is that?''

If she knew the answer to that, she'd know the answer to the whole problem. ''He took some aspirin to start the thing—'' she began an explanation.

''How much?''

Gena had never asked the kid how many tablets he'd taken. Ten-year-olds knew enough to read a bottle and take a sensible dose. Hell. One of the toxic effects of salicylate—aspirin—poisoning was increased respiratory rate. His father had said he'd taken the aspirin to start an asthma attack. Could he have wanted to start one so badly he had taken a whole bottle?

She couldn't tell that by blood work at that point. His salicylate blood load would have already peaked by that time and be on its way down. Besides, it took hours for a salicylate level to be run.

"Thanks, Zack." Gena felt her own respirations begin to slow. "I never thought of salicylate poisoning."

Appleton turned and tossed the bunch of paper towels into the wastepaper basket and stepped out into the patient room. Gena walked over beside him to look at Mark Warren. Stoner had pulled his ET tube so he was breathing totally on his own again. On the bedside stand next to him, the cardiac monitor flashed a good heartbeat pattern. His chest was still tugging, but his ventilation was adequate.

The best treatment for salicylate poisoning was hydration—pushing fluid until the kidneys picked up the toxic level and excreted it. By accident, Gena had been doing for him what she should have been doing for both his asthma *and* the overdose of aspirin. Each hour the aspirin load had to be falling closer and closer to normal. If she could only sustain him short of arresting again, time would slow that respiratory rate and get him fully over this attack.

She opened the boy's chart to start to document the arrest. Read his name, address, and birth date at the top of the page. Why couldn't she have figured out what had been happening there, she asked herself. Zack Appleton might look like a primate, but he obviously had been better able to reason than she had. And why hadn't she been able to guess that Stoner had said he wasn't perfect. Peter Perfect would react the way he had when she'd asked him to help her? She looked at her fluid line to be certain it was free flowing, found herself staring at what she had first thought was a smudge of dirt on the boy's ankle. Suddenly she knew why her stomach had turned upside down: the boy's birth date was February 17, the same day she'd had her baby. And that wasn't a smudge of dirt on his ankle. It was a perfect heart-shaped birthmark.

Chapter Ten

Gena searched through A Building looking for Richard Culbertson. Despite the fact that it had been hours since she'd talked to him, she found him exactly where he'd been last time, lying on a cot in an L and D sack-out room. One side of his face looked crooked as he sat up to talk to her. He rubbed it harder than before, as if trying to convince it to function.

"I just started a new IV in the Warren boy," Gena told him.

Culbertson continued rubbing his face.

"He's my son, isn't he?" she asked. "He has a February 17th birth date. And a birthmark on his left foot."

Culbertson waved at air, started to lie back down again. "Hundreds of children have birthmarks."

"You told me he was in Maryland! I turned down a residency at Hopkins because I thought he was there! And now I find out he's here! You gave him to the Warrens!"

"You signed permission for adoption. You have no right to be angry."

"For Baltimore!"

"You didn't specify."

"I was sixteen!"

"Sixteen-year-old mothers have full authority to sign f adoption."

That wasn't what she was arguing about. "Dr. Culber son! You lied to me!"

The man stopped rubbing his face. He couldn't get th muscle to respond; his right cheek sagged lower than h left. "I gave your son the inheritance the Warrens alway denied you," he said. "You should be happy with that."

Gena caught her breath. As a kid she remembered stand ing on the front lawn of the Warrens' big house, catching glimpse of a birthday party going on in the back yard fo Peter Perfect: balloons, pony rides, a clown doing a magi act. And she had cried, tears pouring down her cheeks fron jealousy. That kind of treatment should have been hers, too She guessed she couldn't quarrel with Culbertson about giv ing that to her son. It was true, that if she *had* specified a family in White Horse who she would have wanted to raise her son, it would have been the Warrens.

"No one knows," Culbertson struggled to speak clearly. "And Peter is sensitive at having to adopt. So I would advise you not to say anything."

Gena stood up abruptly. "Peter *knows* he's mine?" A lot of things fell into place. "The reason he didn't want me taking care of his son didn't have anything to do with the aspirin order, did it? He didn't want me near him, because I might realize who he was!"

Culbertson sat watching her cautiously, not agreeing or disagreeing with her.

"Do you know David Frank is asking me to leave here, because the Warrens are unhappy with me?" she asked him. "Weren't you going to do anything to stop that?"

The man shook his head.

"How dare you talk to me about responsibility?" she returned, hotly. "Ruining my life is not accepting responsibility!"

"I'm not the one who had the baby!" He shouted back at her. "I'm not the one who started this whole thing!"

"But why didn't you give him to someone in Maryland, like you said?"

"The Warrens paid me. And I needed their money."

"That's crazy, Dr. Culbertson." She stepped closer to him. "Next to the Warrens and the Franks, you've got to be one of the richest men in White Horse."

"I have almost nothing! I have spent any extra I ever had building this hospital!"

"Well, that certainly confirms how shitty your judgment is, Dr. Culbertson! Because this hospital is blowing apart!"

"This hospital started in a house with only twelve beds. Two nurses. And myself. I operated on a dining room table! During the Depression, I lived here because I lost my first house! Don't you notice that *I* don't have any children? Didn't it occur to you that *I* wanted your baby? Don't you know that's what I planned from the moment I first diagnosed you? Only then I learned the Warrens wanted one and they offered a hundred thousand dollars. I paid for the surgery suite here with that money!"

"You *sold* my baby!"

"I *sacrificed* having a child of my own! So White Horse could have a decent hospital. You have no right to criticize me for that!"

Gena wasn't convinced all his motivations had been unquestionable. "You had no idea what kind of father he had," she said. "You could have been selling the Warrens a defective child. Actually that is exactly what you did do. There are strange breaks in both his upper extremities—''

''There's nothing wrong with him, Gena. Nothing. You should feel nothing but pride in discovering who he is.''

Gena didn't feel pride, she felt revulsion. Seeing him reminded her of the train station and the horrible, unfeeling Hispanic man who must have fathered him. And revulsion at Richard Culbertson for lying to her about where he was placing him. ''Did you tell the Warrens who the father was?'' She studied his searching expression, and realized the extent of his treachery. ''No! You didn't, did you? In fact, you sold them a baby you thought *might* be defective!''

''I didn't!''

''The one thing you did accomplish,'' Gena said from the doorway, ''is to even things out here. Peter Perfect doesn't like me taking care of his son. Now I don't like taking care of him either.''

At the end of the hallway, by the corner of the building, she stopped abruptly as a blast of wind hit so hard that the entire hallway seemed to tremble from the shock. Plaster cracked over her head and filled the air in front of her with white dust.

She stepped over a fallen plaster chunk and stopped at the door to Leslie Kerr's room, to glance at her monitor and see if William Kerr was there. The man jumped up out of the chair beside the bed as if he had been waiting for her.

''Did you put the cement columns in this building'' Gena demanded of him.

The man straightened his ugly tie, looking dejected that that was all she was concerned about. ''I wouldn't touch a job like this,'' he answered.

Gena glanced from him to the monitor, assured herself

he pattern there was good. "Why not? Was it an impossible job?"

"Price. In-laws or not, I have to make a profit."

Gena left William Kerr standing there and turned to ride up to the third floor, worried because it was taking Bob Haiden so long to get a second pack of blood to her. If that had been stolen as well, she wouldn't be able to stop the baby's brain cells from being destroyed. She was also worried about what Richard Culbertson had done to her, and about ceilings cracking and bricks possibly falling on her head and knocking her into black unconsciousness.

Jack Kissell had already tried three hundred combinations. His fingertips had turned yellow from the gold paint on the combination knob and his legs were cramped from crouching on the floor.

Desperate to stretch, he stopped work and walked over to the window to see if the storm had lessened any. If it had, he couldn't detect it. The radio earphones described no difference: seventy-mile-an-hour winds, snow still falling; the thruway still closed. He rubbed his hands, wishing that he had something to eat, that he had planned ahead better. It would be foolish to leave the office and try to find something, though. One more spin, one more combination, and he might be inside the safe . . .

He stretched, yawned, shook himself awake, and settled down to try another round of combinations.

It was 4:00 P.M. and Gena had finished Appleton's scut work. Down on the labor floor, she had started a fluid line on Leslie Frank Kerr because she'd been in labor for so long without food. On the third floor, Mark Warren ha managed to keep his fluid line intact. But she had a ne report that showed Baby A Dukane's serum level had rise to 16.5 mg.

Murphy was standing by the back counter, pourin dinner-time medicine. "Could you find Mrs. Warren fo me?" Gena asked her.

"If I can have my chair," Murphy answered tightly.

Gena stood up to give her the chair.

"Mrs. Warren went downstairs to put some ice on her eye," Murphy said, moving over to the desk to stand beside her chair, to claim it before Gena could change her mind. "Some plaster dust fell in it and it started to swell."

Gena looked outside at nothing but continuously blowing snow and wind. A piece of plaster had fallen onto the desk and Murphy reached to brush it away to work on records.

"What about Dr. Stoner?" Gena asked her. "Is he around?"

"In the Warrens' room."

Gena pushed herself away from the desk and walked back down the hall, wondering why Stoner had felt it necessary to check on Mark. Probably Ape's directive, she thought. She found Stoner sitting on Mark Warren's bed, teaching him how to juggle. Gena stood in the doorway, first angry, then surprised because Mark Warren was laughing as he achieved three moving balls. That was the first time she'd seen him smile since he'd been admitted. That struck her as funny, because one of the things she remembered liking about Mark on other admissions was a quick, instant sense of humor. This certainly was a different admission for him in a lot of ways.

"Mark wondered if you'd change his IV to his hand,"

Stoner said as she came up to the bed. Mark let the balls drop to the bed cover.

Gena wasn't crazy about doing that. She doubted if there were any more decent needles left in the building, although she had started so many IVs in the last twenty-four hours, she was twice as good at doing them as she'd been the day before. She could probably do them with any size needle by now. "What's the difference?" she asked, studying the boy's face, trying to see the outline of his father's face in him.

"Just put it in my hand like he asked you to," Mark said. His voice was husky, still affected by the respiratory shutdown from the hour before.

"So you can pull it easier?" she asked. She couldn't like him. She would ask never to care for him again after this day.

"So I can go to the bathroom."

That was a fair request, she admitted, but surely not the reason for the swallowed aspirin or the line pulling. She wished Peter Perfect had been fair with her, told her what he had known about him. "Fair warning," she said to the boy, ripping tape off the foot site with more force than necessary. "If this one infiltrates, I call your Dad to tell you to leave it alone again."

The boy cringed from the sting of the last piece of tape coming free; he lay back against the pillows. "You want me slapped, Portobello? Why don't you just do it yourself?" he asked.

That wasn't fair, and hadn't been fair of her, either. After all, he was only an hour's time free from a cardiac arrest. "Is that what the aspirin swallowing was all about?" she asked. "To stop that from happening at home?"

He looked at the ceiling, which was now as interesting to Gena as it was to him. A six-inch track of plaster had come loose and fallen, a result of the twisting stress that had to be radiating along the center of the building every time the wind blew.

"How many aspirin did you swallow?" Stoner asked, standing up to give Gena more room to work.

"How many are in a bottle?"

Stoner picked up the balls he had been using to juggle, and stood tossing one of them into the air over and over, one-handed. "We should talk," he said to Gena, walking toward the door, still juggling. He thought the boy was talking suicide, Gena thought. She didn't. She thought he was talking Warren supremacy; a sense that what a Warren wanted, a Warren could get. An aide in the hallway called Stoner to the phone and he left to get it at the desk.

Gena started to look at the back of the boy's hand for a new fluid site. He squirmed it just enough that she was looking at a bad angle.

"Do you go with him?" Mark asked her after a moment.

Gena took another moment to locate who he meant. Stoner had been the only male around. He had to have meant him. "Stoner?" she asked preposterously.

"He looks at you like he likes you."

Stoner hated her. Gena shook her head at his misconception.

"What if he wanted to make out with you, and you didn't want to do anything?" Mark asked. "What would you do?"

"Stoner wouldn't ever do that."

"Suppose someone else did."

Calmness and patience, Gena thought. A role model on how to handle stress. "Curse a lot," she answered.

"You ever have anyone make you do anything with you? You know, like hold you down or—something?"

Gena wondered how many people in White Horse Dan

Gallagher had told his story to, his version of what had happened to her in that train station? Did Mark know the story of his own conception? "Why are you asking that?"

"I wondered, that's all." The boy concentrated on talking to the ceiling. "I'm readin' this book where the guy has to beat up his wife before he can get off. I wondered how often that really happens."

Gena ripped new strips of tape and waited for him to say something else.

He tightlipped it.

What a strange conversation from a boy who had said almost nothing since admission! "You worried that you'll have trouble with that?" Gena tried.

The boy continued concentrating on the ceiling. "I just wondered what you thought, that's all," he said.

He wouldn't let Gena turn his hand so that she could have a decent look at what veins he had left there.

"What I think," she said, "is that you are an egocentric, bad-mannered—"

"Stuff your opinion." He jerked his hand away from her.

"—irresponsible—"

He sat up glaring at her, gasping for breath again.

"—attention-getting—"

He lay down. Absolutely quiet against the sheets.

Gena looked up at him quickly, to be certain that the reason he hadn't responded to that was because he was too out of breath to respond. No. He simply wasn't fighting her accusation. Of those three things, attention-getting was the one he was certainly most guilty of. He had almost killed himself swallowing aspirin; he had compounded that problem by pulling out a fluid line, not once, but four times. Although he had sat there laughing and joking with Scott Stoner, he had done nothing but treat her like shit since admission. He just spent his time quietly scrutinizing her from behind half-closed eyelids, as if he were weighing her reaction to his attention-getting. *As if it were her attention he most wanted to get.*

"OK." She dropped the IV line to show that now he had her undivided attention. "You have my attention. What do you want to tell me?"

"Put the IV in my hand."

"I *said* I'm listening. What do you want?"

"I don't want to have to go home again."

A lot of ten-year-olds said that. Tired of coming in at nine o'clock on school nights, of picking up their rooms, keeping their elbows off the table, of doing homework. She had thought he was going to tell her something important; instead this was nothing more than a typical parent/child quarrel.

"Sometimes we don't have much choice about such things. It comes with being ten."

"Aspirin is cheap, Doc. And over the counter. Don't tell me I don't have a choice."

Gena took his hand to examine for a vein again. Stoner had been right; he was talking suicide. Whatever was bothering him was important enough to him that he was prepared to kill himself over it.

"What do you expect of me?" she asked.

He made a fist to help her find a vein on the back of his hand, cooperating like his old self, the kind of kid he had been back in August. "Talk to my mother."

Gena set the needle into a vein that suddenly popped into view. He was so used to having those started on him, he knew all the quirks; he reached up and turned on the fluid line for her.

"I haven't had time to talk to your mother," she said

tiredly, "because I have been so busy restarting this so many times."

His eyes gave away a lot. "This'll probably stay in all right while you do that," he said. He even tried to grin. Apparently he thought better of it at the last minute, and buried it with a halfhearted cough.

Cornell Nelson wanted to be a hero so badly he could taste it.

He had felt inadequate, explaining how he had lost a snowmobile, but now he was in charge again. He had a new snowmobile, a new unit of blood—the last O negative that the local Red Cross had available—and he was accelerating along the side of the river, guard rail posts passing him in a quick staccato order on his way to the Bird Island bridge.

Not that he could tell there was a river beyond the posts, with the wind blowing snow along the surface of the water and up onto the roadway.

He heard the whir of a snowplow motor before he could see it. When he could make out the plow, he realized he was not going to be a hero this day. Despite all the plow's work, the Bird Island bridge was still packed with a six-foot drift of snow, up above the guard rails. A snowmobile attempting to run over that would be swept off by the wind. He couldn't cross the river on the ice either. It was too patchy and weak to support a snowmobile. There was only one way over to the island, and that was by the bridge, and snow was still blocking it.

Cornell pulled in next to a maintenance building and watched a forklift truck try to lift a load of snow away from the bridge. The snow blew back as soon as it was lifted away. He shook his head, disappointed. If he stayed there too long watching—even with an insulated container—the blood would freeze and be worthless. He would have to take it back to the Red Cross and leave it with them. And wait until some other day to be a hero.

Murphy stretched a telephone receiver out to Gena as she walked out into the third-floor hallway. "Gena?" Bob Haiden's voice had an edge of concern to it that definitely hadn't been there earlier. "No snowmobiles can get over the bridge."

"A helicopter—"

"Can't get up."

"Haiden! You're telling me that you're not sending any blood!"

"That's right. That's the scoop."

"But I just told a mother I was going to do right by her. What am I supposed to do now?"

"Unless you can get some blood from inside there, the ball game's over."

Gena dropped the phone, thinking of the way that mother had stood by the isolette, watching her son's fingers curl around her own. In another four hours, that baby would be convulsing as his brain cells were infiltrated with poison. Four hours more, and he would be lying limp as a rag doll. His face would be a dull blank. And neither the position of the arms or the expression of the face would ever change again if he lived to be a hundred years old.

In a train station with a knife held against her throat, or riding a merry-go-round that would not stop, she had never felt more helpless in her life.

* * *

Jack Kissell had to use a bathroom.

Of all the dumb things to go wrong in his plan, that had to be the dumbest. He had spent almost an hour in a basement bathroom earlier in the day. Why hadn't he thought of that *then?*

He spun a combination, tried the door, checked the number off on his list as ineffective. Then he had to stop. The feel of a full bladder was too uncomfortable to ignore. Should he take a chance and try and find a john in the hallway? Maybe go back to the locker room? No. It wasn't safe to leave the office.

Sitting on David Frank's desk was a large silver bowl with the words "For Richard Culbertson, In grateful appreciation of long years of service to the White Horse Medical Center" engraved on the side of it. A gift waiting to be presented to Culbertson as soon as he announced his retirement, Kissell guessed.

Hell, Kissell thought. Culbertson expected more than a silver bowl at that occasion. He expected a plaque on a wall somewhere; a whole building renamed for him. He would shit when he realized that that bowl was all he was going to get.

Kissell unzipped and urinated into it, then knelt back behind the desk, and started a new round of numbers.

It was eight o'clock. Gena looked up from a blood slip that showed the Dukane baby's blood level had risen to 17.5 mg. At the same minute, she saw Elizabeth Warren step off the elevator. At first, Elizabeth said she didn't have time to talk to her, then she nodded that she'd walk down to the conference room at the end of the third-floor hallway with her.

The woman's left eye where the plaster dust had struck it was partially hidden by a scarf. The part which did show was red and swollen. The women covered it with her hand self-consciously as she walked. "I must look terrible," she said.

She did look terrible, Gena agreed. Her eye was as swollen as if someone had punched it. "Do you want someone to look at that?" Gena asked her.

"It's really nothing," Elizabeth insisted. "Just a little irritated."

It didn't look like nothing to Gena. "Mark told me he deliberately took the aspirin," she said to the woman inside the conference room. "What I want to talk to you about is the possibility an attack like this happening again."

"Of course it will happen again, Doctor." The woman peered through the window at the blowing snow, rubbing her arms as the wind struck the corner window and the entire room rattled and shook. "That is the kind of disease asthma is."

Thank you for the asthma tip, Gena thought. But she already knew that. "Mark admitted that he knew he was taking aspirin. Why would he need your attention so badly that he would risk doing that?" she asked.

Elizabeth visibly shivered and took her hand away from her eye to rub her arms. The eye was looking worse every minute, Gena thought. She must have had a super allergy to plaster dust to make her eye swell that much.

"This isn't the only time he's acted this way," Gena continued. "Dr. Hamilton said that last fall he deliberately started an attack to avoid a science test."

"Dr. Hamilton has been our pediatrician for a long time," Elizabeth agreed.

Gena interpreted that to mean: Get the message? Don't mess in. "What was happening last night?" Gena pressed, messing in, "That was so unpleasant that Mark took the aspirin to avoid it?"

The woman sighed and looked back at the window, as if she wished both the snow outside and those questions would go away. "My husband has always had a difficult time accepting the fact that Mark is adopted, Doctor," she said finally, "I'm certain that's not an uncommon feeling."

Gena didn't understand what that had to do with anything. She had given Mark up for adoption because Culbertson had told her that he knew a family who wanted him very much.

"Actually, the fact that we *had* to adopt is what he finds difficult to accept," Elizabeth modified what she had said.

Gena was still having trouble relating that to what was happening. "A lot of women can't have children," she tried a sympathetic route.

Elizabeth Warren rubbed her arms in that funny I-just-can't-get-warm way again. "I am not the one who is infertile, Doctor. It is Peter," she said coolly.

Peter Perfect wasn't perfect? The thought barely registered with Gena it was so scary. But OK. That didn't make him the only infertile person in the world. So she still didn't follow what the woman was saying. "How does that relate to swallowing aspirin?" she asked.

"Peter is impotent, Doctor. Has always been. And he gets very angry when he realizes that soon Mark will be capable of things he is not. That Mark is growing up."

The more Gena looked at the woman's arms and the black marks there, the more they seemed to form a pattern. As if someone had gripped her arms so hard each finger had left a distinct round bruise. For that matter, the multiple bone breaks in Mark could be interpreted as a pattern, too. As if someone had pushed or shoved him so many times, he had that many snapped sites.

"Peter gets so angry—" Elizabeth seemed unable to complete that thought.

Gena could finish it. "That he beats Mark," she finished it angrily. And Culbertson had given her son to this man!

Elizabeth looked at her as if she were unbearably stupid, unable to understand the simplest thing. Slowly, she untied the scarf from her head so that her eye, purple and swollen, was completely visible. "Isn't it obvious, Doctor?" she asked, turning so Gena could see the eye better. "He gets so angry, he beats *me!*"

Gena couldn't believe what she'd just heard. The woman had been walking around here for almost a full day with black and blue marks all over her arms, and now her eye was almost swollen shut. "Mark got himself sent home from school last fall—swallowed the aspirin last night—to stop *that?*" Gena asked.

"*I* can't stop it."

Gena pictured a ten-year-old coming into the house, stepping between his parents, raising his arms to ward off blows, getting a broken ulnar bone for his trouble. Shit! She had no idea what living that way had to be like. And couldn't believe it happened in a Warren household! She had been raised to believe that the Warrens were perfect people. She had stood on their front lawn and cried because she wasn't one of them! "Why *can't* you stop it?" she asked, angrily. Elizabeth Warren wasn't a stupid woman. She was sure she'd heard her say once she was a Radcliffe graduate.

"What do you want me to do?" Elizabeth Warren asked helplessly. "How do you expect me to stop it?"

"You could get in your car as soon as this damn storm is over and keep right on driving for starters."

"Without any money, Doctor? I couldn't live that way."

"How can you live this way?"

Elizabeth Warren looked from the snow outside back to Gena. Her face was animated; her eyes frightened. "Peter is an excellent provider, Doctor. I have a lovely home, nice clothes—"

"You have a black eye! And last night, your son poisoned himself. What if the next time he swallows so much aspirin he kills himself, Mrs. Warren? Is your home lovely enough to let you live the next forty years with that?"

Gena left the woman standing staring outside at the snow and walked back to the desk. It was crazy how people wound themselves into such tight corners, cocoons they could break out of if only they could get the courage to do it. She sat down in Murphy's desk chair, thinking, hell, who was *she* to criticize? What had she ever done that was really worthwhile? She was letting a baby die in front of her eyes today. Was that any worse than letting a man beat the hell out of her?

How much did she want the baby to be all right was the question. Just enough to sit and think about it? Enough to bleed off some more blood to transfuse? She hadn't had anything to eat all day. She had a hell of a headache. Draining blood would use up every bit of energy she had left. Damn it. She didn't really have any choice. That would still be better than calmly sitting by and watching a baby's cerebral centers come unconnected from his brain stem.

Moving before she could change her mind, she dialed the lab and told the tech to set up for another crossmatch. She hung up, looked for Murphy, and walked back to the medicine cabinet to search it for an aspirin bottle.

"What's the word on the Warren kid?" Scott Stoner asked by her elbow. "What are you going to do about him?"

"Do you know where Lynn is?" Gena asked him instead, pushing aside bottles of cough syrup and mouthwash in the medicine cabinet.

"I told her to lie down," Stoner answered. "She's too tired to work anymore."

Gena could believe that. The woman had been limping from pain as far back as midnight. But she was the one nurse Haiden had mentioned as being able to help with a transfusion. What was she supposed to do without her? "Is there another nurse in this damn place who could help with an exchange transfusion?" she asked him.

"What's it matter? You don't have any blood."

"I was born with lots of blood."

"You can't use your own again. You'll wipe out."

"I don't have any choice."

Stoner watched her push aside three new bottles. "What are you looking for in the cupboard?" he asked sympathetically.

"Aspirin."

"Tylenol is the only thing there."

Gena hadn't even seen that. She pushed aside a purple bottle of potassium elixir, still looking.

"Red bottle on the top left."

Gena looked at the bottle of sticky red syrup. "I don't want a liquid, Scott! I'm over three. I can swallow pills!"

"The liquid is the only kind there."

Gena grabbed the bottle and started to read the label.

125 mg per 5 ml. Damn! Computing an adult dose of the stuff would take her all evening. Maybe even into the night.

"Two point five ml is one grain," Stoner calculated it for her.

Gena couldn't process any meaning to that.

"That makes twenty-five ml equal to ten grains," he continued.

"Jesus! Isn't there anything you think you don't know how to do better than me?" she asked him.

He started to turn away, disgusted. She didn't want him to do that. She wanted him to stand there and give her as good an argument as she felt like having.

"I think you know how to make a fool of yourself about Braxton Hershey better than me," he accommodated her, turning back, suddenly seeming more than willing to argue with her.

"It really kills you to know someone could prefer him to you, doesn't it?"

"Does he know about the baby?"

Gena picked up a plastic medicine glass and started pouring the Tylenol.

"Don't you think a guy who paid that much money for a ring deserves to know that?"

Gena set her lips in a firm hard line. Unwilling to talk about that part of her life with him. "You'll have to help me with an exchange transfusion," she said instead. "As soon as I get more blood. Please tell me you know how to do one."

He looked at her as if he were reacting poorly to being told what she wanted to do, but she didn't have time to salve his feelings. Her head was splitting and the baby was running out of time. "Can you do a transfusion or not?" she demanded.

"I've never done one. I guess I know the theory."

Gena guessed that was the best help she was going to get. "I'll get the blood—" She started to turn away. He put a hand on her shoulder to stop her.

She jumped from his touch.

"Jesus, Gena. Won't Asshole Hershey suspect something happened in your life when every time he touches you, you jump three feet?" he asked her.

Gena brushed off his hand. "I jumped because you startled me, not because you touched me."

He nodded, then put his hand back on her shoulder to stop her from moving. "If you really want to transfuse that badly," he said solemnly, "I'll get you some new blood."

Gena jumped from his hand on her again. How could he get blood? What did he know that she didn't? "You have some secreted away that you've been saving for Gallagher, don't you?" she accused him hotly. "You discovered the blood from his surgery and hid it somewhere!"

He pulled his hand back from her, crossed his arms, and spread his legs. "About the only thing I discovered is that you only jump when *I* touch you."

"Where do you have the blood?" she demanded.

He looked as if he wasn't going to answer her. Finally he said through clenched teeth, "I'll give you some of mine. I'm O negative, too."

Gena had forgotten that, although at one time in her life she had known it very well. "Why would you do that?" she demanded. Was he setting her up?

"Maybe I don't like to see babies die any more than you do."

Gena stood staring at his back as he walked away, amazed that he was willing to do that. I do only jump when you touch me, she thought, but not because I'm startled. Be-

:ause I wish your touch meant more than a fellow-resident-vake-up-and-get-moving response. I wish it meant that you :ared about me.

Jack Kissell spun the safe dial left, then right, then left again. He tried to open the door. No response. He checked off the combination on his list, spun the dial right, then left, then right again. He tried the safe door. No response. Spun again. Tried the door again. He was so used to feeling the door solidly oppose him that he almost missed the sensation that the door was opening.

He had hit the right number! He had the safe open!

A terrible thought hit him as he inched open the door. What if opening the safe triggered a silent alarm somewhere? What if right that minute a bell in the security office was clanging, announcing that he had succeeded?

No. He corrected that thought. He had watched Lynn Curtain open the safe the day before and no bells had rung. At least none that he knew of. Still a little unsure, he eased open the door the rest of the way. Far back in the safe, he could see an envelope with bank receipts; on the bottom shelf was the manila envelope Lynn Curtain had helped him place there. On the center shelf was the huge stack of money he had glimpsed over Curtain's shoulder two days before. Reverently, he pulled it out and rifled through it. One hundred, two hundred, three—a thousand, two, three—the bills seemed endless. A total of one hundred thousand. All held together with a rubber band and a hand-scribbled note: *Bastard.* No signature. But then Kissell didn't need a signature to know whose handwriting it was. He read doctor's orders every day. He recognized the slant of the letters, the almost microscopic-size printing. For a reason he didn't understand, he had been lucky enough to have gotten into th safe. The money he had—for another reason he didn't understand—belonged to Richard Culbertson.

Scott Stoner drained a unit of his own blood off in under ten minutes and was carrying it down to the basement lab in another five. He was feeling light-headed. He hadn't eaten or rested nearly enough all day to give blood comfortably.

In the lab, the technician leaning on the dutch door to the dark hole he called a work space, looked up at him, then instantly looked away again. "I need a STAT cross," Stoner said to the man's back.

"I'm not doin' a thing for you," Eddie Deer said emphatically. "You want something done, you give me back my radio."

Stoner glanced at the place on the counter where the man's ghetto blaster usually sat. Puzzled as to why the man would think *he* had it. "I don't have your radio," he said.

"I saw you take it."

Stoner unfastened the bolt that held the lower half of the door closed and walked in closer to the work counter. "I don't know anything about your radio," he said. "But I do need a STAT type and cross. Can I get it or not?"

Deer turned his back on him even more surely. "You're so damn sure you don't have my radio, you can damn well do your own cross."

Stoner took a minute to evaluate if he could do that. He'd done that as a laboratory experiment in college, but he didn't trust himself enough to risk giving blood to anyone based on what he knew. "Actually I don't need a type," he said. "This is my own blood, so I know that. I just need a cross."

"I'll show you what you can do with your blood," Deer reached over him, pulled a pair of shears out of a drawer, and slashed the plastic in two. The blood splashed onto the counter in a red blur.

"Hey!" Stoner grabbed for the split bag to save it. Too late.

"I told you," Deer said, "you want some crossed, you give me back my radio first."

"You stupid ass!" Stoner grabbed the man by the shirt collar and pushed him back against the wall. "Do you realize you just killed a baby?"

"What are you going to do to me?" Deer asked. "Cut off my fingers?"

From the strength that was holding him against the wall, Deer seemed to catch on to the seriousness of what he had done. "Dead doesn't impress me," he managed. Tough. Macho. "We're all going to be dead some day."

"You think of how I can get some more O negative blood, or I'm going to kill you!" Stoner thundered at him. "Tell me how to get some O negative blood!"

Deer looked as if he had never meant to hurt anyone, hadn't really thought about the consequences of his act. "Some patient might have O negative blood," he said, squirming under Stoner's fist. "You could get some more that way."

"The reason patients are patients, Deer, is because they're *sick.* You don't take blood from sick people!"

"All the Warrens are O negative. You could try one of them."

Stoner dropped his hand. That was true. That was how

Gena came to be O negative. "What makes you think a Warren would be that helpful?" he asked.

"A baby is going to die if one of them doesn't?" Deer asked.

"No." Stoner guessed he ought to level with the man. "He isn't going to die. He's going to live to be an old man, but he'll be so retarded he won't be able to learn to tie his shoes. So uncoordinated he won't be able to handle a fork to eat."

"Let go of me. I'll go and ask Peter Warren if he'll give blood." Deer picked up a transfusion bag off his work counter, holding the bag awkwardly, the missing fingers in his hand prominent against the counter. "If he says no, I'll ask him if I can take it from his son."

Stoner sat down on a laboratory stool and watched the man stride toward the door. "Why the change to being so cooperative?" he asked, used to having "cut off my fingers" as the man's only reply.

Deer stopped by the doorway, he looked back solemnly. "Dead I don't give a shit about," he said. "Not being able to handle a fork, I can understand."

Stoner watched him punch for the elevator and disappear into it a second later.

By the time Gena Portobello reached the second-floor nursery, Stoner was already there, ready to begin an exchange transfusion. He was standing beside a radiant-heat warmer, the Dukane baby positioned beside him. A sterile cutdown pack, syringes, needles, blood tubing—everything she'd need was arranged on a Mayo stand over the warmer.

By the time she had scrubbed and gowned, the lab had promised at least half a pack of blood would be ready, he aid. Gena watched for a second as he started to attach cardiac monitor leads, thinking, Lord, she didn't want to start that thing. She wanted the wind to suddenly change and blow all that snow off the bridge. Let Bob Haiden get in to do it. There was no chance of that happening from the whiteout blowing by the big nursery window, though. If she was going to make the attempt, she guessed she was going to have to make it with Stoner. Which meant accepting the level of responsibility that came with that. I've got it straight, Culberston, she thought grimly. I understand this is not fun and games.

By the time she was scrubbed and gloved and gowned, Stoner had the cardiac leads firmly attached to the baby's chest and was handing her a scalpel. The trick to getting that started and done safely was to locate the umbilical artery in the cord stump, then thread a catheter into it without rupturing its very thin, very easily penetrated wall. Gena picked up a catheter from the instrument pack and cut away the baby's cord clamp. A newborn's cord contained two arteries and a single vein. At birth, telling the difference between the vein and arteries was easy; as the walls of the vessels sclerosed and closed, though, distinguishing which was which grew much harder. *Make a decision,* she told herself, recutting the cord to a new depth and studying three openings that all looked alike. Pick out an artery.

Stoner stroked the baby's cheek to keep him quiet while she made up her mind. She chose the opening she thought had to be an artery and began to thread the catheter into it. The tube threaded easily for about three centimeters, then suddenly stopped.

That was all right. Fetal anatomy flashed in front of her. That was happening because the catheter was bumping the bend of the artery as it entered the abdomen. To counter that resistance, all she had to do was exert a little more pressure and the catheter would turn and enter the aorta the main vessel of the baby's body where she wanted it to end. If that wasn't the reason for the resistance, of course if she had met an abnormality of some kind or was really in a vein, not the artery, because she had picked the wrong vessel—or a hundred other things she couldn't even think of to list—her next push might send the catheter through the side of the blood vessel. The baby would start to bleed internally. She wouldn't be able to do the transfusion. The baby's bilirubin level would continue to rise. Or he would bleed to death. Game over. Sweat began pooling on her forehead from listing those things.

"Dr. Portobello, Dr. Frank is on the phone for you." A nursery aide with clicking teeth held out a telephone to Gena from the desk area. Gena couldn't take a phone wearing sterile gloves, and besides, she had to get the catheter passed. "Tell him I'll have to call him back," she said firmly.

"Dr. Frank doesn't sound as if he wants to be told that," the aide said. Click. Click. Click. "He sounds very angry."

Gena stood hesitating about what to do. If she pushed the catheter into the wrong place, she wouldn't be able to live with herself for messing that up. On the other hand, if she stood there delaying, she'd never know one way or the other if she had an artery or not. No ass-easy decision there.

She motioned the aide to bring the telephone over and hold the receiver up to her ear so she could hear what Frank had to say without touching it with her gloves.

"My son-in-law just phoned me, Portobello," said the man who administered that building of broken windows and falling plaster. "And he sounded very upset."

"Your daughter is fine, sir," Gena said, looking up at

Stoner, hoping he would nod and confirm that was so, worried that something could have happened in the last few minutes that neither of them knew about. His daughter was an entire floor down from where they were.

"William is upset that Leslie isn't making more progress," Frank continued.

Gena was upset that the men shoveling out the bridge weren't making more progress, but she bit her lip and didn't say that. She was equally anxious to get that transfusion started. To see if she could do it before Appleton learned that she had more blood and took it. The lab tech hadn't delivered any more blood yet, so maybe Ape had already taken it. Overhead, she heard a creaking sound and a ceiling crack crept visibly farther out into the room. "Dr. Frank?" She felt a necessity to talk about more important problems with him than his daughter's early labor. "The ceiling is this building is cracking badly. Is this building safe in this wind?"

"How do you mean cracking?"

"Plaster is cracking. I think that the whole Swamp—"

"Please, Portobello," Frank returned impatiently. "Why do I always have to remind house staff of that facility's right name?"

"I think the A Building of wherever this is, sir," Gena said, "is beginning to twist apart."

"I know house staff doesn't like the extension facility, Portobello, but your judgment of buildings—"

"I'm not talking judgment! I'm talking about broken windows and plaster falling down as if this building twists sideways every time the wind hits it!"

Frank cleared his throat. Paused a long moment. "I'll have to call you back," he said quietly. And hung up his telephone.

Gena waited for the aide to take the phone away from her ear. For better or worse, she thought, she touched the umbilical catheter again and gave it a gentle push. It slid free of the obstruction into the abdominal aorta. When she looked up, Stoner was holding an empty syringe and bilirubin tube out to her. Gena didn't take either of them. She was confused about what she was supposed to do with them.

"A lot of people take a beginning baseline level of blood," Stoner said.

That was teaching talk for, the *first* thing you should do, dummy, is draw off some blood to show where the level is when you begin, so you'll know what you have accomplished, when you are finished. "Right." Gena fitted the syringe to the catheter and pulled back for blood. The catheter worked easily. Certainly a good sign. As she finished, Eddie Deer appeared at her elbow with a plastic blood pack in his hand. He huddled with Stoner about the cross match. "After all those people have taken a baseline, are they ready to transfuse?" she had to interrupt Stoner to ask him.

Stoner nodded, making an OK sign with his fingers to the lab tech. The lab tech put the blood up on the warmer and left to talk to the aide with clicking teeth. Gena picked up a second syringe and removed five ml of blood from the collecting bag. She started to add it to the baby's bloodstream through the catheter. The baby's heartbeat jumped and pounded for a second before it steadied.

"Phone for you, Dr. Stoner." The clicking-teeth aide held the phone up to Stoner's ear the same way she had to Gena's, and he leaned sideways to talk to whomever was calling him. That would be Frank calling back to see if anyone else thought the building was in trouble, Gena guessed.

"When are you going to get here?" Margo Torning demanded in Stoner's ear.

Stoner looked pained. He started to turn away from the lephone, then apparently changed his mind. "This is a ad time to talk, Margo," he said to her. "I'm in the mid-le of something."

"A woman just called here, Scott," Margo sounded as if he wanted to talk very much, "and called me names. For eing here."

Stoner looked up at Gena, as if he wondered if it had een she. As if she kept track of everyone he slept with.

Margo blew her nose with such a loud honking sound it carried over the line. "You are coming home soon, aren't you?" she asked. "I've been waiting for you for almost a whole day."

"I'll be the first one over the bridge when it's clear, Margo. I promise." Stoner looked at the monitor to see if the baby's vital signs were still OK. "But now, I really have to go."

"I love you, Scott," Margo seemed to miss his message that he didn't want to talk to her. "And I wanted this to be a very special day for us. I found some wine. The two of us could have just stayed here in bed all day."

Stoner continued to concentrate on the monitor, still frowning.

Gena studied the readout, decided after a long look that Scott was definitely frowning at what Margo was saying, not at anything he was reading on the monitor.

"Instead, I'm here by myself, and I'm lonely as hell," Margo continued. "I'm being shouted at by a strange woman. I can't stop sneezing because of your cat—"

"I have to go, Margo. Honest." Stoner insisted. "I'll get back to you, when I'm through here. But she probably wasn't a strange woman. It was probably my wife."

"You're sure you'll call me back?" Margo asked.

''Promise.'' Stoner pulled back from the telephone receiver and worked silently at pulling up a second supply of
blood for Gena. The baby's heartbeat jumped again as Gena
injected it. She felt her hand begin to tremble as she started
the cycle over again. She remembered what Culbertson had
said—that the danger to the baby grew more and more haz-
ardous as the procedure went on, because the heart was
asked to adjust time and time again to lesser, then greater
blood volumes. No comment from Stoner on anything. Just
quietly keeping track of the total blood exchange. Vital
signs. Heart monitor readout. Keeping the baby still.

''Phone again, Dr. Stoner,'' the nursing aide held the
phone up for Stoner again. The silence became intense.

That would be David Frank, Gena thought. Angry, she
hoped, because she was been worrying about the structure
of that building, when he claimed there wasn't anything to
worry about. Instead of Dr. Frank, though, she heard Sue
Ellen shouting at Stoner.

''I called our house to see if you were home yet, Scott,
and a girl answered! Do you know there is a girl at our
house?''

Good God, Gena thought. A baby could die in front of
them, and the woman was calling to lecture her husband on
something she knew he did all the time. ''I'm in the middle
of something, Sue Ellen,'' Stoner began again. ''I can't
talk.''

''The girl—''

''I'm in the middle of something, Sue Ellen!''

Sue Ellen clicked a glass against her receiver. ''I don't
know how much longer you expect me to put up with your
acting this way, Scott! My nerves are shot. If it wasn't for
Ed Cronkin next door bringing me over some spiced
tea—''

"What are you spicing it with?" Stoner asked.

"Don't tell me I drink too much! If you were home trying o watch kids in this lousy storm, you'd be drinking, too!"

Stoner helped with another exchange, not saying anyhing.

"The least you could do is take me to a party tonight, to nake up for everything you've done to me." Sue Ellen licked her glass against her phone one more time before she slammed it down. Stoner twisted his head free to add up the total amount of blood Gena had removed and injected. He looked up from his column of figures, as if there were a different step she needed to take at that point. But he didn't tell her what it was.

Gena looked over the setup, satisfied the baby was hanging in very well. "I give up," she said.

"You need to add some calcium gluconate to counteract the action of the preservative in the blood," he said.

A good point. If the baby's calcium level wasn't protected by some means, it would fall so low from the reaction of the blood preservative that the baby would start to convulse. And develop brain damage from hypocalcemia. Her cure would be worse than his original condition.

The nursery aide came back and Gena turned her back on her, afraid that she had the phone in her hand again. Instead, she said she was there to tell her that the third floor was out of prednisone and needed a doctor to get a dose from the pharmacy. She also wondered if she could sit down for a while. Her back and legs ached.

"This might go faster—so all of us can be free sooner—" Gena said to Stoner, "if you didn't spend most of your time talking on the telephone."

"Are you angry because I've been talking on the telephone, or because part of the time I was talking to someone at my house?'' he asked her. ''If you wouldn't spend a your time keeping track of who I'm currently fucking, you' have a lot more time.''

''I don't control who you talk to,'' Gena said. ''Or who you fuck.''

''Some people are interested in knowing whether they are sexually as well as intellectually suited for each other before they make any long-term agreements.'' Stoner stopped working to make that point. ''Believe it or not, it's done all the time.''

The baby started crying and Gena reached to place a hand on his abdomen to keep him from turning. She tried to keep from looking amused. ''What intellectual agreement do you have in mind with Margo Torning?'' she asked. ''Under Margo's fall-back-into-place hair, she has the intelligence of a toad.''

''Not jealous of her, are you?'' Stoner asked.

''Of course I'm jealous.''

Stoner frowned at her as if she were trying to set him up.

''I'm jealous of everyone on the other side of the bridge,'' Gena finished.

Stoner withdrew some more blood silently. All in all, Gena would have to replace about eighty percent of the baby's blood. Despite all the time she'd put into that already, the process was only a quarter done. Stoner worked beside her for ten more minutes without a word, until a blast of wind shook the room so hard a six-inch strip of plaster fell down, pounding onto bassinets and the floor around them like grenades going off, sending a cloud of plaster dust and splinters across the room.

Why wasn't David Frank calling back to assure them that despite the fact the building seemed to be falling apart, it was really all right, Gena wondered. What if he had discovered that something was structurally wrong with that building, but couldn't get through?

"Margo is at my house," Stoner returned to talking, "because the only good thing about what's left between Sue Ellen and myself is that she doesn't jump when I touch her."

Gena didn't need his aggravation. "You could do better by her," she said. "Things like last July—"

"It would never enter your mind, would it?" Stoner asked, "To think that maybe Sue Ellen cheated on me first."

Gena felt her cheeks flush. Because obviously that had not occurred to her. She thought of him as the one at fault. "If your marriage is so bad," she suggested, because she didn't believe that, "why don't you divorce her?"

"I don't know what would happen to the children. Sue Ellen isn't always sober enough to take care of them."

That was an excuse not to take responsibility. The kind of thing Culbertson had accused them both of. "A lot of men get custody of their children today," Gena said.

"They're not my children."

Gena froze, needing to start another exchange. Stoner nodded that the cardiac monitor was all right. She could go on.

"Whose children are they?" she asked.

"Whoever was in a bar on the same night that Sue Ellen happened to be in, nine months before each of them was born."

"You don't know that," Gena said critically. She wasn't used to thinking that Scott Stoner might have redeeming qualities; might have something positive going for him, such as knowing they weren't his children, but being a better father to them than Sue Ellen was a mother.

"Why do you think that isn't true?"

"How can I trust you? You lie to people all the time."

"You can believe they aren't my children."

Gena didn't believe anything he said to her.

"The night of the train station, when one of those men sliced a knife into my abdomen?" Stoner asked. "You want to know what it hit?"

Gena felt her eyes widen. She knew the man couldn't have been castrated, or she wouldn't have had to scream outside the recovery room like a jealous witch six months ago.

"Not that bad," he assured her, allowing himself a cracked smile. "But I have a lot of broken connections. I've been sterile since I was sixteen."

Gena had never known that. How was it that everything in their lives always went back to that night? That nothing had ever been right with either of them since then?

"I married Sue Ellen because she was pregnant. I *thought* with my child."

Did that mean he had never felt much for Sue Ellen? That maybe he had loved Gena more, but married Sue Ellen because of the baby? Gena felt her heart jump. If she had told him that Mark Warren was his, would he have married *her?* Why couldn't she have been as savvy as Sue Ellen to have realized that? To have made that ploy?

"How do you know the baby wasn't yours?" she asked.

"Blood type."

That was possible. With O negative blood, the types of blood his children could have were limited.

The ceiling beam over Gena's head creaked and groaned again, bringing her mind back to where they were. That had to be a main ceiling support groaning! If that let go, the whole floor above them would break through.

"David Frank is on line three for you," the aide came back to the table with the telephone and held it out to Gena's ear, looking exhausted from the effort.

"Portobello,-" Frank's voice carried to her, very subdued. Very serious. "I have talked to the engineer who designed the support columns for those buildings, last year. He is a very reliable man. He has assured me that if we followed his specifications exactly in construction, that building is in no danger, no matter what the wind velocity."

So why had cracking that had started on the fourth floor of that building now spread to the second? Why was a ceiling beam over her head sinking lower and lower every second? A beam that so obviously held up the three floors above that one?

"However, on the possibility some danger does exist, Gena," the man continued smoothly, "I'll order that building closed next week."

Think, Gena commanded her brain. How could a building be absolutely safe one minute, and yet there be some possibility it was not the next? Able to be open one week and not the next? Which was which? Maybe more important, why had Frank just called her by her first name? He never did that with residents. He always called her Portobello, as surely as he called that building by its complete name. "*Were* his specifications followed exactly?" she asked. She waited to be blasted by him for questioning his recommendation. "Sometimes, no one thinks the Swamp—"

"The name of that facility is—"

"*Were* his specifications followed exactly?" Gena shouted. When two stories of the hospital had crashed down on her head, it wouldn't make a damn lot of difference what all that cement and steel had been named.

David Frank sounded as if he were choking on something. On a resident having the audacity to question his judgment, she guessed. Nice going, Portobello, she thought. Really putting your foot in it good here. If the man had any doubt that you were an ass prior to this conversation, he certainly has had that confirmed for him now. Except that she could see the beam above her head sinking lower and lower from the weight above.

"I can't reach the company that did the construction," Frank returned to the telephone as if he were trying to answer that question. "Bob Haiden did the actual request for the work to be done. I have to believe that he didn't order any corners cut."

"What would be the advantage of doing that?"

Gena knew Frank was still there because she could hear him breathing. But he didn't answer. He just didn't expect his residents to question things that way, she guessed.

Gena tried to think through the answer herself. She had talked to Haiden one night about funds for the laboratory space. How so much of the total sum had been earmarked into maintaining A building, that there had been no money left for equipping D Building for research space. William Kerr had said that the money offered to him to do the cement columns hadn't been much. What if Haiden had spent the money for cement columns to buy laboratory equipment instead?

"Do you have any reason to think that money went for equipment in D Building rather than cement over here?" Gena asked.

"Of course not, Gena," Frank returned surely. "D Building is just empty space waiting for me to locate more contributions."

"How can I get into D Building?" Gena asked him. "To check if that's true?"

"You can't get in there. All that new laboratory space is locked."

"Dr. Frank!" she thundered at him. "Tell me how to get into D Building!"

Heavy breathing again on the other end of the telephone. Or reluctant breathing. She couldn't decide.

"Your daughter is in this building, Dr. Frank! Earlier, you tried to get her moved, but couldn't. You wouldn't have been trying to move her because you were worried that there might be something wrong with this building, were you?"

"No. Believe me. I trust Bob Haiden. Implicitly."

"I'll ask security to open up D Building for me. I'll go and look at it."

Frank seemed to struggle with that thought. Then conceded that it was not a totally bad idea. "I'll call one of them for you," he said. "To open up for you."

Gena jerked her head away from the telephone and started working on the final exchanges of blood. If D Building was equipped, it would mean that the cement columns which were supposed to be reinforcing this building, were as crumbly as piecrust. Which meant that the force of the wind outside was registering on the original frame and not on the columns at all. On a building rated as structurally unsound over a year before. Her hand started to shake thinking about that. Stoner reached a hand to steady hers—and she jumped from the sudden quick contact with him.

"Jesus, Gena!" he drew back his hand quickly. "You can't hate me forever because I couldn't stop you from being raped. I was sixteen!"

Gena sucked in her breath, trying to keep from thinking

about that night. "I don't hold you responsible for tha night," she said.

His blue eyes searched her face. "Your trouble is you didn't let that night end," he said. "You had a baby. And of all dumb things, I can't believe you didn't have it aborted. Knowing who the father was."

He didn't know anything about what she had been thinking. He had been too busy screwing Sue Ellen Morrison the minute she left town. "I thought I might want it," she said.

He raised his eyebrows as if she were hopeless. *"Nobody* wants a baby from rape, Gena. That's pathological."

"I thought it might be your baby. From the week before."

Stoner's face whitened. He concentrated for a moment on looking at the almost empty blood pack. As if that thought had never occurred to him, but now that it had, he didn't like it very much. "How did you know it wasn't?" he asked weakly, looking away at the desk area as he handed her the final syringe of blood from the pack. As if he really didn't want to know the answer.

"By blood type. The only possible blood type a baby the two of us could have had would have been O negative. Culbertson typed him. He was B positive."

Stoner's job was done. He watched her intently as she began the last exchange.

"You want the whole story?" she insisted. "The Warren boy is the baby. The reason Peter Perfect doesn't want me anywhere near him doesn't have anything to do with a botched aspirin order! It is because he knows Mark is my son."

"Mark Warren?" Stoner asked.

"Not over an hour ago, I saw the birthmark on his foot."

"A birthmark is not much proof! I told you that before!"

"I'm not wrong. Richard Culbertson confirmed it for me."

Stoner's face had drained to a stark white. "You've got to be wrong!" he insisted.

"When you think about it, Mark has my green eyes—"

"We're using his blood!"

Gena dropped the syringe she was holding. Thinking what that meant. First of all, it was impossible. Because if she was putting B positive blood into an A positive baby, she was killing him. "You said this was *your* blood," she protested.

"The lab tech ruined mine. So he replaced it with Mark Warren's! He said he knew all the Warrens have O negative blood."

Gena grabbed the empty blood pack and turned it so she could read the label: Written in a left-hand script, it read, "Mark Warren." Shit! She had just administered 250 ml of the wrong type blood to a seven-pound baby. There was no way the infant could survive that shock. The wrong type cells would clot in his veins and stop his heart and kidneys and brain. There was no way out. Step by step, while he talked on the telephone, and she criticized him, they had killed a potentially very normal, very bright baby.

"It might be right," Stoner said. "All the Warrens do have O negative."

"I just told you Mark Warren's blood type! Even if I'm wrong—even if he wasn't the baby from that night—I know he's adopted! What are the chances he's O negative?"

Stoner picked up the blood pack to read the label one more time, as if he could make the type change to O negative if he only read it enough times.

"Put the baby back under the lights for me!" Gena barked at him, stripping off her gloves. What a stupid, stupid man he was! Accusing *her* for being at fault for assuming things, and now letting a lab tech assume a blood type! She tore off her gown and took off down the south stairway of A Building to the basement tunnel that lead to D Building. At the end of the short tunnel, she jerked open the door the guard had unlocked for her and stared in at an expensively furnished lobby area; red leather chairs, steel and glass tables, an area in the center which would be, when it was filled and operating, a fountain and collecting pool. The whole thing looking like something out of a public relations suite, not a sparse research lab.

The first three side doors along the hallway that Gena tried were locked. As she put her hand on the fourth one, Stoner came up behind her and jerked it open. Inside, Gena could see three rows of laboratory counters stretched across the room with microscopes standing on them about every four feet. Not simple microscopes. Fiber optic viral ones. Each one of those cost more than Gena made in a year, she bet. Along the wall stood five spectrophotometers, each looking more like a space age computer than the one in the present lab. Even the countertops, the equipment racks filled with endless numbers of test tubes and measuring cylinders, the overhead lights, the Bunsen burners looked expensive. Gena hadn't even known that you could find expensive Bunsen burners.

She left Stoner staring at an equipment rack and strode back to the main lobby. She grabbed the desk telephone and punched familiar numbered buttons to reach Bod Haiden at home.

He answered after five insistent rings.

"This is Gena, Bob. I'm over in D Building."

"Hey! You're not supposed to be over there, Gena," he interrupted her quickly. "That's all new lab space."

"In all my life, Bob, I have never seen such an elaborate .b setup as this. You told me there was nothing over here, nd yet it's completely furnished."

"Yeah, it is nice, isn't it?" he asked. Behind him, a female voice purred. "Feel good?"

"I didn't do bad for a little black kid from Harlem, did ?" Bob added.

"I'm calling, Bob," Gena hoped he was paying enough ttention to her to be able to comprehend quickly what she vas saying, "Because A Building is cracking like hell! Is he money that was supposed to be in A Building's cement olumns over in this lab space?"

The voice behind Bob said, "Come on, hang up. You can talk later."

"Hit me with that again, Gena," Bob laughed, as if someone were tickling his ribs. "I missed what you said."

"Every floor in A building is cracking as if it's coming apart, Bob. How much of the money for cement really went into the columns?"

"Stop it, Jennifer?" Bob hissed to the person with him and came back to the phone. "I'm sorry, Gena, but you've caught me at a bad time here. *Stop it, Jennifer!*" he shouted loudly, but not very firmly, laughing again. *"Wait 'til I get off the phone."*

Gena leaned back against the lab counter. Feeling very tired. Thinking how she had always been envious of Bob Haiden. He had a cute son who liked to play with him; a wife who obviously enjoyed going to bed with him; he had a firm future at one of the most prestigious centers in the country nailed down. What more could anyone want?

"Bob—please." Gena heard her voice growing desperate. "I have to know about A Building."

Haiden's voice came back more serious, finally sounding

as if he comprehended why he was being called. "You car blame me for anything, Portobello. I had no way of know ing a storm this bad would come up." He started to sour panicky. "It wasn't predicted. Or if it *was* predicted, I didn know about it."

"Are the support columns here good or not, Bob? *Answ me!"*

Haiden mumbled something she couldn't catch.

"What did you say? she shouted at him.

"The support columns won't hold in anything over sixty-mile-an-hour wind," he said softly.

There had been seventy-mile-an-hour winds hitting tha building for the last twenty-four hours. "We should get ou of A Building, shouldn't we, Bob?" she asked.

"Stop it, Jennifer! For God's sake, *stop it!"* Haiden shoutec at his wife. "You have to understand what is going on Gena," he said to her. "I couldn't see putting any more money than necessary into patching up a hole like the Swamp. Not when it could be spent for equipment I needed in the lab area."

Gene dropped the phone receiver, picked it back up again immediately, and dialed David Frank. Frank answered so quickly, he must have been waiting all that time with his hand still settled on the phone waiting for her to call.

"Haiden says the cement is worthless in A Building against a seventy-mile-an-hour wind, Dr. Frank," she said. "And there's been a wind that strong for twelve hours."

"Better get people out!" Frank snapped. A man conditioned to making sudden decisions. "You'll find emergency evacuation routes for the Swamp buildings posted—"

Gena started to drop her telephone receiver on him, because no one needed special instructions on how to get to the basement tunnels. Everyone knew where they were, be-ause they used them all the time. She stopped with the receiver a hairsbreadth away from disconnect, unable to believe the last of what she had just heard him say. *"The name of this place is the Sylvester A. Warren Medical Pavilion!"* she shouted into the receiver, feeling some small comfort at having found the administrator with his pants down. She realized, as she ran for the tunnel again, that it would have been better to have found out that the cement columns in A Building were sturdy and could hold up under any kind of stress.

Stoner hadn't believed, when he followed Gena over to the D Building lab, that they were going to find it filled with equipment. Or that A Building was really that unstable. He grabbed the telephone on the lab desk across from Gena and dialed Murphy on the third floor to tell her to evacuate children into C Building.

"This building is creaking and groaning like it's coming apart," Murphy said. In the background there was a loud crash and a child started crying. "I think the whole ceiling is coming down! My God, a ceiling beam just fell in the hallway!"

"Get the kids into C Building through the tunnel!" he shouted at her.

Beside Stoner, Gena started to run toward the stairway, calling over her shoulder that she would tell the second floor to clear out. Stoner dialed Debbie Chemielewski on the fourth floor and told her the same thing he had told Murphy. "Something's happened in the lockup," Debbie said. "A second ago, there was a big crash in there. And now everyone is screaming."

Stoner took off for the south stairway of A Building. He

stopped as he ran past the first floor to call to Sally Yates tell her to clear out. She was standing by the labor de listening to the television set describe preparations in Tim Square for the New Year's Eve celebration starting in a other few hours. Stoner grabbed her shoulders to be certa he had her attention, and then ran past her to the secor floor. He stood at the top of the stairs, as Murphy, carryir a crying toddler—three children and a parent following b hind her—hurried past him on the stairway. "Anyone kno where Lynn Curtain is?" Stoner shouted after her.

"I haven't seen her for hours," Murphy answered. "Sh must be lying down somewhere."

Up on the fourth floor, Stoner helped Chemielewski an an aide push Grishaven's bed onto the elevator. In the roor where Dan Gallagher had been, he glanced at a pile of plas ter rubble where the entire ceiling had fallen in. Lucky mar to have been taken over to B Building and not have beer under that, he thought. He stood fumbling with his lockuj keys. Immediately inside the entrance foyer of the lockup freezing cold struck his face. From the nurse's desk he coulc see that part of the hallway wall had torn away; snow anc cold wind were blowing in through the ripped open portion. A gaunt-looking man, the one who thought there was nothing left to do in life, was standing in the hallway shivering in loose hospital pajamas, his bare feet almost covered with blowing snow. The girl who had tried to commit suicide because her parents were divorcing, her hair pulled back into a blond stringy ponytail, was standing straight backed against the hallway wall. The woman who was sure everyone was talking about her was staring at the hole in the wall. How terrible, Stoner thought, to have difficulty separating out reality from whatever was happening in your ınd on a good day. How scary when reality became even ɔre frightening than your imagination.

Fairy Tale Mary seemed to be in charge of people in the ay room: six men and two women. She had everyone there ated in chairs at the center table and was talking about eakfast being served soon, as if nothing unusual had hap- ened. "Where's the nurse?" Stoner demanded of her. The urse shouldn't have left her patients alone that way.

Everyone seemed to look at everyone else and no one nswered. *Jesus, Stoner, why are you asking questions, as if you pect answers from these people,* he asked himself. They are here ecause they have trouble with answers. Some of them have rouble with questions.

"The nurse left," the man in loose pajamas said helpfully s Stoner turned to urge people toward the stairway. 'Through the wall."

There was a uniform nodding of heads around the table. Agreement among all of them that that was what had hap- pened. "Come on," Stoner waved for people to start down he stairway. The man in bare feet didn't want to leave the nallway. The eighteen-year-old girl started screaming.

"It's all right." Stoner pushed the man ahead of him, took Crazy Mary's arm. "It's warm in C Building; go to get warm." He ran after them down the stairway, on a hunch he strode back through the back corridor, opening doors to resident sleeping rooms as he went. He found Richard Culbertson sleeping in the first room. Roughly—no time for special treatment—he woke him and told him to get over to C Building. Out by the nurse's desk, a ceiling beam had fallen and plaster dust had rained down, obscuring his view. He wanted to check the last room, a room nurses used for charting. He didn't know if it had a bed in it or not, but originally it had been a sleeping room, so he guessed might.

Sitting on the edge of the cot there—looking stunned all the confusion around her—was Lynn Curtain. She h to be aware that plaster was falling down all around t building. No one could miss that. It was like the sound a hundred gunshots. But she seemed too tired to be able pull herself to her feet.

"Come on, Lynn." Stoner offered a hand to help her u "We have to get out of here."

"I can't." She shook her head and tried to lie down agai her face taut with pain. "It hurts too much to move."

"The roof is falling in. You *have* to move."

He took her hand and pulled her to her feet. She walke as far as the doorway with him, then stopped again with new surge of pain.

"Are you in labor?" Stoner asked her. That would mak her two months early, a complication he hadn't expected "No." She leaned heavily against the stair rail and edge herself on down into the basement tunnel. "Just so tired it's hard to move."

Stoner ran the stairs again to the second floor and glance in at the nursery. It was empty of babies. Out by the foyer, Gena was just pushing the Isolette of one of the Dukane twins into the elevator. "This is the last," she called back to him. He ducked back into the stairwell. "This is the last from Three." Murphy said, hurrying past him in the stairway, a boy in one arm, a toddler crying and kicking under the other.

Stoner grabbed the toddler from her and ran with her down into the C Building tunnel. He turned to go back to the fourth floor; he was sure Peggy Ferris wasn't out yet.

There was a final loud tearing sound. He looked at a

nter wall and saw it crumble and lean; chunks of plaster ıd tile and wood supports rained down. The cement sup- ›rts were giving way. Plaster and steel, and what had been alls and floor, began to crumble inward. The fourth floor ⸗ A Building crashed down through all the other levels into ıe basement, smothering everything under layers of plaster ıd steel as it came.

Jack Kissel had heard Gena Portobello shouting for ev- ryone to get out of A Building into the tunnel.

He didn't pay any attention because it wouldn't be safe ɔr him to leave Frank's office. If he left before the bridge ṿas clear, people would see him. The next day, when they ıiscovered the money missing, they would remember he ıad been there. If he stayed in the office no one would ever ːnow he had been there.

Up above him, he heard a distant rumbling sound, like ı freight train roaring down on top of him. Kissell looked ıp and saw the ceiling begin to crack. A moment too late, ıe realized what was happening.

A steel beam crashed down onto the marble-topped desk and split it in two. Kissell stared at the way the marble was cleanly halved, as if a sculptor had been readying it for a statue. He didn't see the second steel beam that struck him on the head or observe his own skull open with the same ease that the desk had split. He didn't see, either, that with death, his hand opened, releasing the hundred thousand dollars. Bill by bill, the money was swept upward by the wind, like a thousand Bird Island gulls startled into flight.

Chapter Eleven

Scott Stoner looked around the C Building basement, now jammed with patients from A Building. Halfway down the crowded hallway, the path was blocked by four patients in beds. Stoner couldn't see Leslie Kerr among them and hoped that someone had had the good sense to take her up to the third-floor surgery suite, ironically just where David Frank had wanted her moved hours before. On his right he could see Dawn Brady, the nursery nurse from 2A, plugging in one of the Dukane twins' Isolettes. In front of him, two mothers were holding crying babies. To his left, children from the third floor were huddled into a group and parents and aides were trying to quiet them. Mark Warren was standing at the far end of the hallway next to his mother. Fairy Tale Mary was standing in the doorway of the nurse's locker room with a group from the lockup, an elaborate curly blond wig pulled down onto her head.

"Where's my other baby?" a quiet voice asked by Stoner's elbow. Good point, he thought. He should take a firm count; any one left behind in the building would have been killed. He could spot everyone from the lockup, he was sure, because he knew exactly how many patients had been up here. He couldn't remember Medicine A's census off the top of his head, but he didn't see Peggy Ferris or Evelyn Corning anywhere. There was a possibility that Debbie had not been able to get them out. He had trouble breathing, thinking how scared Evelyn Corning must have felt watching a ceiling crashing down on her head, unable to speak. Trusting them to keep her safe because she could not call for help. Then not safe.

Debbie Chemielewski, the little nurse from 4A was there, bending over Howard Grishaven's bed, fussing with his fluid line.

"Where's my other baby?" the quiet voice beside Stoner asked again. Right, he thought. Newborns. That would make an easy count. There should have been four who were in bassinets. He located them in the crowd. One twin in his Isolette. The other twin—the one he and Gena has just transfused—he couldn't see.

"Dr. Portobello went back to get him," Dawn Brady said, counting beside him. "When I last looked, she was waiting for the elevator with the Isolette."

Stoner had seen her pushing the baby onto the elevator. But where was she now?

Off to the side of the hallway, the C Building elevator opened and Zack Appleton with about ten men—visitors, maintenance men, a medical resident from B Building—spilled out into the hallway. "What happened?" Appleton demanded. He started to run into the tunnel to A Building, then stopped as he looked at the pile of crumbled walls and floors and plaster and snow.

Stoner followed him to the entrance of the tunnel and pulled a couple of boards free to see if the whole building had come down or not. He was hoping there was a chance

that Gena and an Isolette could still be safe up there. H
peered into blowing snow, almost pushed back by the forc
of the wind. In front of him he recognized pieces of yellov
tile from the fourth floor. A medicine cabinet marked 2A
A lockup bed. The elevator had to be buried somewhere i
the center of that, he guessed, under snarling electric cord
and pieces of flooring. Could Gena still be in it?

"Portobello might be in the elevator," he said to Ape.

Two men behind Appleton crowded in to see how everything looked. In front of them, an electrical cable flashed
sparks as it was moved by the wind. Another overhead beam
loosened and fell. "I could cut off the power to there," a
maintenance man said. "So you could move those cables."

Appleton's face had turned white from just the few minutes he had been standing there letting snow blow against
him. For one more moment he stared at the heaped pile of
rubble in front of him, then bent and started to lift and
throw aside everything in his path as he forced his way in
toward the elevator. Working along beside him, Stoner
watched the man lift pieces of fallen furniture and throw
them out of his way, pieces that Stoner would have sworn
it should have taken two men to lift.

About ten feet short of the elevator, Stoner raised his
head from helping lift a shattered toilet, and recognized the
sound of a baby crying. Ape raised his head and shouted
for Gena. There was no answer from inside the elevator,
just the baby's continuous crying. Maybe just the baby was
in there, Stoner reasoned. Maybe Gena was still up on the
floor and was safe. He glanced up through jagged steel supports and twisted metal, saw nothing but black sky and
blowing snow. That was impossible. There was no second
floor above him to be safe *on.* If Gena wasn't in the elevator,

he was dead. If she was inside the elevator, she could still e dead. She didn't answer.

The Ape tossed aside an examining table, a crib, and a oom sink to reach the elevator and literally ripped away its loor. Shouldering everyone else aside, he stretched inside and tore open the sideways Isolette. He lifted out the baby and handed him to a maintenance man behind him to run back to the C Building basement. Appleton disappeared again immediately into the black hole of the elevator while everyone waited. It seemed a long time before he straightened again and lifted Gena out. Her hair was filled with plaster dust and wet from snow and blood. Her blouse was blood-stained; her skirt smeared with grease from an elevator cable. Rapidly, Ape bent into a blast of wind and strode past Stoner, carrying her into C Building. Stoner stood at the entrance to the tunnel unable to move while Ape carried her past him. Because from the first quick glance—the way her eyes were closed and her head hung to the side—it was obvious to him that she was dead.

Never good enough for White Horse people—always an oddity to them—she had just been killed because of their carelessness. Trying to extend the life of a building whose days should have ended the fall before.

Only that couldn't be! Stoner couldn't go on with Gena dead. He turned to do what he knew needed to be done. He should take the baby upstairs and examine him. He had to be cold, and cold killed newborns. He might have a head injury from the Isolette tipping. He might need oxygen . . . although, what was the sense? That baby was going to die from kidney failure before morning from receiving the wrong blood type anyway. He found himself standing frozen, watching soundlessly as Appleton strode the length of the tunnel to C Building carrying Gena. He hated himself for never fighting hard enough for her, never telling her that he loved her. And now he couldn't do that.

"Sally Yates must still be in there somewhere." Ethel Murphy gripped Stoner's arm to get his attention. She moved to stand beside him in the blowing cold, turning her head to search for any sign of a white uniform in the mound of junk that had been floors and ceilings only minutes before.

Sally would have been on the first floor, Stoner reasoned. Which was terrible. Because if she *had* been there, she was now covered by the weight of the entire building. Maybe she was up in C Building with Leslie Kerr and out of there. Maybe that's why no one could find her. She would have gone with the Kerrs, certainly—.

"William Kerr says she left them in the basement of C Building and went back for their coats," Murphy said.

The group of men beside Stoner began lifting up debris again, searching farther into the pile of rubble. Past a scrub sink Stoner had leaned against the evening before when the twins had been born, chagrined by the pop-up of a rubber mouse; past a cupboard marked 3A. Past a broken copper plaque of half of the profile of Sylvester Warren's head and the word ENDURING.

"I see her!" a man in a red mackinaw coat shouted. He pointed toward a pile of rubbish near what had been a sack-out room. The man straightened and shielded his eyes against blowing snow to peer closer. "Jesus—it's only the top half of somebody."

Stoner looked over the man's shoulder, and then pushed past him. Because it definitely was Sally he had spotted. She was lying on her back under a mound of fallen ceiling tiles, pinned there by a fallen ceiling beam. He knelt beside her and started to brush plaster dust off her face. She was alive.

She blinked as he crouched under a teetering overhead steel beam and lifted up her head to free it from so much dirt. Her hair was dirty from plaster dust. Jesus, he thought. If there was anything Sally Yates hated, it was dirty hair. She washed it every day no matter what.

She looked up at him anxiously, clutching at Leslie Frank Kerr's sealskin coat in her hand. "I can't feel my legs," she said. Her eyes glazed, went out of focus, focused again. Blood from intestinal bleeding filled her mouth and she coughed it free. "Will I be all right?"

Stoner started to try and lift her free of the beam, then stopped. The lower half of her body was completely covered by the beam. Her pelvis had to be broken, he reasoned. The plaster dust under her was soaked with blood . . . her back might be broken . . .

"Of course, you're going to be OK, Sally." He stretched forward to try to estimate better her total damage, to see how bad it was going to be to move the beam. Then he saw what the maintenance man had first seen. Sally's legs had been cut off by the beam. They were separated from her body by at least six inches. Only the pressure of the beam against her pelvis was keeping blood from gushing out of her broken body and killing her. No matter what he did, she was minutes away from death. Left there, she would die of exposure. If he moved her, she would hemorrhage. Either way, he was helpless to do anything to save her.

"Move it, Stoner!" the Ape burst through the corps of maintenance men. "That beam over your head is about to let go!"

"We can't move her," Stoner said.

"You have to move her!" Ape insisted. He pushed his way up beside Sally: triage chief. "If you don't, when the beam comes down, it'll crush her." He looked down at

Sally, then didn't seem able to close his mouth as he realiz the problem. He wasn't enjoying being a triage officer an more. He knew that if he said to move her, it would k her. If he said to leave her alone, it would kill her. He stoo silent rather than say anything more.

"Scott?" Sally turned her head to look up again. She wa operating under shock, from some body command to kee functioning, even when it had almost nothing to functio with. "Are you sure I'm going to be all right?"

"Sure," Stoner answered, reaching and squeezing he hand.

She turned to try and loosen the coat under her. Th movement sent at least a quart or more of blood gushin out of her. Helplessly, she collapsed back against Stoner' hands as everything important to her body—heart, lungs and brain—ceased to function.

"Better move it back, Stoner." Appleton said very quietly. "Before the beam overhead breaks loose."

Stoner lifted what was left of Sally's body, wrapped it in the white coyote coat over her, and fighting against wind, carried it inside.

"Get that baby inside checked over! Let me know how you think he is!" Appleton had regained his former sergeant's tactics by the time Stoner reached the C Building basement and handed Sally's broken body to a maintenance man to take upstairs.

Stoner didn't move any farther than the tunnel entrance. He was determined to stand there in the hallway forever, because until he moved, until he made that moment pass, he could pretend that nothing had happened to Gena Portobello.

"Stoner! For Christ sake, get the lead out!" Appleton

outed at him. "I'm triage officer here! When I tell you to ove, you move!"

For what, Stoner asked himself. Everything he had ever anted was over. He had no job anymore. Gena was dead . . .

"Move! Move it! Move it!" Ape plunked a hand down n Stoner's shoulder and shoved him forward. Numbly, toner rode up to the third floor and let Lori Dukane lay er first twin up on the table in the anesthesiologist's inuction room for him to examine. Amazingly, the baby was kay. He wasn't even as cold as Stoner thought he would e. A sturdy fellow. Although ultimately that wasn't going help him. His kidneys *had* to be failing right that minute. Getting ready to kill him. He'd be dead by morning from he wrong transfusion.

The induction room was littered with bagged but not renoved garbage. Stoner straightened a bag of it as he handed back the baby to his mother. He walked into the surgical uite next door to tell Appleton that the baby wasn't suffering from cold exposure. He wasn't prepared for who was ying on the operating room table there: Gena Portobello. Her face was stark white in death. Appleton was holding a gauze square against her temple, trying to stop blood from a cut beside her eye from dripping down onto his shoe. His shoes were scuffed from A building rubble, and now a cut on Gena's body was bleeding on him. He must have hated that, Stoner thought. There was nothing the Ape hated more than dirty shoes.

But wait a minute! Stoner whirled to look back at Gena again. If she was bleeding, she had to bc alive! Only live people bled.

As Stoner watched, Gena opened her eyes and blinked. She looked up at Ape and managed a half-smile. "Sorry I'm getting you bloody," she said.

Stoner couldn't decide how he felt watching her. R lieved, certainly. But also jealous! Watching her joke wi Appleton that way, he felt so jealous it physically hurt. made him feel like screaming as loudly as she had screame outside the recovery room door when she had seen hi fucking Lynn Curtain.

Appleton pushed some tape into place on Gena's temp and turned to Stoner. "You OK?" he asked.

Stoner didn't have any words adequate to express how h felt.

"Something hurt somewhere?" Ape asked him.

Stoner couldn't describe the kind of pain he had. H shook his head instead of trying.

Appleton turned back to Gena, reapplied the gauze to he temple. "I'll get a nurse for you," he said. "And find a bed."

"No, don't do that." Gena pushed aside his hand and sa up on the side of the table to demonstrate that she was fine She took the gauze and pressed it against her own temple. "A shower will cure me of the thing most wrong with me."

Gena looked up at Stoner and reached for his hand to help her down from the high operating table.

Stoner felt his hand start to tremble so badly he could barely steady her.

"You sure you're all right, Stoner?" Appleton asked him again, watching his hand shake.

Stoner was very sure. Standing there with Gena Portobello momentarily pressed against him that way, certain that she was all right—all the blood on her was from that one small cut on her temple—allowed to stand for a long moment together that way, it seemed the only moment that had ever been totally right in his whole life.

* * *

David Frank sat by his kitchen telephone waiting for it to ring. For Gena Portobello to call him back and tell him she had safely evacuated the S.A.W.M.P.'s A Building. When he finally did hear the telephone ring, he didn't reach immediately to pick it up, afraid that someone might tell him she hadn't been successful at evacuation. Finally, he realized he could not delay either good or bad news any longer and picked up his receiver.

"David?" Richard Culbertson's voice asked in his ear.

Frank shuddered at the thought of hearing any more.

"How could you be such a goddamn ass?" Culbertson asked him.

Frank tried to breathe smoothly. Keep from panicking. "How am I an ass?" he asked.

"All that money I gave you, *paid you,* all these years and all you did with it was keep it to yourself. Didn't have the sense to put it into those buildings."

"I'm trying to move research—"

"All you moved was a lot of building this day, David. The A Building just moved all the way down to the basement."

David Frank held his breath, waiting to hear what that meant.

"You killed a lot of people," Culbertson finished.

David Frank breathed out. Pulled a breath in again with an effort. Trying to think through all the ramifications of what Culbertson's message could mean. Culbertson had paid over a hundred thousand dollars a year for thc last ten years. Bribe money, because Culbertson had made a bad mistake: he had lied to a young mother about her baby. So big an error, Culbertson had been willing to pay for his silence.

"Did Leslie get out?" Frank heard his voice break.

"Don't you want to ask about what's really important to you, David? Don't you want to know if your office safe got out?"

"Did Leslie get out?" he repeated.

"Yes. She still might have trouble with her baby though. She isn't home free."

Frank dropped his telephone into place, grateful, but ashamed. Because if he had thought sooner, or better, he could have averted that disaster. And because his safe *had* been what he had thought of first.

"Telephone for you, Dr. Stoner."

Stoner was reluctant to unfold his arms from around Gena's shoulders to get the telephone, although he realized the caller was probably David Frank, trying to explain how his whole damn building had come down on their heads. After another long moment, he let Gena go and snagged the wall telephone to talk to him. "Happy New Year, Scott!" his ear stung from the volume of Sue Ellen's voice against it. "Listen to the noisemaker I found in the attic!"

"Sue Ellen! The whole damn A Building just collapsed here!"

She couldn't hear him over the whooping shriek of the noisemaker she blew. "I've made a list of New Year's resolutions, Scott!" She acted as if she had no idea that he didn't ever want to think about another year with her. "I want to move back home again. I want to take a Spanish course at the high school. I want to lose ten pounds—"

Stoner glanced at his watch—five minutes before twelve—

as a man's voice beside her interrupted her list to tell her the ball in Times Square was about to fall.

"Ed Cronkin from next door is here helping me celebrate, as long as you're not here."

"Sue Ellen—" Stoner tried to get her attention again. To make her hear him better.

"I know what you're going to tell me, Stoner. To be careful what I drink. Well, don't worry, I'm going to be very careful. I'm not going to drink anything with an alcohol content over a *hundred* proof."

"Sue Ellen!"

"Don't be a spoil sort, Stoner. I mean a sol *spoit,* Soner. I mean a soil sort—" Sue Ellen laughed at her inability to get through the string of words and still laughing, dropped her telephone back into place.

She had already drunk too much, Stoner thought. It was too late for her to listen to his advice not to. Angry, he turned back to talk to Gena. Only she was nowhere to be seen. Something else it was too late in his life to try and reverse, he guessed. That one moment with her, helping her step down from an OR table, was probably the last meaningful one he was ever going to have with her.

Gena had showered and changed to a clean green scrub dress.

"Would you check Leslie Kerr for me?" a nurse she recognized as one from C Building asked her as she came out of the locker room.

Leslie Frank Kerr's problems seemed to belong to another time, a sensible time when people had checked into the S.A.W.M.P., and despite the poor condition of the building around them, got better if they were sick or had healthy babies if they were on maternity, and went back home again. Not had rubble crumble down on their heads.

"She's going to need a cesarean. I know it!" She could hear William Kerr shouting before she even got to the door of the operating room where his wife had been moved. "I saw the pattern on the monitor! You told me yourself, Doctor—" he grabbed Stoner's arm as he came up behind Gena to make that point. "Look at this!"

Gena picked up a strip of paper from the monitor beside Leslie's table and examined it. There was the dipping, rising pattern of distressed fetal heart tones, all right. A definite pattern of cord compression. A cord being pinned between her pelvic bone and the baby's head. Gena glanced at the woman to see how she looked. She was lying on her side on the table as she should have been. With the constantly maintained position, why had that odd pattern returned?

Although the monitor said that everything was fine right that minute, Gena looked at the strip again and counted the seconds that had passed while the cord compression had existed. It had been only a fleeting incident. Not long enough to cause any damage.

Not an innocent happening, however. If there had been a question as to whether Leslie Kerr could have that child normally before, a repeat of cord compression that late in the game meant that the question seriously needed to be reevaluated.

"Find Richard Culbertson for me," Gena barked at the nurse.

She stopped to place her hand on Leslie's abdomen to evaluate a contraction. What she felt was strong. The monitor showed it had occurred about two minutes after the last one. It was the type of contraction that was long and strong nough to bring the woman very shortly to a point of no eturn. A point where a final delivery decision had to be nade: to let Culbertson try a section even when his hands vere shaking, or to try and luck out a vaginal delivery. No natter what, her labor was moving too fast now to hope hat she could wait until the bridge was clear. No matter vhich way Gena chose to go, no matter which way she umped, it could end in disaster.

"I can pay for anyone in this city!" William Kerr shouted. The heavy lines in his face were deeper and made him look even more like a bulldog than he had before. "What's the advantage of being married to someone important, if you can't get help when you need it, for Chrissake?"

His wife had mentioned that earlier, Gena remembered. He wanted a baby more than he wanted her. He saw being married to her as convenient and flattering, rather than something that made his life start and end.

"Dr. Culbertson wants to talk to you on the phone, Dr. Portobello," the nurse came back into the room holding out the wall phone to Gena.

But Gena didn't want to talk to Culbertson on the telephone! She wanted him to come up to the operating room and talk to her *there.* She needed help on the spot, and he was the chief of staff in charge of giving help. Reluctantly, she stretched the telephone until it reached into the anesthesiologist's induction room, so she could talk in private. The room was a mess, bags of garbage that hadn't been removed for twenty-four hours, beginning to smell from rotting bloody sponges. She kicked one as she walked by it, and the spoiled odor rose out of it like a cloud of steam.

"Gena?" Culbertson's voice seemed to float to her from a long way off, as if he had a very bad connection, although he had to be somewhere in the hospital, so it wasn't th connection or the distance. "I'm not going to come up there."

"I *need* you, Doctor Culbertson."

"I can't move my right arm anymore. I'd kill that woman trying to do a section."

"I need your *judgment,* Doctor Culbertson. Your judgment isn't in your arm."

"I'm too old a man to help you," Culbertson's voice wavered and broke. "Those twins this morning are going to be the last babies I ever help deliver."

"You can't do this to me! I need you!"

"Men I went to high school with have become all kinds of things. Accountants. Lawyers. Real estate brokers. One of them is even an acrobat. But none of them, Gena, have been as happy as I have been. I have loved doctoring."

"Help me help Leslie Kerr."

"Redhoe put me under this strain to ruin me. Because he wants my position so much."

Gena suspected that was half true, but that didn't help anything. "The baby is starting to get cord compression again, Dr. Culbertson! I need your opinion—"

"I have *paid* to stay here as chief. He doesn't know he'll have to pay, too."

"Cord compression—"

"That's why you have no right to be angry with me about the baby, Gena. I've paid over a hundred thousand a year to David Frank, because I lied to you about the baby. It's left me with almost nothing. I have given it all to the hospital or David Frank."

Gena couldn't spend time sympathizing with his charity. "Cord compression—" she tried to explain the problem again.

"I can't come," Culbertson whispered into his receiver. "The best I can do for you is to tell you to ask Leslie Frank *why* she had old stretch marks on her sides."

Gena already knew the answer to that. The woman had said she'd been overweight once. "Cord compression—" she tried to spell out the problem one more time.

"It may mean the head was moving over the brim, and now she's going to deliver free and clear."

Or it could mean she *couldn't* deliver free and clear! That was the problem! That was why she was calling him.

The man dropped his receiver back into place and broke the connection.

Shit! Gena literally dropped the telephone receiver. *Grow up,* the man had told her the day before. Face responsibility. And now *he* was backing away from it. Leaving her with it. Letting a baby die. Helplessly, she walked back into the operating room to stand by the side of the table and try to think of something comforting to say to a woman she had no comfort for. "Don't worry," she promised. "We'll do something. There are still options."

"I'm not worried," Leslie smiled at her.

Gena recognized the strange bizarre feeling she'd had earlier that Leslie Frank Kerr *wasn't* worried. As if being David Frank's daughter, she had an inside track that told her everything *was* going to be all right. Although why she felt good about being David Frank's daughter, Gena couldn't understand. David Frank had almost killed them all by being careless about who he assigned to contract for cement.

"The baby is fine right now," Gena said, trying to sound as if she really believed that or as if Culbertson had just assured her of that. "You're getting really strong contractions. I'm sure you're uncomfortable—"

"I'm all right," Leslie assured her. She offered anothe[r] thin-lipped smile. "I know contractions don't get an[y] stronger than this. I can handle this."

Gena patted the woman's arm and stepped back into th[e] anesthesiologist's induction room to use the telephone again thinking one more time that Leslie Frank Kerr *didn't* seem worried. *She* was the one who was sweating about Leslie's baby. What she should do was call Frank and let him know what had happened, she thought. And then try Norm Redhoe. See one more time what *he* thought about his patient. She stepped over an empty bag of blood that had spilled out of a broken garbage bag—an O negative bag. Too bad it had been used in surgery and not been available for the Dukane baby, she thought. She stopped dialing Frank and dialed the lab instead, ready to demand to know how the tech could ever have made such a mistake with blood types as he had with Mark Warren's. Although, even if it had been his mistake, the bottom line said she was the one responsible for the baby's death. Because no matter how mixed up the blood cross had been, she had actually administered it. Don't worry Culbertson, she thought, kicking the bag of blood back inside the garbage bag as no one answered in the lab. I appreciate the level of responsibility that comes with doctoring now.

Elizabeth Warren appeared at her shoulder as Gena stepped back into the hallway. She was wearing her coat and her scarf as if she was still having trouble feeling warm. "I thought you'd want to know Mark is fine," she said. "Has been since we came over to this building."

One thing going right here, Gena thought. Almost too good to believe. "What about your *life?*" she asked her, thinking that was the real problem. "If morning ever comes, can get you in contact with the association for battered omen."

"Peter wouldn't like that, Dr. Portobello. And I don't e to upset him. Although maybe, when he wakes up, he'll el different."

Lucky Peter Perfect to be sleeping through everything appening here, Gena thought.

"He was sleeping in an empty room on the third floor hen the building collapsed," Elizabeth added. She brushed t the sleeve of her coat, as if she were trying to get snow r plaster dust off it, when there wasn't any on it.

Gena comprehended her final sentence slowly. Snapped er head up to look at the woman better. "He got out all ight, didn't he?" Gena asked, looking around for him. "He is OK, isn't he?"

"I haven't seen him since we came over here. I don't now."

"Mrs. Warren!" Gena shouted at her. "Why didn't you ay something sooner? Even if he was trapped but all right n the other building, he'd be dead by now from exposure!"

The woman looked at her as if that was interesting, but not important.

"Mrs. Warren! You didn't tell anyone he was there on purpose! *You left him there to die!"*

The corners of Elizabeth Warren's mouth curled into a faint smile. An elemental connection had snapped in her head. She continued smiling warmly, as if this were a simple conversation about nothing more important than the color of her best china or her living room drapes.

"Does Mark know?" Gena asked. "What do you think is going to happen to him, when he realizes what you've done?"

Elizabeth Warren bundled her coat around even tighter

than before and started to walk back down the hallwa
"Don't worry," she said. "The Warrens take care of the
own."

Gena felt the pain between her eyes begin to bore in
the synapses of her brain. He wasn't a Warren! He w
hers! And because she had been only sixteen, and too stup
to know what was happening, she had given him to Richar
Culbertson!

Beside her, the aide from pediatrics shouted that th
phone on the desk next to Gena was for her. At the sam
instant, Gena's intercom buzzed that a 4A lockup patien
was screaming that she was being attacked by needles an
needed something ordered to quiet her. William Ker
grabbed her arm and asked her what she was going to d
for his wife. The whole scene was like some kind of drean
where she ran and ran and ran, but couldn't get her legs t
take her anywhere. Or she was on a merry-go-round tha
some joker had turned on and let run, and now there wa
no one to stop it and she couldn't get off. Dully, she settle
a hand down on the telephone near her and dialed for Norm
Redhoe. Busy signal. She paged maintenance to see if they
could find Peter Perfect in the A building rubble. Paged
Appleton. Desperate to hear an experienced man's opinion
of what she should do.

"I'm awfully busy," was all he said when she told him
she was having trouble with Leslie Kerr. "And besides, I
thought I made it clear before. I'm not going to take her
off your service."

"I need help, Zack! Not a lecture on responsibility. Stoner
has a broken arm and I don't know what I'm doing! Come
and help me!"

"I had to tell you before. You can't push patients on me

is way," Ape said. "There's only one of me and I can nly do so much."

"But you're a chief, Ape! And you told me to be more ssertive. Now, when I'm doing that—*demanding* you help ne—why are you making me out a fool this way?"

For a long moment there was no sound on the line. Then Ape erupted. "Wake up!" he shouted into his telephone. "Don't make me spell the whole fuckin' thing out for you!"

Gena grasped the problem. He wanted work done for him n return. "What scut work do you want me to do for you, Ape? What's the price?"

There was another long moment of silence from the Ape. "The reason I didn't take Leslie Frank before, and the reason I can't help you now," he returned finally, calmly instead of angrily, "is because I don't know a fuckin' thing about women in labor."

Gena stood staring at her receiver, her mouth open, saying nothing. That had never occurred to her. She thought of him as being all-knowing, all decisive; triage expert.

"Now do you know who's the fool?" he asked, his voice barely audible. "I am. Because I *can't* help you." His telephone receiver clacked back into place.

"Hey, everybody!" an aide ran the length of the hallway, a streamer of toilet paper trailing behind her as she ran. "It's New Year's Eve!" The woman tossed a handful of confetti (made from chart forms) up into the air, and the colored pieces scattered over everything: people, the desk, green surgical-tile walls, the telephone, Gena. "Happy New Year!" the aide shouted again, tossing an ever bigger handful of homemade confetti as she reached the end of the hallway. All around Gena, the building erupted with general noise and whistling. Someone flicked the hallway lights on and off. In the distance, she could hear a siren wailing. It

was midnight and the start of a new and prosperous beginning for everyone. At the far end of the hallway, she watche
Scott Stoner put his arms around two nurses and begin t
sing "Auld Lang Syne" to the accompaniment of a Rock
ettes' chorus line.

The time and date were the only two things Gena wa
sure of—just basic orientation, just being able to determin
who lived in the real world and who lived in fairy tales
Desperately trying to orient herself more firmly, she plunge
her hand down onto an extension button and tried to ca
Norm Redhoe again. His line was still busy. The worl
outside was too busy celebrating a new year to be able t
connect telephones lines to help with problems from the pas
one.

Wearily, she dropped the receiver again and leaned back
against the wall, sliding down from the weight of her body
to sit on the floor. She buried her head in her hands, trying
to black out the singing all around her; the pain flashed
through her brain in jarring stabs.

She looked up finally at the sensation of someone pouring
a handful of confetti directly on her head. "Happy New
Year," Scott Stoner said, standing over her.

She had no time for celebrating, nothing to celebrate.
"What do you want me to do for Leslie Kerr?" she asked
him. "Try a section?"

He crouched beside her; reached and brushed confetti off
her shoulders. But didn't answer.

Both telephones rang on the desk in front of them and
Stoner plunged a hand down on top of one to answer it.
"Jesus Christ, Stoner!" Braxton Hershey thundered at him
over the line. "It was just on television what happened over
there! Is everyone all right?"

"As right as they're going to be."

"What about Gallagher?" Hershey demanded. "Did he ·t out all right?"

"Gallagher was already in C Building. Ape brought him ver earlier."

"Actually, it's his *chart* I'm interested in," Hershey connued. "Did his blood results get out all right?"

"Don't you want to know how people are?" Stoner asked.

"My research—" Hershey began.

Stoner dropped the telephone back into place before he ould finish.

Even more tired than before, Gena pressed her back gainst the wall and buried her head in her hands as a new ireworks display of pain passed through her brain. Thinkng, as she had earlier, that Stoner should have given her he phone to talk to Hershey when he was through. And he adn't done that again.

What she should do, she decided, was set up for a cesarean section. Because, no matter what, she couldn't just let Leslie Kerr go on and have the baby's head slammed mercilessly against her pelvic bones until the baby's circulation was cut off and he died inside her. Or her uterus tried so hard to extract the baby that it ripped wide open and *she* died.

Stoner reached again, and in a helpless kind of motion that said he had no suggestion, brushed a piece of confetti off her knee. Shit, that was a bad situation. Craziest of all, Gena thought, was that the only help Richard Culbertson had given her was to ask about stretch marks on Leslie Frank's sides. As if that were important! It was probably the least important finding that the woman showed.

"Why did Culbertson think the old stretch marks on Leslie Kerr were important?" she looked up at Stoner to ask.

He flopped down beside her and leaned against the wall

the same way. "Old stretch marks *usually* mean someo
has been pregnant once before," he said. "But Mrs. Ke
has them because she lost a lot of weight once. I think yo
were there when she said that."

Gena reached and touched his knee to keep his attentio
focused on that. "When stretch marks are from weight los
women usually have them on their legs, too, don't they?"

"I don't know, Gena," he smoothed his hand over hi
forehead, as if his head ached as much as hers. "Fat wome
don't particularly appeal to me. If you like, I'll be mor
observant in the future and report back to you."

"I'm serious. You see a lot of women. You must hav
noticed that."

"I don't fuck with everyone in White Horse, Gena! Th
only thing I know is that Leslie Frank doesn't have stretc
marks on her belly because she had a baby once before.
Think about it. What kind of possibility is there that Leslie
Frank, daughter of David Frank, who isn't going to give
me another year here because I had a nurse in his recovery
room, wasn't an absolute virgin when she first met William
Kerr?"

Gena let her silence speak for her.

"Even if that's true, Gena—" Stoner seemed to be trying
to follow where that thought led. "How could I, David
Frank's least favorite resident, ever tell him that his daughter had a baby before she was married?"

"How could you tell him that if you *were* his daughter?"
Gena asked.

"But if that were true—" it seemed to be taking Stoner's
brain a long time to get that into perspective. "Redhoe
would have said that. Instead he's had Culbertson worrying
for almost twenty-four hours now that he might have to

ction. Sure Redhoe wants Culbertson's job, but he ouldn't do that to him, would he?"

"Better ask how could he do that to *us!*" Gena said. Because that was what had been happening! They had been orrying for a full day that Leslie Kerr might have trouble aving a baby! Yet she had been able to remain so calm, ven bored, because she knew all along that everything was oing to be all right. She had had a baby once before, and hey had told her that was the ultimate test of whether a elvis was adequate or not when she'd first been admitted.

Angry, Gena pushed herself to her feet and walked to the loor of the first operating room. William Kerr popped to is feet like a threatening shadow as she approached his vife. "I'd like to talk to your wife alone," Gena said to im.

"We don't have any secrets," Kerr said, "You can talk with me here."

"Alone," Gena repeated.

Kerr looked at her for just a second more, as if to ask, who in hell do you think you are? Then he backed away.

Gena let the swinging door of the room close shut after the man, sealing everyone but Stoner and Leslie Kerr and herself outside. Then she flipped aside the sheet covering Leslie's abdomen and touched the old stretch marks on her right side, ran a hand up to the top of the woman's uterus and palpated a contraction—long and hard—the kind that was either doing the work of dilating or jamming a baby's head against an immovable bone. None too gently, she took a glove off the side counter and checked her bottom. Leslie Kerr was a hairsbreadth away from being fully dilated. On top of that, the baby was in the best possible delivery position: left occiput anterior. If she'd really had another baby, she was going to have this one without any trouble at all.

"You bitch!" Gena could remember the woman sayin that she knew labor contractions didn't get any worse tha those she was having. *Because she had been there before!* Gen kicked a metal bucket halfway across the room from ange "Why didn't you have the decency to tell me this is you second baby?"

Leslie Frank caught her breath, then screamed with th pain of a contraction.

"Do you think we give a damn about your fuckin' mor als?" Gena asked. "Do you think we care where you'v been or what you've done before? All we want for you is a good baby! Why, for Chrissake, didn't you tell us you' had one before?"

The woman's face blanched white. She bit her lip to keep from screaming as another contraction hit her. "It isn't easy to be ugly! You've always been pretty! What do *you* know?"

Gena had never felt pretty since Scott Stoner had asked Sue Ellen Morrison to marry him nine years before. And she knew very well what it felt like never to get what she wanted out of life. "You've had Richard Culbertson worrying for twenty-four hours that he was going to have to do a section! When you knew all that time that wasn't going to happen! How could you to that to *him?*"

"You don't know how lucky I am that William Kerr asked me to marry him!" Leslie Kerr burst into tears. "Can't you understand that I can't keep him if he knows I ever . . . did that kind of thing?"

What kind of thing, Gena asked herself. Let down her guard some night in a parked car? Be human for an instant? Find some companionship away at college? Since when were those crimes?

The woman groaned and Gena connected again that she was a patient, not a punching bag for her words. She atched Leslie Kerr draw up her legs against her abdomen nd strain and push; a patient in labor very close to deliv- ry. And a damn ass-easy delivery it would be since this vas really her second baby, if the baby's head stayed in its resent position. Too angry to be rational, Gena gave a netal stool a kick and sent it sailing across the room in the ame direction as the kicked bucket. The rattling of the stool gainst the ceramic tile echoed over and over before it fi- ally rolled completely out of the room into the induction area.

Whether women pushed at that point or not in labor depended on the number of children they had had, and how rapidly anyone could predict they would deliver from that point on. "Do you want her to push?" Gena asked, turning to Stoner. That was his decision.

Stoner had followed the stool into the induction room and was quietly rescuing it for her, acting as if Gena was not out of line there, kicking stools *was* part of a routine labor exam. "I'd like the whole Frank family to shove it," he answered, loud enough so that no one in the hallway could miss hearing. "Gena!" He picked up a blood bag from the floor next to where the stool had come to a halt and held it out to her. "Do you know what this is? The O negative blood bag from Gallagher's surgery! And it's empty! That means Kissell *must* have given it to him!"

"He couldn't have. Hershey said he took it back to the lab."

Stoner stood shaking his head. "He couldn't have," he said. "He cleaned up but didn't take it back."

"What *I* don't believe out of all that, is Lynn Curtain saying Braxton Hershey helped clean up in OR. That isn't like him."

"I believe her," Stoner said.

Gena should have known that he would think Lynn Curtain's opinion was superior to hers. That was one of those things that never changed.

"I believe Braxton Hershey helped pick up blood sponges, because he wanted to use the opportunity to throw out a guilty bag of blood. *He* gave this to Gallagher after we all left the room to cover up a blood loss. And because he touched the blood pack, he contaminated his gloves. Then didn't have the sense to admit he'd done that and caused an infection."

Gena knew that he was right. Braxton was the one who had lied about the blood. And because he had lied about it existing, they had been left short of blood.

"Dr. Portobello? Dr. Haiden is on the phone for you."

Gena was startled at hearing an aide say Haiden's name. She didn't have anything to say to him, and he shouldn't have had anything to say to anyone here. He had almost killed all of them by trying to save money on cement. Angry, she grabbed the telephone on the operating room wall to tell him that.

"Gena?" Haiden's voice was soft, but very concerned. "I know what happened. I'm sure you think that was my fault. But it wasn't! After all, how could I have known this storm would happen? I don't know anything about cement or storms."

None of them knew about cement. That was why they had trusted—every time they worked there since the columns went in—that he had done everything he should have done to protect them, Gena thought.

"I've been trying to call Lynn Curtain," he continued as if this were a social call, "to check if she's all right. But no one seems to know where she is. I wondered if you did."

Gena didn't. And hadn't even thought about her since ne'd left A Building.

"No chance she didn't get out of A Building, is there?" Iaiden asked.

Gena dropped the phone receiver on the man's ear and noved over to a sink to start to scrub for Leslie Kerr's lelivery. Haiden hadn't even realized everything that had appened yet, she thought. Not bad for a little black kid rom Harlem, he had said. Not bad for letting his ambition get ahead of his common sense, that was closer to the realty. Now he was ruined. David Frank wouldn't want him in charge of his laboratory space any more. Frank, whose favorite story was about scraping shit, expected far better things of people than that.

"Dr. Portobello?" Murphy came up to her side, nodding toward a second operating room. "You have a second delivery waiting for you."

But that was impossible. The only pregnant people in the place were Leslie Kerr and Lynn Curtain.

"It's Curtain," Murphy nodded. "She says she's been in labor for hours."

"Is this her first baby?" Gena turned to ask Stoner.

"Jesus Christ, Gena, stop believing that story," he said. "You know it can't be my baby. Start worrying about what to do because she's two months early and we don't have resuscitation equipment."

"I'm sorry," Gena dipped her hands under the scrub sink faucets to begin to wash. "How many times do I have to tell you that when Haiden called me, he told me you were in the recovery room with a *patient?*"

"Haiden called you?" Stoner opened his mouth in amazement. "I was *in* the recovery room because he bet me twenty dollars I couldn't get Lynn in there."

No time to wonder over a six-month-old happening ar longer. Gena picked up a glove as she passed a sterile pac open on the instrument table and came up to Leslie Kerr operating table. Doing her best to remember that peop under stress did funny things, she gave her instructions. I was such a privilege to be married to William Kerr, sh thought, that Leslie had been willing to let them worry al that time, rather than let them know that she hadn't bee as chaste when she'd married him as Kerr might have pre ferred. So wonderful to be a Frank and get upset at resi dents, but not get upset at your own daughter. Althoug Gena guessed David Frank didn't know about that firs pregnancy, anymore than the woman's husband did.

The baby's head delivered perfectly. Murphy came up on Gena's right side and suctioned. The baby's head turned and the shoulders delivered. The baby slid out effortlessly into her hands.

"A boy!" Murphy said, sounding as if she were enjoying herself, past a point of tiredness and ready to take on all comers. Laughing, she lifted the baby up and laid it on Leslie's abdomen. A healthy, perfect baby. Good cry. Good respirations.

"You're all right, Portobello." William Kerr came forward from his place at the head of the table. "I don't know how you knew for sure that this would be all right, but you sure pulled it out."

Gena looked at Leslie Kerr, biting her lip, tempted to tell Kerr how she had known and stop Leslie's merry-go-round. Rising above the problems the patient caused—professional confidence—Gena turned back to the foot of the table. "We lucked out," she answered instead. "That simple."

"I need your help, Gena!" Stoner called to her from the opposite operating room. Gena tossed her gloves and walked ross the hallway to face a new problem. Lynn Curtain, r long blonde hair tangled and needing to be combed, as lying on the table. Despite the matted hair, she looked diant, extremely pleased. At the foot of the table, Stoner as holding a dusky-colored but term-sized baby.

"Boy, boys, boys," Gena said, slipping a new pair of loves into place, feeling happy for Lynn that this year of er life was finally over. "That's all we have any more."

She was worried, because although the baby Stoner was olding was a good size—he was closer to nine months than even months—his color was still dusky. Stoner stroked his ack to make him cry harder. The baby whimpered as if nnoyed at being disturbed, then broke into a more forceful ry, the kind of cry that immediately pinked up the duskiest of newborns. Only he didn't pinken. Gena felt her breath coming more rapidly: infant resuscitation equipment was buried under A building. She kicked a three-legged stool into position at the foot of the table, put two clamps on the cord, and one on Lynn's bottom where she had a small tear. Puzzling about what she could do without good equipment.

"Are you OK?" she looked up at Lynn to ask. Because Lynn had not said a word since she had come into the room.

"I'm OK," Lynn whispered, breathing with short catchy inhalations. Her eyes were so filled with tears of happiness, they were overflowing onto her cheeks.

"Fine time you picked to have this baby," Gena said. Although for Stoner she guessed it really was a good time. It made it very clear that nine months from January first was March, not July. No one could hint any more that this was his baby from the recovery room afternoon. He hadn't even been there in March.

"I was so scared that I'd have it at home," Lynn

breathed. "I can't believe it's over, and I've had him, a
he's all right."

"I never did understand why Bob wanted you to ha
him at home," Stoner said. Gena didn't understand wh
Haiden had called her back in July and told her that Lyn
and Stoner were in the delivery room together. It was a
most as if he had set him up. As if he'd wanted it ingraine
on everyone's mind that this was *Stoner's* baby.

Stoner turned to carry the baby up to Lynn's side an
Gena touched his arm to stop him. She was worried abou
the total dusky, dark color that still hung over the baby.

"Get a stethoscope," she barked at Stoner, motioning t
him to put the baby up on Lynn's abdomen so she coul
listen to the chest. The baby had to have a heart defect
Aside from that, he looked all right: black curly hair,
broad flat nose, a deeply pigmented scrotum. But he was sc
dark . . . something had to be wrong! Gena pressed a stethoscope against the baby's chest, listening for the heart defect
she knew had to be there. She couldn't hear anything unusual in the heartbeat. She listened to lung sounds. Nothing
out of line there either. Funny . . .

She turned the baby over. Perhaps there was some pos-
terior defect on his head that was interfering with his breathing center. Nothing. The baby had a perfect back. Except
for a dark pigmented area across his buttocks, like a lot of
black or Asiatic babies were born with: a mongolian spot.

Gena looked at Stoner to see if he had some clue to the
baby's poor condition, but Stoner was standing at the head
of the table chatting with Lynn as if he wasn't concerned at
all. Damn him! When was he going to get concerned?

"He's a good baby," Stoner said.

That couldn't be true! Gena turned the baby back and
looked at him once more. She realized what was going on:

s Stoner already knew, there wasn't anything wrong with .e baby's heart. Or lungs. He was so dusky, so dark be-ıuse his father was black.

Hell. Her reaction level had been way off base. She had ıissed the fact that Leslie Frank Kerr had been pregnant efore. She had missed the reason why Bob Haiden had een so interested in this baby, why he wanted to deliver nis baby at home. And damn him! With the morphine in .is bag, he wanted to make sure the baby never breathed, o that no one—particularly David Frank, who had strong eelings about what his residents and his research fellows lid in their free time—would ever see him.

"He's a good baby," Gena said reassuringly to Lynn, :ossing aside the stethoscope. "Absolutely perfect."

Ethel Murphy, out of breath from running the length of the hallway, poked her head into the room. "I'm going to call Haiden," she said. "To give him his birth rate report. What should I tell him he had in here?"

Gena moved to the head of the table to stand next to Lynn. Maybe Haiden had planned on killing *her* with the morphine as well as the baby; she didn't know. The woman's tears told Gena that Lynn realized most of that.

"Tell him to add a boy for his count in the other room," she said simply. She looked to Stoner to confirm what she had guessed. "Tell him he had a son in here."

Chapter Twelve

At 6:00 A.M., an orange-colored White Horse plow broke through the last drift of snow on the bridge.

Gena Portobello was checking over the Dukane babies one final time—amazingly, even the one she had transfused looked good—as well as Leslie Kerr's and Lynn Curtain's new boys, when a nurse in a clean, unwrinkled uniform—a sight she hadn't seen in two days—nudged her shoulder. Gena pulled her stethoscope away from her ears to listen to her message.

"This phone's for you," the woman said, holding out the desk receiver. "And Dr. Frank left a message that he would like to see all his house officers in the auditorium before anyone leaves."

Gena had no wish to talk to anyone on the telephone or listen to David Frank talk about anything in an auditorium. All she wanted to do was get a fast shower and fall into bed for about twenty-four hours. She cupped the receiver to her ear and said hello groggily.

"Dr. Portobello? It's Margo." Margo Torning sneezed. "Can you give Stoner a message for me?"

Gena grunted.

"A really cute guy just came by with a plow." Margo ggled. "And is going to give me a ride home." She eezed again. "He's really cute," she giggled again. "And esn't like cats."

Gena dropped the receiver back into place and pushed e foot ahead of the other to make it to the elevator and de down to the C building lobby auditorium. The lobby C Building was filled with people, night workers making eir way toward the entrance where a yellow school bus as waiting to transport them home, their cars hopelessly owed in for another week; day people spilling off the bus relieve them. Everyone was taking time to look at the xposed beams and sides of patient walls of the demolished Building. A blond woman in a red coat was standing by he front door directing traffic in general, checking off night orker's names on a clipboard as they boarded the bus.

Standing by the water fountain, looking tired and lost, lutching a black purse under her arm, Gena recognized Ryan McFarland's wife. She was still wearing the black coat he had worn in, pink matted bedroom slippers on her feet. "Dr. Portobello," the woman reached to attract Gena's attention. "How good to see you again."

"How is your husband this morning?" Gena asked. McFarland had been transferred out of the emergency room to the ICU, so he had been safe while the building had been coming down.

The woman's face went crooked and she struggled to regain composure. "He died about an hour ago," she said sadly.

Gena remembered how his first heart tracing had shown that was going to happen. All the time since he had first been admitted had been borrowed time; all the efforts for him were no more than them trying to put a tire patch a totally blown tire.

"I wish you could have taken care of him longer," th woman said, gripping her arm. "He was doing so well wh you were with him."

That wasn't fair to those who had come after her, Gen thought. Because no matter who had been with him, that ou come would have been the same. "I know Dr. Stoner prob ably led you to believe everything would be all right— Gena said. She remembered Stoner standing with his arm around her, letting her cry on his sweater.

"It's all right," the woman reached to comfort Gena "No matter what he was saying, I knew the only reason busy doctor would let me use him like a Kleenex that way was because my husband was dying." She squeezed Gena' arm a final time and moved off to ask the woman in the re coat if she could find a place on the bus for her.

I've always underestimated Stoner, Gena thought. Al ways worried he didn't know what he was doing when he usually knew very well. She watched the little woman walk out the door, then turned away from the noise of the lobby to enter the auditorium.

The front platform of the room was filled with house officers, contrasts between soiled and clean: Scott Stoner, Ned Browster from C Building, Harry Cummings from B Building, Bert Lewis from Peds. Bob Haiden was conspicuously missing. A row of attendings stood at one side of the platform drinking coffee from white styrofoam cups. Gena recognized Violet Hamilton who had gone to med school when women had to be men; Norm Redhoe who had kept her in suspense all night worrying about Leslie Kerr, Clarence Watts; Dick Bertnam; all grouped around a black man who looked familiar to her but she couldn't place. The Ape was ınding near the front table. He had changed from his iled whites to a clean scrub suit. She noticed that no mat- : how much he had tried, he hadn't been able to get his oes completely sparkling again. He spotted Gena and ɔdded to her.

David Frank was leaning on the edge of the wooden table the front of the room. He looked impeccable, a gray tweed ıit, black shiny wing-tip shoes on his feet. He popped to ıs feet as he recognized Gena and came forward to shake er hand. "You know the debt of gratitude all of us owe ɔu and Stoner," he said.

Gena managed to nod her head. No other muscle in her ody had enough strength left to function.

"I called everyone here," Frank leaned back on the edge f the table and addressed the group at large, "because last ıight's tragedy will have repercussions for the medical cen- er for a long time to come. Our reputation as a hospital ıas been severely damaged."

Braxton Hershey—wearing a gray pinstripe suit and a ɔright red tie—let himself into the room and waved to Gena.

"I've called you all here to announce that I am resigning ıs the medical center administrator. I'm certain you know :here will be lawsuits against the center. I take responsibil- ity for the bulk of them. A number, however, will rest with house staff. I give you fair warning, that I will not protect you from those, anymore than I ask for protection for my- self."

Gena felt a grudging respect for the man.

"I'm concerned," Frank continued, looking from face to face in the room, "about rumors that during the time this facility was closed off, people didn't receive equal care. There's a rumor that doctors played favorites—so-called im-

portant people receiving attention that others didn't
ceive."

Ape looked uncomfortable. He started to turn away
stir his coffee, then looked back to defend that. "Prioriti
weren't that easy," he said. "But there's fault both way
Portobello and Stoner spent the bulk of their time takir
care of a Dukane baby who was a fuckin' nobody."

There was a murmur along the row of attendings. The
were thinking that what she had done was kill a nobod
Dukane baby, Gena thought, by transfusing the wrong typ
blood.

She took a step toward the door, interested in nothing a
much as in getting home, just getting out of there. Sh
glanced at Stoner to see if he was leaving, too. He wa
looking at his coffee cup. Lord, don't anyone ask me wha
was the craziest thought I had during the time I was here
she thought. *Because it would be, that I don't want the experienc
to end.* She wanted to go back to the operating room hallwa
where Scott Stoner had knelt beside her and brushed confetti off her shoulder. Because once this night was over, she
would have to face the fact that she was going to be asked
to leave there, that she would never work with Stoner again.
Possibly never see him again.

"Excuse me—" the black man who had stood with the
attendings pushed himself forward to intercept Gena's path
to the door. "I think it's time I formally introduced myself
to you. I'm Joe Elliott, the man who's about to be the new
Obstetrics Chief here."

Gena looked from him to Norm Redhoe. Redhoe was
staring down at his coffee cup. What in hell had Frank put
in there that was so interesting, that monopolized people's
time so, Gena wondered. Then she realized that Redhoe
was looking at his cup because he was trying to hide his

appointment that *he* wasn't going to be appointed chief Culbertson's place. He had wanted that so much he had en willing to submit Richard Culbertson to twenty-four urs of stress. "Get some sleep. We'll talk about everyng that happened here in twenty-four hours," Elliott finied his introduction.

Gena couldn't shake the feeling that she had met him fore. At least someone who looked like him.

"I won't be here in twenty-four hours," she clarified that r him. "I'm being asked to leave staff."

"Of course you'll be here." Elliott stretched an arm over r shoulders and walked with her to the door. "I owe you great deal. What kind of a person would I be, if I let *you* ?"

Gena let him usher her outside into the hallway. Stood aring at his familiar-looking face.

"I'm Lori Dukane's father," he said, smiling exactly the ame way as his daughter did. "The *nobody* you took care f all night is one of my twin grandsons."

Gena recognized the face. She had focused on a miniature eplica of it for two hours while she replaced a baby's blood. *Replaced it with the wrong type blood!* "Doctor Elliott—we used he wrong type of blood for that baby. I *killed* your grandon."

"Ridiculous." The man waved to the woman in the red coat in the lobby to catch her attention. "I saw him myself not fifteen minutes ago. He could only be that good if he had received O negative blood."

Gena caught her breath, unable to believe that because they had used Mark Warren's blood. Across the lobby, the woman in the red coat turned and smiled at them.

"Have room in a bus for house staff?" Elliott asked the woman.

"Come right this way," the woman said, smiling a
extending a hand to Gena.

Gena let the woman throw a blanket over her should
and walk with her to the waiting bus. She was all the w
outside, stepping into the bus, settling into a front se
before it occurred to her that she should mention to som
one that the blond woman was not the PR person s
seemed. She was Crazy Mary, still wearing the curly-hair
wig and the red coat she had snatched from the nurse
locker room. Gena didn't say anything. Later on would
time enough for her to mention that the person in char
was one they had certified as incompetent to function.
seemed a fitting end to the S.A.W.M.P.'s last day.

Wearily, she sank back against a seat and closed her eye
trying to determine what had happened with the Dukar
baby. The reason the blood for Mark Warren hadn't r
acted had to be, as Elliott had said, because it was O neg
ative blood.

She had had her baby because she had thought he migh
be Stoner's. But then, after he'd been born, Richard Cu
bertson had typed his blood and said it was B positive, an
so she had given him up for adoption. Damn Richard Cul
bertson! The man had said he had paid David Frank a
those years for his mistake. She had thought he had mean
his mistake giving the baby to the Warrens, not leaving him
in Baltimore. *He had meant he had deliberately lied about the bloo
type so she would give up the baby!*

How strange . . . how different . . . her life could have
been if she hadn't walked along a train track late one night.
How different it could have been if Richard Culbertson
hadn't lied about a blood type. But what could she do now?
She couldn't leave Mark with Elizabeth Warren any longer,
she knew that. If she fought for him in court, his father's

ntity would be revealed. And that would help nothing. cause Stoner probably wanted nothing to do with Mark with her.

Someone sat down next to Gena, but she was too tired en to open her eyes to check who it was. Poor Sally Yates, thought; poor Peter Perfect. Poor Evelyn Corning. All pped inside A building; all dead.

"Do you think the Dukane baby is really going to be all ht?" the person beside Gena asked.

Gena caught the old, very familiar scent of English eather shaving lotion. "I guess so," she answered.

"What are you going to do?"

"For the baby? Get a final twenty-four hour bilirubin and matocrit—"

"For Mark Warren."

She didn't know.

"You know I would have married you," Stoner said.

"I didn't want to be married just to be married."

"That's what you're doing with Braxton Hershey."

She wasn't going to marry Braxton Hershey. She had no ntention of spending the rest of her life with a man who ad tried to avoid the responsibility for what he had done y denying he had administered that blood. A man who vas more concerned with research results than people.

"I loved you back in high school," Stoner said. "I would ave married you because I loved you."

In front of them, the bus driver, a fat man with a stomach hat bulged out of his jacket like a large department store Santa Claus, pushed back on the lever by his feet and let he bus doors close.

"Loved." Gena said the word out loud as the bus lurched forward. Thinking how strange it was that in a few minutes things could change so completely. A building that had stood

for fifty years could suddenly come crashing down. Yet ot
things never changed. She was riding out of there wit
bus load of people, but she was really riding out alone.

"As much as I still do," Stoner added.

Gena dared to open her eyes. The bus was pass
through a tunnel of snow; there seemed to be nothing
either side of the bus but a wall of heaped snow as it
proached the bridge. She looked at Stoner. At how terri
he looked. His face was covered with blond stubble. Th
were dark rings under his eyes. His eyes were red and
ritated as he fought to keep them open.

"As much as I still do," he repeated.

Gena slipped a hand into his, confident he would noti
she was no longer wearing Hershey's ring. As she did,
band of bright morning sunlight burst through the sno
clouds overhead and slanted across the snow banks, startlir
a hundred gulls into flight. The bus thrust forward, ov
the bridge, and off the Island.